To Inspector Hound
from Taylor

AMBITIONS

AMBITIONS

a novel by
Joseph Dobrian

REX IMPERATOR, New York, N.Y.

BOOKS BY JOSEPH DOBRIAN

FICTION

Willie Wilden (2011)
Ambitions (2014)

NON-FICTION

Seldom Right But Never In Doubt (2012)

La lutte elle-même vers les sommets suffit à remplir un cœur d'homme. Il faut imaginer Sisyphe heureux.

The struggle toward the summit, in itself, is sufficient to fill one's heart. We must imagine that Sisyphus is happy.

— Albert Camus

To Professor Carol de Saint Victor, who told me in 1976, "You must not go on to law school. Stay in this vale of tears and keep writing!"

AMBITIONS
by Joseph Dobrian

TABLE OF CONTENTS

I. CHRISTINE WAINWRIGHT AND ANDY PALINKAS

II. MELISSA WAINWRIGHT AND CONNOR LOWE

III. CHANGES IN LIFE AND CAREER

IV. DAVID WAINWRIGHT AND MERCY BLAHA

V. THE PLOTS START MIXING A LITTLE MORE

VI. A ROMANCE, A MARRIAGE, AN ELOPEMENT, A WEDDING

I. CHRISTINE WAINWRIGHT AND ANDY PALINKAS

1. Christine Disappears

Let's start with me: Andy Palinkas. I lived next door to the Wainwrights for 26 years and I watched a lot of this story go down. What I didn't see, I heard about, with varying degrees of accuracy.

This story's not about me; it's about the Wainwrights, and especially about the youngest child of that family, Christine, who disappeared in June of 2008.

It surprises me, how little of this story I've had to make up, and how much of it I've been able to piece together from other people's accounts, from gossip, from rumor. I'm not on oath as I tell it. Sometimes I'll be stating the plain facts. Sometimes I'll be repeating what was common report. Sometimes I'll be conjecturing. Speculating, postulating. Guessing at what might have happened. Guessing at what one person or another might have been thinking or feeling. My imagination will tell me: "This is how it must have been, or pretty close."

In any town, you'll find a few people who know practically everyone in that town, and the story behind each of them.

In State City, Iowa, which has 75,000 people (counting the students at State University), it would be an exaggeration to say of any one person that he knew *everyone*, let alone claim that he had all the dirt on everyone. But I know a lot of the people here, and I know a lot of the dirt – and I can imagine a lot more.

State City is a gossip town. It's not a metropolis like New York, where people don't know each other at all, and stay out of each other's business. But neither is it a village where each person knows every other person, so that everybody's afraid to do anything out of the norm. It's a university town, so you're authorized to be weird if you want to be, and people won't care – but they might talk about you.

The townies complain about the students – they're noisy, they're rowdy, they party too much – but without State University, State City wouldn't be "the smallest big city in the world," as we like to call it. State University has a terrific teaching hospital, and a first-rate School of Engineering. Its sports teams – the Rivercats – tend to be strong.

State University also has a world-famous School of Music. State City has been designated by UNESCO as one of six "Cities of Music" – along with Vienna, Sydney, Milan, Dresden, and Caracas. The School of Music's headquarters is the Janscombe Center: a massive structure that sits on the banks of the State River and combines indoor and outdoor performance spaces with classrooms and rehearsal studios. The Janscombe Center is a regional equivalent of Tanglewood in Massachusetts, or Lincoln Center in New York City, or the Sydney Opera House. Janscombe is almost a holy place in State City.

State City is in Eastern Iowa, which was mostly settled by Germans, Irish, Czechs, and Slovaks in the 1840s. Names like Cermak, Blaha, Stasny, Prohaska, Kerchak, Scrofula, and Spatula have been here ever since then. Everybody knows those families, some of which are pretty well off and some not so well off but in any case those families are sort of the hereditary aristocracy of this town. State City is so ethnically mixed now, though, that on any given day an Aziz might be sitting next to a Zylstra on the bus. You'll see Africans with tribal scars, covered Muslim women, and lots of people from the Eastern Hemisphere.

This is the town Christine Wainwright grew up in – and disappeared from. For most of her life, Christine was the kind of girl you wouldn't have noticed: ordinary looking, not especially talented or bright, from a family that was perfectly respectable and completely unremarkable. But by the time she'd turned 17, when she was finishing her junior year of high school, Christine was getting noticed as a singer. People who knew what they were talking about – and there were a lot of those, in State City – were saying she might have "it": real star quality. Then she went missing.

One of the strangest bits of gossip to come out of that case was that this normal-seeming teenaged girl had as her closest friend a man 43 years older than she: a man literally old enough to be her grandfather.

This feature ran in the State City *Examiner*, a few days before Christine's disappearance. Like a lot of newspapers in towns the size of State City, The *Examiner* publishes occasional profiles of local businesspeople, community activists, or village idiots – and on this day, it was this village idiot's turn. I'd say it provides a better description of me than I could have written myself in 1,000 words or less.

The State City Examiner – June 1, 2008
MEET ANDY PALINKAS

Andrew Gabor Palinkas has made it his purpose and passion to send people out of his store and into the world looking good. He knows how to dress – and he teaches his customers how to do the same.

"I dress the way a lot of guys in State City wish they dared to dress," says the 60-year-old owner of Rosen's Men's Store, in downtown State City. "I won't pretend that I don't dress well. My attire isn't just something that goes with my business. It's part of who I am."

A tall, husky, tough-looking man with a meticulously shaven head, Andy's a familiar figure in State City, with his upright posture, sharp double-breasted suits, crusty personality, and (as he puts it himself) "the only pair of piercing green eyes in the world." He's often seen at State University sporting events, and at the Janscombe Center for classical music concerts and recitals. You'll also see him on stage, in productions by the State City Community Theatre.

Andy has been working at Rosen's since he graduated from State City High School in 1966 ("back when I had hair"). He worked there while attending State University, and bought the store from its previous owner, the late Jacob Rosen, in 1986. Just over a year ago, he opened Rosen's Silhouettes, which specializes in formalwear for men and women as well as bridal gowns.

Andy's a member of the State City Rotary Club and the Chamber of Commerce, but he hates to think of himself as a communitarian.

"I don't buy the concept of 'giving back to the community,'" he insists. "If I'm nice to people it's because I want to be, not because I owe anybody anything. Not that everyone would agree that I'm nice."

"I love sports even though I'm a hopeless athlete, and I love classical music even though I don't know a darn thing about it," Andy says. "I'm six-three, so people ask me if I used to play basketball, but, no: I can't even jump six inches! As for music, maybe some knowledge has rubbed off on me, but I'm still an ignoramus. And I never pursued acting as I might have, once I got involved in business. Clothes are the only subject I know well."

Andy says he has all his suits and shirts made in his own store, in Rosen's custom department, designed to his own specifications.

"I dress with style, but I don't dress fashionably," he explains. "My clothes belong to me, and they never go out of fashion."

Andy is full of advice for the boy or man who wants to be well-dressed – or for the woman who's dressing him.

"First," he says, "your shirt collar has to fit. Almost without exception, I find that men wear their shirts a full size too small in the neck, at least. That's why men hate to wear a tie.

"Second, never buy the latest fashions. Find a look you like, and stick to it. Third, always wear just one patterned garment. Mixing patterns is a woman's trick, but it doesn't look good on a man. Men often make that mistake, though, because women buy their clothes."

"It's fun to dress a little better than necessary, no matter what kind of life you lead," Andy concludes. "Obviously I don't advise you to wear a suit and tie on the job if you're a construction worker or a fisherman, but, trust me, you'll feel better if you put on a suit to go to church or to a nice restaurant."

Andy says that for many years, he's been investing quietly in commercial real estate in the State City area, and building a second career as a landlord. But for now, he hopes to keep on keeping State City clothed. Andy admits that he might be fighting a losing battle in his efforts to persuade more men to wear jackets, ties, and dress shirts, and he wonders how much longer traditional men's stores like Rosen's can survive.

"It could be that in a few years there won't be any need for a store like Rosen's," he sighs. "I'm fighting against a horde of men dressed in shorts, T-shirts, and flip-flops."

But, Andy says, *"Il faut imaginer Sysiphe heureux."* That French phrase means, "You have to imagine that Sisyphus is happy," and it refers to the ancient myth of Sisyphus, who is condemned to spend eternity pushing a huge rock up a hill, only to have it roll back down again each time he gets near the summit.

"I enjoy speaking French," says Andy. "I've founded a French-speaking chapter of Toastmasters Club that meets every Tuesday after work: just a few local people."

Andy says he's "single and always looking." He's a life-long bachelor who lives in a quiet neighborhood on State City's east side.

"I'm what the French call a *'vieux garçon,'*" he explains. "I never met the right girl. Or it might be more accurate to say that I've met several whom I thought might be right – but they all had a different opinion. I have noticed, though, in the past few years, that bald heads are suddenly stylish, so maybe there's hope for me yet."

"Some people say grass doesn't grow on a busy street; others say it won't grow on concrete regardless of how little traffic there is," Andy laughs. "Anyway, I'm still looking for a nice girl who'd like to run her fingers through my air."

§

What that feature doesn't tell the reader is that Andy despised Jim and Gail Wainwright, who up till a few months before had been his next-door neighbors in that "quiet neighborhood on State City's East Side." Jim and Gail, and their youngest daughter, Christine, had recently moved to a smaller house (more suitable to empty-nesters) in another part of town – an event that's pivotal to this tale.

Jim and Gail Wainwright are hard to describe because they're so ordinary-looking. They're just a bit younger than Andy. Jim is kind of tall, though not as tall as Andy. He wears glasses, and has short brown hair and a face you forget. Gail is of absolutely average size, a bit hippy, but otherwise attractive for her age. She also has greying mouse-brown hair, which she wears in one of those short Midwest Mom cuts, now that she's older. Again, you don't notice her, you don't remember her, as far as her looks go.

But the Wainwrights, too, are known in State City, and a similar article appeared on them the very next week:

The State City Examiner -- June 8, 2008
MEET JIM AND GAIL WAINWRIGHT

A fixture in downtown State City since 1978, State City Podiatry is celebrating its 30th anniversary this year, and Dr. Jim Wainwright says he's looking forward to another 30. "Retirement's a long way off," says Jim, 57. "I might not literally keep working at this job for another 30 years, but I do hope the practice outlives me. I like to think that I've made myself and my business useful parts of the community."

Jim enjoys jokes about his profession – all in good fun.

"What I like about being a podiatrist," he kids, "is that your patients don't die of anything you do to them, and they almost never get well."

But Jim takes podiatry seriously too – whether he's treating an ingrown toenail or a stress-fracture.

"What I do is more of an art than a science," he says. "Every patient's different and you have to keep that in mind.

"The best part of my job is getting to meet a lot of people. Your feet might not hurt now, but one day they probably will, and when that happens, if you've seen my ad in *The State City Examiner* or in the entryway at one or another of the supermarkets around town, I'll be your first call. I hope I'm known as a square-shooting guy who treats everybody right and assumes everybody else will do the same."

Jim was born in Grand Forks, N.D., and got his training at North Dakota State University, where he met his wife Gail (Edgren) Wainwright. He worked in South Dakota before buying a practice in State City.

"I try to balance the duties of being a wife and a mom with my obligations to the community," says Gail, 56. "I've never been 'just a housewife,' or a 'stay-at-home mom.' I've always kept active by volunteering, and getting involved in local politics to some extent. I've always been a big believer in fairness for everyone. I also owned a gift shop in downtown State City that doesn't exist anymore – but I guess that taught me that I'm not really a business person."

The Wainwrights have three children, only one of whom is still at home. David, 31, is already the author of one novel, with a second one in progress. He and his wife Mercy live in State City and have two children: Juliet and Theo. Daughter Melissa, 28, is a schoolteacher who has just completed her Master's degree in education and will be marrying Connor Lowe of State City at the end of July. Daughter Christine, 17, is ready for her last year of high school this fall.

"I'm almost done," Gail jokes. "No, that's not true. Once you're a mother, you're a mother all your life long to all your kids."

Among her other interests, Gail lists movies and art, reading (mostly novels and self-help books), gardening, and exchanging ideas with good friends. Her pet peeves include violence – in sports, on TV, and in movies – and people who don't fulfill their social responsibilities.

"'I' is the least important word in the English language," Gail says. "Except in the sense of 'I am responsible to others.'"

Now that her son has set an example, Gail says, she'd like to have a career as a writer when her youngest child is grown.

"I feel I have something to say about parenting, that might be helpful to other people," she explains, "and I might even have a novel or two in me. People don't always appreciate how little time you have to yourself when you're a wife and mother. But life is all about the demands it places on you."

Gail was born in Zap, N.D., and attended North Dakota State University, where she met her husband.

"If I ever came close to having a regret, it's that I never got a post-graduate degree," she reflects. "Maybe when there are fewer demands on my time, I'll go back to school."

For fun and relaxation, Jim's tastes aren't as sophisticated as Gail's.

"I have to admit I enjoy romantic movies," he says. "I didn't used to, but Gail usually does the choosing, when we go to a movie or rent one, so I've learned to like them." Jim lists *Pretty Woman*, *Autumn In New York*, and *Like Water For Chocolate* as among his favorites. "I'm all about chocolate," he says. "My favorite dessert is chocolate cake with chocolate frosting, with chocolate ice cream and chocolate sauce on top. But I leave off the chocolate sprinkles if I'm dieting."

Jim also likes music – "But it has to be music I can tap my toe to, or sing along with," says Jim. "I never understood this 'headache music' that kids listen to these days, and rap isn't even music as far as I'm concerned. I know I should like classical music, and I've tried to, but Beethoven and Mozart and that stuff is way over my head. I like the Carpenters, if you remember them, and I can tolerate Janet Jackson – her tamer stuff, anyway."

"Our marriage has worked because we share the same values," Gail concludes. "That's so important, and so many couples don't consider that, when they get married. If they did, there wouldn't be so many divorces."

§

Two days after that feature ran, Christine Wainwright took off, or was taken off. Apparently she left home after breakfast that morning – she told her mother she was going to go hang out with some friends – and never came back. She texted her mother that evening that she would be spending the night at the home of one of those friends – it was summer vacation, so that wouldn't have been so strange – and it wasn't till late the following day that her parents missed her, and started calling around, and finally called the cops.

According to the information that Andy Palinkas was able to piece together, when he decided to get to the bottom of this story, the cops didn't want to take the report at first. The officer who spoke on the phone to Jim Wainwright explained that without evidence of foul play, the police usually don't get involved in the disappearance of a minor over 16. They almost always turn up unharmed, of their own accord, in two or three days. But when Jim Wainwright heard this, from the police officer he spoke to over the phone, he was less than accepting.

"I pay taxes in this town," Jim said to the policeman. "I pay your salary. I pay you in case an emergency like this comes up, so that you'll be there to respond to it. And you're not going to take my report? Put me through to your supervisor!"

Jim was passed up to a Lieutenant – who, after a minute or two of listening to the same sort of talk, said that this wasn't what they usually did, but he'd see to it that a detective was assigned to the case, and he'd send a patrol car over to the Wainwrights' house right away to take their report.

Almost certainly, Jim Wainwright had hoped to take care of the whole matter over the phone, and probably for an instant the Lieutenant was tempted to give Jim a chance to hem and haw and back down and agree to just wait for his daughter to re-surface – but he must have decided that it would be even more fun to send a black-and-white up the Wainwrights' driveway for all their neighbors to see, so he thanked Jim for the call and hung up. It was probably all the Lieutenant could do not to order the prowler to show up at the Wainwrights' house with sirens going and lights flashing.

The Wainwrights were properly mortified to have a patrol car sitting in their driveway – at any rate, that's what one might suspect – but they made their report, and allowed the officers to take Christine's computer with them. The police advised them to call their bank, next morning (it was already early evening), and see if anyone had cleaned out Christine's account.

At about the same time that the Wainwrights made their first call to the police, another local woman reported that *her* daughter, who was Christine's age, was missing. When the police learned that the two girls knew each other, they had a better idea of what was going on.

Next morning, the Wainwrights found that Christine's bank account had indeed been closed. That further increased the probability that she was a runaway. Jim and Gail didn't know the password to Christine's email account, but it wasn't hard for a police technician to hack into it.

Also on that following day, when he started reading Christine's emails – going back weeks – Detective Sergeant Tom Brown of the State City Police Department noticed that the girl had been corresponding with one Andrew Palinkas. From their exchanges, this was evidently *the* Andrew Palinkas, the guy who owned the men's store. It was the morning after that – three days since Christine had disappeared – when Sgt. Brown visited Andy at his store, to ask about this connection.

That's the way a lot of people in State City first meet Andy Palinkas: They see a big, tall, bald guy, with mobile, high-curved eyebrows and rimless glasses that make his green eyes all the more noticeable. He's dressed immaculately in a conservative custom-made double-breasted suit, or a blazer on weekends. He's usually leaning against one of the mahogany display counters at the front of his store, one hand over the other, ready to step forward and greet the next person who comes through the door: just as old Jake Rosen used to do it, when he'd owned that store and Andy had been a salesman. It was early on a Thursday morning, so nobody was in the store but Andy and a couple of associates. Andy was wearing a light grey tropical-weight wool doubled-breasted suit, since it was June, with a pink-and-white-striped shirt with French cuffs and a contrasting white Windsor collar, and a black tie.

"Good morning," said Andy, in a big hearty voice – and just that greeting had been an effort for Andy, when he was first starting out in the business world, because he's shy and introverted. "How can we help you today?"

Sgt. Brown introduced himself, and asked Andy if he knew a girl named Christine Wainwright. Andy said he did. Brown stated the situation bluntly, keeping his voice down so that nobody else in the store could hear.

"We noticed that you and this girl had been emailing a lot, back and forth, and she seems to have told you a lot about herself. Is there anything you think we should know?"

Andy weighed his words, then spoke slowly and deliberately, deadpan.

"I know she has an adventurous nature. And I know she was unhappy with her home situation, in some ways – but what teenager isn't?"

"Do you have any information as to where she might be? Any idea where she might have gone?"

"No. I'd tell you."

"When did you see her last?"

Andy thought.

"In person, it's been a while. Weeks, anyway. You know, we were next-door neighbors for years, but her family moved to another part of town, last year, so our paths don't cross much. But if you've been in her computer, you know the last time we had any contact." Andy thought again. "And that's a thing. She and I have always emailed each other a lot, ever since she's had email. I'd say more days we do than we don't. And I haven't heard from her in several days and I did think that was unusual."

"There were concerns that maybe you knew where she might be," the detective persisted.

"No idea. I know she was having problems. I know that specifically she was unhappy about that move. It's possible that she just took off."

"That's the angle we're pursuing. We're checking to see if anybody might be sheltering her locally – because, you know, that can be kind of serious considering she's still a minor."

Andy caught the detective's meaning at once.

"Maybe someone is, but the only way it would be me is if she broke into my house without my knowledge – and if she did that, it would only have been an hour or two ago at most."

"Didn't anybody think it was kind of strange that the two of you were friends?"

Andy bristled, inwardly, but forced himself to keep his voice down.

"I don't think it was generally known. Her parents knew she was friendly with me. And I don't think they minded. I kind of kept her out of their hair, maybe."

Sgt. Brown looked more intently at Andy.

"We looked at some of your emails," he said. "We're still going through them. But it looks like you two talked about a lot of stuff. Her private issues, I mean."

"Yeah, we did. And some of it was stuff she wouldn't have felt comfortable telling her family. I won't pretend otherwise, since you have access to all of it. And probably some of it is stuff that her parents wouldn't like other people to know. Just my guess. And I have a feeling I won't be too popular with them, if they read her emails."

"Are we going to find anything from you that you shouldn't have sent her?"

"Can't think of anything. I mean, I never advised her to break the law."

"Any sexually suggestive materials?"

Andy still acted calm; he knew the detective had to ask these questions.

"I never sent her any pictures of my dick, if that's what you mean," he replied, and Sgt. Brown looked startled, as though it wouldn't have occurred to him that this impeccably dressed gentleman would have used such a word.

"If you go through her emails," Andy continued, "you'll find that she was pretty frank about her private life. But you'll see that I mostly just let her tell me – or maybe I advised her to be careful."

Brown drummed his fingers on the glass top of the display case.

"I don't suppose you'd mind if we came over to your house and took a look around," he said.

Andy straightened up – he was considerably taller than Brown – and looked stern.

"Not without a warrant, you don't. If I get home tonight and find her there, I'll let you know fast enough. Or do you suspect I might have other bodies stashed in my house? Am I a person of interest in some unsolved case that I don't know about?"

"Not as far as I can tell you."

"I expect you'll start a file on me now, though."

"Oh, we have one on you. Goes back a long time."

Andy had never even had a traffic ticket.

"Really? What have I been suspected of?"

"Oh, just that we've had complaints here and there, over the years. Three or four over, I don't know, 30 years or so. From women. Just that you made them uncomfortable."

"I?"

"Well, they'd complain that you looked at them, in the street, or smiled at them, or said hi to them, in a way that gave them the willies, I guess."

"And they *reported* me?" Andy's voice rose an octave in pitch, and got louder. "They filed a *complaint* against me?"

"Here and there." The detective's expression didn't change. "They complained, verbally, but we'd ask them if you'd threatened them, or touched them, or exposed yourself, or anything like that, and finally we had to tell them that we can't tell you not to smile at people or not to say hi to them. But apparently you have a way about you." The detective shrugged, as though advising Andy not to take it too hard.

"Oh, sometimes I scare myself, believe me." Andy tried to smile, but couldn't quite bring it.

Brown smiled for him, and said, "It goes without saying that we need you to contact us if you hear anything, if you learn anything that could help us, and especially if this girl gets in touch with you."

"Understood," said Andy – but he started to wonder: would he inform the police if Christine contacted him? Especially, would he, if she requested that he not betray her?

§

Andy Palinkas is a constant. A constant in downtown State City. A constant at the Janscombe Center's recital halls. A constant at Rivercat Stadium during the football season. He had been a constant next door to the Wainwrights – somewhat to Jim and Gail Wainwright's annoyance – till they'd moved across town. People see Andy, they notice him; they notice that he's noticing them. Andy Palinkas is warp-thread in the State City fabric: never a community leader, but a presence.

You have to understand this about Andy Palinkas: Not only has he never married; he's never had a serious long-term relationship with a woman. He's apparently straight; he's seen in the company of single women now and then; it's rumored that he's had carnal knowledge of some of them. But you'll search in vain for a woman who'll cop to it. Andy has that intensity of manner, and the distinctive appearance. It's not every woman who wants to be publicly associated with such a fellow.

Andy knows how he's perceived (although, as noted, the police dossier was news to him), and thus the interview with the policeman hadn't shocked him. But it had outraged him – and terrified him. Andy has an overactive imagination. He got to envisioning the cops subpœnaing his computer and finding porn on it, plus other embarrassing material – and then maybe he'd be jailed for some sort of thoughtcrime.

The first thing Andy did after Sgt. Brown had left his store was to text his friend Teresa Blaha. He'd known Teresa slightly in high school (she'd been Teresa Feldevert, and two years behind him, and she'd gone to Visitation High while Andy went to State City High, but they were both interested in speech and drama, and the speech kids all kind of know the speech kids from other schools, just as the jocks know the jocks and the music nerds know the music nerds), and he'd gotten better acquainted with her when they were older.

Teresa Blaha is another State City constant. "Big Mama," some people call her. "Teresa Badass." "Her Majesty."

Teresa had been a plain girl in high school. She had those grey tetracycline teeth, and had been not much shorter than Andy Palinkas (fully six feet when she'd gotten her full growth), but by her freshman year at State University she'd blossomed into a statuesque dark-blonde campus beauty, despite the teeth. She'd always been interested in her Roman Catholic faith, and serious about it, and this had intimidated many young men – although some were all the more attracted to her for her intelligence and their desire for what they couldn't touch.

Teresa had married Ted Blaha right out of college. Ted's family had owned a jewelry store in State City for a couple of generations, and young Ted was helping his father to expand it into a chain, with stores in Cedar Rapids, Coppertown, Waterloo, and Muscatine. It was clear, though, that Ted's bride was cut out for more than selling jewelry.

Despite her teenaged interest in theatre, Teresa had never been artistic. The way Ted and Teresa's marriage worked out, Ted concentrated on the sales end of the jewelry business, while Teresa managed the real estate. She also started buying commercial buildings in downtown State City, and on the outskirts of town, and by the time the story joins us, in the late 2000s, Teresa had become one of State City's bigger commercial landlords. And the Blahas were one of the town's wealthiest families.

Teresa isn't generally disliked. She's not a mean or malicious person. But she's not popular. Too rich, too businesslike, too opinionated, and too assertive: that's Teresa Blaha.

Teresa has an office in the same building as Rosen's Men's Store, one flight up. She owns the building. She and Andy see each other almost daily. She's given Andy some good advice on owning and managing commercial property, over the years. Andy now texted her to ask if they could meet.

Time for lunch? You heard about Christine Wainwright? Cops actually interviewed me.

What are you talking about? Sure: Mainliner at 12.30. She's not dead, is she? In jail?

Not dead. Run away. Tell you more at lunch.

Teresa and Ted Blaha have a daughter, Mercy, who married David Wainwright, the son of Jim and Gail – and thus the Blahas know the Wainwrights pretty well. Ted Blaha is a soft-spoken, easy-going man who gets along with everyone, and his verdict on the Wainwrights is, "Oh, they're harmless. In the long run." Teresa, who is considerably more assertive, simply doesn't like Jim and Gail – and she especially doesn't like her son-in-law.

Long ago, she'd discovered that Andy Palinkas shared her dim view of the Wainwrights. Occasionally Jim would sit with them at Rotary luncheons, and his conversation would usually give Andy and Teresa something to roll their eyes about behind his back. The two of them referred to their fascination with that family as "Wainspotting." Gossiping about them was "Waindishing," or "Waintrashing."

The Mainliner is a bar/restaurant, got up to look like a mixture of a club car and a dining car of an old-fashioned railway train. It's been in downtown State City since the 1930s. It's popular with students in the evening, and with local businesspeople and State University faculty for lunch. Decent food, dependable.

Teresa Blaha and Andy Palinkas turned people's heads as they walked in, that day, even though they were both known around town, because they are both such noticeable people. Teresa, as mentioned, is tall, and she isn't fat, but heavy the way one would expect a woman in her late 50s to be heavy. Just as Andy favors his somber double-breasted suits, Teresa prefers flowered or patterned dresses in bright colors. She has a terrific sense of what colors look best on her, so you can't say she doesn't dress with taste, but some people might call it ostentatious. She usually wears quite a lot of jewelry too. She's a jeweler's wife; what do you expect? She has a loud voice, and she's the sort who speaks her mind – and what makes her annoying, to some people, is that her mind is usually right.

"I'm not surprised," Teresa said, once they'd sat down

in the Mainliner and ordered, and Andy told her what he'd heard. "David's the only one of their children I know at all well, but I always felt sorry for little Christine. I have the feeling that the rest of the family resents her – I mean just for existing. I try to stay out of it – and goodness knows that's not easy for me, since I always know what's good for everybody else."

"They seem to just not like Christine," Teresa continued. "They seem to neglect her, or they act like she's being unreasonable when she asks for the same kind of consideration that any child could expect. Jim and Gail have both told me Christine is 'spoiled,' whatever they mean by that."

"Yeah," said Andy. "She'll tell me that they call her spoiled, but I've never seen it."

"Believe me, I have seen spoiled children," said Teresa. "Christine is normal, that's all. And I've tried to find a way to bring it up to Jim and Gail: that Christine feels like she's a fifth wheel in that family. Once I came out and said something like, 'I think Christine feels that she's not appreciated. She really is a good kid,' and Jim just said, 'She's a spoiled little princess. We keep hoping she'll outgrow it.'

"Honestly, Andy, they talk about that poor child as though she were a problem to be dealt with. And when I compare her to other children I've seen – children who really are problems – I don't know what Jim was talking about. And I told him that. I told him, 'If you don't want her, I'd be glad to have her.' I was smiling when I said it, of course, and he said, 'Don't tempt us.' And he was smiling too, but I couldn't help but wonder if he meant it."

"I'm sure you only improved the Wainwrongs' opinion of you, telling him that."

"Oh, and I caught some grief from Mercy too, for bringing it up. Jim and Gail can never be mistaken, as far as Mercy's concerned, and if I say anything remotely critical of them she says I'm 'playing family politics.' Mercy has always had the idea that I try to dominate her. And I guess now she thinks I try to dominate *everybody*. So that makes me the bad guy, when I notice that that poor youngest child has to sit there and take it because apparently sitting there and taking it is her job in that family."

The food arrived, and Teresa bowed her head, said a quick silent grace, and crossed herself. Maybe many years ago, early in their friendship, she'd have added, "I said it for you too, Andy," or Andy might have said, "The food's pretty good here; it probably doesn't need prayers."

"You know," said Andy, as they started eating, "Jim Wainwright came into my store three days ago – it must have been the day Christine took off, only he wouldn't have known it yet – and he was looking to shnorr some tuxedos for his other daughter's wedding. You believe that shit?"

Teresa tsk'd, either at what Andy was telling her, or at his use of the word "shit." Probably both.

"Yeah," Andy went on, "he came in the other day, all good fellowship, way friendlier than usual – he's been suspicious of me for years, you know – and he starts telling me about how Melissa's getting married, which of course I knew.

"Then he says something like, 'It's amazing how all our friends are chipping in.' And he starts telling me how this livery-service guy is donating the use of a limo as a wedding present; how his son's old buddy who's now a florist is donating the flowers, all that, and then he says, 'You know, the groom's party is going to need tuxes. And gosh, we're all such a big family, all of us and our friends, and we've always considered you part of our family too, since, heck, we've known each other since forever. We thought you might like to participate.'"

"And you weren't invited to the wedding, were you?"

"No, and thank G... I mean, thank Beëlzebub for that, or I'd be tempted to show up and go all medieval. But listen to this: it gets better. Then Jim says to me, 'After all, if it weren't for Gail, you wouldn't have that formalwear operation.'"

"No!"

"Can you fucking beat that?" Andy demanded, and Teresa tsk'd again. "I bailed his wife's saggy ass out of that lease on her gift shop, and now somehow that was *her* doing *me* a favor? Anyway, I'm not good enough to be invited to the wedding, but I can *participate* in it by donating a few monkey suits."

Can we doubt that most American towns — or towns in any other part of the world for that matter — have at least one family like the Wainwrights? Here's a family so much of its time and place, so gloriously ordinary — and to a superficial glance, they're such fine people.

But it's all in how you look at them. The ordinary intercourse of ordinary people can strike you as unremarkable unless you go looking for the drama — in which case there's no family that won't offer some.

No family flies under the radar. The best they can hope for is that they'll pass: not unnoticed, but unobserved. Let them be remarked upon, and it's unlikely that any person, let alone any family, will escape the direst judgment. And oftener than not, that judgment will be richly deserved.

Opinions vary, it goes without saying. A person or group despised by some might be admired by others. If someone had ever brought to Jim and Gail Wainwright's attention the fact that Andy Palinkas abhorred them, they'd have been astonished, and if his reasons were explained to them, however sweetly, they'd have refused to find merit in them.

Andy certainly disliked what he felt was the Wainwrights' sense of entitlement. But there was also this grudge that he'd carried against them for years and years: by then, just over 13 years.

2. That Little Incident

Andy had lived next door to the Wainwrights for a long time before he'd had any kind of emotional reaction to them, one way or another. He'd moved into his house on Crestwood Street in 1981, a month or so after the Wainwrights had moved into theirs. It was still five years before he would buy Rosen's Men's Store, but he'd been working at Rosen's for a long time by then. He was Jake Rosen's right arm; he was making good money. The Crestwood Street house was bigger than he needed but he had still hoped, then, that one day he might bring a wife to it. It was a two-story house with an attached garage; the main floor had a small formal dining room off the kitchen, a half-bath, a front parlor, and a back room that would work as an office. Upstairs were three bedrooms and two full baths.

The Wainwrights' house was similar to Andy's in design. It stood to the left of Andy's house, if you faced them both from the street; to Andy's right, if he were coming out his front door.

Andy hadn't had much to do with the Wainwrights. They never spent time together; they didn't have the same friends. Andy almost never exchanged more than the briefest pleasantries with either Jim or Gail. He sometimes tried to engage the two children (this was before Christine was born), but they would seldom talk to him beyond "Hi," and Andy supposed that there was something about his own aspect that put them off – or perhaps they'd been instructed not to have much to do with "that strange man."

The first time Andy had a conversation of any length with either David or Melissa was when he'd lived in his house for almost 10 years. David had been 14 and Melissa 11. It had been "trash day" – a muddy, gloomy day in March – and Andy had just gotten home from his store and was fetching his garbage bin back into his garage, and Melissa was out doing the same thing, so they were within a few feet of each other.

Andy said, "So, I suppose you're getting ready for a big event over there." Because Gail Wainwright was very pregnant, as though she might give birth any day.

"Yeah, real big," Melissa growled, with such a world-hating expression on her face that Andy almost started away from her. "Like it'll ruin my whole life. I've just had the next seven years taken away from me till I go to college – if I can afford to go, now that we have another mouth to feed. All my friends will get to be normal teenagers, and I'll get to be a baby-sitter full-time and not get paid for it. I hate my life."

"I can see your point," Andy conceded.

"Plus we've only got three bedrooms. And where do you think they'll put this new one?"

Andy shrugged. "I understand. I had to share a bedroom when I was a kid, too, and I hated it. I know that doesn't make you feel any better. Sorry."

Over the next few years, then, with this slight rapport established, Melissa would at least smile at Andy, and she'd reply if he asked her how she was doing. As Andy observed her, through adolescence, it did appear that Melissa got stuck tending little Christine pretty often. Much more than her brother did. Maybe because that's supposed to be girls' work. At least, Melissa reported to Andy, her father had renovated the attic to turn it into a nice bedroom for her, so she had a little privacy.

It also seemed to Andy – although it could have been his imagination – that Jim and Gail didn't pay much attention to their "tail-ender" child, once she'd got past the cute baby stage. Gail seemed to have kind of a short fuse around Christine. Andy never saw any abuse – nothing near it – but he'd hear Gail unhinging her jaw at Christine, louder and more frequently, it seemed to him, than she'd done as her two older kids were growing up.

Mind you, if she did, that would be understandable. If Melissa Wainwright felt that she'd had her teen years taken from her, it's possible that her mother was not entirely without the same sort of resentment: being saddled with another child when she'd thought she was past all that.

Then in the early spring of 1995, when Christine was four years old and Andy would have been about 47, came the incident from which grew Andy's almost obsessive loathing of Jim and Gail Wainwright.

If Andy hadn't happened to be washing dishes, and looking out of his back kitchen window, right when he did, Christine would probably have died. As it happened, his casual glance included the Wainwrights' back yard. He couldn't see fully into that yard, because a paled wooden fence surrounded it, but because of the angle he could see the top of the far side of the fence, where there was a gate.

Andy saw the gate swing open. A few minutes later, Christine Wainwright came into view, sort of half-skipping and half-prancing the way a girl that age will do, coming around the fence so that she was walking along the periphery of Andy's back yard.

A creek runs behind that house, and behind the Wainwrights' house. It's not a broad creek, nor deep. Ten to 12 feet across, and maybe two feet deep most of the year. It's a long creek that meanders through State City for several miles before feeding into the State River. Where Andy and the Wainwrights lived, there's a bank, fairly steep, between the creek and the back yards of the houses on either side, so the surface of the creek, at its usual depth, is about 10 feet down.

Here it was late March, though, and the ice had broken up, and the creek was swollen, so it might have been more than three feet deep in some places. It did occur to Andy that it might not be a good idea for this little girl to be playing so near a body of water, with no supervision. He watched her for a couple of minutes, and wondered whether he should go out there and tell her to go back behind her fence, but she looked like she wasn't doing anything especially dangerous.

Still, it occurred to Andy that now would be as good a time as any to step outside, check out his own back yard, and incidentally make sure the kid was all right; maybe remind her to be careful of the water. It was a gorgeous spring afternoon, a Sunday. Andy wasn't a gardener, but he had planted a few bulbs here and there in his front and back yards, and he wandered across his back yard, now, looking at the croci and making sure the tulips and daffodils were beginning to sprout. He heard a rustling near the creek and strolled over to it. To his left, about 50 feet away, he saw Christine standing on the very edge of the bank, poking at some dead leaves on the ground. Then he saw her lose her footing.

She shrieked as she slid down the bank into the creek, and Andy shrieked, too – falsetto, like a woman. That sound – his own – would stay in his mind for the rest of his life. Andy would remember that shriek above anything else in that whole incident, and years later he would feel slight shame at having emitted it.

Maybe Andy remembered the shriek because he wasn't thinking about what he did next. He just did what it occurred to him to do. He scooted down the bank, slipping more than stepping, and before he was aware of it he was in the water almost to his waist, and it must have been freezing cold but he didn't realize it for the instant it took him to catch Christine and grab her. The current was sweeping Christine right at Andy; she was thrashing, and she couldn't have got by him because he was standing right in the middle of the creek, like a shortstop waiting for a ground ball to come to him.

Andy fielded Christine, and his instinct was to carry her out of the creek and run with her up the bank, but her clothes were full of water at that point so that she must have weighed twice her normal poundage. Andy tried to pick Christine up as best he could by just grabbing hold of whatever parts of her he could get a grip on.

To lift Christine, Andy had to hug her to him, which meant that his whole body was drenched and the creek's current was almost strong enough to knock him down. He didn't believe he could walk the couple of steps out of the creek – the mud nearly pulled his shoes off when he tried to take a step – *and* climb up the embankment while he was carrying a soaking-wet four-year-old girl, so instead of carrying Christine out of the creek he more or less hove her onto the bank: flung her, as though she'd been a sack of fertilizer. Then he scrambled out of the water as best he could, which was difficult because his trousers had become waterlogged. Christine was starting to roll back down the bank toward the water again so he had to shove her, heave her up the hill, by inches, and she was too terrified to help the process.

At the top of the hill, Andy had an awful premonition that his hold would slip and Christine would roll back down again, and this time he wouldn't be able to stop her. It took him a good minute to somehow manhandle Christine up onto the dry grass above the embankment to a point where she wasn't going to do that, and at last Andy was able to start scrambling up, himself. To get up onto the grass, he had to crawl on his belly, because he couldn't get a purchase with his feet. Once onto the grass he lay prone, next to Christine, for a few seconds, trying to gather his senses and catch his breath.

Andy sat up. He could see that Christine was moving, her eyes were open, she was sputtering, so obviously she was breathing, which was a great relief to Andy because he wasn't sure he'd have known how to resuscitate her.

Andy got to his feet and grabbed Christine again. He picked her up in a bear hug, and she started to shout – not scream, it wasn't loud – and Andy slung her over his shoulder in a fireman's lift and moved toward his back door as best he could: slowly, because he was carrying not only Christine, but several pounds of water in his clothes. Somehow, he got the door open. He carried Christine into his kitchen and set her on the floor.

Andy ran into the hallway and up the staircase to the upper floor, to a linen closet, from which he dragged out a blanket, then ran with it back downstairs to the kitchen, where Christine was still sitting on the floor, looking stunned, not saying anything. Andy wondered whether she was going into shock, and how he could tell if she were.

If he'd had his wits completely about him, Andy would probably have carried Christine over to where the gate in the Wainwrights' back fence was still ajar, and carried her through the Wainwrights' back yard and pounded on their back door. As it was, all he could think to do was to carry her – wrapped in the blanket, now – out the back door of his house again, and around his house to the front, where he could beat a tattoo on the Wainwrights' front door.

So far, Christine hadn't said anything. Andy carried her up onto the Wainwrights' front porch and hammered on the door with his fist – didn't knock, but hammered – and hollered, *"Open up! Open up! Your daughter fell in the creek!"*

Only, nobody opened the front door for him. Instead, a few seconds later, Andy could hear Gail Wainwright in the back yard, calling "Christine? Christine?" He still had Christine in his arms; she was still making no sound. Andy ran around to the side of the house, to the paled fence, and yelled over it, "Gail! Over here!" He held Christine up so that her mother could see her over the fence. He had to call twice. Gail had actually gone through the gate on the other end of her back yard; Andy could see the top of her head. She was evidently scouting the banks of the creek. Finally Andy got Gail's attention and she ran around the outside of the fence, through Andy's back yard, so that at last they were face to face and Andy could hand the bundle to her.

Gail moaned, "Oh, Christine, what have you been doing?"

"She might be in shock," said Andy. "I'm going to run inside and call an ambulance."

"I don't think that'll be necessary," Gail said, but Andy turned and would have run back into his own house, except that when he turned he was face-to-face with Jim Wainwright, who had presumably come out the front door of his house, in belated response to Andy's hammering, and had followed the noise outdoors and to the side of the house.

"What?" Jim asked Andy. "What's the trouble?"

"Christine had a little accident," said Gail, in what struck Andy as a calmer tone than he might have expected.

"She fell into the creek," Andy told Jim, still breathless. "She was out playing back behind your fence and she slid down the embankment and went in. I got her out. She'd have drowned." Andy was panting.

"Gosh!" Jim exclaimed. "How'd she get outside the yard?"

What Andy wanted to do was explain to Jim that she'd got outside the yard by tripping the latch on the gate and walking out, and that if he and Gail didn't want that to happen, they should get a fucking lock for that gate – but Gail was standing right there, and Andy understood that neither she nor Jim would thank him for saying that.

"We ought to call an ambulance," Andy reiterated to Jim. "Or take her to the hospital."

"I'm sure she'll be fine," said Jim. "Let's get her inside."

Jim stepped past Andy, took the blanket-wrapped Christine from Gail, and carried her into their house, through the front door. Gail hurried after him. Neither looked back.

They must have seen that Andy was soaking wet. But it must all have been overwhelming to them, almost losing one of their children, and the confusion and all. Maybe some people would accuse Andy of having been petty, and indeed he even accused himself of it, later on, but at any rate he stood there, outside, for another minute or so, noticing that he hadn't heard a "thank you."

Andy scolded himself for being unreasonable and self-absorbed as usual. Jim and Gail wouldn't think to thank him in the heat of the moment, he decided, and he should be ashamed of himself for resenting not having been thanked.

He wondered why the Wainwrights would veto his idea of seeking medical attention. He remembered that Jim Wainwright was a doctor, but in the next instant he remembered that Jim was a podiatrist, and Andy didn't know if podiatrists were proper physicians or not, only he knew they weren't M.D.s.

It finally registered on Andy that he was freezing and covered with muck – he could hardly feel his legs, and what feeling he had was intensely painful – so he went into his own house and took a long hot shower.

That evening, Andy considered going over and knocking on the Wainwrights' door to ask after Christine. But he was afraid Jim and Gail would think he was being intrusive, or maybe looking for some kind of reward.

It was the next evening, a Monday evening, around 7:00, when Jim Wainwright knocked on Andy's front door. He was carrying the blanket in which Andy had wrapped Christine. He looked abashed, it seemed to Andy, and wouldn't come in when Andy invited him. He just said, "Hey, thanks for getting Christine out of the water yesterday. She couldn't tell us too much, except that you got her out, but thanks. Looks like she'll be okay." He handed over the blanket, which had been laundered and now smelled of fabric softener.

"You know, Gail and I had no idea Christine was tall enough to reach that latch," Jim added. "They grow so fast. And then before you know it they're ready to leave you." Jim then offered his hand, which Andy shook.

"Thanks for coming by," said Andy.

"You bet," said Jim, and left.

Andy didn't see Gail Wainwright for about a week after that incident, nor Christine for that matter, but on the following Sunday he and Gail were in their front yards at the same time. Gail was weeding, and Andy jokingly asked if she'd care to start on his yard, next. Then he asked how Christine was.

"Fine," said Gail. "No harm done, apparently. Except she won't take baths now, ever since that little incident. Jim and I have to *force* her into the tub." And she laughed.

Then she looked away, and walked back into her house. It was quite a while – months – before she would give Andy anything more than the barest greeting when their paths crossed. Even after that, Andy seldom got much more than an uncomfortable "Hrm… hrm," from either of the adult Wainwrights, unless further conversation were necessary.

It's hardly uncommon, if someone does someone else a big favor – particularly if it involves rescuing someone from some true calamity – for the beneficiary to resent the benefactor forever after. Could that have been what was happening? Or was it more a matter of the Wainwrights being forever mortified that Andy had caught them being neglectful?

Or – and this is an awful thing to think, but it might bear consideration – was Gail secretly a tiny bit sorry that Andy had saved the child?

It's fun to find certain people contemptible. It gives you a tingle, sometimes, to look upon your fellow man and curl your lip in distaste, or scorn, or (on special occasions) utter loathing. But Andy thought about the Wainwrights more than was good for him, and he knew it.

He once asked himself: was there a moral horizon that Jim and/or Gail Wainwright had crossed, that made him feel the way he felt? Could he point to a deed, or event, that was so horrible that it made him say, "Okay, that's it, that person has crossed the line from being just sort of a jerk, to being irredeemably bad"?

Andy concluded that Gail had crossed that line, *not* when her negligence had allowed Christine to fall into the creek. That had been bad, but Andy could have forgiven it as the kind of mistake any parent could make. And it was not when she couldn't even thank him for saving her daughter's life. That was shame taking over, Andy supposed, and he understood about shame.

No: When Gail crossed the line was when she told Andy that she and her husband had to *force* Christine into the bathtub, now. That was when she went, in Andy's green eyes, from being a neglectful parent to being a malicious, sadistic abuser. And she'd said "Jim and I," which indicated to Andy that Jim was in full collusion. That, coupled with the way Jim, too, had acted immediately following the accident, convinced Andy that the Wainwrights were actively evil. Moreover, Andy decided, they were *obliviously* evil.

Even a psychopath or a sociopath, if you explain to him why some people would call his deeds evil or immoral, will usually be able to see what you're talking about. He might not agree with you. He might rationalize his actions, rationalize them so well that he could almost convince *you*, as well as himself. But he would at least understand why some people might think he was doing wrong.

Jim and Gail, though (at least, Andy believed this): If you tried to explain the wrongness of their behavior to them, you would probably not make much impression on them. They'd be amazed, and they'd flat-out refuse to admit even a possibility that you weren't holding that opinion simply out of malice or perversity. They'd be deeply hurt at the sheer *unfairness* of your position.

The Wainwrights, Andy concluded, were a type of sociopath that's never been explored by the academic or clinical communities, because coupled with the pathology of that sort of person is a sort of absolute ordinariness that renders them highly functional in everyday life and – and this is crucial – *keeps them under the radar of evil.*

3. Christine Grows Up

Another 10 years passed. Although Andy continued to regard Jim and Gail Wainwright with secret loathing, he never developed any ill-feeling toward their children. A few months after "that little incident," David, the eldest, went off to college, and Andy had almost never had any interaction with him. Melissa, the elder daughter, was more forthcoming. She would sometimes stop and chat, when her path crossed Andy's, and Andy had the impression she didn't dislike him.

Christine showed no permanent damage. She became more and more friendly with Andy as she got old enough to have conversations with him – probably because she could tell that he was making a point of paying attention to her. Andy felt just a bit proud of himself, whenever he saw Christine – although he was also ashamed of himself for feeling that pride. He'd only done what anyone would have done, Andy would tell himself – and yet it was because of him that Christine was around at all. Andy felt that having rescued Christine once, he'd accepted a duty to look out for her forever after.

From then on, Andy would greet Christine warmly whenever he saw her, and converse with her whenever she was inclined to. He'd question her about her interests, school, and whatever else she might want to tell him about.

Christine thought "Mr. P" (as her family called him) was kind of strange – but she considered him her friend, probably her only adult friend. He really did look like an evil guy from a movie, like one of those mad scientists who plots to take over the world and sits in his spaceship or his submarine laughing about it. Christine might have wondered why Mr. P was interested in being friends with her, and why she hardly ever saw visitors at his house.

When Christine was five or six, she asked Andy, "How come you don't have a wife?" and he replied, "My dear, I can't explain that to my own satisfaction, let alone to yours, but it's my misfortune." Thus Christine learned two new words – "satisfaction" and "misfortune" – and it occurred to her that Mr. P taught her a lot of new words.

She liked him for that, and sometimes when she saw Mr. P she'd ask him, "Do you have a new word for me today?" And Mr. P would always come up with one; in fact he would usually have one prepared, just in case.

For example, he might say, "I have, indeed. The word for today is 'persevere.' It means to never give up, to always keep trying. Just as I persevere in my efforts to find a wife, and I suppose you persevere in your schoolwork or whatever else might interest you." And he'd tell Christine how to spell it.

Melissa, the elder daughter, grew up to be quite a pretty young woman, but Christine was a plain little girl. She was slightly chunky in her early years, but she lost the baby fat when she hit puberty at about age 11, and from then on she had a slight, spindly figure, almost spidery.

Christine had a snub nose, prominent front teeth, hazel-brown eyes, and straight dark hair that she wore in a pixie. When she got older she wore her hair more shaped, but still chin-length, except that she took a hank of it, over her left ear, braided it to about the caliber of a drinking straw, and let this grow out till it was past her shoulder. She also took to painting the least fingernail of her right hand (the right, she explained to Andy, to balance the tail over her left ear) a different color every day to complement whatever clothes she was wearing.

Otherwise, Christine's appearance was unremarkable. As she entered her teens she became what might have been called cute – in a skinny, toothy way – but never pretty.

Christine seemed an absolutely normal girl, with ordinary interests. She was moderately athletic, didn't do a lot of reading, got average to above-average grades in school. She liked music. She started taking violin lessons when she was eight, but within a year she was more interested in the guitar.

This met with resistance from her mother, at first.

"I really don't want you learning the guitar," Gail explained. "You'll want to start playing rock music, and you'll want to join a band, and then the whole bunch of you will be practicing in our basement and driving the rest of us crazy..."

But Christine took her case to her father, and found him a little more lenient. Jim reassured Gail, apparently, because for Christmas, when she was nine years old and some months, Christine got her guitar. It was an acoustic guitar, not made to be amplified (Gail had insisted on that), but it made Christine happy, and she immediately sent her violin into retirement and began taking guitar lessons.

She was a willing pupil. The young man the Wainwrights found to give her lessons was mainly a classical and flamenco guitarist, but he started Christine on simple folk tunes, and soon she was picking out songs that had been made popular by Bob Dylan, and Peter, Paul, and Mary: what her parents had listened to as teenagers and college students. Jim and Gail both thought that was funny. And as long as she played that kind of music, the guitar was quieter than a violin.

Here and there, by making friends with other musical kids, Christine had opportunities to try an electric guitar. She learned to play some rock songs, and to improvise. Her preference was for folk – and classical guitar struck her as far too much trouble to pursue – but she liked playing rock because it was more sociable. It was a way for her to get to know cooler kids, who might be interested in forming a band – which would make them cooler yet.

As Christine got older, Mr. P seemed especially interested in hearing about her musical aspirations, so when she got involved with a band for the first time – this would have been the spring of 2005, when she'd just turned 14 – he was the first adult she told, even before she told her parents.

They called themselves the Dragonflies. Three boys and two girls. They played covers of pop songs, plus a few original songs that were truly terrible. One of the boys had a background in bluegrass, and he gave the band that influence.

Christine was the rhythm guitarist. The other girl, Léa Burns, was lead vocalist and played violin; Justin Vauks played bass, Rob Caslavka played drums, and Aaron Roos played lead guitar. Christine told Andy Palinkas all this in an email.

I shoulda been lead guitar cuz I know I'm as good as Aaron but A I don't have an electric guitar of my own (gotta work on this, maybe will buy a used one cheap, but for now I hafta borrow one of Aaron's) and B he's a boy so naturally he hasta be lead. What guy is gonna agree to play rhythm guitar behind a girl, right? And Léa is an awesome singer, way better than me I gotta admit so it makes sense that she's lead vocal but she's kinda full of herself U know? (U can tell she's full of herself cuz she uses that accent over the E in her name. She writes the accent bigger than the letters, like some girls will put a big round dot over their i's.) She thinks Aaron's bluegrass stuff is corny, but I kinda like it. I wish we did more of it and less rock. I also wish I could sing like her. It's hard to imagine that we're ever gonna get real good cuz we don't have a regular place to practice so we're lucky if we can get together a couple times a week and usually one of us is missing at least.

We tried using our garage but Dad has his wood shop stuff in there & he doesn't like us messing around. And Mom doesn't like the noise. Its not music shes used to so she complains. She and Dad call it Headache Music. :-P

Dear Miss Christine:

I like that there's an element of bluegrass to your band. I don't know a lot about that kind of music, but my younger brother played accordion when we were kids, including a lot of bluegrass, so I developed a taste for it.

Yes, it's true. Most boys (almost all boys, face it) would die before they would let a girl play lead guitar ahead of them. Maybe one day you'll form a girl group and play lead for them. Life is unfair that way.

It's good you've got an "awesome" lead vocalist, but Léa will probably have a lot to say about the creative direction your band takes, and that might mean less bluegrass and more of what she likes to sing. Ideally you'll all work something out so everyone's tastes and inclinations can be accommodated.

Re your parents' reaction to your "headache music," let me tell you a secret: Grownups have had that attitude since music was invented. Every generation complains that what their kids listen to is nothing but noise, compared to the sweet wonderful perfect music they used to listen to when they were younger.

Here's a suggestion: If you need regular practice space, why not use my garage? Use it whenever you like. Just let me know in advance when you're going to be there, so I can move my car out for you, and be out of there no later than 11:00 at night; it shouldn't be a problem.

Best,

Andrew Gabor Palinkas

Dear Mr. P,

Thank you thank you. I think we will take you up on that but we hafta come up with a cover story cuz Mom & Dad don't know I'm emailing you and it might freak them out if they found out. Ill tell them you & I were talking & you offered the garage but you need to back me up on that if they ask you OK?

A few months after that e-mail conversation – Christine and her friends had started using Andy's garage two or three times a week, on average – Andy had his first substantial exchange with Mrs. Wainwright since Christine's accident, years before.

Andy and Gail happened to run into each other in the Hy-Vee, near the tea and coffee section, and Gail thanked Andy for letting her daughter use his garage.

"Only doesn't it bother you, having that noise blaring into your house?"

"It's only a couple nights a week. I don't mind. Matter of fact, it's kind of fun to have them around, and they're getting better now that they're practicing more. And either they'll get good, one of these days, or they'll outgrow it."

"That's what Jim and I are hoping. Christine's talking about music as a career, now, and I know she's just a kid, and all kids have fantasies like that, but still I worry that she might actually try it."

Christine's group wasn't bad: not good, but decent by the standards of 14- and 15-year-olds. Andy would sit in the garage and listen to them, sometimes. He couldn't help noticing tensions within the group, and they seemed to be largely attributable to one member or the other wanting to be the leader. The bass player and the drummer were more interested in being team members, but Aaron, Léa, and Christine each seemed to think that they knew best and/or should have larger roles.

Dear Mr. P,

Something came up and maybe you can give advice. There's this girl in our school who gets picked on cuz she's kinda slow and has like a learning disability which I guess is the polite name for retarded cuz you're not allowed to say retarded anymore. Anyway I feel bad for her and I thought it might be fun to invite her into the band and let her do something simple like background vocal if she can sing at all, or play some kind of rhythm instrument or something.

I mentioned it to the rest of the band and they didn't like the idea and Léa was specially PO'd. She said something like "This isn't a sandbox where you have to let everybody play. This isn't the second grade, are we trying to have a real band or what?" Which made me kinda mad cuz Léa is stuck up and she's always trying to be the leader and where does she get the idea she's better than the rest of us? But then all three of the guys backed her up on it and I'm thinking I should quit the band if they're all gonna be like that. Plus what do I tell Imogene now? I already invited her to come practice with us next time.

But if I quit I won't have a band and they're my friends supposably, so what am I gonna do?

Dear Miss Christine:

You just learned not to invite a friend to a party before you know she'll be welcome. You can employ several strategies here. First, you can never mention it to Imogene again. If she asks you when the next practice session is, you can say something like, "I'm not sure, but I'll let you know." But if she's insistent, you might have to bring her.

In that case, warn your bandmates beforehand that you're bringing a guest: not a prospective new member, but just a friend who wants to observe. They can't object to that without showing that they're jerks, and they won't want to do that.

If she comes, you'll probably intimidate her by how well you play, and she won't even dream of trying to join your band. You can also put her off by casually remarking that it's *so* much work to get good, and you and your friends put in hours and hours, every day. Even if that's not true, say it.

Now, re Léa's attitude, and the question of whether you should quit the band. First of all, I would advise you not to quit. This is one of those squabbles that will blow over in no time. Also, we have to admit that Léa does have a point. If you guys are trying to be the best you can be, it doesn't make sense to let someone into the band who is going to stick out on account of her ineptitude, and bring down the overall quality of your music.

About Léa being the leader, that kind of thing happens in a band. Usually the most musically talented person will emerge as the leader, although it doesn't always work that way. From the few times I've heard you guys play – to be brutally honest – Léa does seem to be the most talented musician. And as lead singer, she'll be front and center most of the time. If she's becoming your leader, that's normal and natural and it might be best to let it happen.

That doesn't mean she has to always get her way, or be the boss of the rest of you, but you can regard her as "first among equals," and acknowledge her superior musicianship.

Having said that, I'd advise you not to worry. This band won't last forever. I expect Léa will leave the band before you do. Whether or not she really is that good, if she believes she's that good she'll either go solo, or find a band that's cooler than yours.

When that happens, wish her all the luck in the world and stay friends. That is absolutely important. You mustn't let artistic differences damage a friendship. I hope this helps.

Best,

Andrew Gabor Palinkas

A few weeks later, one night when a practice was breaking up and the kids were packing up their equipment, Andy stepped into the garage, from inside his house. "Hi, Mr. P," said all four teenagers.

"So, all okay?" Andy asked.

"Guess so," said Christine.

"I haven't seen your lead vocalist lately."

"Yeah, Léa found another band," said Christine. "You know, we weren't good enough for her."

"What you mean, 'we,' paleface?" Aaron Roos inquired.

An SUV pulled up in front of Andy's house: a parent, evidently. Rob Caslavka hauled his drum set down Andy's driveway and into the vehicle; the two other boys piled in after him; the SUV drove off into the night. Andy and Christine still stood in the garage.

"It made sense," said Christine. "Her leaving. She found a band that actually gets gigs. We just play for fun; it's not like we're ever going to be professionals."

"I thought that was your ambition."

"It's something I think about sometimes." Christine was standing tip-toe on one foot, her other leg behind her knee, one finger on the top of her upright guitar case for balance. "My parents would hate it. Oh, you know what my Dad said, when I told him about Léa? He said, [Christine gave an impression of her father's voice, making him sound sententious] 'She'll be back, when she learns that music should be for fun.' Oh, and then he was like, 'A musician's life isn't all it's cracked up to be, and she'll find that out the hard way.'"

"That sounds almost like your Dad is telling you ambition is bad, huh?"

"Well, Mom and Dad think I should have some kind of career where I'm helping other people. When I grow up I mean." Christine switched to standing tip-toe on her other foot. "Like Melissa, she's a teacher? They ask me why I don't want to be a teacher and all I can tell them is I'm not Melissa. And David's wife, Mercy, she's a nurse – and, same story."

"But your brother, he's a journalist, right?"

Christine smirked, and tsk'd. "Maybe he thought he could help humanity by being a journalist." Christine tried stretching her free leg straight out behind her, still leaning one finger on her guitar. "Or maybe because he's a boy it's not as important for him to be in a helping job."

Andy had to smile at that, because he believed Christine was probably right on.

"It's not my place to advise you," he said, "but you should do what you want most. If that's the career that will make you the happiest of all, go for it. Seriously."

Christine put both her feet back onto the floor of the garage, but continued to lean on her guitar case.

"Is that what you did? Did you grow up wanting to own a men's store?"

The question might have sounded insolent, but it was clear to Andy, from Christine's expression, that she was asking it without guile or sarcasm.

"No, and let me be a lesson to you. I don't mean to say I don't like what I do. I've learned to. I love running a men's store – now – and I make more money at it than I ever thought I would. But Rosen's was where I ended up because I didn't have the gumption to go for what I wanted.

"I loved to act, in high school. Speech and drama. I wasn't an athlete, didn't know crap about music, but I did love to act. It's a long story, why I didn't pursue it, and maybe I'll tell you one day, but I just didn't. If music is what floats your boat, then do it. Chase it down, don't let anything or anybody stop you."

"It's something I like doing," said Christine. "I guess some kids know what they want, right away, and they go after it. I wish I was like that."

"Not too many people are. I wasn't. I told myself I wanted to be an actor but obviously it didn't matter that much to me – or I'd have done whatever it took to become an actor. But you do have to work at it to get good. Like, a lot. I mean, if Léa is a better musician than you are, I bet it's because she earned it. I didn't have it in me to work that hard, and I knew it, so I never tried."

"You could try acting again. Like, community theatre or something. I bet you'd be great."

"I haven't acted a lick since high school. More than 40 years ago, now."

"And next year it'll be more than 41 years." Christine picked up her guitar case and headed out of the garage. "Night."

Dear Miss Christine:

I was thinking about what you said last night, about if I don't go back to acting, I'm just going to get older and older, and you're right. I checked the State City Community Theatre website, and they're doing *One Flew Over The Cuckoo's Nest* this fall, which is a play that's got lots of parts for older men. So I'm going to audition. Thank you for giving me a push.

Now, with regard to your band. With Léa gone, you have a chance to put yourself forward as lead singer. Have you thought of taking voice lessons? You'd probably find them useful in all kinds of ways. One thing that held me back as an actor was that I always hated my own voice. I should have studied voice as a young man.

You sing fine now, from what I've heard in the garage, but you'd probably benefit from formal training. Do ask your parents about getting you some lessons. You can always remind them that it'll make your "headache music" more bearable for them.
Best,
Andrew Gabor Palinkas

Dear Mr. P,

Good idea. I mean both are. You acting and me taking voice. Difference is, you can just do it. I hafta ask.
:-p

Christine reported to Andy that Jim and Gail's first response, when she asked them if she could take voice lessons, was to object to the expense. Gail said Christine had too much on her plate already to add another activity – a costly activity that her parents would be expected to pay for, at that – but then Jim gave that indulgent smile of his and told Gail that this was just a phase Christine was going through.

"I never saw the attraction, but I never saw music do a kid harm," he might have told Gail in private. "It'll keep her busy anyway. And every minute she spends practicing her voice will be one less minute that she's whanging on that guitar."

So, it was decided between the two of them that Christine should have voice lessons – if she'd drop the guitar lessons.

"I just got an idea," Jim added. "Connor, and what his wife's going through. Maybe this would be, I dunno, occupational therapy for her. If she was to give Christine lessons. I could ask Connor if he thinks she'd be up to it."

§

Connor Lowe was a friend of the family. He'd been teenaged sweethearts with the Wainwrights' elder daughter, Melissa, but after high school they'd drifted apart, and now Connor was married to another girl, and had an infant daughter. Jim and Gail were still fond of him, and had stayed in touch.

The girl Connor had married was a graduate student in the School of Music. A soprano, several years older than Connor: a strikingly beautiful woman named Tanya Cucoshay. Jim would have reasoned that it might be Connor's decision, whether he'd let Tanya take that job, with their new baby and all. Then there'd be the issue of whether Tanya would be up to it mentally. Connor had told Jim a little about how Tanya had been acting crazy, that summer, although he hadn't gone into too much detail – to protect Tanya, Jim supposed. So Jim's first call was to Connor Lowe, rather than to Tanya directly.

Connor put Tanya on the phone, and Jim Wainwright introduced himself.

"I've got a daughter here who might be looking for a voice teacher," he said. "Your husband's an old friend of our family – you know, he went to high school with our daughter Melissa – and he said you might be interested."

"Yes, I know you," said Tanya. "You were at Connor's and my wedding, and then at our housewarming. You and Mrs. Wainwright gave us that beautiful garden angel. Thank you again for that."

"I haven't been giving lessons lately," Tanya went on, "what with grad school and the new baby and all, but I have been thinking I should start again. I'd be glad to meet with your daughter, and we can see if we're a match. I charge $25 per half-hour lesson, and I ask you to pay for each month in advance, so unless we arrange otherwise it'll be $100 or $125 a month, depending on whether we have four or five sessions in that month. I'll give her all my policies on paper when we have our first lesson."

"Oh," said Jim, for all the world as though he were

taken aback that Tanya was proposing to charge for the lessons at all. Possibly, Jim had expected them to come at no charge – since he was doing her the favor, offering free therapy to a woman who'd recently had a mental breakdown.

"Oh," he said again. "You know, we've almost come to think of Connor as family, we've known him for so long. Any chance we could work out some kind of a special deal?"

Being reminded that the Wainwrights thought of Connor as family was probably not pleasant to Tanya.

"You can ask around," she replied. "I'm pretty sure my rates are what anyone in town would charge, if not a little bit less."

So Jim Wainwright did agree to the arrangement, on the understanding that the first lesson would be paid for on a one-off basis, and then they'd see. But we can suppose that this gave Jim another reason to dislike Tanya, whom he'd heard was a difficult, willful young lady if not just plain mentally unhinged. So it was with misgivings that he told Christine that her first lesson with Tanya would be on the following Tuesday afternoon, after school.

Christine had never had a conversation with Tanya; she'd just seen her a few times, and she'd heard her talked about, mostly referred to as "that woman Connor married." Her mother had said Tanya seemed "cold," when they'd returned from the couple's housewarming party.

"But let us know how it goes," Gail told Christine. "I can't wait to hear what you think of her." She said this conspiratorially, as though she and Christine had an understanding that Tanya would be a subject of gossip.

Speaking of gossip: To understand what happened later, we now have to talk about Connor Lowe and his relationship with the Wainwrights' middle child and elder daughter, Melissa.

II. MELISSA WAINWRIGHT AND CONNOR LOWE

4. Melissa and Connor in High School

In any high school in the world, you'll find a few kids whom most other kids (and teachers) barely notice, and are forgotten once they're out of sight. That was Connor Lowe, in his middle school and high school career, in the 1990s. Connor had friends, but no close ones. Nobody disliked him, either.

What's remarkable about Connor – what some people might find admirable, and maybe enviable – is that he can fit in anywhere. He's had that quality all his life. He's a plodder: a hard worker who gets it done and never gets in anybody's way. As a teenager, he kept a low profile, deliberately not drawing much attention to himself. This was partly because that was how he preferred it – he was quiet and not outgoing – and partly because he was unsure of himself. He wanted to get along with people – and he almost always did – but he never wanted them to feel that he was imposing on them. Therefore, for him, getting along with others wasn't so much a matter of making himself pleasant as of making himself unobtrusive.

Connor wasn't "in with the in crowd" at any time during his childhood and adolescence. He was never an outcast, either. He blended well, so he was able to hang with the cooler kids sometimes, even though they would never have considered him one of them.

By middle school, Connor was getting his growth. He was lanky, and like many such boys he was clumsy. He had ginger hair that would never obey a comb; he wore braces on his teeth; he required fairly strong glasses for his nearsightedness. He was weedy, but not hideous; awkward, but not hopeless at sports. He was, like most boys of 13, insecure about his worth as a human being – but no more so than most boys. Indeed, a superficial observer might say he was outstanding in his sheer ordinariness.

Only, Connor wasn't ordinary. He was brighter than he looked. He was a good student in general – maybe not because he was especially apt, but more because he just showed up and did the work – and he had one subject at which he excelled: mathematics. But he never felt inclined to show off his skills. None of the other kids seemed to notice that in that one subject, he was the smartest in the class. Or they'd notice, in the way of "Connor's real good at math," but they'd think nothing more of it.

Connor wasn't much of an athlete, but he enjoyed basketball, and it disappointed him when he didn't make the varsity team in middle school. But he persevered. He practiced when he could. He sought out the better players, and when they outplayed him, he learned to understand how they did it.

At 13, Connor began to notice girls. No girl seemed to hate him, but most of them weren't interested in talking to him – just as they didn't talk to any but the coolest boys, or the boys who were kind of girly themselves. That's how it works at that age, and it didn't bother Connor. He was just as glad that no girl was taking a shine to him, since he figured it would lead to embarrassment if one did. And he understood that the cooler boys would naturally attract more notice.

A few girls appealed to him. Strangely – he even remarked, himself, that it was strange – he wasn't much interested in the girls who were generally regarded as the prettiest and most popular. One who did catch his eye was Melissa Wainwright.

Most people would have considered Melissa mousy-looking. She was of average height and build, but she looked shorter than she was because she slouched. But so did Connor, a little. She wore glasses, as Connor did. Her hair was a sort of dishwater-brown. She had a sprinkling of freckles across her nose, although not as many as Connor.

Melissa would smile at Connor in the hallways, and say, "Hi, Connor," and every so often they'd find themselves in the same clump of kids who might be discussing any subject you might think of. In art class, they often shared a table.

It could be that Connor was pleased and flattered that Melissa always acknowledged him and seemed to like him – and her occasional attentions might have made him think that maybe he had something going on after all.

Connor saw past Melissa's mousiness. He thought she was pretty: pretty enough that he would fantasize about kissing her, or even taking it further, somehow. He would practice kissing her, on his pillow at night. He knew she was not, in a purely æsthetic sense, the best-looking girl in his class – but she was attractive enough to make him crush on her.

The trouble (from Connor's viewpoint) would have been an apprehension that Melissa liked him back. Maybe even in *that* way. What if she did? What would other kids think, if the two of them became a couple? Would he be laughed at? Especially, would he be laughed at by the coolest guys, the prettiest girls? He'd have known – as most boys know, on an intellectual level – that he shouldn't let that idea worry him, but it did. After all, Melissa was nothing special. Her glasses were even dorkier than his. She dressed plainly – jeans and a hoodie, usually – and didn't wear makeup, and didn't try to look sophisticated like some of the other girls.

In a word, she was almost as nerdy as Connor believed he was – and while he was willing to accept Melissa as she was, he must have wondered whether he'd be lowering himself, so-cially, by being known as her boyfriend.

In eighth and ninth grade the two of them were kind of a couple. They started hanging out together at school. They were each other's dates for dances. But outside of school they didn't see much of each other. Connor was still at an age where his guy friends would have considered him less than manly if he'd been spending inordinate amounts of time with a girl in preference to them. (They'd have been envious, too, if they didn't have girls of their own.)

Connor still thought, every so often, about kissing Melissa, and finally at the beginning of ninth grade he worked up the nerve to do it: clumsily, rather roughly, and Melissa didn't seem to enjoy it. She writhed a little in his grasp, and sorta-kinda kissed him back, but then she laughed, nervously, and ducked out of his embrace.

For the next few weeks, Melissa remained friendly – but she had that same nervous laugh every time she saw Connor, and he didn't dare repeat the gesture. By the end of ninth grade, everyone (including the two of them) seemed to have forgotten that Connor and Melissa had ever been more than friends.

So it continued, through their sophomore year. But in their junior year, when they were both 16, they couldn't help but see each other differently. Connor had settled into his gawky, gangling body so that while he was still a bit awkward, he appeared to be more comfortable with it. And his persever-ance had finally paid off. He made the basketball team, and while he only ever got to play in the closing minutes of a game he was at least on the varsity squad. His grades and test scores were high enough that he'd have no trouble getting into a good college. He mostly hung out with the computer geeks and the gear-heads, rather than the jocks, so he was still not considered a cool kid – but he continued to attract so little notice that he was accepted everywhere.

Melissa, meanwhile, had blossomed. She still had the mousy hair, but she wore it with more style; she'd exchanged her glasses for contacts; she sometimes wore skirts, now, and light makeup always. She and Connor started spending more and more time together in school, and now that Connor had a car, he would take her for rides. Before they knew what had happened, they were back to being a couple.

The relationship progressed slowly, especially the physical part. They managed to be off by themselves, occasionally, long enough to indulge in some make-out sessions, and they forgot the embarrassment of the bungled kiss of a few years before.

Jim and Gail were always welcoming, when Connor came to their house, and Connor liked them. They were relaxed, unpretentious, and they seemed to be more involved in their kids' lives than his own parents were. Connor's mother was a commercial photographer and his father ran a plumbing supplies business, and Connor got along with both of them, but neither of them had ever had a lot of time left over for him. Connor was an only child, and had always been pretty self-sufficient.

It occurred to Connor that maybe one reason why the Wainwrights paid him so much attention was that they didn't want to leave him and Melissa unsupervised. They certainly weren't allowed to study in Melissa's attic bedroom. And Christine, Melissa's pesky little sister, was usually underfoot.

It may be, also, that the relationship was both helped and hindered by the involvement of Jim and Gail Wainwright – neither of whom missed an opportunity to oh-so-casually mention to Melissa that Connor was a wonderful young man.

"So serious," Gail remarked to Melissa once, "but he's nice, too. So polite and soft-spoken. And, you know, even if he's not the handsomest boy in the school, he's one of that type that's going to get better-looking as he gets older. You couldn't do much better than Connor. I'm glad my daughter's got such good taste!"

On the one hand, Melissa was glad to hear that. She agreed with her mother about Connor, and she was pleased that she'd pleased her parents by dating him. On the other hand, she started to wonder: How great could Connor be, if her parents approved of him? Could she not do better?

Another concern, for Melissa, was that Connor seemed to her to be just going through the motions. She wasn't sure how she felt toward him – she knew she liked him, but didn't think she loved him – but she was certain that Connor didn't love her. She sometimes felt that Connor was only with her because a guy needs a girlfriend, to prove his worth, and she was available, so why not choose her?

Melissa knew there was plenty of time in life for romance and passion; she knew that she would probably have both of those, eventually – but she wasn't feeling either, with Connor. It was a comfortable relationship. Companionable.

The bond was not always as strong as Melissa would have liked. Connor mostly hung out with his guy friends. Melissa's mother would tell her, "You have to give him some space. Boys don't like to feel that they're being smothered."

"I know," said Melissa, "but in some ways we still have the same kind of relationship we had in eighth grade."

"And that's a good thing," Gail said.

The question Jim and Gail Wainwright often asked each other in private was never answered to their satisfaction. They never knew whether Connor and Melissa had "crossed the line." Nor did anyone else, aside from the two parties themselves.

The most likely answer, till the end of their high school careers, would be Third Base. Manual-genital contact. Probably no orgasms, and pretty certainly no oral. And even Third Base didn't happen till senior year – which is when, if their relationship could ever have been called romantic, it seemed to backslide into a friendship with some desultory sexual touching included. They talked a little about going to the same college, but only in passing.

In the late fall of their senior year, Connor mentioned to Melissa that he wanted to look into broadening his work experience. His father paid him a wage for helping in the plumbing supplies business, but he had advised Connor to try working with one or two other employers before he started college, to get a better idea of what the commercial world was like.

"Some of the stores'll be hiring for Christmas," Connor remarked to Melissa, one evening at the Wainwrights'.

Jim Wainwright overheard. "Why don't you ask Andy Palinkas, next door?" he asked. "I bet Rosen's does a lot of seasonal hiring."

Connor showed up at Rosen's for his interview wearing his father's blue blazer as a concession to being "dressed up." Otherwise he was dressed as for school, only with a white Oxford button-down shirt instead of his usual plaid one.

Still, he got a job. "I've got plenty of people on the sales floor," Andy explained to him, "but do you know computers, accounting, spreadsheet, all that shit? That's the one part of my job I hate. I can do it, but I'd rather not if I can help it. If you can take some of that off my shoulders, you can work here."

Connor was careful, thorough, and accurate, and Andy kept him on after Christmas – and through his senior year. Connor took to the work. He told Andy he was pretty sure this was what he'd like to do for a career: accounting, or maybe computer programming for financial services.

By spring of their senior year Melissa had a job too, bagging groceries at Hy-Vee. What with the work, and all the excitement attendant on the last semester of high school, Connor and Melissa's relationship cooled even further, although they remained close friends and spent a lot of their free time together. Connor felt a pang when Melissa told him she'd be going to Devaney College, in Northstar, Minnesota. He'd hoped that she might decide, after all, to stay put and go to State University. But her decision didn't surprise him.

It's not a stretch to imagine that when Connor heard this news from Melissa, shortly after Christmas of that senior year, it triggered an emotion that felt almost like love. An actual tenderness, a longing, that he'd never felt for Melissa before, although certainly he'd been attracted to her for many years. Now, all of a sudden, he started to wonder whether this was the girl he was meant to spend his life with – and she would be lost to him before he could act on his feelings.

It's like that, so often, with boys and girls both. They might be lukewarm in their feelings for someone – but then when they feel that person slipping away, they tend to romanticize the relationship. They tend to build up that person, and to develop feelings that past experiences don't justify.

As the end of the school year approached, Connor daydreamed about proposing marriage to Melissa. They'd be engaged through college (he fantasized), then formalize it when they'd graduated. But he dismissed that idea as ridiculous. Such early engagements had been commonplace, in many parts of the U.S., in generations past, but by the 1990s that sort of thing was strictly lower-class, and Connor would have realized this. The fantasy lingered, however.

That spring, Melissa told Connor, as though she'd been reading his mind, "We'll be entirely different people four years from now. But we'll always be friends."

And indeed Connor could sense Melissa drifting farther and farther from him, in the closing weeks of the school year: less inclined to spend time with him, more interested in hanging out with her girlfriends.

They went to the senior prom together because neither could have imagined going with anyone else. And for the sake of a good story, let's stipulate that it was that night, on Connor's parents' living room floor, when Melissa finally gave it up – quickly and furtively. To oblige Connor, more than anything: to honor a sincere request from a dear friend who, she knew, wanted this thing more than just about any other thing in the world.

It was probably a disappointment to both of them. Especially for Connor, who must have wondered why Melissa seemed to be allowing it – rather than enthusiastically getting into it. Maybe he sensed, as he was doing it, that this was not likely to be offered to him again, at least not for a long time.

As for Melissa, she might have been impressed, and rather touched, by Connor's emotional investment in the act.

But it had hurt like crazy – she'd recall that it felt like she was being torn apart, just as some of her friends had warned her that it would hurt, the first time – and it was over in a few seconds and left Melissa wondering what was supposed to be so great about it.

Indeed, that turned out to be Connor's one and only chance, that spring. Melissa never mentioned it, in the succeeding days, and reacted with indifference when Connor tried to show any physical affection. They continued to spend time together now and then, but at their graduation party – this was held outdoors, in a campground outside of town, and couples were slipping off into the woods at a pretty good rate – Melissa was sticking mainly with her girlfriends, paying Connor very little notice. She left early, with a couple of her mates, to go get a pizza and then head home. It was as though she were deliberately, gradually, shedding all that was high school – and Connor was part of what she was shedding.

Connor brooded about this, but he found other ways to keep occupied, that summer, and he told himself that there would be plenty of time for him and Melissa to get back together one day. When they were both more mature.

5. Melissa and Connor in College

This is a part of the story with which I'm less intimately acquainted. As with the last chapter, some of this I know to be true. With regard to some of it, I know most of the truth. A little of it, I admit I'm surmising. But it's truthy. And you'd be amazed at how much of the truth you can piece together, if you know enough people and if enough of them are talkative.

Two years passed, and a little more. Connor dated different girls, here and there, as he attended State University, and no doubt he got a couple of them into bed, but he never met a girl who aroused any real emotions in him. Whenever he was "seeing someone," he had to admit to himself that he was only with her because it was expected of him. A guy should have a girl, at least one. It must have rankled, that he never seemed to attract girls he really liked. He had to take whatever was available, whichever girls had any interest in him. And he couldn't have imagined himself getting serious with any of them.

He continued to hold Melissa in his mind, and probably he continued to idealize her, remembering her as far closer to perfection than she ever had been.

Many languages have a single word that describes a rather complicated idea, and has no exact translation in any other language. The Portuguese word *saudade* is one of these.

Saudade can best be described as a wistful longing for an idealized version of something past, or something lost. *Saudade* is not quite the same as nostalgia, which is a fond remembrance of something you'll never recapture. It's not the same as sadness, either, because it contains an element of enjoyment. *Saudade* always includes a vague hope that one day you'll recover what you're longing for – even if you know that that's unlikely to happen. It also suggests a longing for something that never really was, or that was never as wonderful as you remember it.

There's a sort of deliciousness about *saudade*. Were it otherwise, we wouldn't dwell so fondly upon it. Such emotions have their uses. Without them, hardly any songs or poems would ever be written. Connor didn't have a poetic bone in his body, but *saudade* was what he felt for Melissa, over those two-plus years.

Melissa and Connor had continued to see each other, casually, during summer breaks and at Christmas. But in their junior year of college, when Melissa didn't have time to see him when she came home for Thanksgiving weekend, Connor began to worry, and when she was about to come home at

Christmas, he emailed her to remind her that he didn't want to miss seeing her. She replied:

I'm sorry, I'll only be there for a few days and it'll be hard to get together what with the Christmas rush and all. Maybe we can get coffee sometime before I go back up to Minnesota. Let's play it by ear when I get there.

Connor was just experienced enough to know what "let's play it by ear" meant, and he immediately suspected what was behind this response, but he couldn't bring himself to ask Melissa to confirm this. She never did call to arrange a meeting. It wasn't till mid-January that Connor got up the nerve to email her again.

Long time, no hear. I still feel bad that we didn't catch up at Christmas. Are you mad at me for something?

Dear Connor:

No, I'm not mad at you; I could never be mad at you. I'm afraid I didn't get together with you because I would have been uncomfortable with the situation, and I know that was really selfish of me and I'm sorry. I should have seen you.

Especially I should have seen you to tell you face to face that I've met someone. His name's Gary, and he's an English major like me, and the strong safety on the Devaney football team. I didn't even know what a strong safety was till I met Gary! It's way too early to tell if our relationship will continue beyond college but for now we're in love and we're a couple, which is why I haven't emailed very often lately. I'm just not home all that much.

How are you? I bet you're wowing some nice girl in State City, right? Or more than one?
Hugs,
Melissa

Melissa had gone to Devaney with vague ideas of majoring in English, and probably teaching it, eventually, at either the high school or college level. She had to admit to herself that that was largely because she wasn't dead-set on any sort of career, and teaching English seemed to her the least uninteresting of all the options that might appeal. And it wouldn't be fair to say that her mother had pushed Melissa in that direction, but Gail had been an English major herself – and not having followed up with a post-graduate degree was one of Gail's lifelong regrets.

Melissa was the middle child, and thus was eager to please, eager to prove that she was as deserving of her parents' love and attention as her elder brother, David. No doubt Melissa also had some of the resentments that middle children often bear, stuck as they are between the more-respected eldest and the "baby" who needs more attention. What else Melissa might have wanted out of life, at that age, isn't clear. How many of us, at age 18, are purpose-driven? How many of us think about what we are?

Melissa interests me, perversely, because she's so passive. Because she allows events to sweep her along. Her decisions are largely reactive. It could be that she didn't need much encouragement from Gail: just a suggestion.

So an English major she became, without great enthusiasm. But as she worked her way through her four undergraduate years, she became more engaged. She developed a fairly serious interest in the 19th-century English novel. She devoured Jane Austen, and while George Eliot didn't rank quite as high with her, she liked Eliot's work too. Dickens she considered somewhat less of an artist than either of those two, since she noticed that Dickens had a way of twisting plots in implausible ways to fit his desired ending.

As Melissa's interest in literature grew, she thought she might like to write a novel or two of her own, one day, although she wasn't sure she had anything original to say. She didn't date a lot, or develop many close friendships, because even at an academics-oriented school like Devaney she didn't know many people who liked to talk about books and poetry as much as she did – till she met Gary Engel at the beginning of her junior year.

Melissa had never dated an athlete before (Connor, who'd ridden the bench for the State City High basketball team, didn't count), and in any case she assumed that the jocks all majored either in Business Administration or Physical Education. Gary didn't look like a jock to Melissa. He wasn't that big: six feet, and slender rather than husky. Safeties, he explained to Melissa, usually were the smallest players on the field.

Gary looked like a "student athlete" from an old movie, with an easy grin and a big mop of blond hair. His face was apple-shaped, and apple-cheeked. He usually wore a crew-neck sweater, and chinos. He had a real All-American look to him, and he was quiet, thoughtful. It was evident to Melissa that while he took football seriously, he was a scholar first. He would get his doctorate, he told her, and be a professor of English even though he knew it was difficult to find that kind of job these days.

"There's always room at the top," he said. "And in the worst case, I'm minoring in Chinese, so I can get a job over there. Or teach ESL."

This was the first boy Melissa had ever truly admired. She'd liked Connor; she'd felt – still felt – a strong and honest affection for him. But she'd never admired Connor, never looked up to him. She'd felt comfortable with Connor, was all. She felt comfortable with Gary, now, too, but Gary also made her feel all sort of fluttery inside.

Almost as soon as they'd met – in a class on Woolf and Strachey, in the fall of her junior year – Melissa had attached herself to Gary. She'd make a point of sitting with him in class and walking with him afterwards. She started taking his sleeve as they walked, then his arm. Gary didn't seem to mind. They started spending more and more time together, and they were officially a couple by the first of October.

The physical part of the relationship was so utterly different from what it had been with Connor. With Gary, Melissa was wanting to do it, rather than doing whatever she'd done with Connor simply because it was expected of her. It wasn't what she'd dreamed it would be, from the fiction she'd read on the subject, but it was close enough.

Melissa had never been a football fan, but now she was going to every home game and some of the away ones, to cheer Gary on. She felt lucky that his position – strong-side safety – was one of the easiest to follow and understand.

By mid-October, Melissa and Gary were spending more nights together than not. "Maybe I don't know what love is," she emailed one of her high school girlfriends (while swearing her to secrecy), "but this sure feels like it."

Melissa and Gary both stayed at school in the summer between their junior and senior years, and when their leases expired at the end of July they moved in together. On a visit back to State City, Melissa presented this development to her parents as a *fait accompli*. Gail asked her whether they were going to have separate bedrooms at least, which made Melissa fall apart laughing. That laughter seemed to disturb her mother more than the fact that Melissa was having sex, which after all Gail had suspected for some months.

Melissa didn't bring Gary for a visit to State City, since she knew pigs would fly before they'd be allowed to sleep together in the family mansion. She did meet Gary's parents, several times, since Northstar was only a short drive from the Engels' home in Edina. Gary's father was a civil engineer; his mother played cello in a local orchestra.

During the fall of their senior year, Melissa and Gary were almost a married couple, and they talked a bit about getting married, but Gary was planning to continue his studies, working toward a Ph.D., and Melissa had had enough of school and would be (she supposed) getting started on a teaching career. She assumed she could get a job teaching high school

English almost anywhere in the country – near wherever Gary decided to go to graduate school.

Gary didn't have a lot of leisure during the football season, what with studies and athletics. He was working hard – Melissa could see that – whereas she was taking a fairly light course load in that final year. She became almost a housewife: doing their laundry, keeping their apartment nice, having dinner ready at a regular hour every evening. Gary never seemed to take this for granted. He was as sweet and kind to her as he'd been a year ago, Melissa remarked to herself.

It was early in their final semester that Gary's attitude seemed to change. He was never less than pleasant to Melissa, but he seemed more distant, and was certainly less interested in sex. He suggested as how they might have to accept living apart for a while, because it looked like he'd be going to graduate school at Columbia, and did Melissa want to follow him there and look for a teaching job in New York City? Or might she want to get a graduate degree too? If so, it would probably be too late for her to get into Columbia.

The way the scenario played out, then, was so predictable that it hardly bears telling in any detail. Melissa started perceiving what she thought were little clues that Gary was developing other interests: specifically, an interest in a young female professor – Phyllis Rooney, a Joyce scholar – the one who'd been encouraging Gary to go to Columbia.

Melissa never caught them: at least, not in the act. Instead, Gary caught Melissa – tailing him. One night when he'd told her he'd be walking to the library, and Melissa had told him she'd be studying at home, Gary made a detour en route to that same library: a considerable detour. To a residential neighborhood. It was night, but the snow on the ground, combined with the street lights, provided plenty of illumination: enough that he recognized the make, color, and license plate number of the car he saw parked in an alley near the professor's home.

Gary took an unanticipated turn down another street and brought out his cell phone.

"I've been spotted," he told his professor friend. "Or at any rate I just spotted her, trying to spot me. She's parked round the corner from your house. I've got to double back to the library. You should probably just stay there. Though it might be fun to go out, and see if she tries to tail you. No, I'm totally kidding. But I'll have to figure out what to do, now."

Gary did indeed walk to the library, stayed there a decent interval – including some minutes in a men's room, on the phone, discussing with Prof. Rooney how they might be able to get together in the future – and then he walked back to his and Melissa's apartment, pretending that he hadn't been anywhere else and that he hadn't seen Melissa's car. Melissa, after waiting nearly another hour near the professor's house, had driven back home and waited for Gary – hoping he wouldn't get home till the chill was off her skin and clothes so that he couldn't tell that she'd been out. And when Gary did get home, she couldn't admit she'd been tailing him.

Gary knew they were done; Melissa knew they were done; neither of them could say anything about it. They went through a few days in which Gary more or less tried to ignore Melissa, and Melissa didn't speak to Gary at all except to snap at him – and she would cry herself to sleep at night.

Gary didn't dare ask what was wrong – because he knew that she knew that he knew what was wrong. Prof. Rooney, meanwhile, told Gary that since he was only committed to 50 percent of four months' rent on that apartment, she'd be willing to advance him that amount herself, while he found himself another place. (He couldn't have stayed with the professor: Devaney College frowns on faculty who openly romance their students.)

Gary and Melissa had That Conversation, the weekend following the fateful evening. After which, Gary spent several days moving out by stages, taking some of his stuff back to his parents' house in Edina and transferring his necessities to a crummy room that rented month-to-month. This allowed him and Prof. Rooney to get together discreetly, and didn't cost the professor a lot of money.

The emotional impact of all this on Melissa was considerable. She hadn't lost her virginity to Gary, but he'd been the first guy she'd felt she was in love with, certainly the first guy she'd ever thought she might like to marry. And here she was, dumped – for a woman more sophisticated, probably more intelligent, and overall simply *better* than she. She didn't have any real evidence that the professor had stolen Gary – he would admit to nothing, he'd never been actually caught, and she wasn't going to go on with the detective work now that she'd irretrievably lost him – but one way or another, she *had* lost him.

Melissa was teary, off and on, for a good month after the breakup. Her academic performance suffered, although it didn't make much difference in that final semester. She put herself out there, looking for other guys, but found nobody to appeal to her, not even for recreational sex.

As graduation drew nearer, Melissa would sometimes party too hearty and become susceptible to the blandishments of one boy or another. If she'd stayed at Devaney beyond that semester, she might have developed an alcohol problem as well as what used to be called "a reputation."

Another issue was Melissa's plan for the following year. She didn't have one. The breakup, and the ensuing depression, had made it all she could do to get through her classes. She didn't know if she could hack graduate school, and in any case she hadn't applied anywhere. She had applied, half-heartedly, for a few teaching jobs – but not many.

Bottom line: Melissa didn't know, that spring, what she'd be doing in the fall: whether she'd be unemployed, teaching school, working retail, or taming lions. This did not help her overall mood, her sense of personal security, or her expectations for the long term.

Melissa graduated from Devaney in spring of 2002 with a Bachelor's degree in English, and discovered that it wasn't all that easy to get a teaching job unless she wanted to teach in an extremely undesirable district. She spent June and July living in Northstar, working at a garden center selling flowers and seeds, and occasionally traveling to an interview. She hadn't secured many of these, because she'd restricted her job search to the North Central U.S. She hoped for employment somewhere near State City, but found no such opportunities. She dreaded the end of July, when her lease on the apartment would run out and she'd have to either stay in Northstar in a smaller place that she could afford without Gary's contribution, or move back into her parents' house in State City – unless she found work that paid better than what she currently had.

She especially didn't want to tarry long in State City if she would have to see Connor. This was partly because it would have mortified her to let Connor know that her relationship with Gary hadn't worked out, and partly because she wasn't sure whether – after Gary – Connor could hold any appeal for her. She didn't see Connor all summer. During the few days she spent in State City, she avoided any place or situation where she might run into him.

"You could go to grad school," her mother advised Melissa. "You could probably get into a post-grad program here at State. But it wouldn't make a lot of sense to spend the money on that if you don't have a specific goal in mind. It might be better to teach for a couple of years – and then go for a degree with a better idea of what you want to do with the rest of your life."

Melissa's first and only job offer came during one of her visits to State City: an email, followed by a call on her cell phone, from the administrator in the Detroit public school system who'd interviewed her a couple of months ago. At first she considered turning it down right then and there – but then she realized that this might be the only offer she'd get for the coming school year. She told the administrator that she'd need a couple days to think it over. He gave her 24 hours.

When she ended the call, Melissa was 90 percent sure she would turn it down – but when Gail reacted by crying, "Oh, my God, *Detroit?* Oh, *please* don't take that job. God knows what would happen to you there!" Melissa reconsidered.

"I'm going to take it," she told an old high school friend, Liz Prohaska, over a beer in a downtown tavern that evening. "For one thing I'm curious to find out whether I'm a racist. I don't think I am, but I've wondered if I might be. For another, Mom is kind of a snob even if she isn't a racist, and I don't want to disappoint her but I don't want to end up like her either. And more than anything, I do *not* want to move back home while I work at a clerical job at the University and hope some medical student falls for me."

"Besides," Melissa's friend said, "your mom might not like it at first, but pretty soon she'll be telling everybody how she's so proud of her daughter who's teaching in Detroit and 'making a difference.'" Liz used the air-quotes, and Melissa laughed and conceded that that was probably true.

And so it was that in August of that year Melissa Wainwright moved to Detroit, into a modest apartment in a not-too-bad neighborhood, to teach at Amos Fortune High School – which was not just an inner-city school, but was described thus, on its website:

"Amos Fortune is an alternative high school for students who have trouble with language arts and social studies. The school offers a full curriculum featuring math, science, social studies, language arts, technology, music, art, and other subjects. The school focuses on providing hands-on instruction for students throughout the district."

This – as Melissa knew going in – was a nice way of saying that Amos Fortune was the school of last resort for incorrigibles: the last stop before prison, or a way-station between periods of institutionalization.

§

Connor had soldiered on through his junior year. He tried not to think about Melissa, and usually he didn't, but every now and then, if he were alone and in a foul mood, he would – he couldn't help it – and he'd wonder whether he'd made a mistake, and wasted a couple years of his life, carrying this torch.

He continued to earn extra money by handling Andy Palinkas' accounts, at Rosen's, and otherwise he spent most of his time studying. He socialized little. He got the feeling that his old friends were distancing themselves from him. He suspected this was because he was no longer interesting to them.

He studied hard. He went into his senior year as one of the outstanding undergraduates in the College of Business; he could have gotten into almost any post-graduate program.

As in high school, Connor remained the sort of guy who could gain entry to any crowd, by being insignificant and inoffensive. He belonged to several study groups, and he brought knowledge and hard work to the table.

A couple of young ladies from those study groups seemed interested in him – one was a Sikh girl named Agampreet, and the other was a girl from Chicago named LaShonda – but he didn't find either of them attractive physically. The three of them were probably the top business undergraduates, academically, who were not Korean or Chinese. Connor was able to laugh and kid with LaShonda, but Agampreet didn't seem to get any of his jokes, and he had to concentrate hard to understand her English.

Connor went through the first semester of his senior year, and part of the second, in a general funk. Christmas break was the worst of it. He was living alone in an efficiency apartment in downtown State City; the town was dead; for the second straight Christmas he hadn't gotten to see Melissa. Indeed, he didn't know whether she'd come home at all. He had no girlfriend. Despite his high academic standing he felt he was going nowhere. He felt like a dull person, and he had to admit it was because he *was* a dull person. Connor was not introspective by nature, but every now and then he could assess himself pretty accurately.

He wished he liked to drink.

By the time his final undergraduate semester was a few weeks old, Connor felt nearly despondent. He was not the type to spill his guts to anyone, but on this occasion – it was a few days from Valentine's Day, and he was aware of it – he was feeling lousy enough that he took the opportunity.

He'd run into LaShonda at the downtown Starbucks; they'd sat down together, and LaShonda had asked him, "You doing anything with your Valentine on V-Day?"

Connor had had to admit that he didn't have a Valentine to do anything with.

"*You* don't? No way!"

"Way," said Connor, shrugging. "I haven't been thinking about it lately."

"Yes you have. You wouldn't be looking all gloomy if you wasn't."

Connor shrugged again, and decided it wouldn't do any harm if he told LaShonda what was on his mind. So he told her, as briefly as he could, about this girl he'd liked in high school and how he'd still had his hopes up till a year ago, and how he was still gun-shy about hooking up with anyone else, after that.

"You can't let one monkey stop your show!" LaShonda exclaimed. "Plenty of young ladies out there."

"Maybe I'll meet one, one of these days."

"You have to make it happen! Connor, look at you! You all grey-looking; you look like the change of life. You don't look healthy, at all. Join a club or something. Go to church at least. Go where you can meet people. Listen, on Thursday I'm taking you to my tango club."

Connor did not know what tango was; he thought at first LaShonda had said "tangle," and wondered if she was referring to some sort of co-ed wrestling.

"It's a dance, silly," LaShonda said. "It's way fun."

Aside from the body-shaking type of dancing that everyone does in high school and college, and square dancing in elementary school, Connor had never danced a step in his life. But he assumed that a dance club would have a lot more girls in it than boys, so he might as well give it a try.

And it was there, on the following Thursday evening, that he met Tanya Cucoshay.

6. Connor and Tanya Cucoshay

She was tall – almost as tall as Connor, close to six feet – and slender but with curves. She wore a tight neon-pink cocktail dress that left her arms and shoulders bare; it had a short skirt that showed most of her legs. She also wore pink spike-heel shoes. Her hair hung loose past her shoulders, brown with a slight reddish cast – dark auburn, you might call it – wavy, but with not a lot of body to it. Her jaw was broad and angular; her mouth was remarkably wide, with full lips that curved upward in a discreet suggestion of a smile. Her nose was slightly aggressive. Her cheekbones stood out to an almost surreal degree.

Her eyes couldn't be compared to anyone else's. They were a silvery-greenish-brown, like polished jasper: large, wide-open, with flecks of yellow in them. They were somewhat slanted, Oriental-looking, and they seemed to dance and laugh all by themselves. Above them, her eyebrows were meticulously plucked and penciled; her forehead was high and broad, with her hair swept back from it. She had a slight widow's peak.

If Connor had been a woman, he would have noticed that this woman's pink dress didn't go with her autumnal hair, sallow skin, and speckled eyes. Women might have assessed her makeup pretty harshly, too. They might have called it just a bit overdone, with little sense of color or unity. But Connor only observed that he'd never seen a face as compelling, as stunning, as hers.

LaShonda introduced them.

"Connor never danced the tango before," LaShonda told Tanya. "He doesn't even know what it is."

"We'll fix that," said Tanya. She had a clear, loud voice. She looked Connor right in the eye and turned her full smile on him. She grabbed Connor's hand and led him away from the drinks table, onto the dance floor.

"The first thing you need to know," Tanya told Connor, facing him and locking eyes with him, an almost-serious expression on her face, "is that there are no mistakes in tango." Because of her odd-sounding surname – he'd never heard one like it – Connor had expected to hear a foreign accent, but, no: Tanya had a noticeable Iowa twang. Her speckled eyes twinkled, and Connor's knees felt wobbly: he could hardly stay on his feet.

Connor didn't have a good sense of time or rhythm. Tanya saw this as a challenge. She explained to him the basic tango step: slow... slow... quick-quick slow...

Connor didn't care about the dance; what he cared about were those eyes, and that enormous mouth smiling at him as Tanya back-led him across the floor.

"Just relax," Tanya said. "Trust me. This is how everybody learns."

They ended up working together for nearly two hours, and when they'd worn themselves out, Connor invited Tanya to dinner. He took her to a noodle shop that catered mainly to students, and they exchanged basic information as they ate.

"You're lucky to have a normal name," Tanya told him. "I'm always having to spell mine, and correct people's pronunciation – over and over, sometimes." She did a slight pursing of the lips that was not quite a simper and not quite a smile, which was a sort of signature expression of hers.

"Everybody wants to rhyme it with ricochet, but it's cu-*co*-shay. Sounds like a sneeze. And I'm Titania, like in *A Mid-*

summer Night's Dream. Not Tatiana. And I'm ti-*tah*-nya, not tie-*tay*-nya. It's a mess. Anyway, just call me Tanya."

Tanya was older than Connor, he could tell: about 28, he estimated, and he'd just turned 22. She had this semester, plus one more year, to earn her Master of Music degree.

"I got sidetracked," she explained, "so I started college kind of late."

As a business student, Connor had never had anything to do with students in music, theatre, or the visual arts. He knew nothing about music. But Tanya told him that music was all about math, and thus should be easy for him to understand.

"I'm completely left-brained," she added, not laughing. "That's the part of the brain that works with numbers and analysis; I guess that's why I'm a musician."

§

Tanya Cucoshay had never had a lot of friends, even when she'd been small. She wasn't generally disliked by any means, but she'd never grown especially close to any other girl or boy. The first thing you noticed about her, when she was a girl, was the liveliness of her speckled eyes. Next, you noticed the cheekbones and the width of her mouth. Those two factors, combined with an apparently innate mobility of her facial muscles, gave her an amazing vivacity and variety of expression. Adults would remark on it. She was not pretty in the classic sense – that would come later – but the energy of her aspect made her a beauty.

Few children lived in her neighborhood in Indianola, Iowa, because her father was an otolaryngologist and the Cucoshays lived in a part of town occupied mainly by professionals and wealthier businesspeople. She had few playmates.

To adults, Tanya was invariably pleasant and correct, and the standard comment was, "What a delightful girl she seems to be." "Seems to be," because no adult got to know her better than any of the children did. The only adults to whom she was at all close, aside from her family, were her voice and dance teachers. From the first, she was light on her feet, and loved to skip about, inventing dance steps for herself from the age of three onwards. She could also sing: could carry a tune sooner than most children could, and she sang loudly, too.

Tanya was closest to her sister, Danuta, who was five years older and treated Tanya as a special pet. Five years seemed the perfect age difference: far enough apart that they were never competitors; not distant enough for the younger child to be a nuisance to the elder. Danuta was not as pretty as Tanya, so Tanya became Danuta's doll. Danuta would dress her baby sister's hair and show her how to use makeup – if rather clumsily and excessively – which Tanya consequently wore to school before any of the other girls did.

The makeup was one way in which Tanya stood out; another was that she was a better student than most. She wasn't of deep intelligence, but perceptive and a quick learner. Teachers liked her because she was tractable. She did as she was told; got consistently high grades; never gave trouble. Boys mostly left her alone, because they didn't know what to make of her. If they tried to tease her, she would tease back till they gave it up. She wasn't a tomboy, didn't play sports, and most of the boys didn't understand dance.

Girls respected her; some admired her. Only a few liked her. She was polite to everyone, and she'd laugh and kid, but always in a somewhat distant way, so that most of the other girls thought she was stuck-up: condescending, if they'd known that word at that age. Tanya tended not to involve herself in the politics of childhood.

Seldom did another child cross her, but if one did, Tanya didn't forgive easily – and the list of children to whom her behavior would never again be more than correct grew slowly during her elementary school and high school years.

Tanya had always been tall for her age, but at 11 or so, she shot up to about 5'10". Her skin started erupting, too, but somehow this didn't much affect her overall attractiveness. She was aware of the looks that she was starting to get, from boys, and she probably knew, on some level, that boys found her intimidating. No doubt she had plenty of insecurities, even at that age, but she covered them with aloofness. Through the ninth grade, Tanya never came close to having a boyfriend, but by the 10th grade a few of the taller boys started showing some interest. She dated basketball players, although she had no aptitude for athletics, herself, nor any inclination to them.

She didn't like the basketball players, either. They weren't interested in what interested her. They tended not to be very good-looking. And they were sweaty and didn't smell nice. One, though, she especially liked: a boy named Mark. He was much better-looking than the others. He had a sweet face with full lips, and thick wavy black hair. And he liked to write poetry. It wasn't good poetry, so far as Tanya could tell, but it was something that passed for poetry.

Tanya and Mark dated in senior year. They were the "glamour couple" of Indianola Central's class of 1992. They went to the prom together; they lost their respective virginities to each other. Not necessarily, but probably, in that order.

They talked about getting married, one day. But Mark went to Creighton University on a basketball scholarship; Tanya to the San Francisco Conservatory of Dance. Tanya had hoped, at first, that their relationship would survive this separation. She had fantasies of being a star ballerina married to a top pro basketball player. But as often happens in these situations, the two of them found other friends, and lost touch, quicker than they'd anticipated.

§

Running all through Tanya's childhood and teen years was her musical training: singing and dance. And she gave Connor the full story on it, over dinner at that noodle shop. Connor had little opportunity to talk.

It's probable that Tanya told this same story to anyone – any male, anyway – who was favored to hear it. There'd come times, years later, when the version of this story that she told to other men would include her relationship with Connor. But Connor wouldn't have known how many men had heard her story before she told it to him. He must have felt that Tanya was paying him a particular compliment by revealing so much of her history when they'd only met a couple of hours earlier.

"I always wanted to be a dancer," she told Connor, "I think I was five when I started telling my family and my friends that I wanted to be a ballerina, and I started asking for lessons. I had no idea about ballet – didn't know anything about what went into it – but I'd seen all the Disney cartoons and I'd fallen in love with the concept.

"I had to wait till I was in third grade – the best instructors don't like to start kids on ballet too soon, because if you're too young you're not disciplined enough – but we found the most wonderful teacher. Stella Rhodes, I don't suppose you've heard of her. She'd been a principal at some very prestigious company, I forget now which one, and she was such a dear woman. Very kind and patient, really good with children, but strict. You couldn't talk inappropriately; you had to wear the black leotard, pink tights, pink shoes. That's why I love pink to this day.

"Then there'd be the summer camps, when we went to Oberlin or such places. I did that, several summers, but mainly I just did lessons year 'round. Indianola's another college town, you know, although not as big as State City, and there was a dance school in Des Moines that offered classes to the general public. I tried everything. Classical dance, several types of modern dance: the Martha Graham style, the José Limón style. I loved learning both, because they offered such different points of view."

By this time, Connor had no idea what Tanya was talking about, but he knew guys were supposed to be good listeners if they wanted girls to like them. Mainly he was just gazing at Tanya as she talked.

"Then instead of going to college, when I graduated high school I got accepted to the San Francisco Conservatory, where I had this one teacher – his name was Peter Baughan; I'm sure you've never heard of him, either – who was such a melodramatic figure! I had the worst crush on him. He had this dark wavy hair – although he was over 50 then – and a beautiful body, muscular, carried himself with enormous grace. When he spoke he'd use a lot of arm-waving, grand gestures.

"And he was critical like you wouldn't believe. He would criticize every aspect of you: your hands, the arches of your feet, your weight, the proportion of your legs, your hair, your backline. He would actually measure you, the circumference of your ankles, the width of your behind, and all. He was looking for the perfect ballerina: long legs, short torso, super high arches – and if you didn't have that, he could be nasty.

"One of the girls I studied with looked like a fairy, ethereal, so light and delicate, and Peter would fawn all over her. But he was always telling me, 'You're too tall! You're far too tall! You'll never dance professionally!'

"And yet I got involved with him. I had a relationship with him. I admired him so much; I was willing to be his slave if he would make me the dancer I knew I could be.

"I was determined to prove him wrong. I liked the modern dance department a lot better, but I was going to have a career in ballet to spite Peter – even while I was essentially living with him. That was my big mistake.

"Of course he eventually took up with that other girl. Of course he did. Of course he did. He was using me to get to her. I see that, now."

Tanya's expression conveyed a gentle but dramatic sorrow. Connor scrabbled in his brain for something to say so that she'd know he was there.

"Were your parents okay with your being a dancer?"

"Funny you should ask," said Tanya, with that trade-mark simper. Then her eyes twinkled in a way that almost made Connor reach across the table and embrace her.

"They'd expected me to go into the sciences, probably as a medical doctor. That's what they both wanted for me, when I was in high school, and I had perfect scores in all my math and science classes, so everybody assumed that that was what I'd do.

"But I did some research, when I was in high school, about what it would take to go through pre-med, and medical school. I was especially worried about how I'd handle doing experiments on animals, and killing them in the process. That whole idea horrified me. And I had no desire to deal with sick people. I finally told my parents I'd rather be a stripper than be a doctor.

"So they said they'd support my dance studies, on condition that if it didn't work out, I'd go to a regular college and major in, you know, one of the sciences, or math, or engineering.

"I lived in San Francisco for eight or nine years; I took courses in dance, fitness, gymnastics; I took up tap and ball-room and salsa dancing. Plus I was studying music, as much as I could find the time for it. I'd been in choir in high school, and I'd taken voice lessons, and in my last year of high school, one of my math teachers pulled me aside at a recital – his daughter was in my class, and she was taking voice lessons from the same teacher – and he told me not to study medicine or any-thing else, and to study music instead because of my voice.

"I was still committed to dance, but I tried to keep up my vocal training all those years I was in San Francisco, al-though I had limited time for that. But the thing is, a dancer and a singer have way different life-cycles. A dancer, if she hasn't made it by her early 20s, she's not going to. But a singer, her voice won't mature till she's a lot older. And by the time I was 20, 21 – yeah, I was too tall. And I could dance, but I was only pretty good. I was never going to be a star. I wasn't getting any serious gigs. That's when I started feeling that singing might be something I could do.

"And at the same time, my parents started running out of patience, and started putting pressure on me to go to school and get a degree and learn to do something practical. So I started taking courses at the University of San Francisco. I started out with a double major – music and business administration – but the business classes were incredibly boring and I wasn't doing that well in them. Meanwhile my music professors were passionate about the material and I enjoyed music so much more, and that's most of the reasons why I dropped out of business.

"It took me an extra year to graduate, because I also met this amazing math professor, Henry Sullivan, and he absolutely transformed my life. I'd always been good at math, but his calculus classes were an incredible experience for me – like Helen Keller learning to spell 'water.'

"I'd always thought that math was too esoteric to be of any use to me, but Sullivan taught me about applied math, math functions, solving equations so that I could approach almost any situation in math terms – and I realized that if I wanted to have a career in music, math would be a big help. So I switched my business major over to math, and with one thing and another I was 25 before I finally graduated.

"If I'd had it to do over again I'd never have tried to be a dancer, but you never know what other paths you'll discover if you think you're on the road you want to be on."

Tanya concluded with a triumphant beam at Connor, and a little exhalation, as though she'd come to the end of a song and was expecting applause. Connor almost did want to applaud, but he forced himself to find a question instead.

"So you came back here for your Master's?"

"I could have used math for all kinds of careers," said Tanya. "As it turned out, I got a job as an investment associate at Wells Fargo, there in San Francisco, and I put music aside for a couple of years.

"I was making pretty decent money. But I couldn't be satisfied with that. I realized finally that I *had* to be a musician; I had to make my career in music, one way or another, or I'd never forgive myself."

As Tanya said that last phrase, she looked at Connor so serious and sorrowful, simpering again, a bit, but with a slight hardness in her expression.

"I also wanted to prove a certain reviewer wrong," Tanya said. "My last year at USF, I was in *La Bohème*, I was Mimi, and I actually got written up in the San Francisco *Chronicle* – I still have the review, and I know it by heart."

Tanya straightened up, assumed an even sterner expression, and recited it to Connor in a deep voice:

"Miss Cucoshay has no business singing opera. She has a rough, brassy voice that might do for a pop career. We advise her to shift her focus to that, or to character roles in operetta and musical theatre."

Tanya looked disappointed that Connor didn't react with more indignation, but perhaps he couldn't appreciate how deeply such a review would cut.

Connor couldn't intellectualize it. He'd seen women whose beauty was more flawless than Tanya's. Melissa Wainwright had been prettier, in the wholesome Midwestern way, while Tanya was more exotic-looking.

He and Melissa had had similar backgrounds, similar values. They'd always understood each other. He hardly knew how to have a conversation with Tanya. Her interests, aside from mathematics, weren't his. Her story was alien to him. But he could listen, and Tanya was talkative about herself. After she'd told Connor about her dancing and singing, she went on about her personal life for quite a while – in a dramatic tone of voice, for the most part, keeping her eyes riveted on Connor's.

"I'm starting to figure out," she told him, "that a lot of my problems come from my getting involved with abusive men. One way or another. Verbally abusive if not physically."

Tanya presented Connor with quite a list. The high school boyfriend who'd started cheating on her as soon as he'd gone off to college. Peter Baughan, of course, who'd been her mentor, her artistic and spiritual guide, and her lover till he'd tired of her and dismissed her. (Connor would almost certainly have noted that Baughan had been an odd sort of spiritual guide, if he'd constantly told Tanya she was a flop as a dancer – but he'd have had better sense than to ask Tanya about this apparent paradox.)

Then later there was the co-worker who'd cost her a job, in effect, by spreading false stories of her sexual promiscuity after she'd refused to sleep with him. Another boyfriend who constantly cheated on her. And another boyfriend who constantly cheated on her. The night she'd almost been dragged into an alley and gang-raped by street thugs who had only let her go when the screams from her trained voice intimidated them. A Bulgarian boyfriend ("Never date a Bulgarian. Horrible people. They're criminals and they treat women like shit.") who sometimes threw her around when she displeased him.

Connor gazed back at Tanya, and shook his head. Tanya seemed so vulnerable. Connor wondered why it was (it seemed to him) that women so often were attracted to men who would treat them so. He wanted to say something about how it was too bad that men were such jerks, but he was afraid it would sound obsequious, so he kept silent.

"I was afraid to stay in the Bay Area," Tanya went on. "So much had happened to me there that finally I was sure I'd be killed, literally. And I'm convinced – I *know* – that this was some higher power speaking to me, somehow, telling me that I had to get out of this life and get back to music, which is where I truly wanted to be. I knew I'd never be satisfied if I didn't have a career in music. I'm a very spiritual person; I'm very tuned into what the Universe is telling me."

Connor continued to find it hard to say much to Tanya without prompting, and she seemed to sense that he was awkward socially. They met again at tango the next week, spent almost all evening together, and went out to dinner afterward.

This time, Tanya gave Connor a little time to talk, and he was able to tell her that he, too, had known a girl in high school about whom he'd had thoughts of marriage.

"And then she went away to college and I stayed here, and I lost her," Connor told Tanya. "It's taken me a while to get over it. I mean, it's funny: Sometimes you don't appreciate what you have, when you have it – and then it's not there anymore, and you spend a lot of time beating yourself up because you let her get away. Like, I don't know, maybe it was my own fault for not fighting for her."

"You thought she was your true love, huh?" Tanya replied. "Yeah, I thought I had that in high school too. But, life happens and you move on."

And at the end of the evening, Tanya invited Connor back to her place – and he spent the night there.

Connor felt in awe of Tanya – as though he suspected that she regarded sleeping with him as more of a thing to do, for recreation, than the result of any real feelings for him. She didn't act sentimental to him, at first, and she seemed amused, impatient, even scornful when he tried to act mooshy with her. It wasn't impersonal, the sex – in fact, Tanya could get downright histrionic in bed – but it wasn't particularly affectionate on her part.

Tanya taught Connor more about tango, and other types of ballroom dance, and she could talk intelligently about anything that involved numbers or money. Connor didn't understand the whole concept of majoring in music, or studying for graduate degrees in it. Tanya would sing for him sometimes but he didn't understand that kind of singing. He had to admit, though, that she came so alive when she sang; he loved watching her face light up; he loved the intensity that would come to her when she sang.

Sometimes she would sing instead of talk. That is, in the course of a regular conversation she'd sing part of a sentence, all of a sudden, just three or four notes, in a tune that

Connor supposed she'd improvised on the spot.

Connor couldn't tell a good voice from a bad one, but Tanya's voice reminded him that she was there. Hearing her singing lifted his spirits. She even taught him to sing, some. Connor had always thought he was tone-deaf, but Tanya got him to where he could carry a tune and stay on-key.

Connor was impressed with the magnitude of Tanya's ambitions, which involved becoming either a principal soprano with a major opera company, or a professor of voice at a major university or conservatory. But he had reservations.

"Don't you want kids?" Connor asked Tanya one afternoon, as he walked her from the Student Union to the Janscombe Center. It was that "false spring" day that happens around the first week of March in State City: a quick thaw where the temperature rises into the 50s or 60s and everyone feels happy and full of energy because they know they're on the downhill side of winter.

Tanya gave a little snort. "Hell no. People who have nothing better to do can have kids – or people who don't think they're worth anything till they've had one. Cleaning up baby shit isn't my idea of fun."

Connor felt intimidated. He wanted a family – at least two children – and he always had assumed that that's what he would have, and that everybody else wanted children unless they were just weird. Or gay. But he was afraid to say this to Tanya. It looked – to his amazement – as though Tanya were reacting to him as a possible boyfriend, not just a sex buddy, and he didn't want her to think he was wrong for her, or too ordinary. He laughed, and somehow that laugh struck Tanya as the closest to "sexy" that she'd ever seen from him, and she stopped him – right there on the path along the riverbank – and kissed him the way a girl kisses a boy when she means it.

Before either of them knew it, they were a couple.

§

"It's like you're the other side of me," Tanya told Connor once. "You're the side of me that wanted to continue in math, once I'd understood how to appreciate it. It's like I see, in you, what I might have been if I hadn't spent all that time on dance – and doing what I do now.

"You're going to be the success that maybe I could have been, or what my parents might have wanted to see me do – and it makes me feel... I don't know, *completed*, spiritually completed, by enjoying what *you* do, vicariously."

This was an eye-opener for Connor: the first time he'd had any clue that what he did – math, equations, computer science, business administration – could be sexy.

People looked at them, when they walked together, and Connor must have known it wasn't because of him, but he carried himself taller, straighter, to make himself more worthy of Tanya. Tanya, a woman of 28, and him only 22. Tanya, a worldly, accomplished woman, a woman far more alluring and glamourous than any he had ever imagined being with, even in his childish fantasies.

Connor was reluctant to introduce Tanya to his friends – most of whom weren't University students at all, but his old car-crowd friends from high school, and most of whom had gone to community college or to no college at all. They were all a lot younger than Tanya, and obviously wouldn't know how to talk to her, nor she to them.

But in May, to celebrate Connor's graduation with a Bachelor of Business Administration degree, Connor's old friend Brett Norton and his *fiancée* Beverly Ricci offered to take the two of them out to dinner.

Brett and Bev were Connor's age, but they'd settled into heavy, middle-aged bodies and comfortable working-class manners. They were what Connor's father would have called "salt of the earth." Good people, and Connor liked them, but he was afraid of embarrassing himself by showing them to Tanya.

Sure enough, the evening was kind of a frost. They met up at Red Lobster. ("You know, I've never been to a Red Lob-

ster in my life," Tanya had admitted to Connor when he told
her what the plan was for the evening.) Everyone was friendly
and on best behavior, but Tanya was clearly trying to keep the
boredom out of her face as Bev talked about her clerical job at
MRC (a big data analysis company in State City) and her side-
line business as a seamstress, and when Brett described his job
at the city's power plant.

Also, Brett, Bev, and Connor kept referring back to
their high school days – not a lot, but every now and then –
and to the times when this girl named Melissa had been the
fourth member of their gang: not Tanya. Tanya wouldn't have
minded this, except for the wistful look she thought she saw in
Connor's eye when Melissa's name came up.

Brett and Bev appeared lost when Tanya described
what went into an M.M. degree, and what would presumably go
into a D.M.A. degree later on. Connor hardly said a word, but
he was never a talker in any company.

"That might be the right girl for you," Brett told Connor when the two ladies had gone together to the powder
room. "She's smart. You need someone smart and... you
know, sophisticated like that. But she's sure way different from
Melissa. Gonna marry her?"

The idea had occurred to Connor before, but he'd
never allowed himself to consider it. In the course of that meal,
though, Tanya had been talking about where she might get her
D.M.A. – and she hadn't mentioned State University. This time
next year, she'd be off somewhere else, and lost to him.

This almost certainly would have set Connor to worrying, there at the table. He'd already let one girl get away, and he
didn't want to make the same mistake twice. So when Brett said
"marry," Connor must have told himself he'd better make up
his mind about Tanya, by the end of summer at any rate.

Tanya shrugged, when she and Connor were walking
back to his car and he asked for her assessment of his friends.
"They're fine, I guess," she said. "They're just not the kind of
people I'm used to knowing."

Connor and Tanya continued to be a couple that summer, almost but not quite living together. They drove to Indianola to meet Dr. and Mrs. Cucoshay, who were pleasant to Connor but a bit reserved. Tanya kept Connor busy, taking him on little road trips around Iowa. Connor talked about camping together, but Tanya laughed.

"I don't sleep on ground," she said, "and I don't poop in outhouses, much less in a latrine, and I don't go without at least one shower a day. Sorry."

Connor considered going on a camping trip with Brett and Bev and a few other friends, without Tanya, but worried about whom Tanya might meet if he left her alone for a few days. He always worried that she might eventually lose interest in him, in favor of someone older than he, someone more established in life, who had more money and more sophistication to offer her.

Two things happened at the end of that summer vacation that convinced Connor to act. First, the day before the new semester started, Tanya told him, "Now that you're working on your M.B.A., you should start looking more businesslike, just to get you in practice." She was smiling when she said this, but Connor could tell she meant it. "I'm going to take you over to Rosen's, and we'll pick you out a few nice shirts for you to wear to class. And, listen, no shorts or anything but regular shoes on school days, okay?"

Connor wouldn't have minded showing off his girlfriend to Mr. Palinkas – he'd mentioned her to his boss, offhand, more than once – but the boss wasn't in the store on the day Connor and Tanya visited. It was in the store – standing next to Tanya, looking at her as she studied a couple of dress shirts to decide which would look better on him – that Connor felt he'd never seen Tanya look so beautiful. He'd once seen a photograph of Michelangelo's *Pietà*, and he'd been struck by the calm gentleness in Mary's eyes and mouth, and it was this same look, this heart-melting look, that he saw then in Tanya's face as she stared at the shirts. He had been in love with her before, but never so much as just then, with the afternoon sunshine coming through the big front window and reflecting light off her hair.

He said it barely loud enough for her to hear it: "I love you, Tanya, I do."

And Tanya smiled just a little and said, "I love you, Connor," and kissed him on the cheek, which was somehow, in the moment, more intimate than kissing on the mouth.

It was the following Sunday morning, over the kitchen table in Tanya's apartment (he'd stayed the night, and gotten up paying special notice to the perfumey smells of her bedroom and bathroom), when he said to her, "Tanya, I don't ever want to be apart from you, ever. Would you marry me?"

Tanya didn't laugh, as Connor had feared she would; she didn't look horrified or sorrowful or even at all surprised.

"I can't see myself marrying anybody else," she said.

Once they were engaged, issues of logistics came up. They talked about marrying as soon as possible, but Tanya said that wouldn't be practical till they both had a better idea of their futures. She suggested waiting till Connor had completed his M.B.A., which would be nearly two years out. That way, she'd go wherever she decided to go to get her D.M.A., and when Connor had his degree it would be easy enough for him to find a job near wherever she was.

"But I can't wait two years," said Connor, with a big half-forced smile. "Can't you do your D.M.A. here?"

"It's a consideration. It's not my first choice. The professor I'm working with now is retiring, and there's one other professor here I'd love to study with, but I'm not sure she'd take me, and otherwise State doesn't have much to offer me. And the whole School of Music is so political here. I'd hate to get involved. But this does change things, doesn't it? I'll tell you what. I'll see what I can do about getting into Professor Jespersson's studio – and if I can, I'll stay here."

Why did Tanya love Connor, or tell herself she did? Connor must have been lovable at first. The way he'd gaze at Tanya as though she were something unattainable: She'd seen that look from other guys, but it could be that Connor, being younger and gawkier, struck a sentimental note with her. Her boyfriends in the past had mostly been exceptionally handsome, studly men – or ethereal beauties, like Mark, in high school. Connor wasn't unappealing, but he wasn't an Adonis.

Connor would have been something new to Tanya. He wasn't weak or ineffectual; he was bright and a hard worker. He was what she, Tanya, might have been had she taken a different path. To see him crushing on her the way he was – and she could not have missed it – would have made her feel tender toward him, and from there it's easy to see how a romantic attraction could have grown.

She knew Connor wasn't a loser. She knew he might be going places, career-wise, and we can't pretend that that isn't attractive to a woman. Women are attracted to men who look like they've got something going on.

It may have been that Tanya perceived Connor as a perfect foundation on which she could project and build some of her own dreams, the non-musical dreams. It's a cliché, and a rather cringeworthy cliché at that – but maybe Tanya felt that Connor would *complete* her.

Connor was serious, but Tanya probably thought she could loosen him up. And if he was a little nerdy, he was a different kind of nerd, a non-musical nerd, one who could talk about math, and symbolic logic, and other subjects her musical friends never touched. No doubt she felt that she and Connor could continue to have fun together.

And they did, too. So when Connor proposed to her, Tanya thought, why wait? She'd never felt that strongly for anyone else before, and maybe she honestly couldn't imagine feeling that way for anyone else – and she probably did feel, on some level, that Connor was a catch.

7. Melissa and Leander Washington

At Amos Fortune High School, Melissa Wainwright encountered a lot of new experiences – many of which she reported in emails to her parents, brother, and sister. The first eye-opener came on the first day of school, in a remedial reading class, when a hulking young man of about 19 rose from his desk in the middle of the session and headed for the door.

"Wait, where do you think you're going?" Melissa demanded.

"My parole officer," said the young man, and continued on his way.

And that young man never gave Melissa any trouble. Others did. She'd never had to break up a fight before. She'd never had to deal with a boy trying to set a girl on fire in the middle of a classroom session. She'd never had to consider how she'd handle it if she told a student to stop doing something (such as rapping aloud in class), and he replied, "Make me," or how she would go about confiscating a weapon.

It could be that Melissa had had dreams of going into this undesirable school and "making a difference" to these troublesome kids, à la Sandy Dennis in *Up The Down Staircase*, or Sidney Poitier in *To Sir, With Love*, or Jon Voigt in *Conrack*. But she found, quickly enough, that the best she could hope for was to avoid any serious classroom disruptions – and influence one student, maybe two, every semester, to take her studies seriously. She could persuade a few students to do the work and get through. But with most of them, she could tell she was getting nowhere, and in no case did she feel that any student would say of her, "Because of Ms. Wainwright, I went out and made something of myself."

She'd been warned in her English education classes in college that for a teacher, the biggest problem was never the students, and it was never the administration: it was the parents. That might have been true in an ordinary school, but at Amos Fortune almost none of the kids were from two-parent households; many of them were parents themselves.

Then there were the prevailing behaviors Melissa observed, constantly: behaviors she despised, but could say nothing about. The amazingly high number of out-of-wedlock pregnancies. The constant obstreperous behavior of all but a few students. The baggy jeans, the neck tats, which did not directly interfere with her work but which nonetheless disgusted her. She tried to tell herself that her dislike of all this was due to her own ethnocentric prejudices, but that wouldn't wash.

She and two other women were the only white teachers in the school, and Melissa had little to do with them since they were in different departments and quite a bit older. She was off-hand friendly with the other English teachers, but when she became aware of their methods and abilities, she developed contempt for most of them – and again, she wondered whether she was being unfair, and prejudiced, by feeling this way.

Melissa told her family about her frustrations with these teachers, but she gave only passing mention to her growing friendship with a social studies teacher named Leander Washington. He was older than she – about 30 – and he was lean and athletic, dark-skinned; he dressed neatly in dark pressed slacks and immaculate white or light blue shirts. He had rimless glasses, and wore his hair short, in a perfect fade. He didn't smile a lot, although when he did, Melissa thought it was one of the most charming sights she'd ever seen. He wore a wedding ring.

Leander would speak seriously with Melissa, as though he were genuinely interested in hearing what she had to say about the subject under discussion – usually school matters, or they'd talk about current events, or a movie they might both have seen.

It was Leander to whom Melissa tentatively voiced her concerns, one day in the teachers' lounge. She said, naming no names, "It kind of worries me that one or two of the teachers in my department don't seem to have any business teaching English. I mean, I've seen some of the emails they send, internally. They're almost illiterate."

Leander looked grim, and immediately named three of the "one or two" teachers Melissa was thinking of. This was a great weight off Melissa's conscience.

Leander rolled his eyes. "You'll find that there are two kinds of teachers at schools like this one," he said, softly enough that nobody else could have heard him. "There are teachers like you and like me, who came here out of some sense – perhaps a misguided sense – of idealism and altruism. And then there are the teachers who can't be fired but are too incompetent to be exposed to students who might be able to read and write and calculate better than they can. And I have just cited examples of the latter."

Melissa's neighborhood wasn't the worst of inner-city Detroit, but its squalor oppressed her. Some of her neighbors were clean and respectable, but many weren't. She'd routinely hear gunfire at night. She carried pepper spray in her purse.

She complained to Leander that she wished she had more of a social life, that she would be willing to be friends with some of the families in her neighborhood, but they didn't seem interested in cultivating her.

"Go to the A.M.E. church," Leander advised. "It doesn't matter if you're religious yourself. Just go; you'll meet some of the decent people. They'll be older, mostly. But it's a way of introducing yourself to the community."

The Wainwrights went to a Methodist church, usually just on Christmas and Easter. Melissa had had almost no religious instruction. But she knew the reputation many black American churches had, for theatrical demonstrations during the services. The only black church service she'd ever read or heard a description of, though, was in *To Kill A Mockingbird*, where the festivities had been low-key. It was thus at the service she attended in Detroit, although the congregation prayed and sang more energetically than she was used to. The women wore dark dresses and flowered hats, for the most part, and Melissa felt woefully underdressed. But many of the congregation smiled at her, and she was welcomed to the buffet brunch following the service. She started attending services weekly, not because she had any religious beliefs in particular, but because she enjoyed the society – and she began wearing a dress and a hat on Sunday, and bringing food for the buffet.

After a few weeks, the principal of Amos Fortune – he was a gruff, stocky black man, 50ish, named Tolliver; the students and teachers called him Mr. T – remarked to Melissa in the hallway one morning that he'd heard she was attending the A.M.E. church. He mentioned it jocularly, with a little grin.

"Good for you," Mr. T said. "But be careful who you make friends with. You can't let yourself get too close to these people."

"It's not an unfounded concern," Leander said to Melissa when she told him about this conversation. "One thing we're fighting here is low expectations. Maybe he thinks that if you 'get too close to these people,' you'll be just one more bleeding heart white girl who tolerates the ghetto culture."

"It's not like I'm hanging out with the worst elements," Melissa protested. "I'd say the opposite."

"Maybe Mr. T is thinking that it doesn't matter if it's just church. Eventually you'll become influenced by those worst elements – or by the worst traits of the respectable elements. Mr. T is probably afraid you'll 'catch nigger.'"

Melissa gasped.

"Chris Rock wasn't kidding, when he said it was our private civil war. There's black people and there's niggers. And if you refuse to tolerate niggers, that doesn't make you racist."

Melissa looked offended.

"I'll consider myself warned," she said.

"Don't take it too seriously. It's great that you go to that church. That's where the black people are. Just do what you're doing; it'll be fine."

Oh, and that situation where a student was rapping aloud in class and Melissa asked him to stop, and he replied "Make me"? Melissa dispatched another student to Mr. T's office to ask him to come to her classroom for a moment. When he did, and Melissa explained the situation, Mr. T turned to the student and demanded, "That right, boy? You said, 'Make me'?" Melissa could almost see the student physically shrinking. She'd never seen anyone so cowed simply by the force of someone else's personality. This was a kid who might have defied a policeman, or might have tried to – but was powerless against Mr. T.

"How do you *do* that?" she asked Mr. T, later.

"It starts when you're little," Mr. T explained. "Every kid's got a dog in him. Every kid's a coward. You have to teach yourself when you're starting out, to control that dog. You don't go looking for trouble, but anyone tries to give you trouble, you let him know you're gonna rip his head off and shit in it. Even if you can't back it up, if you *act* like you can back it up, most likely you're never gonna have to. And if you have to back it up – you *do*. You're not gonna win every fight you get into, but if you refuse to be defeated, you won't lose, either. I took that boy's heart as soon as I walked into that room, did you notice? Because I developed good habits, long ago."

Melissa recounted this conversation to Leander, who said, "He's right."

By the end of her first semester at Amos Fortune, Melissa felt that she was getting by, better than she'd expected to. The rest of the faculty, and the people at church, seemed to like her.

But she couldn't get past the hopelessness of working with these students, most of whom she was pretty sure would end up as career criminals, or living at the bottom of society no matter what she tried to do for them. She didn't hate her students, but with only a few exceptions she found them repellent. She truly liked maybe two or three of them.

She also feared that as young as she was, she was already on the shelf romantically. There was nobody to date; no way to meet anyone suitable in her neighborhood. She was beginning to think the world of Leander. He'd become her closest local confidant, because he was brighter than her other colleagues, and his company refreshed her. He explained things to her; he listened to her ideas. And Melissa thought he was beautiful to look at. But he was married, and she wasn't going to mess with that.

§

Melissa was home for the holidays, at the end of that first semester, and it was at a New Year's Eve party that she and Connor saw each other for the first time in more than a year. Tanya was spending the holidays back home in Indianola with her parents. Brett and Beverly (married, now) had invited Connor to a party at the house they'd just moved into – and there was Melissa.

She had become much prettier, Connor thought. She was a grown young woman now, not a near-teenager anymore. And she was looking at him, now, in Brett's and Bev's living room, in a way he couldn't remember her looking at him back in the day.

Who can explain this look she was giving him? It was unmistakable: not a look of love or infatuation exactly, but clearly a look of attraction that went beyond affection.

Could it be that Melissa was still feeling the hurt of her experience with Gary, and living a life of solitary misery in Detroit, and had come to this party hoping to rekindle something with Connor? Either a brief fling to make her feel better, or some kind of permanent if distant relationship? Something, at any rate, that might make her feel less frustrated with the idea

that she was spending her better years teaching juvenile delin-
quents in Detroit?

Unlikely. More probably, she'd gone to the party that
night with no such ideas. But maybe, when she saw Connor
there, he was suddenly more attractive in Melissa's eyes because
he now had a girl – even though Melissa didn't yet know that
he had one.

It works that way for men and women both. If you've
got someone – especially if it's early in the relationship and the
first flush of love hasn't yet faded – you'll carry yourself more
confidently, pay more attention to your appearance, and look
healthier. People will notice, and will find you more attractive.

In any event, once they'd laid eyes on each other, Connor and Melissa hardly had a thought for anyone else. It was a
good-sized party – 20-odd people crammed into a small house
– but Connor and Melissa might as well have been alone. They
sat on Brett and Bev's couch, side-by side, sipping beer while
Connor asked for the full story of Melissa's teaching career, and
she told it.

Melissa was surprised – she noticed it as it was going on
– that she was enjoying telling Connor about her life in Detroit,
even though she was describing a life she considered drudgery,
a life she'd have been glad enough to leave.

"But I've been going on all about me," she said at last.
"I guess we sort of lost touch. And it was way more my fault
than yours. Anyway that guy... Gary... he's long gone. I'm just
an old maid schoolmarm, now."

She gave Connor a glance far more flirtatious than anything she'd bestowed on him in years past. "How about you?
Seeing anybody?"

Connor all of a sudden didn't want Melissa to know the
truth – but in another instant he realized that he'd have to tell
her, or she'd hear it from someone else. And if he withheld the
information from her now, she'd feel that he'd lied to her, if
only by omission, when she did find out.

"Actually I'm engaged."

Connor saw the blood drain from Melissa's face, and saw a look of dismay come into her eyes for a moment before she could force herself to banish any such expression.

"Oh," she said. "When did this happen?" Melissa could not keep a quaver out of her voice.

Connor told her the story.

"I thought we were done," he said, "so I... y'know..."

"Sure."

"You okay?" Connor asked. "Want to get some air?"

Connor saw, out of the corner of his eye, that Brett and Bev were giving him knowing smiles as he helped Melissa on with her parka.

"Back in just a few minutes," Connor called to them, over the hum of the other guests, and then he wondered why he'd felt the need to tell them that.

Connor and Melissa went down the porch steps, and out onto the sidewalk. It was a typical New Year's Eve for State City: bitter cold, and blowing. This was a quiet, lower-middle-class residential neighborhood, so there was no partying on the street, indeed no other people so far as they could see. The two of them snuggled against each other as they walked, partly to stay warm and partly to hear each other above the wind.

"Want to go for a drive?" Connor asked. "Easier to talk that way."

Once they were in Connor's Jetta, the conversation started flowing again, as easily as it had done when they'd been in high school. They drove east along Highway 6, and Melissa told Connor all that had happened between her and Gary, as plain as she could make it.

"I'm sorry," said Connor. "I wish we could have... I mean, we never really had to break up... I mean..."

"Maybe we did have to, for a while," said Melissa. "It was, you know, how kids feel when they get out of high school. It's the end of something, and you go on to something else. But tell me about this girl!" Melissa sounded almost cheery.

Connor told his story.

"I still don't know anything about music, or about what she does," Connor concluded, "but she seems to have a lot of ambition, and she makes me want to make more of myself, too. To make her happy and to make me feel better about myself, too, you know?"

"She sounds like a good match for you."

"She challenges me."

"Be careful," said Melissa. "When Gary and I split up, he told me he wanted more 'challenge' out of a relationship, whatever that means. And I'm sure that's what he got, but I wouldn't be surprised if he regrets it now."

It was past midnight before Connor turned the car around and drove back to State City – they'd gone almost to the Mississippi River – and they stopped at the Rivercat Truck Stop, just outside of town, for a snack before driving back to Brett and Bev's house. By the time they got back there, the house was dark, so Melissa asked to be let out next to her car.

"Congratulations, Connor." Melissa leaned over and kissed Connor, on the cheek. "Let's stay in touch."

"Yeah." Connor kissed back, also on the cheek. "Let's not..." He couldn't find exactly the words.

"Let's not be strangers," said Melissa, and she exited the car, waving Connor goodbye in the dark. He drove back to his apartment, and she to her parents' house.

It had attracted notice, at that party, that Connor and Melissa had left together and not returned. And how the word got back to Tanya was practically a fluke. She shouldn't have found out: It's unlikely that any of her friends would have been at that party. But she did run into Brett Norton, on the street, when she'd returned to town a few days later, and just about the first thing he'd said to her, once they'd exchanged greetings, was, "Are you and Connor not seeing each other anymore?" And when she said they still were, so far as she knew, Brett had looked terribly embarrassed, and admitted that it was just a matter of his not having seen her at the party the other night, and Connor's old high school girlfriend had been there, and she and Connor had left together and…

And then Brett apologized for his dumbness. "It wasn't anything," he reassured Tanya. "They were just catching up, you know."

Tanya had waited for Connor to get in touch with her – and she waited a day longer than she'd expected. This gave her time to get angrier and angrier – although she did her best not to show it, at first, when Connor did finally come over to her place on the evening following her return.

"Connor, I know this might be nothing, but I'm kind of concerned," she told him, almost as soon as he was in the door and had gotten his coat off. Connor could tell from the set of her mouth, and the glint in her eye, that she was upset with him, which had hardly ever happened before.

"Someone told me that he saw you on New Year's Eve, leaving with some young lady…" Tanya told Connor what she'd been told.

"That was just Melissa Wainwright. I've told you about her. We're old friends. Really. We just wanted to talk. I was telling her about you, actually. About us. And, yeah, maybe she was a little sad to hear it – but that's all it was."

"Okay. I believe you. It unsettles me, though, when I hear that you left a party with some other girl and never came back. And obviously it gives other people the wrong idea. If they were wrong."

"I'm sorry. I guess it could have looked that way. It was dumb. I didn't think."

"Okay. But try to think harder from now on."

§

It wasn't till the following May, with just a few days left in the school year, that Leander told Melissa that he'd split from his wife. He'd come to school one morning minus his wedding ring, so it was natural for Melissa to ask him, when they were in private, whether that meant anything. He said it did.

"We grew apart," Leander added. "No hard feelings. It's good that we found it out before we started a family."

"You never told me anything about her."

"She's a lawyer. Very passionate about what she does, very dedicated. Maybe too much so. You might not believe it, but I'm pretty apolitical. And I have no patience with people who talk about identity politics and 'oppressor classes,' and that. And you know what else? Mumia was guilty and Al Sharpton ought to be ashamed of himself." Leander gave another of his grim smiles.

"I want a family and so does she – but we've come to have such different values that it wouldn't make sense for us to have a family together. So we decided to split while we were still friends."

At this, Melissa wanted to reach out and put a hand on Leander's arm – not sexually, just for comfort, because he did look kind of downhearted – but she didn't want Leander to read anything into it, so she didn't.

Melissa had decided not to teach summer school that year. The idea of staying in Detroit, in her neighborhood, all summer, was sickening to her. She kept her apartment, but moved herself back to the family home in State City for three months, mostly just chilling and seeing some of her old high school friends – although not Connor, till just before she was ready to go back to Detroit for the fall term.

8. Connor and Tanya Get Married

Connor and Tanya had started living together at that same time: in May, at the end of the spring semester. They'd chosen the third Saturday in August – the one right before classes started at State University – as their wedding date. Tanya's parents had lobbied for holding the nuptials in Indianola, but Tanya said she only wanted a very informal ceremony, with no religion and no gowns or tuxes, and she wanted her friends to be there – and that meant a lot of School of Music people, who were in State City. That weekend would be ideal, she figured, since so many people would be coming into town anyway.

The invitations went out in June. Connor and Tanya addressed them; they'd agreed to each limit themselves to 50 people outside of immediate family.

The wedding would take place in the room in which they'd met: the ballroom of the downtown Marriott. A local judge, a friend of the Lowes, would perform the ceremony.

Tanya hadn't bothered to ask who was on Connor's list of 50. She couldn't think of anyone he'd ask to whom she might have objected – till a few days after they'd sent out the invitations, and the RSVPs started coming back. One of them was from Melissa Wainwright.

For the first time in their relationship, Tanya threw a full-out tantrum worthy of a principal soprano. She threw other things, too: books, dishes. Connor knew he was in trouble when he came home from the library that night to find Tanya glaring at him sidelong. When she did that, he could be sure she was seriously angry. And her lips had gone bluish-purple, which meant "take cover."

"You son of a bitch," Tanya hissed at him, as soon as he was in the door of their apartment. She held up the RSVP card and waggled it at him. "Do you think I'd invite any of *my* exes? I do not fucking believe this."

"Tanya, she's a friend. I've known her since we were kids! How could I *not* invite her?"

"Easy. Easier than inviting her. You don't send her a fucking invitation, okay?"

"But you never asked me who I was inviting. If you were worried about it, why didn't you ask?"

"Because I fucking trusted you!" Tanya shrieked. "I never thought you'd do anything like this. And why didn't you ask me? If you'd asked me I might even have been okay with it."

This, Connor felt, was irrational, and he didn't know how to respond to it without making himself as foolish as Tanya sounded to him.

"But I invited her parents too," he said. "They're old friends of mine. It's not like I was inviting her as my ex. She's part of a family that I'm friends with." And Connor saw that Tanya was ready to explode again, and he was even afraid she might try to hit him. "I could have just invited her parents, I guess, but it was through her that I got to be friends with them, and besides, this way we have closure."

"Closure? We've been together for more than a year, we've been engaged since last fall, and now you want *closure?* You fucking weasely bag of *shit!"*

That's when Tanya started picking books and coffee cups off the dining table and hurling them: not at Connor, but against the walls, where one of the cups shattered.

Then she went to the kitchen and brought a bottle of vodka out of the cupboard. She poured a tall glass half full of it, topped it with orange juice, and drank it in about a minute, glowering at Connor all the while.

Connor sank into a chair and sat wondering how he could get out of this jam. Tanya finally sat too, at the far end of the room from him. They stayed thus for what was probably a few minutes but must have felt to Connor like an hour.

Connor finally had an idea.

"I mainly wanted to show you off," he told Tanya. "I want everyone to see what a beautiful woman I'm marrying. Especially all my old friends. I want them all to see you. I want to impress them."

Tanya slowly raised her eyes, and glowered at him.

"You'd better be sure you want to marry me," she said, thick-tongued. Connor had never seen her drink anything stronger than wine or beer before; the vodka had been there for company.

"It's not too late to change your mind," Tanya added.

We can't doubt that Connor did consider changing his mind. Here he was seeing Tanya as he'd never seen her before, and it must have terrified him. But it must have been even more frightening to him to contemplate the end of their relationship. Could he have backed out of the wedding, and continued to live with her, indefinitely? Conceivably, yes – but at that moment he wasn't calm enough to consider all the options thoroughly. All he wanted, right then, was to not have Tanya so angry at him. It was extremely uncomfortable.

He must have been pretty sure that if he had admitted that in fact he was *not* so sure anymore, Tanya would have insisted on a split. And that, he did not want. Even with Melissa in his mind. And we can't know to what extent or in what way Melissa *was* in his mind, then. Connor might have been sincere when he said he'd only invited Melissa as a dear old friend. He did not want to lose Tanya. She still had a strong hold on him. Her beauty, her spirit, the way heads turned whenever the two of them were out in public, the sheer *prestige* that attended his being with a woman like this, a woman far above any he'd ever dreamed of being with: all that would have been much more than Connor would have cared to part with.

Connor was not widely experienced sexually, but sex with Tanya was certainly more exciting than that one clumsy, fumbling, embarrassing liaison with Melissa had been. Connor must have known it would be a grim task, finding another girl who could measure up to Tanya. Now that he was accustomed to having a regular girlfriend – and such a girlfriend – no doubt he was thinking, "She's way the best I'll ever do."

This episode must have added to whatever reservations he might have been developing – but those reservations, he would never express. He spent the rest of the day and evening reassuring Tanya again and again that she was the love of his life, his wife forever; there was nobody in his mind but her. Nobody, nothing. He said it again and again. She *was* his life, he told her.

At last Tanya forgave him: grudgingly, then tenderly.

§

What did Dr. and Mrs. Cucoshay say about this? They probably had misgivings, especially in view of Connor's age. But they'd have known their daughter well enough to be certain that she would do what she would do. And probably they were glad to see Tanya settling down. Of course they came to State City for the wedding; so did Danuta and her husband, from Seattle.

On the morning of August 16, 2003, in the ballroom of the Marriott, Connor and Tanya were married. Judge Chapman performed the ceremony, and there was a buffet lunch after-wards. The bride wore not a wedding dress, but a simple day dress in the lightest possible beige. Connor was wearing a blue cotton poplin suit and a white shirt, and a red and blue striped tie, all of which made him feel uncomfortable. He joked to Tanya that he might wear a tie again when their daughter got married, but not before that. Tanya gave him a sharp little dou-ble-take when he said that, but she let it pass and the ceremony went off easily.

The two of them stood together, as the reception line formed. Brett and Bev Norton were there. Bev was starting to show pregnancy – due to give birth in December, she said –

and Brett was being extra-attentive to her. Brett's pride in Bev, and hers in him, were palpable. Connor grasped Brett's hand and exclaimed, "I'm so glad for you, my friend. A *baby*!"

"You and Tanya are next," Brett said.

Andy Palinkas, Connor's part-time employer, apologized for not being able to stay long, since he had to get back to the store, but Andy made Connor feel even prouder of himself than he had felt before, by absolutely goggling at Tanya.

"My God, Connor, I've never even spoken to a girl as beautiful as that. Congratulations, and every happiness."

Connor introduced Andy to the bride, and Andy clicked his heels and bowed his bald head over Tanya's hand, and kissed it. Or rather, he kissed his own thumb, which was atop her hand, which is how it's proper to kiss a lady's hand if you're back in the Habsburg Empire, which Andy probably wished he were. Anyway it got laugh from Tanya.

"Tanya, I've heard you perform many times, at concerts," Andy said, "but I've gone far too long without being formally introduced to you. I wish you all the best."

Tanya smiled back at Andy and said, "Aww," as though he'd said something that actually touched her. "Thank you."

"Don't let Connor give you any trouble," Andy added. "Kind treatment only confuses him." Tanya laughed aloud, and Andy kind of floated away from her – hopeless, but infatuated nonetheless.

Jim and Gail Wainwright were there. Connor introduced them to Tanya, whom they'd never met.

"You're so lucky, Tanya," said Gail. "You take good care of him. Make him happy."

"You picked a pretty one, Connor," said Jim. He then kissed the bride, a bit noisily, while Gail caught Connor's eye and gave him that little "what can you do?" look.

Melissa Wainwright showed up too, in a classic jewel-tone blue dress and spike heels. Melissa's date, who wore a white linen suit and a bright blue tie of nearly the same tone as Melissa's dress, was an extremely handsome young man named

Chad Thurston. Tanya knew him from her tango club, and knew he was gay.

"You'd think she was the one getting married," Tanya muttered to Connor, when Melissa and Chad had moved along. "Showing off all that cleavage. Still think you chose the right girl?"

Who can know how serious Tanya was about that question? Who can know how seriously Connor took it? But he didn't laugh. He couldn't come up with anything comforting or distracting to say. He started to roll his eyes, then he stopped himself, knowing that that wasn't quite the thing to do, but he couldn't help releasing a sigh, which he was pretty sure Tanya heard. But she went back to greeting guests, flashing her enormous smile again, and Connor was reassured for the time being.

Some of Tanya's friends and acquaintances from the School of Music had provided a small ensemble for dancing, which her parents had paid for along with the rest of the wedding. Tanya had requested that they play mostly tango tunes, so they'd even found an accordionist to be part of the group. But the first dance was a waltz, as is traditional at weddings. Tanya and Connor danced it together, and everyone applauded, then the rest of the bridal party joined in. Another waltz, and Tanya danced with her father, who was a tall, slim man in his 60s, and Connor danced with his mother, and the rest of the "duty dances" were completed.

"And now," Tanya proclaimed in a voice that filled the room, *"TANGOOOO!"*

The little orchestra struck up "Libertango," Tanya flung herself into Connor's arms, and he swooped her across the floor as, once again, the guests applauded – far more enthusiastically than they'd done for the initial waltz.

Anyone was free to dance, but nobody else was dancing once that tango had started. They were just watching as Connor and Tanya gave them a show. But then Melissa and her date began dancing too. Tanya could see that Melissa didn't know how to dance – but Chad did. Tanya had danced with him often enough to know that.

As she continued to dance with Connor, Tanya saw – or fancied she saw – the briefest flash of wistfulness in Connor's eyes when Chad and Melissa came into his field of vision. A flash only, an intake of breath, a contraction of the eye muscles, a slackening of the jaw, nothing more – and then he looked away from the other couple in an instant, and rearranged his facial expression.

With some force, Tanya back-led Connor so that he'd be facing away from Melissa and her young man. Connor looked astonished at her, and perhaps slightly sheepish.

In a few minutes, Chad broke away from Melissa and with a big dimply smile he embraced Tanya, kissed her on the cheek, and said, "Let's cut a rug for old times' sake." Which left Connor to dance with Melissa.

Tanya could see, as she danced with Chad, that Connor and Melissa were just dancing, not talking, so she couldn't take exception to it – but how could she not feel unease, at the least? She allowed them two dances before she broke away from Chad. Then, smiling at Melissa in as friendly a manner as she could muster, she said, "I'm missing my husband; I have to have him back for the next dance." She took Connor by the arm. Melissa returned the smile, demurely and reservedly.

Years later, Tanya would relate the incident to a friend in whom she'd come to confide.

"Duh, she was trying to show me up! Of course she was. Of course she was. I've danced professionally. I *do* know how to dance. And, yeah, I saw what she was up to, and I wanted to show *her* up, but I knew for one thing that Connor wasn't up to it. I mean, I taught him to dance, sort of, but we tried to dance competitively once and he just didn't have it. A girl can only back-lead so much. So after we'd had a few dances, I retired. I let Melissa do her thing. I hope she had fun. I thought she made a fool of herself.

"But Connor couldn't take his eyes off her. I pretended I wasn't noticing, but I was, and finally I couldn't help it, I said to him, 'See something you like out there on the floor?' And he looked at me like I'd gone crazy and taken a swing at him.

"I couldn't believe it. This was the man I loved, and I wanted to kick him to death. At our wedding reception. It was right then that it dawned on me what a mistake I'd made. Or it should have dawned on me. Or I should have known better a long time before we got married. And maybe I did know. But I wasn't admitting it to myself, then. I couldn't have."

That evening, Andy Palinkas had an opportunity to gossip with the Wainwrights. He'd stayed late at the store, and when he came home the sun was not quite ready to set. Jim and Gail were sitting out on their front porch, sipping lemonade. Andy waved to them as he got out of his white Grand Marquis, and walked over.

"I'd forgotten that you two knew Connor," he remarked. "But he used to date your daughter, long ago, didn't he? So of course you'd know him. That sure is a beautiful girl he married. What I wouldn't give, to be in his place!"

Gail shrugged. "I never met her before," she said. "But I'm worried for Connor, a little. She seemed... just not right for him. For one thing she's way older than he is. And then, I mean, a *music* student. I never have been comfortable with arty people. Oh, I admire them in a way. And our son David's a writer, and English was always my favorite subject in school so I can understand that. But..."

"You certainly can see why Connor would be attracted to her," said Jim, with a bit of a leer. Gail glanced sharply at him.

"I mean she has a way about her," said Jim. "And she is pretty, you have to admit. But, I dunno. She doesn't look like she'd be the kind of girl to make Connor a good wife. She looks to me like the type who'll try to dominate him and take advantage of him. And she's probably just interested in his money."

"I didn't know Connor was rich," said Andy. "Not on what I pay him for doing my taxes, that's for darn sure."

"He's not rich now, but there's money in his family," said Jim. "Plus, this girl probably knows he'll make a fortune one of these days. I'm sure she's not stupid."

"She was bright enough to set her cap for Connor," Gail agreed. "And bright enough to know how to snag him. You can tell. Girls like her. They're... wily."

Christine Wainwright – who would have been 12 years old, then – came out of the house at this point. "I'm going over to the Skelleys'," she announced. "You were at the wedding too, huh?" she asked Andy.

"Mr. P can tell you what I was telling you," Gail said to Christine. "The way that woman was shooting looks at Missie all through the reception."

"I didn't see that," said Andy. "I left, as soon as I'd kissed the bride."

"She was," said Gail. "It was pretty blatant. Almost like she thought Melissa was there to steal Connor away from her."

"Wasn't she?" Christine asked.

"Christine!" Gail looked scandalized.

"She got all mad when I called her on it, when she was getting ready this morning. But she dressed herself up like it was her that was getting married. I never saw her work so hard on looking good. Even for, like, for her high school prom that Connor took her to, right?"

"Oh, Christine!" said Gail.

"And why else is she up there moping in her room? She looked great, though." Christine skipped down the driveway, toward a house across the street and down the block.

§

The day after the wedding, Connor gave Tanya a surprise: He announced that he'd decided against taking a full load of courses when classes started that week. He'd take just three graduate hours that fall, and get his M.B.A. eventually, no hurry. Instead, he'd start up his own day trading business. He had a little savings of his own, he explained, and his father was lending him some seed money; so was Dr. Wainwright – on the understanding that he'd give them a solid return.

"They'll all give me good recommendations," he explained. "I can set up my practice here, and it'll be portable; I can do it from anywhere. So wherever you end up going, once you've got your D.M.A., I'll have a career I can take with me. Spending all that money, and all that time, for an M.B.A.: it'd be a gamble; to heck with it.

"Isn't day trading kind of a gamble?"

"Not much of one if you know what you're doing. And I do. I figure I can make quite a lot of money. More than if I were a drone, working for someone else." Connor laughed. "See? You're making me ambitious."

Tanya was a little put-out that Connor hadn't consulted her, but she agreed that it sounded like the sensible course – and she was pleased and flattered that Connor was looking ahead with regard to her own career, and was planning to make himself flexible, to accommodate her. She'd arranged, once it looked like she'd stay at State University, to take her Master's as an "internal degree" that would be part of her doctoral program. She still had two years to go for her D.M.A. And it was getting tougher for her: more work, more involvement in departmental politics.

All academic departments are political as hell, because everybody wants to be the star, everybody wants to be the boss, everybody wants the lion's share of the resources. It's been said that departmental politics at a college or university are so brutal and vicious because the stakes are so small. But in the School of Music it's worse.

This is mainly because among the graduate students in, say, the College of Business, there's less competition. There, each student just has to play his own game as best he can play it, get good grades, and get a good job later on. But in the School of Music, each student is competing with other students to be first chair in the orchestra, or to get the plum roles in an opera or a musical.

At the beginning of the movie *Glengarry, Glen Ross*, Alec Baldwin tells a bunch of real estate brokers about an upcoming sales contest, in which first prize is a new Cadillac El Dorado:

"Anybody want to see second prize? Second prize is a set of steak knives. Third prize is, you're fired."

The School of Music is like that. The biggest fish – the concertmaster, first-chair trumpet, principal soprano, all the musicians who snag the best solos or the best singing roles – get noticed. They get the paying gigs; they get hired by the better orchestras, or one of the better universities if they want to teach. Students who are back in the pack, in terms of standing and accomplishment, might as well get married and start having kids and hope they find a job at some middle school in Bumfuk Egypt: directing swing choir and teaching 12-year-olds to sing "Stodola Pumpa."

And a lot of those students spend the rest of their lives either hating themselves because they didn't have the talent or the drive to be as good as they wanted to be, or because they're convinced (or they convince themselves) that their careers were sabotaged by jealous peers who didn't have as much talent, or by some bitter dog-in-the-manger professor.

That's what you have to look forward to – if you're not at the top of your game, every day. Anybody can learn to sing, or play an instrument, but it's hard, and it takes Malcolm Gladwell's 10,000 hours, at least, to do it at a professional level. So, musicians can be plenty cut-throat. And they're stressed out, all the time. Especially in grad school.

That brings up another area where Tanya and Connor were in the long run not compatible. Tanya could talk about business and math, but Connor couldn't talk about music. It didn't interest him. He'd listen if Tanya felt like talking about it, but he'd never have anything insightful to say in response.

And sometimes it would annoy Tanya that Connor appeared not to be hanging on her words, the way he used to. She used to find it cloying, when he would gaze at her like a stunned ox, before they were married, but if that gaze went away she would miss it. There's the old joke about how many sopranos it takes to change a light bulb: the answer is, "Just one, to hold the light bulb in the socket while the world revolves around her." Tanya was a soprano.

Now that their relationship had settled into a less romantic, less intense, more routine tempo, Connor and Tanya found that they sometimes had to grope for conversation. Tanya didn't find Connor as interesting as she did when she was teaching him to sing and dance. And she was noticing that his being younger – which had attracted her, once – was sometimes a drawback. He still looked like a college kid. He was content to slop around in shorts and a torn t-shirt and flip-flops whenever he could. His table manners weren't bad, exactly, but sloppy and careless, and it wasn't so cute anymore.

They seemed to be living more compartmentalized lives. They still spent time together, but it tended to be quiet time, in the evenings. They'd sit together in their apartment and he'd work on his investment projects, and she'd study; they had little conversation aside from friendly banter. The sex was still frequent. They seemed happy enough – except that now and then Connor would get on Tanya's nerves when he'd mention (always in a jocular tone) that it was too bad she'd never learned to cook. Meals were catch-as-catch can; they almost never had an organized lunch or dinner together unless they went out.

They led pretty separate social lives, too. Brett and Bev were still Connor's best friends, and he enjoyed the company of older people, too, such as his clients Jim Wainwright and Andy Palinkas. Tanya's friends were almost all connected to the School of Music – students or faculty – and Connor had nothing in common with them. He didn't like most of them. They struck him, mostly, as pretentious and stuck-up, and interested in things he didn't know or care about. Tanya didn't seem to like his friends, either. She never said it, but she must have found them unsophisticated, boring, exactly *not* the kind of people she wanted to socialize with on an everyday basis.

Tanya and Connor never talked of it at any length; they just tacitly agreed that they would hang out with different crowds. Not that either of them had a lot of time for a social life, that fall. They still went to tango club occasionally, but less often now that they were both caught up in their occupations.

9. More About Melissa and Leander

That fall, back for another year at Amos Fortune High School, Melissa Wainwright was no happier than she'd been the previous year. The experience was just as frustrating. If she were dealing with it better, it was because she was accustomed to it. She still didn't like many of her students, or hardly any of her colleagues. Outside of school, her social life revolved around church. She was still the only white member of the congregation, and she didn't buy into the religion, but she enjoyed the company of the women she met there. They were funny, and comfortable: just pleasant respectable older ladies. She enjoyed taking part in their community activities. They organized weekly dinners for the needy, rummage sales, bake sales, and various performing arts options for children (which attracted no boys whatever). Several of the women wanted to know if she had a young man, and if not, why not, and Melissa said it was because she didn't get out in the evenings.

"But you're such a pretty girl," one of them told her. "It's a shame you're dying on the vine. You need to move out of this neighborhood. Even if it meant you had a longer commute."

Melissa conceded that maybe she should. There was very little culture in her neighborhood – no concerts or theatre, and not even many movies – and she wouldn't have gone into any of the local bars. She didn't feel safe in her neighborhood at night. But she had to admit to herself that it was inertia, more than anything else, that kept her from engaging in social activities that might be conducive to meeting eligible men.

Melissa enjoyed Leander's company at school, but she sensed that some of the black female teachers were acting less friendly to her, in direct proportion to how often, and how much, she was seen with him. It may have been her imagination, but that was what she sensed. She mentioned it to Leander, and without any smile he said, "No, that's not your imagination."

And thus it was that the two of them started giving each other less face-time at work – and discreetly seeing more of each other outside of school. They started going out to dinner occasionally, or going on little weekend outings – but never anywhere near the school and her neighborhood. Leander appreciated movies, and could talk about them – and with him, Melissa noted, she tended to see a more eclectic mix of movies than she'd have seen on her own, or with any of her old college or high school friends. Melissa had never had any strong musical tastes – music had never been important to her – so she didn't understand Leander's fascination with the compositions of Duke Ellington and Charles Mingus. But she enjoyed Leander's enjoyment of them.

While she was chatting and laughing with Leander, even though sincerely glad to be with him, she would sometimes remind herself that hanging out with him proved that she wasn't a racist. When he kissed her, she felt that kissing him was something praiseworthy – even though she was not unwilling – because it proved that she wasn't a racist. By the time she went to bed with Leander, she wasn't trying to prove anything at all – unless maybe the rumor that black guys are better endowed.

But to be fair, Melissa was just as much taken with Leander's personality as with any of his physical attributes. "I love your big sexy brain," she'd tell him, when they were curled up together on his couch, just talking. Leander was one of the most intelligent men she'd ever known, and one of the most informed. It was November before "I love your big sexy brain" had progressed to "I love you," but it did happen – and when it happened, Leander said it back to her.

It was all the more delicious – but saddening, to Melissa – that she and Leander had to keep their relationship a secret. They agreed that if it were to be known at the school, they'd both be ostracized, and almost certainly at least one of them would be out of a job. Leander told Melissa unequivocally that her friends from church would be no friends to her if they knew.

"Maybe a few of them would pretend they were all right with it," he said. "But only a few, if any. Decent single black men are in very short supply. I know, it doesn't sound right for me to call myself decent – but face facts. I'm a catch for some nice young black girl. And you're taking me out of the mix. You're stealing me from that community. Oh, you are just the kind of grey meat they'd despise."

They never got together at Melissa's place. Leander lived some distance away, in a neighborhood where Melissa wasn't known, so they had their sleepovers at his apartment. Melissa always wore a hat or a stocking cap, and turned the collar of her overcoat up around her face, when they were out together or when she was entering or leaving his building.

If Melissa spent a Saturday night at Leander's, she would almost always bring her Sunday clothes with her, and attend church the next morning as usual, so that nobody would draw any inferences from her not showing up.

Leander didn't want his ex-wife to know about the relationship, because the divorce wasn't final, and while the breakup had been friendly, he wanted to keep it that way. He couldn't tell his parents, either, for they'd never be able to keep it a secret.

"They'd probably be cool," he said. "Misgivings, yeah, but they'd accept you, I'm pretty sure. When the situation's stabilized, I'll introduce you. Maybe after the holidays."

This was more than Melissa could promise. When she went back to State City for Christmas, not a word did she breathe to anyone about this new relationship – despite the fact that the idea of marriage was starting to pop into her head, now and then.

She didn't think her parents would give her any direct grief, if she told them. She was pretty certain they'd claim they were okay with it. They might even claim they were proud of their daughter for being so color-blind. She could almost hear her father saying something like, "It's the color of a man's heart that matters, not the color of his skin."

But if her father were to say it, she would never believe that he meant it – and she was pretty sure that even if they never hinted at it to her, her parents would feel that she had disgraced herself, and them. So, when she was home and Jim and Gail asked her if there were a young man in the picture, Melissa would reply, "Not really. A few guys I'm friends with, but nothing serious."

Connor must have decided there'd be nothing wrong with calling over to the Wainwrights', two days after Christmas, to invite Melissa to join him for coffee before she had to head back to Detroit. He'd returned to State City, from Christmas in Indianola, leaving Tanya to spend a few extra days with her parents – so she would never need to know.

And that's all it was: coffee. Connor had driven to the Wainwrights' house, planning to take Melissa to Starbucks, but Gail Wainwright insisted that he come in and have some Christmas cookies: "They're still good. Jim and I are watching movies in the other room; you two can visit all you want. Christine, let's let them have some time alone."

So that's what Connor and Melissa did. Melissa told Connor about her job in Detroit, but not a word about Leander. Connor told Melissa about his day trading business.

"Your Dad was a huge help," he added. "Getting me started. Your parents... they're wonderful, both of them."

"Are you happy with Tanya? She's beautiful."

"Yes, she is."

"Does she make you happy?"

"Yes, she does."

"Then I'm glad," said Melissa, and that was all they said on that subject. Connor left, after less than an hour – and after asking whether Melissa was sure she didn't need a ride to the airport the next morning.

"Mom's taking me. Anyway Tanya wouldn't like it."

"She's got nothing to be jealous about. But try telling her that."

They embraced – a long embrace, after making sure neither Jim nor Gail was nearby – and wished each other well. Tanya never knew of the visit, although Connor would certainly have had a plausible story prepared in case she ever asked where he'd been that afternoon.

§

So, Melissa went back to Detroit, and to Leander. They went along, through the spring semester, just as before. That summer, Leander was offered a transfer for the upcoming school year. He had the option of staying at Amos Fortune, but the transfer would take him to a better-paid job in a magnet school that focused on the social sciences and "public interest."

Melissa had started to hope that Leander would bring up marriage, but so far he hadn't, although they were together more and more, and were more open about it, as long as they weren't in her neighborhood or at work. Leander told Melissa about this opportunity over dinner at his apartment, one night during the few days' break between the spring semester and summer school.

"I could stay," he said. "I could go on doing what I'm doing, and keep telling myself I'm making a difference, but… I've lost the faith. I've seen only a handful of kids graduate from Amos Fortune that I was pretty sure would fly right the rest of their lives – and not in one of those cases could I be sure it was because of anything I'd done. At Joe Louis High, I'd be working with the 'talented tenth,' at least in theory."

"You should totally take it," said Melissa. "No-brainer."

"Maybe a few years ago I'd have been all, 'No, they need me, those poor disadvantaged kids need me!'" Leander let his voice fly into a querulous falsetto for those last few words. "But I'm not kidding myself like that, now. Besides, I'm burning out. I don't think I could take another year at Amos Fortune."

"And if you get tenure after this next year," he told Melissa, "you might want to put in for a transfer yourself. There's only so many years a person can stand an environment like that. If I'm to continue to play the idealistic young teacher, I've got to get my big black ass away from it."

This made Melissa laugh, but she had to agree with Leander. They both taught summer school at Amos Fortune, and when the fall semester started, Leander went off to Joe Louis. He and Melissa still saw a lot of each other – they usually lived together at his place on weekends, now, and some of Melissa's church friends wondered why they didn't often see her at services on Sundays anymore. A couple of them, on one of the rare occasions that fall when she did show up, asked her after the services why she hadn't been around.

"You found you a young man, didn't you?" said one.

Melissa blushed, and that was all the ladies needed: they laughed as though it were the funniest thing in the world.

"Bring him here next Sunday, honey. We'd be proud to meet him."

"He's not religious," Melissa replied. "But I'll mention it to him."

During the first week of classes in the fall term – Melissa's third year at Amos Fortune – Mr. T off-handedly asked her in the hall, "How's Leander liking it at Joe Louis?"

"He loves it," Melissa said, before it could occur to her to reply evasively. "He's doing great there, so far."

Mr. T guffawed, mouth wide open, showing his teeth. "I knew it!" He strode down the hall toward his office, still laughing.

10. Connor and Tanya Get Pregnant

For their first Valentine's Day as a married couple – this was when Melissa was still in her second year at Amos Fortune – Connor had planned to take Tanya to a nice dinner and present her with a necklace he'd picked out for her at Blaha Jewelers. He did, too, but not before Brett and Beverly had stopped by their apartment with the new baby. Connor had invited them. The baby – a girl – was just old enough to be taken on visits.

When Brett and Bev entered Connor and Tanya's apartment, Bev was carrying little Brenna in a front-pack.

"God, she's beautiful," Connor breathed, offering the baby his finger.

"Isn't she?" Brett replied. "Gets it from her mother."

Connor looked at the baby some more, and imagined what a baby of Tanya's might look like. And he thought of the way Tanya sometimes looked down at him, if she were sitting in his lap or if they were relaxing in bed, and he thought how that face might look, smiling down at a beautiful baby girl.

Connor gave Tanya her necklace over dessert that night. "With all my love," he'd written on the card.

"Connor, you can't know how special you are to me," said Tanya. "I can't imagine ever being without you."

Connor reached across the table and took her hand. "Tanya," he said, "Brett and Bev got me to thinking. Wouldn't it be great if we could have one of our own?"

Tanya stiffened, and moved her head back a couple of

inches as though she'd smelled something. Then she made herself smile again, and replied, in a friendly tone, "I don't want to."

If Connor had hoped that the sight of adorable little Brenna, that afternoon, and the romantic dinner, and his gift, might have put Tanya in a more tractable mood – well, he'd hoped in vain, that's all.

"I don't like babies, I don't like children. You knew that going in."

Connor had to admit to himself that he had known that going in – but he'd been certain Tanya would change her mind once they were married. He was still fairly sure she would, although less so, now. How could she not want a family? He knew that no normal, natural woman felt fulfilled, or felt that she was worth anything, till she'd had a child.

He knew enough to retreat. But he also knew he'd damaged the evening.

Brett counseled him, a few days later: "Be patient. Let her get her degree or whatever it is she's going for. Then she'll be ready."

Connor couldn't be patient. Not for that long. He tried flattery. He dropped hints about how beautiful a child of Tanya's would look. What fun it would be for her to teach that child to sing. Tanya, years later, said something like this to the friend to whom she'd described Connor's behavior at their wedding:

"I can't call it browbeating. It was more subtle than that but not really subtle at all. It went on for months. When we were out in public together, every time we saw a baby, it seemed like, he'd look at it like 'aww,' and then he'd tell me why that baby was so cute, the way you'd explain why a great painting was a great painting, or sometimes he'd look at the baby and then look at me and shake his head like I was depriving him somehow. Or sometimes he'd see an older kid, maybe five, six, seven, and he'd say something like, 'Gosh, it must be fun to watch a kid grow up.'

"Then he started getting all mopey, going around the

apartment, like, scowling at everything, and at first I let him alone. I thought he'd snap out of it. But he didn't.

"It got back to me that the reason why Connor didn't go after his M.B.A. right away was because *I* was putting pressure on *him* to make money, to support me while I got my D.M.A. I don't know if Connor actually told people that, or if he implied it, or if somebody else started that story. But, yeah, that was the story: Evil Selfish Tanya got in the way of his education. Of course I did. Of course I did.

"I do not care about money. I have never cared about money. I don't care what Connor might say. That was never the issue. I wouldn't have cared if we'd lived in a trailer and ate canned spaghetti every night. I'd have been perfectly okay with it if he'd gone after the M.B.A., for his own satisfaction if nothing else. No, he was the one who wanted to make the money right away, have the nice house, the two-car garage. And the kid, to show off how grown-up he is, or I don't know what he wanted her for; I don't know why it was so important to him that I get pregnant right away when he knew I wasn't into the idea. Maybe so as to make sure I'd never go anywhere, never go away from him? And then he went away from me.

"Before we got married we'd agreed. I told him I didn't want children; I told him that even if I changed my mind – which was totally unlikely – I would want to hold off at least till I'd gotten my D.M.A. and established a career somewhere, and I warned him that that would probably take at least six years, maybe more. And he said he was fine with that.

"Oh, he painted me this great picture: how he'd build up his practice while I worked on my singing career, and he'd be okay with me touring if I went back to being a professional singer – he told me all that. And I believed him, I bought the P.R., I married him, and we hadn't been married long at all before he started bringing up the idea again. Just one kid, he said, one to get us started, then we could hold off on any more till we'd both done whatever else we wanted to do.

"It was, you know, you always hear guys complaining how if they're not getting along with their girlfriend, and if they ask what's wrong, the woman will say 'Nothing!' when obviously it's something? That was what Connor was like. I'd ask him, 'Do you want to talk?' and he'd say something like, 'Everything's fine. Evidently.' or he'd do this big sigh, and he'd say, 'I guess there's nothing to talk about.'

"And then sometimes he'd tell me what was on his mind, and of course I knew already what it was, and it was always the same whine about 'This isn't the marriage I expected. It's like you don't want me to be happy. I've told you I'd take care of the kid and you wouldn't have to do anything. Is that too much for you?'

"And naturally I couldn't help believing that Connor was thinking about the life he could have had, with someone else. There was always that uninvited guest, living with us.

"It got unbearable. He brought his mother into it – told her about me not wanting children – and told me he'd told her about it. And according to Connor – I got this from him; his mother didn't say it to me – she very nicely suggested that I wasn't doing what a woman should do, that I just wasn't very womanly and that maybe he'd made a mistake."

It's anybody's conjecture as to what words Connor's mother actually used, and how closely they might have tallied with the way Connor reported it to Tanya. And who knows how accurately Tanya was reporting this whole incident, years after the fact, to her friend? But that was the way Tanya told it.

Could that – the suggestion that she was "not very womanly" – have been the clincher? Tanya was so assured in her femininity, yet her insecurities were never hard to spot. A person might appear utterly self-confident, but if you hit her right, that façade could crumble. "Not very womanly" must have tagged her right on the button.

Or maybe it was the suggestion that Connor had "made a mistake." The mistake perhaps being not that he'd married Tanya, but that he'd let Melissa get away. Whatever Connor might have been thinking about Melissa at that time – and however much he might have been thinking about her – Melissa was never out of Tanya's thoughts for long. Whether or not she was justified in her suspicion, Tanya couldn't stop believing that she was still sharing Connor with someone else.

Tanya's friend then asked her, "Did you discuss this with either of your parents?"

"They told me, if I wanted to leave him, they'd support my decision," Tanya replied. "They even sort of hinted that maybe I should. But they warned me that if I wanted to stay with him, he wouldn't be satisfied unless he got his way, and in a sense they were right – only when he did get his way, he still wasn't satisfied.

"But I didn't want to leave him. I loved him. Hard to believe, looking back, but I did. And I believed he loved me. And I'd married him. I didn't make that promise like it didn't matter, like 'If it doesn't work out we can always get divorced.'

"It didn't sound like a good idea, anyway. It doesn't sound natural to me, for the father to stay home and take care of the kid while the mother hardly ever sees her. I thought, if we were ever did have kids, it would be better if I were the primary caregiver, because that's how nature works – but if I didn't want to care for a child, then it was probably best for us not to have any children. Or at least wait till I felt ready to put the time and work into it. I thought I was being reasonable.

"But Connor, he kept up with, 'But I'd take care of it. I'd do everything. You wouldn't have to lift a finger.' And when I still didn't want to do it, he started, like, glaring at me sometimes from across the room as though he actually disliked me, or at least resented me as though he was asking for something reasonable and making all kinds of concessions and I was just refusing him because I got some kind of pleasure out of depriving him. And finally I thought, well, maybe I could do it, to bring us together and drive Melissa out of the picture."

§

In the summer of 2004, with Connor looking less and less cheerful every day, and paying her less and less attention, Tanya made him an offer over breakfast.

"I'm thinking we could have a baby."

The stunned look on Connor's face pleased Tanya, and even more satisfying was the tone of amazement in his voice when he asked, "Seriously? You really want to do it?"

"I want you to be happy, Connor. That's part of what I married you for. And if you're not going to be happy unless we have a baby, then I guess we should have one. Just one."

Connor practically glowed, his smile grew so big.

"But there are conditions," Tanya said. "First, we'll only have one. That's final. Second, we'll time it. I don't want to put off getting my D.M.A. So I'll have the baby around the first of June next year, and take that summer off, and I'll be able to go back to school when the fall semester begins."

Connor still looked pleased, but a bit less so, as though the edge had been taken off his perfect ecstasy.

"You wouldn't want to take a year off, and, you know, take care of it? Bond with it? That'd be part of the experience."

"No! That's the point. It'd be your baby. I'd be doing this for you. Not for me. For you. You know how I feel about my career. If I do this for you, you have to do what you said you'd do. You'd have to take care of it. It would be your kid completely, and not mine. You can do that; you work at home now. But if we're going to do this, I need your word that that's the way it'll be."

Connor was sure that Tanya would change her attitude once the baby was born. First, he saw that he'd been right, that she'd change her mind about having a child. He'd known that she would come around – and now, she had.

This, we can be pretty sure, was Connor's reasoning: All women want babies, at least all normal women do. Even lesbians want them. Tanya was no different; she was willing to have a baby; it would not be long before she truly *wanted* the baby. And Connor would have been just as sure she'd change her mind about taking care of the baby, once she'd had it. It was a sure thing that when the doctor handed it to her and she nursed it for the first time, she would feel differently. There was no way it *couldn't* be like that.

§

In September 2004, a little more than a month before her 31st birthday, Tanya missed her period, and started waking up with nausea that would last most of the day. Her face broke out, worse than ever, so that she could hardly bear to take it outdoors. Soon thereafter, she started getting terribly tired in the afternoons, which made it tough for her to keep up with her course work. She hadn't been prepared for this, nor for how pregnancy would affect her singing.

Even in the earliest months of pregnancy, the low blood pressure would make Tanya feel dizzy when she sang, and she'd get short of breath. Her voice just didn't sound right to her, although her colleagues insisted that they didn't hear a difference.

She fulfilled her choral obligations – she was a member of Kantorei, the School of Music's élite vocal ensemble – and she arranged to give her solo recital in November of that year, before she was too far along, but she realized that she'd be too pregnant to participate in the spring opera, in which she would have probably been the principal soprano. (Fortunately, from Tanya's point of view, the opera was *Lulu*, which she hated and probably wouldn't have enjoyed performing.)

"Thank God it wasn't *Carmen*," she said later. "I'd never have forgiven myself."

Her recital was, in her mind, a disaster. She didn't make any serious mistakes, but she could hear her own voice and knew it wasn't good. Her former teacher, the one who'd retired, was there, and said, "Don't worry, dear; there'll be others." Her current advisor, Prof. Jespersson, told her, "It's not the end of the world. I know you can do better. It's up to you, now, to set the example for the rest of the studio. About how to bounce back from an off performance."

In mid-December, Tanya had her ultrasound, which revealed that she was carrying a girl. Connor was thrilled. He literally jumped into the air when Tanya gave him the news.

When they were home together, that night, they both felt almost the same about each other as they had before they'd gotten married, before all the arguments about having the baby. For now, it seemed, both of them felt that they'd done not just the right thing, but the ideal thing. Tanya wasn't showing much, yet, but she felt bloated and unattractive – and it did her good to see Connor mooning at her as he used to do.

It was a couple days later when Connor, downtown to do some last-minute Christmas shopping, ran into Gail Wainwright. Before he could tell her about the pregnancy, she said to him, "Melissa's in town, for the holidays. You should give her a call. I'm sure she'd love to see you."

When Gail said that, Connor figured he had better not tell Gail anything, because he didn't want Melissa to hear the news of his impending fatherhood from anyone but him.

He did tell Melissa, after Christmas. He and Tanya had spent Christmas weekend in Indianola, once again, and as usual Tanya wanted to stay a few extra days – so she agreed to take the bus back to State City later in the week, and let Connor get back to his work on Monday. Those last few days of the year would be just when he might find some good stock trades, he explained, with so many companies winding up their fiscal quarters. And that was the truth, but he did welcome the opportunity to see Melissa.

Connor and Melissa met at the downtown Starbucks, which in late afternoon, with the students out of town, was nearly deserted. Connor was shocked at the sight of Melissa.

She looked slammed. Haggard, as though life had whipped her comprehensively and was putting the boot in.

"Is something the matter?" Connor asked as they sat

down at a table with their coffees. "You look preoccupied."

"Mostly I got fired," Melissa replied. Connor looked appropriately shocked. "I've been told that my contact won't be renewed next year. I'll be out of a job as of June."

"But why? You're a great teacher!"

"Evidently not so great. That's a long story. But let's just say I got the wrong people mad at me for this and that. Or maybe they just didn't want to give the white girl tenure."

"Then are you moving back here?"

"I don't know. I might try to get another job in that area, since I'm there. On the other hand I'm not that crazy about Detroit if I don't have a good reason to live there."

"It's not like it was such a great job," Melissa continued. "Matter of fact I hate it. But it hurts that they don't want me there anymore. I'm not even sure I want to go on teaching. It's been a pretty crappy experience. I don't know what I'm going do next. But I have a few months to decide."

"I wish we'd been in closer touch," Connor said, after a longish pause. "Maybe I could have given you some advice, or moral support, or something."

"No, it's okay. It was one of those things. Nothing you could have done. But tell me about you. How's Tanya?"

"Pregnant." Connor had rehearsed a little announcement, he'd had it in his mind how he would tell Melissa the news, but that was how it came out. Then he smiled.

"She's four months along," he added. "May 25 is the due date. It's a girl." And his smile got bigger.

"Oh, Connor!" Melissa sighed, and she reached across the table and laid a hand on each of Connor's arms. "That is so wonderful."

"It is," Connor said, looking down for a moment then looking right at Melissa. "I can't wait to be a dad. I'm... I'm so looking forward to it."

"You'll make a great dad," Melissa breathed, and she patted both his arms again. "Have you decided on a name?"

The rest of their conversation was mainly taken up with

Connor's expectations about fatherhood and – it was inevitable – Tanya's initial reluctance.

"She's into it now, though" Connor added. "It'll work out great."

"I sure hope so," said Melissa. "You so deserve it."

"Let's keep in touch," Connor said, as they walked out of Starbucks. They embraced, and walked away from each other, not looking back.

11. Melissa's Career

A couple of points need to be discussed here: Melissa's job, and her ongoing relationship with Leander.

"You're just not a good fit for this school," Mr. T had told her, "and frankly the Detroit public school system as a whole isn't right for you. Not saying you have no potential as a teacher. Just that this *mill*-yoo might not be the place where you can realize it."

When Melissa had asked him what, in his opinion, she'd done wrong, Mr. T told her, "You don't have a forceful enough personality to handle a roomful of rowdy boys. You let them walk all over you. I don't say you keep a disorderly classroom – but you're so busy managing the class that you don't seem to do much teaching. I'll grant you, lots of the students don't care about that – but some do."

Melissa, now getting a bit angry, reminded Mr. T that there were other teachers in her department that seemed to be a lot less competent, and who had poorer attitudes than hers, and pretty similar approaches.

"That may be true," said Mr. T. "They've got tenure. There have also been complaints that you're not collegial. Now, that might be a cultural thing, I don't know."

Melissa was too flustered to argue further, but once she'd left Mr. T's office she started guessing what the real reasons might have been for her termination.

There was her relationship with Leander, which she had to believe had become common knowledge and must have caused resentments. Who knew? Maybe Mr. T himself was sexually jealous, and was punishing her for having a relationship that prevented her having one with him. She tried to remember any conversation in which Mr. T had come on to her, invited her to socialize, made any suggestive or ambiguous remark. She couldn't think of any, but neither could she get rid of that suspicion.

As for the charge that she wasn't collegial, it's true that she'd never gotten friendly with any of the other teachers, aside from Leander, but she'd also (she told herself) made a special effort to *not* act stuck-up or patronizing, to *not* give even the least indication that she harbored any racism.

Leander, when she came over to his place that night with the news, was more certain than Melissa had been.

"Plain as day," he told her. "Poor T, he knew you were out of his league – oh, he might have tried, but he probably had just enough self-awareness not to – so he didn't like having you around. But your colleagues, that would have been the clincher. I bet they never missed a chance to make little innuendoes to T. Whether it was your teaching style, or your attitude, or calling you a 'ho' behind your back, but one way or another you were not going to win with them.

"Anyway, it's a blessing in disguise. T's right, you don't belong in this system."

Maybe it was because she was upset, but Melissa put the worst possible interpretation on this. All of a sudden – although she didn't say it aloud, then – it seemed to her that Leander now thought of her as a failure, and that he was seizing this opportunity to advise her to get out of Detroit and perhaps out of his life. This, at a time when she'd thought their relationship was as strong as ever and, if anything, getting stronger.

"So I should move?" she asked.

"No, no," said Leander. "There are private schools here. Schools in the suburbs. Lots of options. No, honey, I'd be terribly upset if you went anywhere." And he gave Melissa one of his rare, enormous smiles, the kind that Melissa liked to say made her fall in love with him all over again whenever she saw it. They just happened, those smiles, and they lit up Leander's face and make a handsome man look handsomer. They came so seldom, and they were so clearly genuine when they did come. Any woman might have reacted to them as Melissa did.

And once again, Melissa started wishing that Leander would ask her to marry him, or that she could work up the nerve to ask him – but now, when she was out of a job, didn't strike her as the time to bring it up. She was pretty sure it would look like she was now hoping that Leander would support her financially.

So, she shrugged, and feigned nonchalance.

"Guess I better brush up my résumé," she said.

But when she was back in State City for the holidays, she was indeed frazzled: worried about her career, her income, and her relationship with Leander. She told Connor only about the first two of those items; he didn't even know that Leander existed. Melissa didn't want him to know, and felt that he would not have wanted to know.

12. The Baby Arrives

Connor had been mistaken, when he told Melissa that Tanya was "into" the prospect of motherhood. Tanya was never into it – although Connor tried to convince himself that she was.

Tanya looked back at that horrible recital in November, and blamed her pregnancy. When rehearsals started for *Lulu*, she couldn't stand to overhear any of her colleagues talking about it, and she could hardly endure the presence of Sally Greenhow, the girl who'd been cast in the title role, even though she and Sally were in the same studio and had always been friendly with each other.

Tanya no longer cared that she hated *Lulu*. All that mattered was that she wasn't going to be in it, while Sally – who Tanya secretly feared was the better singer – would get all the glory. She supposed it could've been worse. She could've been in the show, in a smaller part, and had to listen to Sally sing what should've been her part, for weeks of rehearsal.

Sometimes, in the studio, when she heard herself sing, Tanya would burst into tears and have to run to the restroom to get them under control.

Connor had to admit to himself that he made a bad mistake, one afternoon, when he and Tanya were discussing the new baby's name.

Connor swore up and down that his suggestion of "Melissa" had had nothing to do with his old sweetheart: he just had always liked the name.

"Really, I should've thought of that," he admitted when Tanya had calmed down. "I'm sorry. But, gosh, can't you let it go? She's long past. She's history. I don't even think about her."

Tanya rolled her eyes and laughed very unpleasantly.

Connor tried to be attentive to Tanya, as best he knew how. And sometimes she'd appreciate it. Other times she'd snap at him, or look for reasons to criticize him.

"Don't you think I'm fat enough already?" she snarled, for instance, when Connor presented her with a box of Valentine's Day candy. But then she apologized a few minutes later, and thanked him, and ate some of the candy as though she were doing Connor a favor.

"It's just hormones," Brett reassured Connor. "Bev went through the same kind of thing. It's a lot easier this time."

"This time," for Brett and Bev were almost as far along as Connor and Tanya, but it would be their second child. They were also preparing to move to a larger house.

"Why don't you and Tanya buy ours?" Brett asked. "We'd give you a better deal than the asking price. It's just the right size for three people – or it would have been fine for four of us, but we wanted something bigger. It's in good shape."

Connor knew this; he'd been in Brett and Bev's house many times. But when he brought it up to Tanya, she was immediately balky.

"You're trying to tie us down," she accused him. "It was all a lie, wasn't it? You're going to keep sabotaging me with one thing and another till you've made me into whatever the fuck you're trying to make me into!"

"Tanya, no, I swear," Connor protested. "We have to live somewhere, we're going to be here for another two-three years probably, and we'll be building equity. If we do move someplace else, we can keep it as a rental or sell it. And it'll be way good for our credit rating."

Connor sat down with Tanya and showed her the numbers. Tanya was bright, she was as good at math as Connor was. It was there in black and white. It made sense, economically, to buy Brett and Bev's house.

"But that's no neighborhood to live in!" Tanya exclaimed. "It's all pickup trucks with Rivercat logos on them. People who drink Mountain Dew for breakfast! Yeah, I'm a snob. You bet I'm a snob. That's not where I want to live!"

"You don't have to associate with them. It's not a bad neighborhood. It's... you know, good working people, people like Brett and Bev. It's a nice house. A great house for a kid."

"Clear across town from campus. I'd be away from *everything*. You know how I hate to drive, and I'd be stuck there, with a baby..." Tanya was crying again.

And yet she agreed to it. It made sense. More sense than having a baby in their student apartment, and it was easy enough to get out of that lease. And Brett and Bev did their best to make the transition painless for them.

It was April when they moved into Brett and Bev's house, and on May Day – a Sunday – they threw a housewarming party. Tanya was eight months along, and could hardly bear to show herself – it was all she could do to go to classes and fulfill her other obligations – but Connor wanted to show the house to his friends. Tanya didn't seem interested in inviting any of her friends from the School of Music. Connor asked her to do it anyway: "I don't want this to just be my party!" So finally she did invite a few, but not many.

Tanya left most of the planning, organizing, and other work to Connor. The semester was winding down and she still had finals upcoming and other projects to complete. She was also having contractions, now and then, and she wondered whether that was unusual at this stage of the pregnancy – but she didn't tell anyone about them.

Tanya had a minor crisis on the morning of the party: a fashion crisis. There weren't many clothes she could still wear, in her condition, and the idea of a maternity dress was more than she could bear. She settled for a plain shift dress that made her look the least blimpy of anything.

Connor smiled at her and gave her a little hug.

"Why wouldn't you want to show it? Nothing's more beautiful than a beautiful woman who's pregnant."

"You've lowered your standards a lot, honey," Tanya said. "But I do appreciate it."

The party lasted all that Sunday afternoon, and it was almost all Connor's friends, although most of the people Tanya had invited did come. Prof. Jespersson and her husband were there, slightly overdressed: she in a bright multicolored dress with sharp geometric designs; he in a silk sport jacket and tie.

"A sweet little house, dear," said Prof. Jespersson. "I can't say I've ever been in this neighborhood before…" (she looked up and down the street at the tract houses, all built in the 1950s "little boxes" mode) "but it looks charming."

None of Tanya's friends stayed long. They didn't have

anyone else to visit with, aside from each other, and they saw each other every day anyway. The great majority of the guests were Connor's friends from college and high school: business students, or working people, people who'd have been utterly alien to the voice students. Also in attendance were a few older businesspeople: clients of Connor.

Connor's parents would have been there, but they were out of town on business. Tanya hadn't invited her parents; it would have humiliated her to have done so. Andy Palinkas hadn't been able to make it, but Jim and Gail Wainwright were there – as were their son David and his wife Mercy. Mercy had her and David's little girl, Juliet, in tow – and she was about as pregnant, with her second child, as Tanya was with her first.

Tanya probably felt a flush of resentment when she saw Mercy – good God, was *every* woman pregnant? – and she and Mercy hardly knew each other at all, but Mercy gave Tanya a big hug, as best they could embrace each other under the circumstances. Tanya didn't know what to think of Mercy: whether to like her, or be suspicious. But she appreciated the hug.

"You're going to love it, Tanya," Mercy said. She was smiling, but speaking in an earnest tone, as though she somehow sensed Tanya's misgivings about the project, and wanted to reassure her. Probably Tanya sensed this, too, and felt grateful for Mercy's encouragement even if it didn't help.

David gave Connor a big handshake, and clapped him on the shoulder. "You're looking great, Tanya," he added.

Jim Wainwright was especially interested in the construction and layout of the house. Connor walked him around the inside and the outside.

"It's a well-made house, Connor," Jim said. "And this is a stable neighborhood. It should hold its value just fine if you take good care of it. And I know you will."

"Thanks," said Connor. "I hope so. Seriously, this is my dream coming true. A family, a business, a house of our own…"

"You've earned it," said Jim. "You know, Connor – Gail and I think the world of you. And maybe at the back of our minds we kind of hoped we'd end up having you as a son-in-law. But, hey, what happens, happens. Tanya's a great girl."

Tanya, meanwhile, was enduring pats on the belly from people she didn't know. For no reason other than feeling uncomfortable with all these strangers and near-strangers, she felt like she could fall apart crying at any instant, but she held it together. She felt another contraction.

"Dear? Are you all right?" Gail Wainwright asked.

"Yes, fine," said Tanya, in a less friendly tone than she should have used.

"You're not contracting already, are you?"

"Oh, no. No. I don't think it's time for that yet." Tanya worked up a smile.

"You're so lucky," Gail said. "Connor's going to be such a wonderful father. He's so looking forward to this."

"Of course he will. Of course he will." Tanya forced the smile to stay on her face. "Yes, I'm sure he'll do a perfect job."

Jim and Gail Wainwright were among the last guests to leave. They'd brought a small lawn statue – a smiling angel – and a baby blanket as housewarming gifts. Connor set the angel in the mulched area next to the front porch, and he and Tanya saw the Wainwrights to their car.

"That angel's just the right touch to make a house a home," Connor told them. Tanya's teeth clenched.

"Oh, Connor," Gail added as she was getting into the car, "have you heard from Melissa lately? Did she tell you she'll be back here this summer?"

"No, I didn't know," said Connor. "We haven't been in touch." He looked over at Tanya, but she showed no reaction. He hoped she hadn't been paying attention.

Tanya started fighting back the sobs as soon as the last guest had left – and she lost the fight pretty quickly. She collapsed onto the living room sofa, wailing.

Connor sat next to her and tried to hold her.

"Don't," Tanya whined, stiffening.

"What do you want me to do?" Connor asked, as gently

as he knew how to. "Is there anything I can do?"

"I don't think you could do or say anything right now to make it better."

"What? I can't do anything for you unless you tell me what's wrong."

"That fucking angel," said Tanya.

"You don't like it? I guess we don't have to have it in the yard, but it would hurt Jim and Gail's feelings if we didn't. And they've been real good to us."

"*Fuck* Jim and Gail!" Tanya shrieked, flinging herself out of Connor's arms and walking to the other side of the room. "They've been real good to *you*, maybe. Years ago. It's like you still want them for in-laws. And you care about hurting *their* feelings but you don't give a flying fuck for *mine!*"

"But why would it hurt your feelings to have that statue in the yard? It's just a little thing, it's not ugly."

"For one thing," said Tanya, seeming to calm down ever so slightly, "it's the tackiest piece of shit I've ever seen in my life. It's exactly what any of our fucking neighbors might have in their yards. And it's a… a *symbol*." Her voice started to rise again. "That fucking statue sums up everything about… that statue personifies what a mistake we've made."

"Honey, you're not making sense right now. I know, it's been stressful…"

Tanya felt another contraction.

"Let me take care of the cleaning up," Connor continued. "You relax. Go lie down if you want to."

"I don't want to lie down," Tanya sobbed, from behind her hands. "I feel so trapped. I'm in a fucking dungeon and there's no way to climb out."

Connor searched in vain for something to say to this, but only for an instant before he heard Tanya gasp.

"My water."

§

Tanya gave birth in the early hours of the next morning – three weeks ahead of schedule. That turned out to be no problem in terms of the mother's or the baby's health. But Tanya immediately – in the midst of labor, literally just a few minutes before the baby was out of her body – demanded that the doctor give her "that shot or pill or whatever" to halt lactation. The doctor informed her that that medication wasn't available anymore.

When she was handed the baby to hold, Tanya cried, "No! Get it away from me!" She shrank away from the baby, crossing her arms over her breasts and lowering her head as though to physically protect herself.

"No!" she screamed, again and again. "No! No!" She tried to roll over on her face. Her attendants had no choice but to take the baby away.

Because the baby was premature, the issue of breast-feeding hadn't yet been discussed, but now – as soon as she was recovered enough to listen – Tanya was counseled by a hospital employee about the benefits of breastfeeding.

"They tried to bully me," she would recall later. "They tried to guilt me into it, with this nicey-nice counselor basically explaining that I'd be a bad mommy if I didn't breastfeed. They even got Connor into it. I finally started screaming at all of them, like, 'Get the fuck away from me.' I was afraid they would try to force me somehow."

In fact Tanya had to be sedated – or that was what the attending physician decided. But it was also decided that she could not be forced to breastfeed, although Connor looked terribly hurt when she repeated her refusal for the record.

Tanya wasn't in any physical distress following her childbirth, but because of her emotional reaction she was kept hospitalized for 24 hours.

Tanya was home from the hospital ahead of her baby. One of the first things she did was to get onto her computer and find all the information she could on how to prevent or stop lactation. She took all the advice, even to the point of wearing cabbage leaves inside her brassière. She was relieved that at least now she had some time to prepare herself for life with a baby, without having to carry that baby around from the very first. However, the premature birth had caused her to miss a choral performance and fall behind in her course work just as the semester was wrapping up – and she had to take "incompletes" in everything, on the understanding that she'd finish up over the summer.

"Like that'll be easy, with a fucking baby to take care of," she remarked.

Tanya at least felt relieved that the experience hadn't stretched her belly too badly. Her doctor was astonished at how quickly her skin rebounded. "It's as though you never had a baby," he told her. "Would that that were true," Tanya replied, and the doctor said nothing more.

Olivia, or Livy as Connor's parents took to calling her, was healthy if quite small, and she developed normally.

Tanya had found it hard enough to cope while Livy was still in the hospital. She'd have terrors, at night, and wake up almost unable to breathe. If Connor were awake, he'd try to comfort her, but usually he'd sleep through the episode, and Tanya didn't want to wake him because she didn't want him to see her crying – which she'd do, inevitably, once she'd gotten her breath back.

It got worse when the baby was home, from everyone's viewpoint. Connor would complain to Brett and Bev (who was on the point of giving birth to her second child) that even at her best, Tanya seemed to withdraw from him. She almost never smiled. Every day, and sometimes more than once in a day, he'd catch her crying – not just weeping, but sobbing her heart out.

"I've tried asking her what's wrong," he told his two friends, "and she'll say something like, 'Livy'd be better off if I was dead.' And at least she calls her Livy now, sometimes, instead of 'it.' But I don't know if you can call that progress."

Sometimes Connor would have an awful premonition

that he might have to physically protect Livy. It would happen usually when the baby was crying, which would trigger more tears from Tanya. Tanya never menaced the baby in any way, but she'd curl up on a chair or the sofa with her long legs and arms drawn up close to her body and her fists clenched, or clutching her hair (which was often not clean, these days), and Connor would wonder if, or when, Tanya might snap and become violent. He would pick Livy out of her crib and hold her close, keeping his back to Tanya partly to shield Livy – and partly so that Tanya would not have to see the baby.

Connor was already a thin man, and now he began to lose more weight. He was under so much stress that he wasn't hungry. He had to remind himself to eat.

"I can't remember the last time I wasn't feeling scared to death," he confided to Jim Wainwright, during this period. "I was looking so forward to this… this part of my life. It's not what I expected, that's for sure."

"Some women get them," Jim reassured him. "The post-partum crazies. It's a phase. You just have to ride it out; be as considerate as you can, and try to catch Tanya doing something right – and encourage her whenever you do."

Tanya spent as much time as she could at the Janscombe Center, completing her course work. She would practice there, too, for as long as her voice could take it, or she would go to the dance studio and review the ballet and modern dance moves she'd not worked on in years. But as soon as she got home, Connor would tell her that he had work to do – and he had to ask her to take care of Livy at least for a while.

She could cope with this as long as Livy was asleep. And when the baby awoke in the night, it was Connor's job to get up and tend to her. "You promised," Tanya had reminded him, the first time he suggested that they take turns getting up. "I told you it would be your responsibility. And you agreed."

It seemed to Connor that Tanya was making excuses to put in more hours at school.

"Honey, Livy might forget she even has a mommy," he

said once, in what he hoped was a jocular tone.

"I hope she does," muttered Tanya, turning away.

"Maybe Livy would like to hear you sing to her sometimes," Connor suggested.

That triggered another crying jag.

"Why should I?" Tanya demanded. "How can I ever have a career now?"

These episodes came and went – but didn't disappear.

"I had nobody to talk to, nobody," Tanya told her friend later on, looking back. "I don't have any close friends in this town, none I can spill my guts to. I've never been close to my dad. My mom, I can talk to, but I couldn't be calling her all the time, and anyway she didn't understand. I mean she did her best but she's not always... I don't know... she's not very deep. My sister... we were close when I was little, but she didn't approve of the lifestyle I was living for a while; I guess she felt I ought to be more settled, and then when I *was* settled, I almost felt like I didn't want to give her the satisfaction of seeing it. Especially since I was so miserable. I feel pretty alone, still. And it was worse then, as you might imagine."

What Connor had been fearing, happened, on the morning of the Fourth of July. Connor would never experience another Independence Day without thinking of it. He was mowing the back yard. He could still hear Livy crying, inside the house, over the noise of the lawnmower. Then, all of a sudden, he heard Tanya's voice in a shriek that sounded absolutely inhuman – as though she, Tanya, were being killed. He switched off the mower and bounded into the house, to hear Tanya screaming, "Shut up, shut the fuck up, shut the fuck up!" She was in Livy's room, holding Livy up in front of her, screaming into the baby's face, gripping Livy so hard by the arms that her own hands were red and white.

All Connor could think was that Tanya was about to shake the baby to death – if she hadn't already. He managed to get his arms around Livy while at the same time grabbing one of Tanya's wrists and squeezing it till she let go of the baby. Tanya ran out of the room and collapsed onto her and Connor's bed, wailing.

Connor held the baby, whispering to her, rocking her, and eventually Livy quieted. She didn't appear to be hurt. Connor could still hear Tanya bawling in the next room. He wanted to go in there and hit her.

He didn't hit Tanya; he didn't touch her or speak to her or even look at her. He stepped into their bedroom just long enough to scoop up his cell phone, car keys, a change of underpants, and a clean t-shirt. He got his toothbrush from the bathroom, carried Livy to his car, and was ready to drive off when he remembered he had to bring diapers and feeding equipment, so he ran back into the house and retrieved all of that. From the bathroom, he could see Tanya now sitting up on the bed, not crying anymore, but looking stunned.

Again, Connor avoided looking at her. Tanya looked at him like she wanted to say something, but didn't, and he was out the door and gone. He drove to his parents' house.

Connor waited a few hours before phoning Tanya to tell her where he and Livy were.

"Okay," Tanya said in a dull voice. "I'm taking my car to Indianola."

"You're not getting treated?" Dr. Cucoshay demanded of his daughter, that evening, when she'd arrived in Indianola and told her parents what had happened. "And why didn't you tell us all this before?"

"Didn't see any point," Tanya muttered, looking at the floor. "There wasn't anything you could have told me."

"I'm not a psychiatrist," said Dr. Cucoshay in a sardonic tone, "but I am a qualified physician, and I'm just barely bright enough to give you a diagnosis. We're getting you on some medication first thing tomorrow, young lady, and we're getting you fully evaluated, and finding you a therapist. And that boy you married could use one too."

Tanya was warned that the medications would take a while to have a noticeable effect, but at least they gave her hope, and that was enough to bring her out of her depression somewhat. A few days away from Connor and Livy helped too.

Her parents never asked Tanya, "Would you want to leave them both? Just walk away from it?" It seemed they were taking it for granted that she would return to Connor and Livy. However, they strongly advised Tanya to insist to Connor that they get couples counseling in addition to whatever therapy or medications might be prescribed for her.

Connor, at first, was dead against this idea. "What'll people think?" was his immediate reaction, when Tanya told him this over the phone from Indianola.

"You'd better not care what people think, if you want us to go on living together," Tanya replied. "You'll just have to do it."

"If we do it, it'll have to be a man," Connor countered. "I've heard how it works. If it's a lady therapist, the two women gang up on the man and make it all his fault."

It's surmise, certainly, but we might suspect that Connor was less horrified at the idea that other people might find out that he was in couples counseling – after all, it was hardly a state secret by now that he and Tanya were having their problems – as he was at the idea of letting any stranger hear about those problems directly from himself or Tanya.

His own parents didn't seem to blame him for the situation, except for having made a questionable choice of a wife in the first place.

"It's not like *you* did anything wrong," Mrs. Lowe reassured her son. "I feel sorry for poor Tanya, but there's only so much you can do in a situation like that. If she's so dead-set that you have to go to counseling with her, then you'd better do it, but it doesn't mean you have to blame yourself for anything. Just go, and try to be understanding. She's having a real tough time right now. Lots of women get the baby blues. She'll get over it, but you'll have to help her."

Somewhat to Connor's surprise, Brett and Bev recommended couples therapy to him before he'd even told them that Tanya was demanding it.

"It sure helped us," Brett told him. "Saved our marriage, I'd say."

"Yeah, it did," Bev said.

"You? You guys were in therapy?"

"Not for long," Brett said, "but, you know, you gotta work on marriage. You're gonna have your problems. We went to a couple, up in Cedar Rapids, a married couple, they work together sometimes."

"You mean on the same pa… the same couples?"

"Yeah," said Bev. "Maybe the man doesn't want to go to a lady therapist 'cause he's afraid she'll take sides with his wife, or vice-a-versa, and this couple, usually they each handle their own clients, but they'll work together if they need to."

"Man, if you love her, you gotta do it," said Brett.

"I do my best to love her," said Connor. "And I do. Sometimes she makes it hard for me to show it."

Connor wished he could confide in Jim and Gail Wainwright. They, he was sure, would give him the best advice of anyone. But he felt – although he couldn't explain why, to himself – that if he asked the Wainwrights for advice on this matter, it would be a betrayal of Tanya. So, he didn't.

§

Three days after her meltdown, Tanya was back home with Connor and Livy. Connor tried to keep Livy away from Tanya as much as possible, over the next few days. Tanya noticed this, and was more appreciative than hurt. Trying to make it up to him, Tanya, during those same days, started coming up with suggestions for how they might redecorate or renovate the house, running them by Connor and offering to do most of the work, if he agreed. They were both trying to please each other, while walking on eggs.

Tanya seemed a little less miserable, too, when at last she finished her incompletes from the spring semester and was able to plan her activities for the fall: more course work, more studio work, ensembles, various other performances.

The "couples therapy couple," as Tanya called them, were Morris Shawn and Anne Noonan. They were both in their 40s, both terribly earnest. Morris was curly-headed and round, although not fat; Anne was horsy-looking.

At the first session, when Anne asked Tanya why she thought she was there, Tanya was defensive.

"I went crazy."

Anne smiled. "You never go crazy all at once. It's a process, like counseling – and sometimes it takes a lot longer to go crazy than to recover."

"They were kind of intimidating," Tanya said to Connor as they drove home from that first session. "Too good, almost. They're not warm. You get the feeling they're kind of phony. I did, anyway. But maybe that's the way they're supposed to act. I don't know. I'd never had any kind of therapy before."

"It could have been just me feeling this way," Connor replied, "but I felt like they thought I was somehow inferior to them. Maybe they felt less like that about you because you're older, or maybe I'm too sensitive. But it sure wasn't comfortable, talking about that stuff. Let's hope it gets easier."

It surprised both of them that their early sessions, at least, were mostly without acrimony. Anne and Morris controlled the situation pretty tightly and saw to it that there were no interruptions, and as little back-and-forth as possible. They got Connor and Tanya to paraphrase and repeat each other's complaints, and calmly discuss whether those complaints were legitimate.

Most of the problems came out early, and clearly. "I need you to be the sweet girl I fell in love with," Connor told Tanya, during one session. "I need you to be normal."

With some questioning from Morris, it came out that

Connor didn't know that there was a difference between baby blues and post-partum depression, and that it was the latter that Tanya had.

One of Tanya's big complaints was that Connor hadn't kept his part of the bargain.

"We had a deal," she told him, at Anne and Morris' urging. "You agreed to it when I offered to have a child for you. You agreed that it would be your child, that you'd take care of it. Anything I do for the baby is extra."

"Oh, Tanya," said Anne, gently. "Were you being realistic, when you offered him that arrangement? Did you really think that that was how it was going to go?"

Connor looked offended.

"I don't mean anything against you, Connor," Anne said. "It's hard to blame you for accepting an offer like that. But maybe both of you should have realized that it doesn't work that way in real life."

Tanya also had to admit that she'd known all along that she could never love this baby.

"But it's done now," she protested. "I can't force myself to feel what I don't feel."

"Fake it till you make it," Connor advised. "If you tried harder to love her, you might."

"Not a bad suggestion," said Morris. "After all, Livy's the innocent party. Okay, you didn't want her; we have to validate that. But she's here."

"So let Connor keep his word," said Tanya.

Connor shook his head. "I thought you'd change," he said. "I thought once you had a baby in your arms, you'd feel…"

"Like how I'm supposed to feel?"

"Well, yeah."

"I want us to be a family," Connor said, in another session.

"So we're not a family if I'm not the primary caregiver?" Tanya demanded.

"Tanya, do you want to be a family?" Anne asked, and Tanya was dumbfounded, unable to think of an answer that was both truthful, and satisfactory at least to herself.

Probably neither Connor nor Tanya could have said whether the first few weeks of counseling were helping their marriage. But Tanya, at least, was feeling better. Apparently the medication was having some effect, or her depression was resolving naturally, or both, but at any rate as August wore on and the new school year approached she felt more energized, more hopeful. She cried less, and was no longer openly hostile to Livy, although she still avoided the baby. She sang around the house, quite often, something she hadn't done since the late stages of her pregnancy – although she never sang to Livy the way Connor had once fantasized that she would.

Tanya had learned that the University Symphony Orchestra and the University Chorus would perform the Dvořák *Requiem* that winter, and that the spring opera would be – she could hardly believe it – *Carmen*. And she was pretty sure she would sing principal soprano in the former, and the title role in the latter – even though Carmen is for a mezzo voice. She would do what she had to do to get both parts, she resolved.

Connor felt encouraged that Tanya was less moody, less crazy – but she was still not very friendly to him. He felt more like her incompatible roommate than like her husband. She hardly ever smiled at him anymore.

It also perturbed him that it was apparently the anticipation of the school year, and the advancement of her career, that was making her more cheerful – and not her husband or her baby.

He hinted at this, during one counseling session.

"It's like that's what matters to you. Your own stuff. Like your husband and your child are just something you put up with. And you don't even put up with us, half the time. You spend all day and half the night at Janscombe. And it's all you can talk about. I wish you could show half as much enthusiasm for your family as you do for your career. Do you have any idea how it makes me feel when I see what I'm worth to you?"

"*I had a child for you!*" Tanya shouted. "I made myself fucking miserable for you! And that's not enough to show that you're worth something to me?"

She turned to Anne and Morris.

"This is what I go through, every day," she told them. "These guilt trips. Like he's telling me I'm unnatural somehow, or not what a woman should be – and mostly how I'm *huuuurrrrting* him!" She almost sang that last phrase. Anne and Morris both started a little.

"Oh, and how I'm *damaging* my *chiiiiiiild*," Tanya went on, still in grand voice. "And you have to love how he keeps reminding me that he doesn't trust me around her."

"Connor?" Morris asked.

"She calls it 'guilt trips.' I'm just trying to remind her that there's more to life than her career."

"Yeah, that's real helpful. Making me feel like shit every time I do something that might make me happy."

"I just wish other things made you happy too."

And yet it appeared that the possibility of divorce was off the table. Both Tanya and Connor said they didn't want that – although it's anyone's guess how sincere either of them was when they said it – and they agreed that it wouldn't be right, not with a baby that was barely out of the incubator.

Tanya couldn't help saying to Connor, toward the end of that session, "You should have married someone else."

"Honey, there's nobody else I could have married."

"I can think of one."

"What?"

"You know who I'm talking about."

"Whoa! Whoa! I never came close to marrying anybody but you!"

"You still carry a torch for her, though. You're not going to tell me you don't."

"Hold it," Anne interposed. "Whoever this is, I don't think she's come up. It might be important, you think?"

"It's nothing," said Connor. "It's almost the end of the session."

"We can keep going," Morris said. "We've got nothing scheduled next hour. We probably shouldn't leave this hanging. We won't charge you extra."

Connor denied having seen or communicated with Melissa Wainwright since, "You know, since the wedding." Tanya suggested that if she were to hack his emails, he might have to change his story.

"I'm pretty sure I could figure out how to do that," she said, to see if Connor would blench. "But I'm not going to. I might not believe you but I'll trust you."

In any case, Tanya told Connor and the counselors, she knew she was Connor's second choice and that Connor would have dropped her like a hot brick if he could have gotten back with Melissa Wainwright.

"You have no idea how awful it is to love someone, and want to make him happy, and know that he doesn't want you to do it because he'd rather fantasize about someone else making him happy," she concluded.

Connor denied this. But the counselors remarked that this was obviously an issue they'd have to work through.

Connor wouldn't have been too worried. He'd have told himself that he truly had not done anything, in the past six months anyway, for Tanya to be jealous about. He'd known that Melissa was in town for the summer, but he'd made no effort to see her. He hadn't even emailed Melissa more than once or twice after the New Year, and not at all after February.

He knew, from Jim Wainwright, that Melissa had gotten a job at a private school in a suburb of Detroit – a probationary job that might or might not last more than one year – so she'd be out of town yet again and Connor would have no opportunity to see her. And, he resolved, he would make no effort to do so now. It might be an exaggeration to say that this resolution made him feel righteous, but it reinforced his conviction that Tanya's accusations were unfair if not downright malicious.

13. A Proposal

Less than a week later, Tanya came home from the Janscombe Center practically bursting with energy, looking as radiant as Connor had ever seen her. Almost before she was through the front door, she was telling him the news.

"It all came in at once!" she exclaimed. "I've got a gig as a guest soloist with the Davenport Chamber Singers in three weeks, and then this quartet that I'm involved in is going to sing at a wedding in Muscatine – and then in October I'm singing the solo in the last movement of Mahler's Fourth Symphony, with the Cedar Rapids Symphony Orchestra! That's something that's been on my bucket list since I was a girl!" She threw her arms around Connor: the first time she'd done that in months. "When it rains it pours, doesn't it?"

"Finally!" she cried. "Finally it looks like I might be back on track!"

Give Connor the benefit of the doubt and suppose that he wanted to be happy for Tanya. That he wanted to show it. It's even conceivable that given time, he might have had words of support for her. But not having had the opportunity to brace himself, instead of having this news sprung on him, he couldn't help sighing, and getting an expression on his face that might have been classed as "troubled."

Tanya's posture stiffened as she saw this, almost as though Connor had struck her.

"Honey, that's great," he forced himself to say. "That'll take you away from us even more, though. We'll miss you." He tried to smile.

"You've got each other," Tanya scoffed. "I'll still be

here often enough."

"Okay, I'm sorry: I'm glad for you, seriously. It's not always easy for me to be kicking up my heels about your career when I'm taking care of Livy single-handedly and you don't even notice, don't ever say anything about it."

"Should I? Okay, you're taking care of her. You asked for her. Oh, and should I congratulate you for complaining about having to keep your part of the bargain?"

That night, in bed, may have been when it snapped for Connor. It could be that as he lay there, he could hardly stand the idea that Tanya was lying next to him; it may have been at that moment when he realized that he didn't love her anymore, and could never love her again. And although he probably did feel a bit guilty, he told himself that he had to see Melissa.

He emailed his friends Brett and Bev the next day:

Guys, I need a favor. I want to see Melissa before she goes back up to Michigan, but it might be awkward if I tried to arrange it myself. You know, Tanya might take it the wrong way. If she found out. For some reason she has this obsession with Melissa and I can't make it go away. She can't believe that I can be just friends with somebody I guess. Could you come for a visit one afternoon before she leaves town and bring Melissa? Tanya is usually gone all day now and usually doesn't get home till 7 or 8, so if you came in the middle of the afternoon it would be fine and she probably would never know, and if she did it would be OK at least she wouldn't think anything was going on. Let me know soonest.

And so that afternoon, Connor and Melissa were reunited, in Connor's house, with Bev (who was still on maternity leave from her job) as chaperone. Connor, no doubt, had an explanation ready in case Tanya turned up unexpectedly, or if it somehow got back to her that he'd had visitors – but she never did find out. Melissa was fulsome in her praise for Livy's beauty.

"She did look like me when she was first born," Connor explained, "but now she's looking more like her mother."

"That's how it works," said Bev. "Babies always look like their daddies at first so the daddy'll stick around. Then they look more like their mommies till they're grown up."

"That's not such a bad thing after all," said Melissa. "Tanya's a real pretty girl."

"And she *would* hit the diaper right when you two show up," said Connor. "Come on, we can still talk." He motioned the two ladies to follow him down the hall to the bathroom where he would change Livy.

"You do that so well," Bev remarked. "You might be faster than I am, and I'm on my second one."

"But you and Brett get to divide the diaper duty, I bet," Connor replied. "So you each get to change one baby's worth. I change diapers all the time around here, so I'm probably even with you."

"You look so comfortable with fatherhood," Melissa remarked. "It agrees with you."

Connor smiled again. "It had better."

"Tanya isn't around much, huh?" Bev asked as the two women followed Connor into the kitchen, where he prepared a bottle for the baby.

Connor sighed. "She has a lot on her plate. She's getting ready for another school year, and she's got singing gigs to rehearse for – and I don't know what else. She doesn't tell me an awful lot about what she does."

It might be interesting to take that last statement apart. It's probably truthful enough. Was Connor trying to suggest anything more than the face value of the statement? Would Tanya have been more forthcoming about her activities if she'd thought Connor wanted to hear about them?

We have to consider Connor's feelings. They weren't without foundation. He felt neglected, even abandoned. He still had memories of when Tanya had loved him. Might he have sincerely wished that he could recapture that time, those feelings? Or might he have come to think of all that as a part of his life long past, of which nothing but ugly residue remained?

"I guess she'd rather do what she's doing than take care of her baby," Connor continued. "I don't mind. I enjoy it."

He didn't mention that he and Tanya had had an agreement. It was wonderful to him, to hear Melissa softly sigh "Aww" when she heard his declaration.

We might call it cruel to speculate in this manner, but could this little scene have been staged? Might it have been not quite the usual time for Livy's feeding, or for her to be put down for a nap? Might it have been something Connor wanted to show Melissa – and Bev for that matter – as a sort of performance art? A dance, almost, portraying the loving and caring father and perhaps putting ideas in Melissa's head of what might have been – and of what might still come to pass if fortune smiled?

"How much longer you going to be in town?" Connor asked Melissa. He tried to sound casual.

"Sunday," Melissa said. "School starts Monday."

"I'd like to get together once more before that," he said. "We haven't had the chance to have much of a visit today, what with my little distraction here."

"And three's a crowd," Bev added. Connor smiled back at Bev, a bit, but he couldn't catch whether Melissa's facial expression had changed. "Missie probably has a lot to tell you."

"I could get my mom to look after Livy for an afternoon," Connor said. "I know Tanya's going to be tied up, the next couple days. If you'd like to… you know, go for a drive or something."

"If you're sure that's okay," said Melissa. "I mean, wouldn't Tanya mind?"

"Oh, she knows we're old friends. She's usually pretty easy-going about that kind of thing. But, you know, it's probably best to be discreet."

Connor seemed almost to have forgotten that Bev was in the room too. Bev merely raised her eyebrows.

Connor's mother didn't ask any questions, when he emailed her to ask if she could handle the baby for a few hours on Thursday afternoon. The only explanation that he volunteered was, "There's some errands I need to get done."

§

"You're not... seeing anybody now, are you?" Connor asked Melissa as they drove out of town on American Legion Road in his Jetta. It was a hot day, and he must have been glad of the air conditioning, but still couldn't help remembering that one of his teenaged fantasies had been to own a convertible – and take Melissa for a ride in it. The hardtop would have to do for now.

"Here and there," said Melissa. "Nothing serious."

It could be that she was considering whether to tell Connor about the relationship that had taken her out of the Detroit public school system. She had always had doubts about her and Leander's long-term prospects, but she still did think about those prospects, and she and Leander were still a couple. But none of her State City friends knew of his existence, and she didn't feel like letting Connor be the first to find out.

"I sometimes think about what might have been," said Connor. He was driving east, toward Muscatine County: the same route they'd taken on that New Year's Eve drive, which seemed forever ago to Connor now. "You know, if we hadn't lost touch."

Melissa reached over and touched Connor's arm.

"I miss you," Connor admitted. "I've missed you for a long time. You were always so easy to be with. I always felt so relaxed around you – I mean, after I got over feeling so clumsy around you. We had a lot of fun together, didn't we? Lots of laughs. And sometimes it seemed like we had a lot of the same thoughts, almost like we knew each other's minds."

"Yeah, we did have fun," Melissa replied, but now she was looking out her window, not at Connor, as though she were not getting the import of his words.

"We can't just keep on emailing each other every few months," Connor said. "We'll keep drifting, you know, drifting farther apart and… and getting farther away from where we were, back then. And I don't want that to happen. Melissa, I want us to be as close as we were!" Connor said this in a dramatic tone, looking as intently at Melissa as he could while still keeping half an eye on the road.

"What do you mean? I mean, I can email you more often if you want."

"That'd be a start. I mean I want us to be… even if we're not living in the same town, I want us to be… *together*. You know. Like, spiritually. Like we were meant to be."

"Connor, you've got a wife. And you've got a baby. We can be better about staying in touch, if you want to, but I'm not going to be the other woman."

Connor pulled up in front of an old abandoned church, just off the highway, in the middle of Iowa farmland.

"Have you ever been in here?" he asked Melissa. "It's been preserved, kind of. It's in good shape. A nice place to just sit and think. Especially in the summer. I take Livy here sometimes, to sit and have quiet-time with her."

"It's padlocked," Melissa remarked.

"No, I mean around in back. There are benches out back, I guess people used to sit and talk there. When it was still being used as a church."

They walked around the old frame building, and sat in one of the two weathered park benches.

"You wouldn't be the other woman," said Connor, with a great sigh. "It's done. It's like we're already divorced. There's nothing there anymore."

Connor told Melissa his side of the story: Tanya's lack of interest in motherhood, her preoccupation with her career, her hysterical moods, her histrionics, her near-homicidal breakdown, her long hours at Janscombe.

"She says she's studying and practicing. I have to believe her; I don't have any evidence of anything else. But she doesn't love me anymore, that's the bottom line."

"Oh, you can't say that."

"She might have loved me once. But it's looking like I don't have what she wants. You know, I'm a plain guy. I want a nice business, and a nice home, and a family. A family most of all. And that's not what she wants. She still wants a career as a singer – you know, traveling all over the world, being with famous people. She wants excitement. She wants to be famous and glamourous – and I'm just a boring guy."

Connor told Melissa about their counseling sessions.

"I'm doing my best. And maybe she is too, I don't know, but she does seem to think it's all on me because I'm not being supportive enough. The thing is, though, it's not about who's at fault here. It's not going to work."

"You know I care about you," Melissa replied. "I'll always care about you. But what is it you want me to do? I'm not going to have an affair with you."

"That's not what I mean. I know you would never do that. But maybe… She's going to… Our marriage'll be over. One day."

"Connor! You can't know that. You have to try to work things out."

"I have tried. There's nothing to try anymore. And I want to believe there's a future for *us*. For you and me. I want you and me to be together, when it finally is over."

Melissa looked stunned.

"I can't," she said at last. "Promise that, I mean. I don't want you to consider me part of this equation. Whatever you do with your marriage, whatever you decide, you're going to have to do it as though I don't exist. Anything could happen. You might work things out. You never know. And, I don't know, it feels weird to be having this conversation. We'd better get back to town. I still have some things to get done today."

That, Connor probably thought, was as definite a "no" as a "no" could be – without being a complete and unequivocal "no." He might have been saying to himself, "She said, 'I can't promise that.' She didn't say, 'No, no way, not ever.' There's a difference." And that rationalization may have left him with a vestige of hope.

That's how people think in those situations. If someone refuses you, you can't always bring yourself to take it as a final refusal, right away. You have to tell yourself that the window's still open a crack. It almost never is, but you have to believe it, or pretend to believe it, just to get yourself through the day.

Once you do accept it, once you say, "Okay, it's done; there will never be any chance" – once you say that to yourself and *believe* it, then it's amazing how calm you feel, and how maybe it still hurts but the pain isn't so immediate, so unbearable anymore – and sometimes you can even laugh at yourself for having been such an idiot in the first place.

Sometimes it works the other way. Sometimes you accept it and believe it, but instead of making you calm, it makes you angry. Either at the other person or at yourself.

But Connor wasn't at any of those places yet. He hadn't accepted it. He didn't *believe* it.

He went paler in the face than usual, and said, "I understand." And they walked back to the car. And Connor was so flustered that he just got into the driver's seat and waited for Melissa to get in; ordinarily he'd have let her in the passenger side before getting in himself. He noticed this mistake as soon as he saw Melissa opening the door herself, and was embarrassed, but decided it would probably be better if he said nothing about it. In the next moment he tried – for no particular reason – to recall whether he still extended this car-door courtesy to Tanya, and then he remembered that the two of them were hardly ever in the same vehicle anymore. They usually even drove separately to their counseling sessions.

"Connor?"

Melissa had to remind Connor to switch on the ignition; he'd just been sitting there feeling sick. And hopeless, no matter how hard he tried to convince himself that he could hope. But he drove Melissa to her parents' house, and neither of them could come up with anything more to say.

Connor was probably relieved to find none of the other Wainwrights in sight when they got there. Melissa put a hand on his arm and said, "Take care, Connor. Good luck."

Connor didn't dare say anything about staying in touch; he wasn't sure whether it would be good strategy to do so.

Connor was still in a daze when he arrived at his parents' house to pick up Olivia. His mother asked him what was wrong, and he couldn't bear to tell her.

"Just tired, I guess," he said.

"You work so hard," Mrs. Lowe told him. "Dad and I are so proud of you."

III. CHANGES IN LIFE AND CAREER

14. Christine's Voice Lessons

A deep depression doesn't go away all at once, but in some cases it can lift pretty quickly, and in Tanya's case it got a lot better when the new school year began. She took almost no notice of the two other people who lived in the house with her. She got little sleep, what with all her obligations, and she often was up, reading or working on her computer, when Livy woke up in the middle of the night, and on those occasions she would go and attend to the baby, as best she knew how, and let Connor sleep, but we can assume that she only did this to keep the peace, not out of any goodwill to either of the other parties.

It cheered her up, when the Wainwrights contacted her about giving lessons to Christine. It did irk her a bit – or more than a bit – when Jim Wainwright seemed to think she should do it just for the fun of giving lessons, but she wouldn't hold that against his daughter.

It was early in September. On that Tuesday morning, Connor noted that Tanya looked happier and healthier than she had for a year – since she'd gotten pregnant, it occurred to him

– and he supposed she was looking forward to giving that lesson. When Christine arrived on her bicycle, late that afternoon,
Tanya was at the door wearing her biggest smile.

"This is going to be such fun," said Tanya, as she let
Christine into the house. "You've never had any voice lessons
before, right? That's fine, it's been a while since I've given lessons, so we're almost even. And you don't need to worry about
how you sound because you can be sure I've heard a lot worse,
somewhere down the line."

Tanya had set up a cheval mirror next to her small electric keyboard in the living room, and had Christine stand in
front of it.

"So, let's see how much you know. I'll play a few notes,
and you just sing them as best you can, on a 'la.'"

"You've got a good ear," Tanya said, after a minute of
this. "You're on pitch, anyway. Let's see how high and how low
you can go."

After another couple of minutes, Tanya said, "Okay,
let's start you off in mezzo. After you've had a few lessons,
your range is going to open up, and then we'll see. What kind
of stuff do you like to sing?"

"Rock, mostly, and I've done some bluegrass."

"You've got a powerful voice already. Potentially powerful. What we work on is going to depend partly on the kind
of music you like, and what'll be the most helpful in terms of
developing your voice and your know-how. What do you know
about music? Do you play an instrument?"

Christine and Tanya seemed to hit it off, although they were
never close, partly because of the age difference, and partly because of the family association. Tanya never alluded to it, but of
course she knew that Christine was Melissa's sister.

Tanya was pretty sure there wasn't anything going on
here except a business transaction – Christine needed lessons
and Tanya was the obvious person to go to – but she couldn't
shake the suspicion that Christine was being used by the Wain-

wrights to keep tabs on her and Connor, or by Connor to maintain a closer connection with the Wainwrights. Anyway she thought Christine was a nice girl. Christine thought Tanya knew her stuff, and was a patient teacher, although moody.

That is, Tanya was always pleasant to Christine, but sometimes she'd make a remark about how she was going through a rough patch – mainly with her career as a student. She almost never spoke of Connor or her baby.

"It's not easy, if you decide to make music your life," Tanya told Christine. "And if you want to be a real success, you do have to make it your *whole* life. There isn't room for anything else. I don't know if it's worth it."

Before long, it looked as though Christine might one day be in a position to make such a commitment. After three or four lessons, her vocal range did open up, and she felt more comfortable in her upper register. Christine was clearly a soprano. And according to Tanya, she'd never used her voice properly.

"That was a D6 you just sang. And I'm pretty sure you can go higher than that without straining – or you will before long. You definitely have the range that a coloratura soprano needs, if you can learn the technique. You might actually have a voice you could make a career of."

Although she'd hardly ever been exposed to it before, Christine started to develop an appreciation for classical singing. Tanya started her out on brief, easy selections, especially songs from the French and Italian baroque traditions.

"You're taking a language in school, aren't you?" she asked Christine. "No? Start, then. If you want to make it as a serious singer, you'll need to know French, Italian, and German. Those are the singing languages. And it gets harder to learn a language, the older you get, so start now."

It was too late for Christine to add a language to her regular course load at school, but Tanya urged her to learn on her own. She started giving Christine nothing but songs in French, Italian, and German.

Dear Mr. P,

You speak French, right? My voice teacher says I hafta learn it so I'm trying to teach myself. Maybe if you work on it with me, I can test into French II next fall even if I didn't take French I this year. I can sorta kinda get it, written, but I don't have anybody to speak it with. Could we get together and talk French sometimes?

Also are you keeping up your part of the deal?

Dear Miss Christine:

I'd be glad to. French was the only subject I was good at in school. It was another reason I was not liked. Because not only was I real good at French, I was also a show-off. And what's funny is that there was one other kid in the class who was just as good at French as I was – better in some ways – and he was otherwise not that bright. He got pretty bad grades except in French. He and I were also in Bonehead Math together, and we'd sit at the back of the classroom and totally blow off whatever we were supposed to be doing, and be whispering and passing notes back and forth in French. Once we even wrote a pornographic story in French, which is a great way to learn the slang and colloquialisms if you can get your hands on a big, comprehensive French-English dictionary, one with all the naughty words in it. As you might imagine, that was not easy in the 1960s. I won't show you the story till you're 21.

Yes, I'm keeping up my part of the deal I hope. I've been cast as Chief Bromden in *Cuckoo's Nest*. That's an important part. I'm looking forward to treading the boards again.

And so, beginning in September and continuing for the rest of the school year, Christine and Andy started mixing French into their correspondence. They almost never had time to talk in person at any length, but Andy would greet Christine with "*bonjour*" whenever he saw her, and he taught her to say "*bonjour*" in response. He taught her "*comment ça va?*" and "*très bien, merci,*" and "*s'il vous plaît,*" all with a good accent. He explained to her the concept of nasalized vowels, and taught her to make the difficult French "u" and "eu" and unstressed "e" sounds.

Christine mostly had to glean what she could from a borrowed textbook, but Andy told her the Pimsleur CDs would teach her a good accent. He bought them for her.

"The accent is more important than learning the vocabulary and the grammar," he told Christine. "That, you'll pick up, inevitably. But you have to develop a good accent right from the get-go. If you start with bad habits you'll never get them trained out of you."

Dear Mr. P,

Thank you again for the CDs. I'm doing what you said and repeating the words as exactly as I can even tho it sounds weird to be making all those noises that we don't have in English. You hafta twist your mouth up in all kinds of weird ways and it's funny but it's embarrassing to let my folks overhear me. They were laughing, but I got Mom to try it with me and she just couldn't do it and gave up pretty fast, but at least she doesn't laugh now.

I mentioned to Tanya that you had got the CDs for me, and she said "Oh, that big tall bald guy?" She says she sees you at concerts sometimes. She says everybody in the School of Music knows who you are and they call you some funny name that I don't remember.

Dear Miss Christine:

The funny name they call me is "Sibelius." Jean Sibelius was a composer from Finland, dead a long time now, and he looked kind of like me when he got older, with the completely bald head and the big ears and the intense scary aspect. Yes, I know a lot of the music students know me. It's kinda cool that I've earned a nickname.

French pronunciation is a bear at first but once you get the hang of it you'll feel proud of yourself for having achieved such a good accent. Trust me on this.

Tanya encouraged Christine to attend recitals at the Janscombe Center. Once she took Christine up to Cedar Rapids, to a rehearsal for her performance of Mahler's Fourth Symphony, to give her an idea of how a concert like that is put together, and how a singer works with an orchestra. Christine kept working with Tanya, that semester and into the winter.

Christine never considered Tanya a friend, but she figured that was how it ought to be. Students shouldn't get too close to their teachers. She loved Tanya as a teacher. She appreciated how businesslike Tanya was at each lesson. There might be some kidding around, but only a little. And Tanya was exacting, as she'd warned Christine she'd be.

"It might seem that I'm just focusing on criticizing you, but we don't have much time," Tanya explained, "and I've been doing this for a while and I have a very critical ear, so I'll notice things that you won't, and I'll point them out to you because I want you to be as good as you can be. And you're going to be really good – if you develop the best habits at this stage, so that you won't have to think about them later on. And if you work your fucking ass off."

On the whole, Christine appreciated this policy, and Tanya gave her enough praise and encouragement to make her want to keep working, and working harder.

Jim and Gail felt concerned that their daughter was taking music too seriously. "You're turning into a real Bohemian," Jim kidded her one night at dinner, and when Christine replied that in fact she had been thinking she might want to sing the role of Mimi one day, it turned out that she had to explain to her parents who Mimi was, since Jim had been using the term in the sense of "unconventional person," and had never heard of *La Bohème*. Gail had, but she'd been unsure of how *Bohème* was pronounced.

"You're enough of a diva already," said Jim. And he was smiling when he said it, but Christine probably suspected that he meant it.

"At least she's not doing any more of that headache

music," Gail remarked to Jim when they were alone, and it was true. Christine seemed to lose interest in music other than classical. She persuaded her school's choir director to let her join the ensemble midway through the semester, and he was delighted to have her.

"You're going to go farther than I will," Tanya assured Christine during one lesson. "I fucked up; I let myself get sidetracked, and now if I get my D.M.A. maybe I'll get a teaching job somewhere, but it's too late for me to be a real star. And talent's cheap. It's not enough just to be a good singer. You've got to stick to it. You have to keep putting yourself forward constantly, you have to market yourself. It's not just practicing and performing. You can't let up, ever."

"Don't let yourself do what I did," Tanya warned. "Don't let yourself lose focus. Don't fall for the marriage and children shit. And whatever you do, *don't* go to State University. It's too stressful. Find some other school. It's bad enough that one of us is ending up a failure."

A couple of tears rolled down Tanya's cheeks, as she sat at the piano, and Christine was alarmed. She wondered if she should pat Tanya on the shoulder, or give her a hug.

"I'm sorry," Tanya added. "I get these moods. Plus I'm cramping so bad. But I get so tired of life."

Dear Mr. P,

It's so weird working with Tanya because she seems so sad a lot of the time. My Dad says she went crazy after she had her baby and I should be careful of her. She doesn't act crazy to me at all but sad. Mostly about her family sitch, which I don't understand cuz you know about Connor, he's a nice guy. He used to date my sister Melissa, but you knew that, right? Anyway Mom and Dad feel sorry for him for being married to Tanya but I don't see why they would cuz I like her a lot.

Hey, what's the French word for boyfriend?

Dear Miss Christine,

There are several. You'd call a young man you're just friends-friends with your "copain." If you're both grown up, he would be your "ami." If it's romantic, he's your "petit ami" or "petit copain." If you're living with him, he's your "compagnon." But just to make it more complicated, sometimes people will use "copain" to suggest that the fellow is a little more than a friend. Context is everything, as in most areas of life. What's the deal? Do you have a petit copain?

Sorry to hear about Tanya. I don't know her at all except that I was introduced to her at her wedding. She is an amazingly beautiful woman. I'm glad to hear she's nice on the inside too, and I'm sorry she's sad. Be nice to her.

Dear Mr. P,

No, nothing like that. I was thinking of my sister, is why I asked. Melissa has this petit copain apparently. She hasn't told Maman et Papa but they sorta suspect she has one. But here's what they don't know — and I don't for sure either but I'm pretty sure he is sort of noir. As in Afro-American. She hasn't told me, either, but I'm guessing it from the guy's name: Leander. You know, it's kinda a weird name like you think of AA guys having. Apparently he's a teacher too. And she said to me at Xmas that she'd like to bring him home one day but she was afraid Maman et Papa might have a hard time with it, and that made me think it even more. That he must be AA, I mean.

I dunno if they'd have a problem with them staying here (as long as they stayed in separate rooms of course), but what if he turns out to be AA? They'd prolly be all politically correct and act like they didn't even notice what color he was, and prolly they'd start talking about how they love Janet Jackson and they think Chris Rock is the funniest guy in the world, like white people do when they're trying to show off for AA people.

And then when they were alone, you know what I

bet they'd do? I mean Maman et Papa. I bet they'd do the same thing, tell each other what a nice young man he is and how they're so proud of Missie for being so mature and open-minded and willing to do something like that, get with an AA guy I mean. Cuz they'd be afraid to admit to each other that they don't like it. Even tho they've been married for like 30 years I bet they still worry about "what would he/she think."

Also at Xmas Missie was talking about how she could get a lot better teaching job if she got a Masters, but she cant afford to take time off to go back to school and it would take her too long if she just went to school in the summer, and dadadadada, and I heard Mom tell Dad that they should offer to help her out if she'll move back here and live at home and go to State. And Dad said yeah but we hafta make it look like it's her idea.

I'm so tempted to tell Missie about that. But that would mean for sure she wouldn't do it, and if she wants to do it why not let her, nahmean?

Dear Miss Christine:

Are you so sure Melissa would refuse an offer like that, just to be defiant? She might jump at it. I hardly know her, but she never struck me as a rebel. But if she's serious about ce jeune homme – and remember, it's "cet homme" but "ce jeune homme," because of that rule about elision – and if he's in Detroit, she might not want to leave. You might think of a diplomatic way to find out how she'd feel about accepting a deal like that without telling her that your parents might be ready to offer it.

15. Tanya Sings Carmen

At the start of 2006, Tanya would recall, she wasn't much happier than she ever was, but music had lifted her out of her doldrums. She'd taken on a couple of other students, and the spring opera was upcoming. And then she got the news about *Carmen*. She'd been afraid that Sally Greenhow would get the title role, but Tanya did have seniority.

When it happened – she was sitting at her desk at home, and the email popped up on her server from Prof. Riding, who'd be the musical director for the opera, asking her, "Will you sing Carmen for me?" – she felt almost faint, almost nauseated from the thrill, which sounds counterintuitive, but there it is. And then the queasiness passed, and she'd never felt so excited, so rewarded by life, as when she read that email a second time, and a third, and a fourth. She felt the scream building up inside her for several seconds, and then she did scream – it amazed her how loud a noise she could make – and then she screamed again, "*Connor!*"

Connor bounded out of his office, alarmed – probably he feared that Tanya was having another meltdown – and Tanya leapt from her chair and grabbed Connor's arms, tried to dance him around the room. Her exuberance couldn't be compared with the day she'd come home overjoyed, a few months before, because she'd landed those few professional gigs. This was a whole new level of elation, almost of ecstasy – and Connor might have reflected for an instant that *this*, this incredible animation, this delight that Tanya took in her own passion, was what had made him fall for her. And – who knows? – it might have occurred to him that if only he could win *this* girl back...

At any rate, this time, Connor knew better than to not at least try to match Tanya's enthusiasm. He didn't say a word about how this project might take her away from him and Livy. He probably *was* pleased for Tanya's sake; at any rate he congratulated her warmly enough that she wasn't disappointed. He even proposed going out to a nice dinner that night. It would be too late to get a sitter, he warned her – but Tanya laughed and said, "We'll bring her. Red Lobster's fine with me."

And, for the few weeks before rehearsals began, Tanya and Connor's marriage enjoyed a bit of a renaissance. No sniping, no sarcasm, no surliness. They were even affectionate with each other, sometimes. They still weren't happy with their marriage, but they acted, for a while, as though they might be comfortable with each other someday.

§

Tanya must have noticed the guy playing Escamillo – the baritone, the toreador – right away. For one thing, he was terribly young for the part. Only a junior, as it turned out, 20 years old, so that was unusual right off the bat: for someone so young to get such a big part. A lot of people say the State University School of Music is overrated, not nearly as good as it used to be. But it's still way full of talent. You don't see undergraduates singing major roles in an opera there.

Generally, the singers in the School of Music know each other at least a little, but Tanya didn't fraternize much outside her own studio, and she'd never actually met Gareth Rossa. She'd seen him around, was all.

It probably didn't hurt that at the first rehearsal – the first time they'd been in the same room together, so far as Tanya could recall – Gareth was *gaping* at her, from a few feet away, as though he couldn't believe what he was looking at. Tanya thought it was funny.

Tanya would probably have never supposed that this kid had been cast as the principal baritone till Prof. Riding walked over to him and they started talking, and from over-hearing snatches of their conversation Tanya could figure out that this youngster would be the toreador. She also noticed that the boy kept looking at her as much as he could, even while he was talking with Prof. Riding. When the professor had walked away, Tanya walked up to him and asked, "Are you my Es-camillo?" and she introduced herself, holding out her hand.

Gareth shook it, gently. He might have wanted to blurt something, but he didn't; he collected himself and just said, "Hi," perfectly nonchalant and straightforward. And he looked Tanya right in the eye and smiled, and said, "Really looking forward to working with you."

He was so pretty. If Tanya were the most beautiful woman Gareth had ever seen, he might have been the prettiest boy Tanya had ever seen. She wanted to kiss that mouth; she wanted to run her hands through his curly blond hair. He had such bright white teeth, and lips like a bow. He had a light, northern European complexion, although his face looked more Greek or Italian – like Apollo, but Apollo as a boy. He had a couple of days' growth of beard, but somehow that made him look even younger.

That was how they met. The mutual attraction may have been immediate, but neither of them acted on it, during the first few weeks of rehearsals – except that Tanya and Ga-reth would talk together pretty often when they weren't on stage, and they learned each other's information. Gareth found out that Tanya was married, and he told her that he was from the town of Centerville and that he had this year, plus another, before he graduated – and after that, he'd be looking for a post-grad program someplace.

If you know *Carmen*, you know that Carmen and Es-camillo don't spend a lot of time onstage together. But Tanya was a perfectionist, a tireless rehearser, and Gareth enjoyed re-hearsing with her. If nothing else, *"Si tu m'aimes, Carmen"* would be perfect – and they found they enjoyed singing other duets that had nothing to do with the show.

As they got better acquainted, Tanya began to tell Gareth about her marriage, and her child – although she could hardly bear to tell him that part of it. Maybe she would have preferred to somehow deceive him, let him think that she had no child. The fact that she had one was a stigma to her, especially when she confessed it to Gareth. It was as though she were sure it would make her an old woman in his perception – and she didn't want Gareth to think of her as an old woman. Nothing had happened between them, and it's conceivable that at that point she was still only thinking in the abstract that she would love to reach over and kiss him properly – but still she wanted him to perceive her as young enough to be intriguing.

That's human nature. Any man, any woman wants to be considered young and desirable, and they don't like to let slip any information, or any visual clue, that might make them any less of either.

"I guess it was my fault the baby was premature," Tanya told Gareth once. "I don't know: maybe because I was stressing so badly. I can't even give birth right, apparently. I shat it out of my body as soon as I could. At least it didn't do anything to my figure. I would rather just forget that I ever had it.

"Every time I looked at it I felt like shit. I know I'm supposed to love it but I just didn't feel anything about it except that for the first few weeks I wished I could kill it. Now I don't want anything bad to happen to it but I wish I could forget that it was ever a part of my life. I wish I could erase that part of my brain."

She told Gareth about Connor, too. How Connor had pushed her, nagged her, guilted her, moped and sighed, till she'd let herself tell him she'd have his baby. How it was clear to her, now – and had always been clear to her, only she had shut her eyes to it as best she could – that Connor still carried a torch for his high school sweetheart.

"This plain, dumpy girl. You can imagine how that made me feel."

"I can't imagine that. Anybody wanting anyone else when he had you."

"Thanks. But apparently he still has these thoughts."

Tanya told Gareth about the naming of their daughter. And about her depression.

"I was crazy," she admitted. "I guess you could say that. Just not as crazy as *he* thought I was. Or wanted me to be. Or, I don't know, not as crazy as he probably told other people I was. That's another thing. The way he talked about me to other people. Telling them I was crazy, making everyone feel sorry for *him*, like he's this noble creature who's bearing his cross. When we'd had a deal and he tried to renege on it.

"He's still trying to. Still trying to guilt me into giving all this up and being a mom. Meanwhile he obviously sees himself as this wonderful self-sacrificing dedicated father who's bearing his cross because his selfish crazy wife won't accept her obligations. Of course he does. Of course he does."

Gareth at this point reached over and put his hand on Tanya's forearm, and squeezed just a little.

Gareth had never met Connor, never even seen him, and now he asked Tanya what her husband looked like. She brought her wallet out of her purse, and showed him one of the photos she carried – of their wedding.

"Hm," said Gareth. He privately believed that Connor – who was not much older than he was – looked like someone who needed to have the shit beaten out of him.

In fact, the more Gareth thought, the more he wanted to put a shank between Connor's ribs, or blow him away with a shotgun. He even wrote about it in his journal, and long after the fact – long enough after the fact that they could both smile about it – he showed the writing to Tanya:

Tanya's husband has to go. He does not merit being allowed to live. Obviously I won't do it, because I don't want to go to prison, but if I were absolutely sure I could get away with it, I would consider killing him.

I'd like to kill him in a way that he'd be aware of. I don't want it to be slow. He doesn't fucking deserve to be tortured to death. He needs to go. He needs to go fast. And he needs to go in a way where I can look him right in the face and have him know that he's about to die at my hands, for what he did to Tanya.

I've got a pump-action Mossberg, back at my parents' house. I've shot a lot of pheasant with it. That would be the way to do it but I still have to figure out how I'd arrange to meet up with him and have him where I could kill him without his being able to run away or anything, so he would have those few seconds of knowing what was about to happen to him, and why it was about to happen to him, before I blew his face off. Or maybe I'd shoot him in the chest so that he'd have a few seconds to bleed out, and in those few seconds he'd be able to think about why this was happening to him.

If anybody sees this, they need to know that I'm not going to do it, so if this guy does get killed it's not me.

Gareth didn't kill Connor – indeed never made any serious effort to get within shooting distance of him – but he did work on that fantasy for several days, honing it, fine-tuning it, till by the time the rehearsals for *Carmen* had gone into tech-week, he was playing it in his mind, at night, as he drifted off to sleep.

I have to admit I enjoy it. It's how I cope.

I don't know if anything can or will ever
happen between me and Tanya but I can't see
anybody but her. It's like other women don't
exist for me. Only Tanya Cucoshay and her
star-galaxy eyes and sweet breath and my
will to live and fight for her, and die for her
if it ever came to that. I feel that it has to
happen between us and it will happen.

Meanwhile, as Tanya got more and more involved in rehearsals, she spent less and less time at home – and whole days would go by when she and Connor didn't exchange so much as a word. As in the previous few weeks, there was much less animosity than there had been – but the occasional periods of friendliness had disappeared as well. It was as though Tanya and Connor barely noticed each other's existence.

For tech week – that week of rehearsals leading up to opening night – the company met and worked in the actual venue: Yolande P. Janscombe Auditorium, which is the largest performance space in the Janscombe Center.

It was during tech week that Tanya and Gareth had their first kiss. It's impossible to say who started it. They found themselves alone and unobserved for a moment during a break between scenes and all of a sudden their eyes met and then their lips, and perhaps Tanya was thinking, "Oh, shit, what am I getting myself into here, but Oh my God he's so pretty and he wants me so badly," and Gareth must have been thinking "I can't believe this is happening but it's happening, it really is happening," and then Tanya broke it off and laughed into Gareth's face, not like she was making fun of him but laughing because she was astonished as well as enjoying the experience.

Tanya laughed some more, and put her hands on Gareth's forearms to indicate that she wanted out of his embrace, and she said, "Oh, Gareth, what are we doing?"

Gareth grinned and said, "Kissing!"

"That complicates things, doesn't it?" said Tanya, and

she headed back to the stage to resume rehearsal.

Gareth probably had always had his pick of girls his own age, so it would make sense that he'd have been up for a more challenging relationship – and thus understandable that he'd become fascinated by a mysterious older woman. Nor do Tanya's thoughts require profound analysis. She was married to a man who, she knew, regarded her as a liability, as a problem to be dealt with – like a disease or an injury that might or might not be corrected. And here was this pretty boy, the prettiest boy she'd ever seen. There was her husband, who had almost entirely convinced her of her own worthlessness, and now here was this incredibly gorgeous, young, enthusiastic, and crazy-about-her guy...

What's going to happen in a situation like that?

First, what didn't happen. Tanya and Gareth didn't consummate their relationship. Not right then, and not that week. What might amaze some readers is that Gareth was smart enough to *not* pursue Tanya full-tilt after that incident. Most guys 20 years old would not have been so bright, nor would have had that much self-control – and they might have blown it. This guy, though, he lay back and gave Tanya her space.

Gareth, that night, went right back to rehearsing as though nothing had happened, and at the end of the evening, when he and Tanya happened to be standing together when the director started giving notes, he took Tanya's left hand – the one with the engagement and wedding rings on it – in his right for just a second or two, and gave it a squeeze. Tanya squeezed back, and smiled sidelong, before releasing Gareth's hand, and that, apparently, signaled what they both understood: This episode was not over yet.

Tanya must have had to do a lot of thinking in just a few minutes, on the drive home from rehearsal that night. This had been tech-dress, which always takes longer than any of the other rehearsals, and Tanya had warned Connor that she'd be home late, so she hoped he'd have gone to bed already and she'd not have to have any conversation with him.

She must have had to admit to herself that she'd seen this coming from the moment she and Gareth had introduced each other. And now it had come, and she was probably going over her options right there in the car as she drove. The options amounted to these:

• Never act further on this business. Never kiss Gareth again, never flirt with him, never touch him any more than was necessary for the purpose of the opera. Indeed, never speak of this matter ever again. Pretend it never happened, and hope that Gareth would do the same. Likelihood of her wanting to do this, on a scale of 1 to 10: Probably 3. Likelihood that Gareth would go along with it, on that same scale: Probably 2 at most.

• Tell Gareth explicitly that they must never have more than a strictly professional relationship, that there were no hard feelings and no regrets, but it must stop dead, right now. Likelihood of her wanting to do this: 1. Likelihood that Gareth would go along: 8 or 9, she guessed, if she were forceful enough in expressing herself. Which, she probably told herself, was the most compelling argument for *not* doing this.

• Continue to kiss and fool with Gareth, here and there, and see where the situation might go, and figure that what Connor didn't know wouldn't hurt him. Likelihood of her wanting to do this: 6. Likelihood that Gareth would go along: 3. He'd probably insist on moving faster. Likelihood of Connor finding out: 9, at least.

• Jump into a full-out affair with Gareth. Likelihood of her wanting to do this: 6. Likelihood that Gareth would go along: 10. Likelihood of Connor finding out: less than if she and Gareth were just kissing and fooling, since if the were having sex in private they'd be more discreet in public.

• Get into a serious thing with Gareth, and leave Connor once she was sure of Gareth's feelings. Likelihood of her wanting to do this: maybe 4. She was extremely attracted to Gareth, but wasn't sure how serious she wanted to get – and should/could she leave Connor under these circumstances? Likelihood that Gareth would go along: Probably 3. He might think he wanted to, and he might be temporarily swept up in the idea, but could that last? Probably not.

• Leave Connor right now, since if she was even thinking, at this stage, of having an affair with a boy more than 10 years younger than she, she had no business staying in the marriage. Likelihood of her wanting to do this: 1. As she considered it, driving home, she probably didn't want to leave Connor. She was probably feeling guilty, and regretful, and was recalling too clearly that she'd loved Connor once, and hoped that she might love him again – and that Connor might love her. After all, things had been better between them, lately. Likelihood that Gareth would go along: not relevant, since this would be independent of what might be going on between her and Gareth.

The smartest choice, Tanya almost certainly concluded as she pulled into her driveway – and the obvious choice – was to go ahead and have fun with Gareth. If it didn't go anywhere good, tough. Gareth was young enough that he'd never care – he'd have gotten what he wanted anyway – and she, Tanya, would be fully aware of what she was getting into. Connor need never know.

The light was on in the living room, she observed from the car. Connor would've left that light on for her if he'd gone to bed, but he was up, watching TV with the volume turned low, not to disturb Livy. He gave Tanya the barest glance.

"Thought you'd wait up for me?"

Connor smiled on one side of his face. "Why not?"

"Want a beer?" Tanya asked. Connor declined. Tanya went to the fridge and got one for herself.

Tanya and Connor sat at opposite ends of the couch and together they watched *Letterman*, not talking, hardly looking at each other. When the show was over they went together to the bedroom, and got ready for bed at the same time. Their only conversation was to check with each other about their schedules and obligations for the next day. They got into bed, each said, "night," and each turned away from the other and fell asleep, at opposite sides of the bed, not touching.

Tanya, in retrospect, claimed she couldn't remember exactly when she made her final decision to leave Connor, but it might have been right then. Just as she was drifting off, might have been when Tanya resolved in her own mind that she could not continue living with Connor, at least not for long. As for Connor, it's likely that by then, he felt that each day with Tanya was a day without Melissa – or at least a day when he was not free to show Melissa that he was free.

That situation got neither better nor worse, for the next few days, on the surface. But at rehearsal, Tanya and Gareth would sit together regularly when they weren't on stage or getting ready to go on, and they'd hold hands if they were pretty sure nobody could see it. That was on the next night, dress-dress. But by the next night – "invited dress" rehearsal – they were holding hands openly. Tanya, seeing that they were observed, said to nobody in particular, "I'm so nervous. Gareth is imparting his calm."

Before curtain-up, they kissed each other for luck. For several seconds.

At intermission, Tanya avoided Gareth. He was clearly looking to her, wanting to approach her, but he was a singer too. He understood the concept of being "in the zone," and supposed that she was just staying focused on the show. And she was trying to do that, but wasn't succeeding. She was thinking about Gareth, and how to handle him, every bit as much as Gareth must have been thinking the same about her.

At the end of the rehearsal, Prof. Riding and the stage director both addressed the cast, orchestra, and crew. Tanya purposely sat some distance from Gareth and looked away from him, arms folded, as though to make it clear that she didn't want him sitting with her. She noticed, out of the corner of her eye, that he looked dismayed, and for the moment she didn't care. She was brooding about her performance, now, and blaming Gareth for it.

Prof. Riding began, "People, tomorrow night we open. The conventional wisdom is, 'Bad dress, good show.' I won't say we were bad tonight, but I know we can do better. We're all tired, so it's understandable that our focus might have been a little off. But tomorrow night we've got to nail it, so after we've turned you loose I want you to all go home and get some extra sleep if you can, because tomorrow we *will* have a good show – if it kills us.

"Carmen, I'm sorry to bring it up, but you seemed distracted tonight. Anybody can have an off night, and I'm glad that if you had to have one, you had it tonight. You're the star and you deserve to be. You will be so *on*, tomorrow night. I can feel it.

"Escamillo, that goes for you too. There was something missing tonight. I went out on a limb, casting an undergraduate in this part, and I want you to justify my decision – and I have faith in you; I know you'll come through tomorrow."

Tanya and Gareth glanced at each other from across the auditorium, and this time Tanya made a little grimace of sympathy, and Gareth felt relieved by that look, relieved that she was apparently not angry at him.

When Riding had dismissed, Tanya walked over to Gareth, reaching out and putting a light hand on his forearm to keep him from coming any closer.

"Gareth, we're going to have to put it on hold. We've got the show to get through and we can't complicate it now. Wait till the show's over. Then we'll see."

Gareth looked stunned, as if he couldn't tell whether she was blowing him off, or encouraging him to be patient and let it happen – whatever would happen – later. Probably he wasn't feeling reassured, but didn't feel hopeless either. He grasped Tanya's hand for an instant and said, "Okay."

As Tanya recalled the incident, much later, she went home that night as confused as she'd ever felt in her life. She didn't know, herself, whether she was dismissing Gareth or not. Again, that night, she went to bed without hardly speaking to Connor, and didn't think he noticed.

She knew she hadn't done her best that night, and partly she blamed Gareth for distracting her, and partly she blamed Connor for not being supportive, but neither Gareth nor Connor were at the forefront of her thoughts. At that time, rightly or wrongly, she saw her performance as *the* critical incident of her career so far: the confirmation, or the refutation, of what she was re-playing and re-playing in her mind: that old review in the San Francisco *Chronicle*.

"Miss Cucoshay has no business singing opera. She has a rough, brassy voice…"

Tanya cried herself to sleep that night. Connor didn't notice. He never had any trouble conking out immediately his head hit the pillow.

But then the next morning, Friday morning, Tanya got up feeling better, as though she knew she was going to nail it that night, like she'd gotten it all out of her system the night before and was resolved not to let Gareth, or Connor, or anything else bother her.

She was pumped, and Connor must have noticed it, because he said that very thing – "You sure look pumped!" – as Tanya was getting ready to head out the door.

Tanya gave Connor a big smile, the biggest she'd bestowed on him since she'd told him she'd gotten the part.

"Tonight will only be the most important thing I've ever done so far in my life. So yeah, I'm pumped!"

And immediately she knew she'd said the wrong thing as far as Connor was concerned, because he would have preferred it if Tanya had felt that having married him, and having birthed his offspring, were way more important than any opera.

She saw that in his face immediately.

But, those were *not* the most important things Tanya had ever done. Singing Carmen *was* more important. She told Connor, "Just wait, you're going to hear something *amazing* tonight."

It says something about how poorly they were communicating by then, than she didn't know for sure whether Connor would be there for opening night. But she must have assumed it.

"I thought I'd go next week. You know, when you've done it a few times and got settled into it."

Tanya wasn't a great actress, but she did have the dramatic "stop yourself in the midst of whatever you're doing and just stare open-mouthed" thing down pat. Only in this case she wasn't acting, not for an instant. She was genuinely outraged, and for a few seconds dumbstruck.

"I don't believe what I'm hearing," she said at last. "My supposed husband isn't going to be there to hear his wife singing Carmen on opening night?"

"I didn't think it would be that important to you. Anyway I doubt I could get a sitter now."

Again Tanya paused, staring.

"*Get one!*" she screamed, and she was out the door, and in the frame of mind she was in it's lucky she didn't wreck her car on the way to class. She probably could hardly see straight.

Her anger didn't dissipate during the day. Instead she dwelt on it, through classes, through practice, through lunch, through everything else. Tanya kept replaying, in her mind, every injustice that Connor had ever done her, or that she'd suspected him of. She went over and over practically every incident she could recall, putting the worst possible spin on each one. She moved through the day almost by instinct. Her mind was so focused on all the various ways in which Connor had done her wrong, and this – his nonchalantly figuring he'd hear her sing Carmen one of these days, instead of opening night – was the sockdolager. Maybe Tanya had already resolved, in the abstract, to do what she ended up doing, but this was the one punch that truly ended the fight.

When she got to the theatre, Tanya didn't even look at Gareth; she didn't look at anyone any more than she could help. If she'd been paying attention, she might have heard more than one member of the cast remarking that she had her bitch-face on. Unless they assumed she was getting into character.

As she was putting on her costume, Tanya realized that she was going to have to snap out of this, and focus on the show, and her performance. And she told herself, "You're so angry, all you can do is use it. So, use it."

So she used it, that night, at Yolande P. Janscombe Auditorium, to a packed house.

It had to have been the best performance that Tanya had ever given in her life. The best performance of *anything*. That performance would stay with her for as long as she had a memory, but even more vivid in her mind was the ovation she received at the curtain call. It was for her, just for her, and she never would have imagined anything like it. Not mere cheers from the audience: roars. Roars upon roars. For a few seconds she feared she might faint, right there on the stage; she came to herself only when someone ran onto the stage with a bouquet of roses for her – huge red American Beauties.

In years to come, Tanya would go back over the DVD of that performance now and then, and she would see that it hadn't been perfect, that she'd gone flat once or twice – but no performance is absolutely flawless. She'd had energy; she knew she'd had energy. She'd communicated. She could feel the audience responding to her, all the way through the show, and by the end of it she felt exhilaration – and relief – such as she'd never felt in her life. She felt that she'd finally justified all the years of work – and had proven, at last, that that critic from the San Francisco *Chronicle*, who had probably never given her another thought as long as he lived, had been wrong. She did have business singing opera.

The tenor, Dan Wolf, gave Tanya a huge hug as soon as

the curtain had come down, and then Gareth hugged her too, and as Tanya hugged him back she must have felt the electricity between them; she could not have denied it then, and it must have been at that instant that she knew that she had to start taking specific steps – and that was when she no longer gave a shit whether Connor had been in the audience or not.

Connor was there, in the reception area backstage, and he gave Tanya a hug and a kiss. Tanya didn't mind, but it was like being kissed by a stranger.

"I just barely got a ticket," Connor reported. "They were sold out; they had me on standby in case there was a no-show, but I got in at the last minute, and not too bad of a seat. You did terrific."

Trying to be gracious, trying to let Connor know she appreciated his coming to the first night, Tanya said, "Thank you for being here; it means a lot to me."

"Yeah, Jim and Gail said I should bring Livy over to their house. And they said they'd keep her overnight if we wanted to stay out late."

And that took it out of Tanya right there. Like he wouldn't think she'd mind that he'd gotten *them* to sit Livy for him. She couldn't believe it.

Connor did ask Tanya if she'd like him to take her out to a late dinner, but a bunch of the cast had been planning to go out for beer and pizza, and that's what you do after opening night of a play or an opera. So Tanya said to Connor, "Why don't you come along?" and he did – they each took their own car – but Connor mostly just sat there all through the evening. He hardly spoke to any of Tanya's friends. He didn't know any of them, and what would he have talked to them about?

He just sat there looking uncomfortable. And eating pizza. And under other circumstances maybe Tanya would have tried to draw him into the conversation. She did introduce him. She didn't introduce him to Gareth, because Gareth was way down at the other end of the table – although Gareth must have seen the two of them; maybe that was *why* he was down at the other end of the table. Tanya wasn't looking at him either.

What might have been in Gareth Rossa's head as he sat there? He was ordinarily an exuberant person, and so he was on this evening, and he might have been so adrenalized by his own performance that he didn't let the sight of Connor bother him. Or maybe he was so confident that he'd win out, eventually, that he didn't give a shit that Connor was there. But he stayed away from Tanya, and was even flirting with some of the female chorus. And that may have had something to do with why Tanya wasn't looking at him.

The next morning, when Connor got ready to get in his car and get Livy from the Wainwrights, Tanya told him she had to meet her tenor to go over a few rough edges. They'd agreed to do that right after last night's show, she said.

But instead she got into her own car with that morning's *Examiner*, and drove to several of the places that were advertising furnished rooms or apartments that didn't require a lease. By noon she'd found a place not too far from the Janscombe Center – driving distance but not that long of a drive – that she could afford, that she could rent monthly through July if she wanted to. And she brought out her chequebook and put down a deposit.

She then sat in Starbucks for a couple of hours, calculating what she would have to do next. How would she tell Connor? When would she? Would she transfer some of her stuff to that apartment before telling him? Should she do that before or after she went to a lawyer on Monday, and should she go to a lawyer at all? Shouldn't she let him divorce her instead?

She told herself to turn off the questions. She still had a performance to get through that night, and a *matinée* the following day, Sunday.

Second nights usually don't go as well as first nights, because you have a natural tendency to let down after the emotional high of the opening. So if Tanya was off her game that night, it wasn't so noticeable, since most of the rest of the cast was likewise. Gareth gave a less-good performance also, and when the curtain came down after curtain call he whispered to Tanya, "I'm sorry. You couldn't play off me, as bad as I was," and Tanya took his hand and squeezed it and said, "Bullshit; it was my fault. You did the best you could." She left the stage that night telling herself that her subpar performance had, in the last analysis, been mainly Connor's doing.

Tanya remembered having read – in one of the books on business management that she'd studied during those years when she wasn't focusing on music – that the least bad time to fire an employee is the first thing Monday morning. That gives him a full week to look for something else, without ruining his weekend. Having made this decision – and she made it in the dressing room that Saturday night, as she was changing back into her street clothes – made her feel a little better.

She also, perhaps, felt proud of herself that she was not leaving Connor for another man. She'd made this decision in-dependently of whatever might happen between her and Ga-reth; for all she knew, Gareth might have lost interest in her after the way she'd been all but ignoring him. On the way out of the green room, she passed by Gareth and gave his arm a quick squeeze and said, "We'll get 'em tomorrow," and they smiled at each other.

And they got 'em tomorrow. The Sunday *matinée* per-formance was, Tanya felt, just as good as opening night had been. With another weekend's worth of performances coming up, Tanya felt that she was in control of her course – both pro-fessionally and personally.

But still, she made no further moves on Gareth.

§

We have to give Tanya low marks for originality, but to be fair we couldn't have expected anything unusual or artistic from her, in the way of dumping her husband. Tanya could sing, but she wasn't imaginative or profound. She went by the book.

She was home by 7:00 on Sunday night, and she would

have made dinner for Connor from whatever happened to be in the fridge, but he had already eaten, so she made a snack for herself, and later on, when she could be certain Livy was sound asleep, she went into the living room where Connor was watching TV, ran a hand gently across the back of his neck, and sat down next to him, snuggling up and smiling into his face.

Connor looked nonplussed, but he didn't seem averse to whatever Tanya was up to. Once she'd made her intentions clear by running her hand over the fly of his jeans, he became responsive. When she suggested that they adjourn to the bedroom, he became eager. It was the first time they'd had sex in weeks. Tanya allowed Connor a short break before initiating a second round and bringing him off again, for insurance.

"Gosh, Tanya," Connor murmured as he drifted off to sleep. "You're amazing." Tanya gave him a comforting pat on the shoulder before going into the bathroom to pack her toiletries.

Connor thought nothing of it the next morning when he got up and found that Tanya was not in the house. She often got up early and went to the library to study, or to the gym, or to Janscombe to practice, or at any rate that's what she would tell him she was doing. He didn't notice, since he was bleary from sleep, that some of her toiletries were missing – let alone that some of her clothes had disappeared.

He might have noticed, with surprised approval, that Livy had been changed and bottled recently. He hadn't even heard Livy waking up, and now she was lying in her crib, drowsing, apparently contented.

Connor remained oblivious to what else was going on till about 5:30 that afternoon, when he looked out of his office window and saw Tanya's car pulling into the driveway, and a Jeep Cherokee pulling in behind it. From the Cherokee emerged Tanya's tenor friend Dan Wolf, and a woman whom Connor didn't recognize.

The sight of these extra people didn't surprise Connor: Tanya occasionally brought friends over to study, practice, or socialize. But when he saw Tanya getting out of her car with a box of plastic lawn bags in her hand, and saw that the two guests were carrying large plastic baskets, he started to get a seriously bad feeling. He got out of his office chair and was at the door to greet the arrivals as they came in.

"Dan you know, and this is Dan's wife, Sylvia," said Tanya. "They've come to help me move my stuff out."

Connor stood gaping.

"I don't want there to be any trouble. I'm not taking anything except my stuff. The house is yours, Livy is yours, it's all yours. No hard feelings."

Tanya headed into their bedroom. Dan and Sylvia followed her, which prevented Connor from coming after her, which is probably exactly what Tanya had in mind to prevent. Connor was obliged to stay in the front of the house and wait for them to come out with the rest of Tanya's possessions.

"We'll take as many of my books and stuff as we can fit," Tanya told Connor over her shoulder, as she passed through the living room and out the front door with her first sackful of clothes. "We'll try to get all my stuff out tonight, and if we have to come back for anything, it won't be much."

Connor still couldn't think of anything to say. Dan and Sylvia didn't look at him as they walked past, carrying filled baskets. They returned for a second load, walking together as though Tanya had instructed them to stay near her – as she probably had. Tanya folded her electric keyboard, which had stood in their living room throughout their marriage, and carried it out.

Tanya would have been certain that Connor wouldn't want to have any kind of conversation about this final collapse of the marriage where anyone else could hear it. That must have been in her mind, when she'd asked Dan and Sylvia to help her. Or maybe she'd brought them along for physical protection (unlikely: Connor wasn't violent). Let's not overanalyze: she probably just wanted a couple of extra pair of hands. But their presence did keep Connor quiet and out of the picture. Before they'd begun walking the second load of Tanya's stuff back to the car, Connor had gone back into his office, and was looking at the computer, pretending to work. He let whatever was happening, happen, and did not emerge from that room.

At last, Tanya stuck her head into his office and said, "Connor, take care, okay?" She set her wedding and engagement rings on the edge of Connor's desk. Then she was gone.

It's hard to imagine what must've been going through Connor's mind, immediately after Tanya left. He probably felt stunned, and numb, for a while – the way you'd feel right after you'd been shaken up in a car accident but not seriously injured. You have to sit still for a while, and absorb it psychologically.

He probably did have hurt feelings. It's never pleasant to be left. It makes you wonder about your personal adequacy. So even if Connor no longer loved Tanya, this could not have been easy for him.

No doubt he felt some worry, some concern. Most likely he wasn't too upset at the prospect of having to take care of Livy by himself, because he'd been doing that, and he genuinely loved the baby and was glad to do it. But there must have been a bit of "What am I going to do now?" mixed into his thoughts. There might have been some "What can I tell my parents? What will other people think about me? What is Tanya going to tell people?"

There might have been relief mixed in, too. Indeed, once he was over the initial shock, and much as he might have tried to deny it to himself, relief was probably his main emotion. It couldn't have been easy for Connor, living with Tanya, especially for the year-and-a-half he'd just endured.

And it might have occurred to him that this was just what he wanted, just what he'd been angling for all along. Could he have been sitting there rubbing his hands together in glee like a cartoon villain, telling himself exactly that? Probably not literally, but could he have been thinking *something like* that?

No. Almost certainly not. For then he'd have had to admit as much, to himself. No, he would never have thought that he was in any way pleased; he wouldn't have allowed himself to think any such thing. Besides, there's often something comforting, something almost delicious, in convincing yourself that you've been terribly mistreated. It can be as soothing as a wallow in a tub of warm soapy water.

But, ordinarily, life does give us what we want – even if we don't immediately recognize it as such, and even if it's not what we tell ourselves we want.

Tanya had taken her computer with her, and her phone. It took Connor a couple of hours after she'd left to pull himself together and decide how to proceed. At about 9:00, Connor left a voice-message, an email, and a text message, all saying about the same thing: "Where are you? Please contact me."

IT'S NOT IMPORTANT WHERE I AM. I'LL BE BACK IN A FEW DAYS TO GET ANYTHING I MIGHT HAVE LEFT BEHIND. IT'S NOT MUCH.

Is there somebody else?

WHAT DOES IT MATTER? YOU WON.
CONGRATULATIONS.
NO MORE TONIGHT. I NEED TO SLEEP.

Connor almost called the Cucoshays to see if Tanya were with them, but he decided that that was unlikely: she wouldn't go to Indianola with her classes and another week of performances upcoming. And he couldn't even be sure that she'd informed her parents that she'd left him, and in that case it'd be awkward if he broke the news to them.

He almost called his own parents but was afraid of what they might think; afraid of what they might say about Tanya. And despite everything else, it might be that he was afraid of how he'd react if he heard anyone else criticizing Tanya.

Above all he wanted to call Melissa Wainwright. But he must have known he couldn't. At any rate, he didn't.

He heard Livy moving in her crib, starting to make noises like she was about to cry, and he went to her and changed her, then made her a bottle – reflecting that it was a good thing he'd fed her just before Tanya had come in the front door, that afternoon, or he might have forgotten about it entirely. He sat in the easy chair in the living room, feeding Livy in his lap, holding her close.

It's cruel to imagine this, granted, but a cynic might not have been able to help suspecting that Connor was posing for himself: the wronged husband, selflessly feeding the infant abandoned by her mother; the two of them clinging to one another because now all they had to sustain them was their mutual love and dependence. It wouldn't be far-fetched to suggest that in Connor's head, Helen Reddy was singing "You And Me Against The World."

§

Tanya hadn't left much behind, and she didn't come back to fetch anything. Connor gathered up a few of her items and texted her, offering to bring them by wherever she was staying.

You can deliver them to the Wolfs' house, and Dan or Sylvia will deliver them to me. They have the Cherokee. Thank you in advance for doing that.

Connor's phone messages went unanswered. His e-mailed requests for explanations were answered, finally, two days after Tanya had left:

Connor, you must know that our marriage was done long ago. I see no reason to go into any of it now. I'll talk with you if you feel it's necessary but right now I'm too preoccupied with the opera and with other stuff, such as my course work. Maybe next week we can get together for coffee.

At the brush-up rehearsal on Wednesday night, Tanya didn't mention the split to anyone – and she'd asked Dan not to let anyone else know. She kept her distance from Gareth most of the time, but smiled at him now and then, and he'd smile back.

On the Friday, Tanya gave what she thought was technically, if not spiritually, the best performance of her life – largely, she thought, because she'd gone up to Gareth just before the curtain, taken his arm, and said, "Give me a kiss for luck, you fool." And Gareth had done it, and Tanya had grabbed his face in her hands and given him a proper kiss, and as she held the kiss she let one hand lightly touch his ribs the way a woman touches a man when she's into him, and we can imagine what the immediately visible results would have been.

She didn't tell Gareth, that night, about the change in her marital status. She didn't tell him on Saturday either, although on that evening the two of them had gone back to holding hands openly before the curtain. And afterwards, after they'd changed back into their street clothes, she said to Gareth, "You want to go get a drink?"

Ah, to have been Gareth Rossa. To be that attractive, that talented – and above all, to have the degree of *cool* required to win a girl like Tanya. People who have it, don't need to imagine it. Those who don't have it, never could imagine it.

But one could imagine the outcome. One could imagine what it might have been like, and only wish to have been that cool, that attractive – cool and attractive enough to have experienced, himself, that one glorious night.

I can't. I can't bear to think of Gareth Rossa – or any other man who's younger, handsomer, studlier than I – doing it with Tanya. I can admit to myself intellectually that it happened. But imagine it, I can't. Or rather, I could imagine it all too vividly, if I were to let myself, so I'll do my best not to. I only wish I could imagine how I might have done it, if I'd been in that other man's situation.

So slowly, so gently. And maybe, the next morning, the first thing I'd have seen would have been the face of Tanya asleep, smiling the tiniest of sleep-smiles, and I would have never seen anything that moved me so, never seen any other face that I'd ever have described as perfect – perfect, in this case, even because of its flaws, rather than despite them – perfect, as I'd have described Tanya's face, at that moment.

I'd not have wanted to touch Tanya's face, then, for fear of waking her. So I would have just lain there, staring at her face as she slept.

16. Connor Sings the Blues

On the following Monday morning, Connor found an email from Jim Wainwright on his server:

Dear Connor:

Gail and I caught the last performance of the opera, yesterday. Not the kind of thing we like to do usually, but Gail thought it would be good to get exposed to a little culture, and I enjoyed it even if I'm not sure I understood what I was listening to, and even if I kind of dozed off here and there. But Tanya sure did a good job, so tell her congratulations from me and Gail. We didn't get a chance to greet her after the performance but she looked radiant. It's nice that she had a chance to do that. Now she can focus on you and on raising a family. I don't have her email, so please let her know Gail and I were impressed.

Connor emailed back:

I'd better give you Tanya's email so that you can congratulate her yourself.

It's titania_cucoshay@stateu.edu. She and I aren't in touch much right now. She moved out the other day. It's a very sad time for me and little Olivia.

It's a safe bet that Jim never did get in touch with Tanya. But he did immediately invite Connor to lunch, to make sure that Connor was okay, and to offer whatever help he could. They were to meet up at the Mainliner two days later – and Tanya had agreed to meet Connor for coffee at Starbucks the day before that.

She met him there, Tuesday afternoon, right at the appointed hour, and smiled at Connor and greeted him in the way she would have done for any casual acquaintance. She made no move to touch him, nor did Connor make to touch her. He couldn't smile; he looked kind of stunned, Tanya thought. Beyond "Hi," they exchanged not a word till they'd ordered, and sat down, across from each other at a table for two in the center of the seating area. At that point, Tanya just sat, looking at Connor, one eyebrow slightly cocked, her expression otherwise neutral, waiting for him to say something.

"Where are you?" Connor asked. "Where are you staying?"

"I'd rather not tell you. You've got my phone and email; if you need to send me anything I'd rather you did it through Dan and Sylvia. Did you drop my things off with them?"

"No, and I'm not comfortable doing that. It's only a couple boxes. If you want them, they're all ready; you can come get them. Bring a bodyguard if you think you need to."

Tanya shrugged.

"Is there someone else?" Connor asked.

Tanya paused and thought for a few seconds.

"There has been... someone... for a long time," she said, very slowly, as though thinking every word over. "A long time. If you want to know the truth, I'm not sure you're Livy's father. Now you know, and I don't care to talk about it."

Connor physically recoiled, as though he'd been slapped – but his mind started working on this. He had an excellent memory – people who are good with numbers often do – and going back to the months before Tanya got pregnant, he couldn't remember any indication that Tanya had been cheating on him. And she'd been so reluctant to be pregnant, and so angry and resentful, and so completely insane-acting, besides: Connor reasoned that she wouldn't have acted that way if there'd been another guy – especially if for all she knew she'd gotten pregnant by another guy. She wouldn't have been *that* kind of crazy, *that* kind of angry. Connor wouldn't have begun to imagine how differently she would have acted, if another man had been involved: He just had a strong sense that she would have behaved, somehow, *differently.*

And could she have been carrying on an affair during those awful last months of pregnancy? As for the few months after Livy's birth, Connor would've told himself, she was simply *not* having an affair then. No way.

Connor might've had a thought like this: "If she'd had another guy, back then, she wouldn't have been so crazy, because she could have talked to him... ." Could that have occurred to him? To do him justice, Connor wasn't utterly without a conscience. It wasn't highly developed, but he had one. So, maybe that thought came to him. But maybe it didn't.

More probably, he'd have simply conceded that he'd been fooled. He'd have said to himself, "Okay, so there was another guy, all this time. How could I not have seen it?" And maybe his next thought would have been that this proved his worst suspicions about Tanya: that she was, after all, a faithless, amoral, utterly selfish, *bad* person.

Whatever he was thinking, he sat silently for a while, and Tanya did the same. She sipped coffee and glanced now at him, now around the room. Maybe she thought she ought to say something but couldn't come up with anything. Or maybe she was just bored, uncomfortable, and wishful to leave.

"Are you going to be with… this guy?"

"I'm with someone, yes."

Connor looked down at his lap again.

"Connor, I'm sorry it didn't work out. But there isn't anything else to say. I'll listen if you want to say anything."

§

"I guess I should've seen it coming," Connor told Jim Wainwright over lunch the next day. "The signs were there. She just didn't love me anymore. We tried counseling, and I thought things were getting better. I thought I'd done my best to make her happy, but apparently it wasn't good enough."

"Maybe she's not telling you the whole truth about this other guy," Jim said. "Maybe it wasn't going on for that long. It could be somebody from that damn opera."

Connor racked his brain to try to recall what any of the other players looked like, besides Dan Wolf, who was married, so it couldn't be Dan. The guy who played the bullfighter? But he was so young; he looked younger than Connor himself, by a few years.

"I never suspected anything till she moved out," said Connor. "I always tried to think the best of her."

"That's what makes you a good person," said Jim. "You're always honest and straightforward, and you expect honesty from others, and it comes as a surprise when someone lies to you. It's so easy to cheat a guy like you."

Connor smiled a little.

"That's how I like to think of myself."

"So, are you okay as far as the legal stuff is concerned? Do you have a lawyer and all?"

"I guess I'll have to get one, but it doesn't look like it's going to be complicated. Tanya said she just wants out; she doesn't want alimony or support – and she doesn't want Livy at all. She told me that since I wanted her I could keep her."

"No!"

"Yeah, that's what I'll never forget. She said, 'You got everything out of this marriage you wanted, and now you've gotten rid of the part you didn't want, so don't feel so bad."

Jim sighed. "It's her loss," he told Connor. "If she didn't appreciate what she had… then I don't know what else to say. I sure can't understand a woman like that, but then you and I are never going to figure women out, are we?"

"I have to look at the bright side," said Connor after another pause. "At least I'm in control of the situation. It's not like she's fighting me about anything."

"You ought to make sure *she* pays child support," Jim suggested. "You won't get much from her now, not while she's a full-time student, but look at it long-term. She might turn out to be a big opera star, and then she can pull her weight. She brought that baby into the world."

Maybe Connor was decent enough to say to himself that he'd never ask that of Tanya, all things considered.

"For now, I have to try to put my life back together," he told Jim. "At least Tanya didn't throw me out of the house, and she didn't try to use Livy as a bargaining chip."

Connor sighed, and squared his shoulders as best a man can do when he's sitting on a padded banquette.

"I'll get past this. I'll keep building my business, and if I have to I'll hire someone to help me take care of Livy. I'll just do what I have to do; I'm not going to let this get me down."

"That's the spirit. Connor, you're a good man. I admire you. You're going through a bad patch that you don't deserve at all, but you're making the best of it. You've got courage. More than most people."

"I don't know about that," Connor said, looking resolute. "But, you know, there are things that you just have to *do*, if you want to call yourself a man."

"I'll see if Christine has time to do some baby-sitting," Jim said. "She's pretty busy with this and that, now, but maybe she has a friend who's dependable."

And that's how the news of Connor's marital breakup

passed from Jim to Gail and, inevitably, to their children.

And to Andy Palinkas. Andy had little interaction with Connor, although he was still Connor's client. They communicated via email, but hardly ever saw each other.

Andy and Jim usually saw each other at Noon Rotary on Thursdays, in the Marriott banquet room, but they seldom spoke there, beyond a quick greeting. Only rarely did they sit at the same table. Andy usually joined Teresa Blaha at what was unofficially known as the "landlords' table." Sometimes, instead, Andy sat at the "music table," where the regulars included the School of Music's oboe professor; the owner of the town's largest music store; and a woman who ran a Suzuki Method violin school. Other Rotarians who were interested in music sometimes joined them. Jim Wainwright usually sat across the room at the "doctors' table."

On this gloomy, rainy Thursday, as the meeting was breaking up, Jim came over to Andy and said, "Andy, I'm bringing Connor Lowe here next week. I think he needs to get out more – you know, he's stuck home all day – and if we can get him into Rotary, it might draw him out, you know? Might help him make some new friends. He's kind of lonely."

Andy inclined his head.

"So I was wondering if you could help me out," Jim continued. "Help me make him feel welcome here, I mean, and maybe encourage him to join. It'd be real good for him. You know, he's kind of like a second son to me and Gail."

"Sure."

"I don't know if he told you, but his wife just left him. Just up and left him. How do you like that?"

"Wow." Andy was astonished. Not by the news, but it surprised him to notice that he felt an odd emotional twinge at hearing this. "Is there a story behind it?"

"Well, Tanya was always a difficult girl," said Jim. "You could tell. I only met her at their wedding and once or twice after that, but people told me things, and you could tell from looking at her that she was used to having her way. A girl as pretty as that, she can usually write her own ticket. And she's pretty, I'll grant her that. I only ever heard her sing that once, at that damn opera the other night, but I hear she's talented; I'll take other people's word for that. Anyway, that's what she set her sights on: her career.

"We thought – or Connor thought – that once she'd had a baby it'd calm her down, and drive those feathers out of her head so she'd settle down and forget this music business. I mean, careers in music don't make sense for most people. I imagine you'd meet a lot of shallow, phony people, and they're into drugs, a lot of them…"

"But Tanya's more of a classical singer, I understand."

"Maybe. I don't know." Jim and Andy walked slowly from the dining room to the coat room. "But those people, too, they're off on their own clouds, you know, and they're not interested in the real world, they're not interested in things like family, the kind of things that most people get enjoyment out of. Oh, well, it takes all kinds, doesn't it? If that's what this girl wants to do for a career, God bless her, but you'd think she'd have told her husband about it before she married him."

Andy inclined his head again, and Jim sighed, as they put on their raincoats.

"I don't know," said Jim. "Maybe she wanted someone who would finance her graduate school for her. Sounds awfully calculating to me. Almost like she'd planned the whole thing all along, though you hate to think that of anybody."

Andy opened his eyes wide at this; Jim apparently took this as encouragement to continue.

"Apparently," said Jim, "she looked in the mirror and she saw a star. Connor tells me she found another guy. He said he'd had no idea. He asked her who the guy was, how she'd met him, and she wouldn't tell him, for whatever reason. It's too bad. They say you can't cheat an honest man, but I'm not so sure. If there was ever a square shooter, it's Connor – and boy, she did a number on him."

"Too bad," said Andy, as they left the building and walked down the front steps to the parking lot. "Connor's a decent guy."

"Yeah, you know, Gail and I always kind of hoped he'd end up marrying into our family. He and Melissa dated all through high school, on and off, and when they went to separate colleges Gail and I were kind of disappointed – but maybe it's all turning out for the best, now. You never can tell."

17. Melissa's Life and Loves

Melissa Wainwright didn't hear about the breakup at first-hand, and even if she had, it would've been Connor's version. As it was, that was the version she got, second-hand, first from Christine and then from her parents.

As far as Christine was concerned, the top news item was Gail's decision to find an occupation outside the home:

> Mom & Dad are talking about buying that gift shop How Precious so Mom will have something to do, and she's prolly gonna make me work there this summer. I can hardly wait, only SO NOT. Dave and Mercy are same as always. Connor and Tanya split. Dunno all the deets. Mom and Dad prolly do.

So Melissa called her mother, less than an hour after receiving that message, and that was how she heard as much of the story as Gail knew – plus some editorializing, no doubt.

Melissa was into her fourth year of teaching: her first year of teaching at Goodhearts, which was a liberal private school located in an upscale, mostly white suburb of Detroit.

She found Goodhearts an easier gig than Amos Fortune, although the pay was no better. But she had to admit she didn't enjoy it.

For one thing it was a long commute, and while she could have moved nearer the school, that would have meant moving farther from Leander. For another, she felt that she'd lost a lot of her knowledge and teaching skills, in three years at Amos Fortune, and she found it difficult to deal with academic-minded students who were looking for more of an intellectual challenge. When her mother asked her about her job, during this same phone conversation, Melissa had to admit that it wasn't going well.

"Some of the students were complaining to the principal that I'm too easy. Too easy! Like I didn't just come out of a situation where maybe 10 percent of my students could read. I don't even know if they'll hire me back next year, and I don't know that I want them to. It's not like I'm doing anybody any good, here. They all know it all already!"

"You know, Missie, I bet you'd find better jobs here in the State City area than the one you have now," said Gail. "You might want to send out some applications. Not just the State City district, but some of the smaller towns. I could ask around, and see where some school might need some help."

Gail didn't come out and ask, "Why not move back here now that Connor is available?" but that must have been in her head, because it wasn't more than a minute or so later before she'd brought the conversation round to that subject.

"Poor Connor," Gail said. "That crazy woman he married, and now he's a single father. I feel so sorry for him. You know, I always liked him back when the two of you were an item. I never said much about it at the time, because I know at that age kids never listen to their parents, but I was pretty sure he was going to grow up to be a terrific adult. It's nice to see one of my predictions come true, every once in a blue moon. Do you hear from him, at all?"

"No, nothing, since last summer."

"You might want to give him a call or an email, to let him know that people are thinking of him."

Melissa slept on this – probably she didn't want to intrude, and didn't want to give Connor any wrong ideas – but finally she did email him:

Dear Connor:

Just heard your news. I'm so sorry. Hope you're dealing with it okay. Let me know if there's anything I can do.

I don't know that there's anything you can do. Thank you for reaching out. It has been a pretty tough time for me and Livy. But we're making the best of it. I have to say I feel sorry for Tanya. She doesn't know what she's missing. Livy took her first steps yesterday, and any day now she'll be saying her first words, and learning a new word or two every day after that, and Tanya won't be around. It's sad for Livy, too. She'll grow up not knowing her mother, or practically not having a mother.

But I'm not going to bad-mouth Tanya. It's her loss. She thinks she knows what she wants, and whatever she wants it's not me or Livy. I wish her well.

It would be nice to stay in touch with you and hear how you're doing with your career and all. I'm sure you have a great way with the kids you're teaching. I hope when she's old enough for school, Livy will meet one or two teachers who can give her the same attention that I'm sure you pay your students. Who knows? Maybe by then you'll be teaching somewhere in the State City area, and when Livy's a teenager you'll inspire her to do great things.

Seriously, wherever you are, it would be nice if you could make friends with Livy, too. Like if you get back to State City every couple of years, you could look in on her and get to know her – so she could have a grown woman to look up to.

It would be great if Livy's mother were still a part

of her life, or would become a part of it once again, but we can't count on that. She found a new guy. I don't know much about that, yet, but I would be pretty sure it's some other musician. I understand it was going on for a long time without my ever suspecting anything. I have to get used to the fact that I can't trust someone I thought I could trust. That is what hurts the worst.

I'm glad that you and I are still friends; you are someone I can trust and I will always treasure that.

Connor, you know I'll always be there for you one way or another. You've always been one of my favorite people. You're going to have such fun watching Livy grow up, and I agree with you it's too bad that Tanya will miss out on it. But it is her life, her decision.

Here's what you need to know: it will get better. It won't always be easy to be a single parent but I know you're a great dad and you're going to bring up a great daughter, and that will be a source of happiness to you all your life.

I'm so flattered that you want me to be a part of Livy's life too, and of course I will be her friend, wherever my journeys take me. I don't know where I'll be teaching next year. I'm not sure I want to stay in teaching. It's rewarding in some ways and it's all I ever wanted to do, but it might be time now for me to take stock of my life.

Whatever happens you and I will always be friends.

It must be pointed out here that Melissa was still in a relationship with Leander – and Jim and Gail didn't know of the man's existence. And Leander's family didn't know about Melissa. When either set of parents asked whether there were someone serious in the picture, both Leander and Melissa were evasive. On the order of, "There's someone I like, but we're not involved." Or, "I'm dating; I don't want to commit myself to anybody right now."

It might have been that conversation with her mother

that made Melissa decide it was time to introduce her family to the man she was thinking of marrying. She and Leander had been together for more than two years, and while they hadn't discussed marriage at length, it's hard to imagine that the subject wasn't on their minds.

Both of them were afraid to bring up marriage, and children, in the same way that they were afraid to tell their families about this person they were involved with. Leander and Melissa had serious feelings for each other, there's no question of that. But were either of them thinking long-term? Were either of them interested in a life together?

At any rate, the same day she had that email exchange with Connor, Melissa phoned Leander and told him, "It's time for you to meet my family. I'm going down there for spring break, and you're coming with me." (Up till then, she hadn't been planning to go out of town for spring break, and it was only a week away.)

She could hear Leander's discomfort on the other end of the line; she knew him well enough to know his inflections.

"Baby, this is kind of sudden," he said. "Besides, you sure they'd be able to handle it?"

"We need to find out. And when we get back, we're going to see your folks too."

She could hear Leander exhaling.

"Where would we stay? At your parents?"

"They'd probably want us in separate rooms. I won't make a big thing about it. It'd just be for a couple of nights."

§

At the same time, late afternoon – unaware of this conversation – Gail Wainwright pulled into her driveway. She'd been downtown, talking with Teresa Blaha about her purchase of How Precious, the gift shop.

Gail didn't like Teresa any more than Teresa liked her. But if Gail bought this shop, Teresa would be her landlord, since Teresa owned the building that the gift shop was in. This meeting had been a conference about the terms of the lease that Gail would be assuming when she bought the store, and the discussion had been pretty routine, but Gail was feeling steamed, because she thought it was pretty mean of Teresa not to lower the rent for someone who was practically a relative. But, she reminded herself, Teresa probably didn't get rich by giving people breaks, and some people simply are like that.

Gail knew the Blahas looked down on the Wainwrights for not being as rich as they were. She also felt that her family had done the Blahas a big favor by making the Blahas' daughter part of *their* family. Mercy Blaha was such a sweet girl, and maybe the Wainwrights would be a good influence on her, so that she and David would bring up their own children without any materialism or hoity-toity ideas.

And speaking of children, as Gail got out of her Toyota Camry she spied her younger daughter, standing in Andy Palinkas' yard, chatting with Andy, and that was another reason to feel put out. Andy had never behaved inappropriately so far as Gail knew – but his friendship with Christine was an annoyance. It gave Gail, and Jim, one more thing to worry about, because you never knew when an older man like that *might* try something.

Plus, we can be pretty sure that Jim and Gail both resented Andy for being someone with whom their daughter had such an easy relationship. It's common for parents to be unsettled when a child of theirs develops, with an adult, a friendship that might be more confidential than that child's relationship with her own parents. It can make the parents look bad in their own minds.

Finally, seeing Christine and Andy together would have been a constant reminder that Andy had saved Christine's life, long ago, and that if Christine had died it would have been due to Jim and Gail's negligence – and Jim and Gail knew that Andy knew this.

But Gail put on a cheerful face, as she got out of her

car. "You two!" she called to Christine and Andy, "Solving the world's problems!"

"Christine's telling me about her voice lessons," Andy replied. "Sounds like she'll surpass her teacher before long."

"We can only hope." Gail didn't sound enthusiastic.

Once Gail was in her house, Christine went on with what she and Andy had actually been discussing.

"So Missie'll be here Saturday, and *j'ai demandé* last night, *est-ce que cet homme est noir*, and she said 'Yeah but don't tell Mom and Dad whatever you do because I still have to figure out how I'm going to tell them myself.'"

"*Elle doit leur l'annoncer*," said Andy. "She should tell them. She doesn't want to just let them be surprised when they pick her and Leander up at the airport. I mean, that wouldn't be quite *comme il faut*. I were her, I'd email them and tell them, 'Look, just so you won't be shocked, this guy's black.' That way they'll have a few days to get used to it."

"I think she's afraid they'll say he can't come, if they know before he gets here. I don't think they would. They're not racist. I mean, no more than anybody."

§

Jim and Gail gave Leander their full hospitality. They were open and friendly; they did their best to make him feel at home; they both seemed to like him. They might not have been pleased if Melissa had married Leander, but who knows? At any rate they didn't bring that subject up, nor did Melissa. Shortly after Melissa returned to Detroit, her father sent her a rather detailed email, in which he gave her contact information for the State City Community School District and several neighboring districts, and suggested that the leaven had been cast, in the form of good words having been put in, here and there.

Jim also made Melissa what he considered a pretty generous offer.

If you want a career in education, you pretty much have to have a Master's degree. I suppose you could work on one at some school in Detroit, but is there a good one that you would want to go to? If you had a job down here, you could get a Master's from State University, which we all know is a good school. Come down here, work on your degree, and Mommy and I will pay your tuition. Whether you find a job here or not, only I'm pretty sure you will.

You might even ask your young man if he'd like to live in Iowa. It would be a way of finding out how serious he is about you. And even if he's not ready to pull up stakes yet, maybe a year or two of not being in the same town will be a good test for the relationship.

This offer might not have worked, except that when she got the email, Melissa had only just been introduced to Leander's parents. She'd hoped, and expected, that Leander would have brought her to the family home – they lived in Detroit – and she was more than slightly troubled when Leander arranged a meal at a nice restaurant, with Melissa as his date.

"My mother's not a cook," Leander had explained. "You might enjoy her society, but not the cuisine. And she wouldn't be too pleased if I expected her to whip up a meal for company."

And Melissa had to admit that she was taken aback, since she'd assumed that all black mothers like to cook for company – which Leander apparently divined, because he laughed and said, "My experience of down-home cooking did not emanate from my mother's kitchen."

So, Leander had taken them all to a Sunday brunch. And while the Washingtons hadn't been exactly unfriendly, Melissa sensed that they weren't comfortable with her. Leander's father, a manager at the Ford plant, was gruff and almost monosyllabic. Leander's mother was also a schoolteacher, and she wanted mostly to talk about the philosophies and techniques of education. She used a lot of esoteric terms that

Melissa suspected she was trotting out on purpose to test Melissa's intellect and erudition.

Sure enough, when Melissa had worked up the nerve, after the encounter, to say to Leander that she didn't think his parents had liked her, Leander just said, "I'm sure they'll be fine. They just need to get used to you, like they'd need to get used to anybody."

Thus, while Leander and Melissa continued to see each other, Melissa started to wonder whether she could ever bring herself to marry him. She had the impression that Leander kind of did want to marry her – but she didn't want to pressure him by asking him to declare his intentions, and she wasn't sure she wanted him to. She wasn't going to propose to him; she wasn't going to push him. If it were meant to be, it would happen.

And thus Melissa decided not to renew her contract at Goodhearts – she hadn't been sure she'd be asked back, anyway – and she announced to Leander that she was moving back to State City and taking this opportunity to get a Master's degree for free.

"I can understand that," said Leander. "You don't like it here. Sometimes I don't like it here either."

That remark heartened Melissa, and she said, "We'll still see each other. I'll have my own place and you can come down whenever you want to, and I'll still come up here."

On the one hand, there's a good chance that Melissa wanted to keep her relationship with Leander alive – or part of her wanted to. But almost certainly, part of her was convinced it wouldn't work, couldn't work. She saw her father's generous offer as an opportunity not only to further her career, but to ease her way out of a relationship that had no future.

With regard to the race issue: Who can say what her feelings would have been, about having black babies? Maybe she didn't have a big problem with that. And maybe she truly wasn't worried about her parents' attitude. How can we be sure that Jim and Gail wouldn't have been okay with it, even if they'd had misgivings? Probably Leander's parents would have accepted half-breed grandchildren, too, but what they thought of Melissa might have been another story. Melissa never did know exactly what they'd said to Leander about her, if they'd said anything. The most she ever got out of him on that subject was, "They liked you fine." But Melissa doubted this.

Another matter that was weighing on Melissa's mind was that she still thought, sometimes, about a career as a scholar – and maybe as an author – rather than as a school-teacher. This would be an opportunity to continue her studies of English literature – and maybe go on to a doctorate, and a career at a college or university. There might even be a novel or two in her future after all.

So, Melissa moved back to State City. She'd sent out job applications in advance. She had some interviews set up, although she'd been warned that it was too late to count on finding a permanent position for the coming fall.

Dear Mr. P,

It's kinda weird, having my 26 year old sis back home living w/us, but I guess it's just for a while till she gets a job and her own place. She's going on interviews but she's saying it doesn't look too good at least for this year and she prolly will have to be a substitute teacher and find some other kind of job. And prolly she misses her BF but otherwise she says she's glad to be out of Detroit. You know what's funny? Maman et Papa are pretending to be suttal but they really want Missie to get with her old high school BF again for some reason. I don't get it cuz I never thought he was all that. Anyway he's married to my voice teacher or was. I guess they're getting a divorce now. And Maman et Papa are like, a few days ago before Missie got here, Mom was like, "Would it be a good idea to find some way to invite Connor over?" and Dad was like, "We can't throw them together cuz we don't know how serious she is about this Leander – but she can't be all that serious, if she's gonna move back here. Can she?"

That's what Dad said. I think it's kinda funny.

Dear Miss Christine:

     I think the word you want is "subtle." The B is silent. I'll tell you what, though: Distance kills relationships. Kills 'em dead. That might have been on your folks' minds when they persuaded your sister to move back here. I'm only speculating.

     Say, I am re-considering the idea of taking voice lessons. I'm too old to get good at a musical instrument, but I would think that a person can learn to sing (at least somewhat) at any age. And now that I'm back into theatre, it would broaden my acting capabilities if I learned to sing. Do you think your teacher might be able to take on another student?

Dear Mr. P,

     You are a crazy old man! :-D
     At any rate you're not SUBTLE.
     She's got a BF. So I hear. Do you know her?

Dear Miss Christine:

     Please! I'm old enough to be her father, ain't I? So, no, I'm not going to date her, good heavens. I was just curious; didn't mean to suggest anything else. I only know her from kissing her hand at that wedding. I've heard her sing. I've admired her from a distance. Don't know much else about her; Connor never mentions her to me, not that he and I are all that intimate.

Dear Mr. P,

     Yeahright. ;-)
     titania_cucoshay@stateu.edu.

And it was right around then – that same week, in fact – that Jim Wainwright, in the course of doing business with Connor, remarked that his home had recently become a little livelier, what with Melissa having moved back to town.

     "You think she'd like to see me?" Connor asked.

"You'd have to ask her. But I'm sure she would."

So Connor emailed Melissa and asked if she'd like to meet up for lunch.

Nobody had told Connor that Melissa still had a boyfriend back in Detroit; all he knew was that she was back in State City for at least a couple of years. So Connor took her to the Welcome Inn. He didn't want to make it too obvious that he was courting her, so he didn't take her to one of the fancy places downtown. The Welcome Inn is located just off the Interstate: one of those family-type places with the brightly colored booths, and lots of noisy kids and extremely fat adults, and garish photographs of food on the menu. It could be that by bringing her to this place, Connor was trying to trip little triggers in Melissa's mind about having kids herself one day and dining *en famille* at a place like this.

After that, Connor took Melissa back to his house – which now sheltered only him and little Olivia – and showed her how carefully he'd baby-proofed the whole house, and kept lots of baby toys in his office, so that Livy would want to be with him while he was working.

Melissa told this to Christine, when Connor had run her home and the three of them (plus Livy) were sitting in the Wainwrights' kitchen, having coffee, later that afternoon. And Christine subsequently told it to Andy.

...and Missie was telling me all this like it was just the most wonderful thing in the world and I dunno if she was just trying to flatter Connor since he was sitting right there, or maybe it just didn't take much to impress her. Connor was trying to look all modest and I came thisclose to asking him if he wanted a medal or a chest to pin it on.

Anyway after Connor left I asked Missie if she told Connor about her Detroit BF, and she's like "We were so glad to see each other. I didn't want to tell him anything that might make him feel bad."

So I asked her if Connor was still into her but I

know he is so I was just saying that to get her to say something, and she was like, "It kinda looks that way. But I'm not giving him any encouragement."

That's what she told me. I dunno if she still sees anything in him or not. It sounds like it was kinda weird how Tanya dumped him. Tanya doesn't discuss it with me a lot, but from what I gather she was unhappy with Connor once they got married and she was always suspicious that he still had a thing for Missie, and now it turns out maybe she was right, right? But it's none of my beeswax. And if Missie is not into him she oughta tell him about her boy in Detroit maybe, but that's just me and what do I know? Maybe it's more fun to keep Connor on a string just in case. I dunno what's in her head.

And guess what? Tanya is telling me maybe I need to work with some other teacher, or I will need to pretty soon. She says she loves teaching me but she isn't sure she's gonna be able to work with me on the level that she wants me to go to. She says if I work real hard I could be a major opera star, she says I definately have the voice and now I hafta develop it and she says she'll work with me till she's taught me all she can teach me and she says then I should work with one of the faculty here at State U. That's kinda scary but it's great that she wants me to get good.

And have you gotten in touch w/Tanya yet?

Oh before I forget, I tested into French 2 for this fall. That's thanks to you. I reeeely appreciate que vous parlez français avec moi. Merci pour votre assistance.

18. Gail Wainwright's Foray into Retail

In summer of 2006, Jim and Gail Wainwright finalized the purchase of that downtown gift shop, How Precious. Gail had been insisting, for years, that she felt she'd been deprived of a career, having been a *Hausfrau* all of her adult life. Like Melissa, she'd gone into college as an English major, with a view to teaching, but the only post-graduate degree she'd ever gotten was the "Mrs." She and Jim had agreed there was no need for her to work full-time, as long as he was making good money, and after all it was right for the mother to take care of the kids. So Gail had taken part-time, temporary clerical jobs here and there over the years, and had gotten involved with the local Democratic Party during every election cycle – she was a precinct committeewoman, and had even been the vice-chair of the State County Democrats a couple of times – but none of that had really been a career.

Gail had been planning to start following some new vocation as soon as her two children were grown and out of the nest – but then, Christine had come along, and that had delayed Gail's self-realization by several more years.

Betty Friedan, in her classic book, *The Feminine Mystique*, wrote of the housewife who, "As she made the beds, shopped for groceries, matched slipcover material, ate peanut butter sandwiches with her children, chauffeured Cub Scouts and Brownies, lay beside her husband at night… was afraid to ask even of herself the silent question, 'is this all?'" There was more to Gail Wainwright's life than that – in all, she was an active person – but even if she never put it into Friedan's words, she did have those feelings, and more than just now and then.

Jim at first suggested that Gail might start with volunteering – like at a hospital or in a nursing home, or at the public library – but Gail said, "I want something where I'm making something of myself somehow."

"You mean achieving something?"

"I guess. Making money, accomplishing something…"

"We have enough money."

"Well, doing *something*, then. And I don't mean volunteering. I mean, oh, how can I describe it?"

"Something with measurable results?"

"I guess," Gail repeated. "A business maybe. It's too late to go back to college and be a professor or whatever."

Jim and Gail had brainstormed, and discussed possibilities, on and off for several days. Jim had even – without telling Gail he'd done it – spoken with Teresa Blaha at Rotary Club and asked Teresa if she had any ideas, since she was a career woman of Gail's age. Teresa, too, had suggested volunteer work, but Jim explained that that was okay in its place but it wasn't a career.

"I was about to recommend Big Sisters," said Teresa. "But you're right, that's not a career."

"She's got enough trouble with one teenager."

"She might want to start a business that would employ people," Teresa suggested. "That way she can have a career and help other people at the same time. Assuming she knows how to be a boss, which isn't an easy job, believe you me."

"I'm sure she could pick it up," Jim said. And Teresa – once she could recount this conversation privately to Andy Palinkas – rolled her eyes heavenward.

Long story short, the elderly couple that had owned How Precious for many years was looking to sell out and retire, and Jim and Gail took the opportunity. Gail, they figured, would own and manage the store, and she'd hire an assistant manager whom she could groom to take over full management if Gail ever became disenchanted with being on the sales floor.

"We can give Christine some part-time work there too, at least in the summer," Gail had said to Jim when they were in the early stages of deciding to buy the store. "She's at an age where it's best if she doesn't have too much time to herself."

Christine was less than enthusiastic, even when it was pointed out to her that most high-school kids had to work – for spending money and to save up for college. She would have preferred to spend her summer vacation putting more effort into her music, and having fun, which she figured was what the teenage years were for.

Dear Mr. P,

Prolly you've heard I'm getting the "opportunity" to work for Mom. She says she wants to do something "fulfilling." I think she did this to keep me busy with shit I don't want to do, so I won't get too good at music or have S-E-X.

I didn't ask 2B born. Of course I know better than to say that to Les Parents. Or I should say Aux Parents. Last time I tried it I got grounded. So it looks like Li'l Chrissy is gonna have to suck it up and be a store clerk for a while. Prolly that is gonna cut into my music too but I'm pretty sure that as far as Les Parents are concerned that is Bonus. That way there's less chance I might be a real musician. I hate my life.

Dear Miss Christine,

It's a drag, I'll admit. Life is unfair and that's all there is to it. I'd love it if I didn't have to work. I would turn goofing off into an art form. However, this is a situation that you might have to accept, whether you like it or not. It's absolutely true that you didn't ask to be born, and the reason that parents get exasperated, when you bring that fact to their attention, is that they have no answer to it. I'll be bound you weren't the first kid to get grounded for saying that, nor will you be the last.

This probably won't be comforting advice for you, but I'll say it anyway: I've been in retail since I was 18, and it's not always the most fun job in the world, but it does teach you a lot, about a lot of things.

Mostly, it teaches you about people and how to get along with them. I have to tell you, when I was a teenager I was not a nice guy. Some people still think I'm disagreeable, but I promise you I'm less bad than I was when I was 18. I don't mean to suggest that you have any issues with your personality. I think you're an extremely nice girl and I'm sure you know that. But there's nobody in the world who couldn't stand to improve their "people skills," and working in that shop will probably be one of the best learning experiences you'll ever have.

Sorry if I sound like I'm preaching; I'm trying to find the silver lining. I promise you it won't be a totally bad experience, and in the long run you won't be sorry you did it.

Retail is something I know a lot about, so if you ever have any questions on that subject, you know where to find me. And tell your mother the same goes for her.

Christine's employment at How Precious turned out to be less of an inconvenience than she'd feared. The store didn't get as much traffic as her mother had hoped, so Christine didn't have the opportunity to develop her people skills as Andy had predicted, but she was getting paid for doing almost nothing, the way she saw it, and that was better than doing nothing for free. She was working hard on her singing, still taking lessons with Tanya and practicing as she found time to. Once school had started, Christine only put in a few hours per week at How Precious, after school and on weekends – but that was more onerous than in the summer, when she'd been working more hours but still had some time to herself. That fall, Christine hardly ever had the chance to work on her music.

And Christine was not the only staffer at How Precious who didn't seem to want to be there.

Dear Mr. P,

This is a case of "be careful what you wish for." Mom bought the store to get out of the house and be around people – tho I still think it was partly to make work for me – but she doesn't seem to like people much. Not in the store anyway. When I'm out front I see Mom being snippy to a customer now and then. Like once I even heard her say "Did you want to buy something?" in a kind of bitchy voice, and I wonder if she does that a lot, and people aren't gonna wanna shop there if she's like that. Whenever I'm out front I try to be extra friendly to the customers and once I caught Mom glaring at me like she was mad at me. Like she thought I was trying to make her look bad.

And then there was Dana Terwilliger, who was 20 or so, attended State City Community College, and worked part-time at How Precious. Dana was taking business courses, at Gail's suggestion, so that she would be in a position to take over management of the store in a couple of years – and ownership, if Gail ever decided to sell out. But Dana didn't seem to like her job either. She would be pleasant enough to customers – no worse than Gail, anyway – but she hardly ever had a word to say to Christine aside from what was necessary.

Dear Mr. P,

I dunno what to make of this. OK, I told you how there's a girl that Mom is "mentoring" and is going to sell her the store to her one day? Problem is, I see her lifting stuff. I see her slipping it into her bag and taking it.

So I knew I hadda do something, Mom's getting ripped off, right? And if she's getting ripped off that's our family's money too, right? But I didn't wanna rat her out to Mom cuz I know Mom hates any kind of conflict and she'd prolly be madder at me than she would be at Dana, cuz I told her something she didn't wanna hear, nahmean?

So what I did was I asked Dana, in private, "can we talk?" This was this morning and she was surprised that I wanted to talk to her cuz it's not like we're friends or anything.

So I tell her I have a problem or rather a friend of mine has a problem. See this friend of mine, she works in a store and she sees that some of the other associates are stealing stuff, and she doesn't wanna get anybody in trouble but just wants it to stop, nahmean?

And Dana just looks at me for a second and then she says real slow, "you better tell your friend that she's gonna get hurt pretty bad if she doesn't mind her own business."

So tonight at home I told Mom and Dad. I didn't want to cuz I knew it would bug Mom but I'm being threatened, right? By a big girl who could beat the shit out of me. So I told them the whole story at dinner. About the stealing and what I said to Dana and the threats. and you know what Mom said to me? She said, "Christine, are you sure that really happened?"

I about shit. Woodent you have about shit?

Course I kinda knew Mom woodent believe me. She's gotta believe that Dana is a good person deep down and all that, so of course she's not gonna believe me, but I still couldn't believe she didn't believe me. Anyway I got kinda upset and yelled at her that IT REALLY HAPPENED and Dad said stop shouting at your mother Christine in that way he uses when he's really mad, and I don't know what to do and he says apologize to your mother for shouting at her and at that point I got up and left the table before I called them both fuck-pigs or something.

Now its 2 hrs later and I dunno what I'm gonna do.

Dear Miss Christine:

I am appalled. I have a good mind to walk over to your house right now and knock on your door and tell your parents what you just told me, and give them a piece of my mind. I know you'd not want me to do that because you believe (correctly in my opinion) that your parents would be upset if they knew that you and I were corresponding. I don't know what else I could do, but I feel that I must do something if they won't.

Are they still up, right now? Could you walk up to one or both of them and in a calm voice tell them that you must be heard on this issue? I mean, tell them that you were indeed threatened, that Dana is indeed a thief, and that you resent your mother not taking your story seriously? Can you risk that? Please consider it, and then write me back later to tell me what you've done. If that doesn't work, I'll try to think of something else.

Dear Mr. P,

OK I tried it. they were watching tv in the den and I waited for a commercial and then I walked in and said "Mom and Dad we need to talk now."

And dad gave me this fish-look and said, "Are you going to apologize to your mother?" and not losing my shit right there was the hardest thing Ive ever done in my life (sorry about the typos but im reeeeeeely upset right now) and I said thats not important, what is important is that Dana is stealing from you and she threatened me, and Mom how can you call me a liar?

I still cant believe I waznt screaming my hed off at her and I cant belive I didn't hit them or anything cuz I wanted to.

I guess then they could see I was way upset cuz dad didn't say anything and then Mom said "Christine I didn't mean you were lying I just meant there must have been a misunderstanding."

so then I said OK so what are you gonna do about it and Mom said I hafta think about it but Christine are you sure she didn't think you really were talking about some friend of yours and she was just warning you that your friend might get hurt if she said anything?

I said "not the way Dana was looking at me, I knew she knew I meant her."

And Mom said, "I'm sure she didn't mean to threaten you. She wouldn't do that."

And I was just kind of working my jaw cuz I coudnt think of anything to say and I coudnt get a sound to come out of my mouth, and then Dad said "Christine, let your mother handle it."

And I would except I know Mom doesn't like scenes and I cant be sure that she will say anything to Dana about it and meanwhile I have to work there in the store with someone who is going to beat me up if I look at her funny.

Pleeze don't say anything to Les Parents.

Christine wasn't scheduled to work the next day. At dinner that evening, Christine, in as even a tone as she could muster, asked her mother if she'd spoken to Dana.

Gail apparently couldn't bring herself to lie outright; instead she looked away from Christine and said, "Honey, I don't see the point in making a big to-do over this. I'm one hundred percent sure it was a misunderstanding. The way you described the conversation, it must have been. I can't think of any other explanation. And I haven't noticed any merchandise missing."

"That's because you never do inventory." Christine's voice rose a trifle. "I *saw* her slipping stuff into her bag!"

"She's buying the store eventually," said Gail. "She's only stealing from herself."

"Dear, that doesn't quite make sense," said Jim.

"Oh..." sighed Gail, "*Well*... I suppose I'll have to check to see if there's anything missing."

"Meanwhile she *threatened* me," Christine insisted.

Gail sighed again. "If you say so. But come on, Christine, what could she do to you? Just stay out of her way."

"Would *you* want to work in a situation like that?" Christine demanded.

"Nobody's forcing you to," said Gail. "We thought it would be a chance for you to earn a little money and get some experience. If you don't think you're getting anything out of it, you don't have to."

§

When Andy heard about this last conversation, he decided he would have to confront Gail, as tactfully as he could. He advised Christine to keep working at the store and avoid Dana, for the time being, and he waited for an opportunity to speak with Gail when they were both outdoors at the same time. On a Sunday afternoon he spotted Gail in her front yard, deadheading the last of the year's roses, so he came outside and pretended to be picking up debris in his own yard.

"How's the store going?" he called over. He was hoping that Gail would immediately pour out her troubles, but she only replied, "Fine, no complaints," without stopping her pruning. Andy had to persist. He walked over to her.

"By the way, I was talking shop with Christine the other day, and she said you were having some trouble with an employee. Sticky fingers and all that. Christine said you were bending over backwards to give this girl a break, and she said you were just too nice a person to let her go. And that's great. It's great that you're so good to your employees. But I know you haven't been in the business long, so I'll give you some free advice. One bad employee like that can ruin you. It might take her a while – but believe me, she can do a lot of damage."

Gail kept looking at her rosebushes, not acknowledging.

"I've had to let employees go now and then, and it never gets any easier," Andy went on. "It's no reflection on you. Even if it does make you feel like a louse when you fire someone. You have to remember it's their fault, not yours."

Then he stood there, next to Gail, so that she would almost be forced to respond somehow. A few seconds later, Gail sighed as a way of preparing to speak.

"It's complicated. It would be hard for me to fire this girl and find someone else and train her and all. I suppose I could tell her that I'm concerned about her performance – and just warn her that I'm keeping my eye on her."

"You know best," said Andy. "But Christine was upset."

Gail did start keeping a sharper eye on Dana, and checking inventory, and couldn't help noticing that Christine had been right about missing merchandise. She could not bring herself to flat-out accuse Dana of stealing, but she did take Dana aside and give her some earnest mentoring about the importance of keeping an accurate inventory and not letting merchandise disappear. Shrinkage cut into profits, she reminded Dana, and "we all need to be more careful and keep accurate records of sales – and watch out for shoplifters."

The shrinkage stopped, and Dana never repeated her threat to Christine – but Christine would report to her mother that Dana gave her looks that scared the daylights out of her.

"Christine, I can't fire her for the expression on her face," Gail exclaimed. "The two of you are going to have to work things out for yourselves. I just cannot handle a situation where my employees are constantly bickering."

Christine reported this exchange to Andy Palinkas. Andy emailed Connor Lowe, swore him to secrecy, and asked him to do a little number-crunching. When he had the figures in hand, a couple of days later, Andy walked into How Precious, during a slow time of the day, and made Gail an offer.

"The giftware business isn't my bag," he explained, "but I've thought of another use for this store. One that might be more profitable eventually. This would be a good opportunity for both of us, if you want to get out of this investment."

The negotiations didn't take long. Andy offered to buy Gail out for what he believed the concern was worth. Gail held out for a price that was closer to what she considered fair.

Andy encouraged her to shop around for a better offer – and either she did or she didn't, but one way or the other she did finally agree to sell for what Andy was willing to pay. She didn't look pleased, when they met up to sign the papers.

Dear Miss Christine:

When I take possession of How Precious, you'll still have a job if you want it. However, How Precious is not going to be a gift shop for long. The first thing I'll do is let Dana go. The second thing I'll do is to hold a nice big going-out-of-business sale. The third thing I'll do is convert the store into a branch of Rosen's. It'll be Rosen's wedding and formalwear store. I'll call it Rosen's Silhouettes. At first it'll offer men's formalwear and ready-made wedding gowns, but I'll offer custom-made bridalwear as soon as I can find a dressmaker. Meanwhile I've found a candidate to manage the store and handle alterations. You might know her. Beverly Norton. She's a friend of Connor, who recommended her to me, so your sister might know her too. She's a seamstress and very nice and I'm sure you'll find her easy to work with. I'm telling you this now because I want you to study up on formalwear for men, and bridal attire.

Dear Mr. P,

It looks like I can't work for you. Mom said she's mad at you for not giving her a better deal on the store and she said she wondered why you would want me to work for you. She also asked me if you had ever "touched me" when the band was playing in your garage or any other time. I told her you never did but that's the way her mind works. Anyway she said I hafta wait till I turn 16 to look for another job cuz apparently it was legal to work for a family biz when I was underage but its not legal for me to work for anyone else. And I don't turn 16 till next year.

Im sorry cuz I wanted to work for you. It would have been fun. And you know what else? Mom is partly mad at you cuz you embarrassed her. U know, making her face the fact that she's not cut out to own a biz, and besides, now U know that she's not good at it. Course she is mad at me too, for telling you anything. I know you thought you hadda say something to her and in a way Im glad you did but it sucks. Hard to explain.

One silver lining you might say. I didn't make enuf money from the store to even pay for a week of college, so Mom I guess kinda made me a peace offer. I hate hate that kiddie twin bed and white dresser that Ive had since I was 3, so she's gonna drive me around to some of the junk shops where maybe I can find a bigger bed that I can roll around in, and a big dresser that will actually hold my clothes and I think there will be enuf room for a little desk so I can have a flat surface for my computer IN MY FREAKIN BEDROOM for a change. If we can get it hauled for cheap.

IV. DAVID WAINWRIGHT
AND MERCY BLAHA

19. The Long Courtship of David and Mercy

The story of how David Wainwright and Mercy Blaha came to be married and start a family has become a living, breathing document, of which a great many versions exist. As with the other story lines in this saga, the version reported here is pieced together from many accounts.

David and Mercy met in college – not at State University, although they'd both grown up in State City, but at the University of Des Moines. UDM is Iowa's second-biggest university, also state-owned. It started out as an agricultural and mechanical college, in the 19th century, but evolved over the years to become a somewhat posher, slightly more academically prestigious school than State. UDM is best known for its School of Journalism, its Political Science department, and its College of Law. David and Mercy started dating casually during their junior year there, and more seriously in their senior year.

David Wainwright had been dainty-looking, as a boy. Once he'd reached adolescence he'd developed to about five-ten, and lanky, with a coif of wavy brown hair over his forehead and large, long-lashed blue eyes. His nose was small and straight, and chiseled at the nostrils. When he smiled, it was more of a dimpling. Ordinarily, his face took on a rather dreamy aspect, as though he were some distance away from the situation or conversation, perhaps composing a poem or a sketch. This gave him an air of serenity that many girls found attractive, although some found it indicative of pomposity.

He had friends, as many of them as a young man in his time and place might have been expected to have. Some of the girls thought he was a romantic. When he courted a girl, he had a way of alternating between a tender attentiveness, and dismissiveness, so that the girl didn't quite know where to have him. He had an intensity of manner, an effusiveness, an exuberance, a *joie de vivre*, that to some observers appeared self-conscious: as though a person who was not naturally effusive and exuberant were acting the way he supposed an effusive and exuberant person would act.

"Airy," was the way one acquaintance described his usual behavior. "Studied," said another.

This isn't to say he was insincere. Maybe his emotions were genuine but it was his nature to express them puffily.

"I want to be a citizen of the world," he wrote to a high school sweetheart, when he was just turned 18. "I want to explore every corner of this world. I want to gain the compassion of Albert Schweitzer, the kindness of Ghandi [sic] and the knowledge of the Buhda [sic]. I want to become an enlightened person, and share my enlightenment with the world as I travel through it. I know it will be a long journey but I am determined to get there or cherish the journey for its own sake!"

This was the awkward emotionalism that David Wainwright brought to many social situations, and to his writing.

One can understand, if not completely excuse, Teresa Blaha's perfectionistic attitude toward her daughter. Mercy was her only child, preceded and followed by several miscarriages. Teresa's doctors finally had to tell her that it was highly unlikely she'd ever carry another child to term – and that she might endanger her own life if she kept trying.

Even in childhood, Mercy Blaha felt that her mother thought of her as a status symbol to be shown off to the public. Maybe Teresa did think that way, but if she did, it's hard to blame her. Mercy was nearly perfect from infancy on. When she was a girl with white-blonde hair, her mother would habitually dress her in slightly nicer clothes than the other little girls wore – white, or of the lightest pastel shades – and remind her not to get them dirty. Mercy seldom did get them dirty. She played with other children, and got along with her peers, but at a slight remove.

"She was untouchable," one childhood playmate remembered, years later. "Very nice, very sweet, but untouchable. You never felt you knew her, the way you could know other children you played with. She would smile and laugh sometimes, but she was so serious. Not gloomy-serious, but always adult-acting.

"I had the impression her parents had terribly high expectations of her. Her mother especially. They set high standards and she was supposed to meet them without question. And she almost always did. It seemed like she never even considered not being as perfect as she could be. And frankly, I wish more parents would be like that. Including mine."

The Blahas lived on the northeast side of State City, and the Wainwrights on the southeast, and Mercy attended Visitation High, so she and David never met till they were in college, at UDM. David almost certainly would have admired Mercy from childhood, had he known her. Mercy was always the prettiest girl in the room, the best-behaved, and usually the smartest – or at any rate the highest-achieving student.

Her white-blonde hair turned golden as she got older, and Mercy wore it in a bob that set off her large blue eyes and full lips, which usually turned up the least bit at the corners so that she seemed to be smiling with private amusement, a little teasingly, knowingly. She was always pleasant and gracious, but not outgoing. She had a small circle of girlfriends. As a teen-ager, she was part of the student government or "preppie" clique. She was on the Student Council every year of high school, played flute and piano, and acted in Drama Club.

Mercy had boys interested in her, from an early age, but she was hard for them to approach, and in any case she considered almost all the boys her age well behind her in terms of maturity. It wasn't till the summer before her sophomore year of college that she started keeping any kind of company with a boy: Michael Staley, five years older than she was, newly hired by her father as Chief Marketing Officer for the Blaha Jewelers chain. Mercy and Michael met at a party at the Blahas' home – an open house for Ted's employees – and they ended up spending a lot of time together that summer.

This young man came from a well-to-do family in Cedar Rapids, and was fresh out of State University College of Business with an M.B.A. He was exceptionally good-looking, with wavy dark hair in contrast to Mercy's straight blondeness.

During her sophomore year, Mercy saw Michael whenever she was home in State City for vacation, and he'd sometimes come to Des Moines to visit her – and during the following summer, they were almost inseparable.

Michael never did propose to Mercy, during this time, but by the end of her sophomore year the subject of marriage was coming up. Michael would work "when we're married" into their conversations, now and then, like "After we've been married a few years we can do such-and-such," or "It'll be fun to do some traveling once we're married," and so on. Mercy never objected. It was taken for granted that they'd get married – or at least Michael took it for granted. By that summer, even Mercy's mother was making "when you two are married" remarks. Just from time to time, and in a jocular way, but enough to reinforce Michael's conviction that it would happen. Mercy never said a word in contradiction.

Back in Des Moines, in the fall semester of her junior year, Mercy met David Wainwright for the first time, in a sociology class. There must have been some immediate chemistry, because while they didn't become intimate friends right away, they would sit near each other in class, and talk, and sometimes have coffee together. David was the sort who wore his heart on his sleeve, so Mercy knew he was attracted to her. And that was why she made a point of hinting to David that she had a "home-town honey," back in State City – a serious one with a good job, at that.

This made David resentful, although he kept that feeling to himself. So this guy had an M.B.A. and a nice job, he may have thought. Big whoop. There's more to life than making money, and if this girl was too shallow to realize that, it was her loss.

But David didn't think Mercy was so shallow. He found her pretty bright. And to hear her talk, she wasn't especially interested in money. She was studying nursing, she told him, and sociology, and she thought she might put off her career for a couple of years, to join the Peace Corps after college.

"That is, if I don't get married," she added. "Or I might do the Peace Corps thing even then."

This didn't sound good to David. Talking about marriage, so early in life. It's not like this is the 1960s, he said to himself, when everybody got married as young as they could and then got divorced later. But he supposed that people his and Mercy's age still thought about it, still talked about it, still had people they suspected they might marry eventually. David assumed that that was pretty normal. He bided his time, and enjoyed Mercy's company as often as he could get it. And he thought of her quite a lot when he wasn't with her. He had a pretty bad crush, although he tried not to be obvious. He wasn't dating anyone else.

Mercy came back to school from Thanksgiving vacation, in that fall of 1997, wearing the diamond solitaire that Michael Staley had given her in the presence of her parents. Seeing Mercy with that rock on her finger – it was a big one, probably two carats, although David wouldn't have known that – was one of the worst kicks in the guts David had ever experienced.

He pretended not to see the ring. He didn't comment on it; not by word or gesture did he acknowledge its existence. Maybe he thought if he ignored it long enough, it might go away of its own accord. Or he was bright enough to know that there was nothing he could say, one way or the other, that would work to his advantage. So, he forced himself to behave, to Mercy, just the way he'd been behaving all semester – friendly, a tiny bit flirtatious, but not more than a tiny bit – and he bided his time.

And maintained his hopes. Engagements can be broken. Long-distance engagements are notoriously fragile. Engagements contracted at a young age, even more so. David knew all that. He spent the last month of the semester seeing Mercy as he could – which wasn't much, for she had a lot going on – and dreading Christmas, when he knew they'd be in the same town but unable to get together because she'd be spending all her time with her family and the boy she was to marry.

But when David saw Mercy again, back in Des Moines at the start of the spring semester, the ring was gone. Mercy still considered David no more than a friend, but she began to see more of him, to confide in him now and then.

"Michael was the first real boyfriend I ever had," Mercy told David, over coffee one day. "Certainly he was the first boy I'd dated that my mother approved of. And she approved of him a little too much, you know?

"I mean, face it: How likely is it that you'll marry the first guy your mother likes, when it's obvious that she's trying to push you together? Even I'm not as obedient as that. Plus, I'm only 20 years old.

"And what I knew for sure was that I didn't love him. Michael's a nice guy; I like him; I respect him; but no way I love him. I don't even know what love is."

Another factor that probably militated against Mercy marrying this young man was what she had seen of her parents' marriage. Ted Blaha was a successful businessman, but at home his wife, Teresa, was in charge, and Ted had learned early in their marriage – if not before – that to do her bidding was always less painful than to do something else. (He may also have come to learn – again, early in their relationship – that doing Teresa's bidding was usually the right course.)

Mercy, seeing this through the eyes of a girl who loved her father, didn't assess this situation as one parent following the good advice of the other. She saw it as cruel domination by her mother. She saw it as control, emasculation.

Mercy resented her mother for dominating her father; she resented her father for his obedience. In particular, as a child and as a teenager, she resented her father for not interfering, for not supporting her, when she had a difference with her mother.

"Maybe I could have gone to Dad, when Mom was being so controlling with me," Mercy told David, "but I was so used to his telling me, 'Don't make waves; Mommy knows best.' It might have been different if I'd had a really awful relationship with her, and let him know it; maybe he'd have stuck up for me. But I never tried him. And I never went to Mom for any advice on anything because I never had to! She was always telling me how it was going to be."

So David had known, since early in their acquaintance, that Mercy loved her father but also pitied and resented him. David understood, also, that Mercy didn't love her mother – save that she would have said she did, the way almost all people say, as a matter of convention, that they love their parents.

Imagine how a young lady, who already had this attitude toward her mother, would react when that mother started planning her wedding to a boy she didn't love, to whom she'd only become engaged in the first place to please that mother.

And poor Michael Staley! He had the M.B.A., the semi-executive job at his future father-in-law's company, the good looks, the likable personality, and the beautiful girlfriend – and yet apparently he lacked the gumption to formally propose to Mercy, in private. At least, that's how a person could take it. And who knows how Mercy would have reacted, if he'd done the business of going down on one knee, or some comparable gesture, when nobody else was watching? Might she have felt flattered enough to accept, and eagerly enter the contract? Might they have had a successful marriage – if not happy ever after, at least happy enough, for most of the time thereafter?

There's no way we can know, but maybe it would have improved Mercy's attitude, and Michael's odds of success, if Michael had made it clear to Mercy that he considered her a prize to be fought for and won, rather than claimed.

"Also," Mercy told David, "all through this past fall while I was here at school and couldn't do anything to stop her, Mom was going crazy, planning our wedding. She'd even picked out a date. For next June, after I'd graduated and moved back to State City – which of course she assumed I would do. Mom said it would take more than a year to do it up right – and, yeah, obviously it would, if it was going to be as big a thing as she wanted to make it. And every day I felt more and more like I was being dragged into an arranged marriage, like a Hindu or a Muslim. Like I was involved in something I had nothing to do with, and I was just watching it go on because I hardly had any choice.

"And Mom actually went with Michael to Dad's store, and the three of them picked out the engagement ring."

Perceptive people might suspect that Teresa Blaha knew that if she'd advised Michael to invite Mercy to go pick out a ring together, Mercy might not have gone along. If she had forced her daughter's hand, that way, Mercy might have flat-out said, "I'm not marrying Michael. So just forget the whole thing, right now."

Perhaps Teresa felt that a bought-and-paid-for diamond ring would be a lot harder to refuse, than the mere offer of one yet unbought.

"Anyway," Mercy told David, "they bought the ring together, and on Thanksgiving Day, right after the big family dinner, Michael presented it to me with both sets of parents watching, and how could I not put it on?"

David tried to think of a clever response, but all he could do was nod.

"And thank God for Christmas. Mom was so caught up in getting it together for the holidays that she didn't have time to do any more with the wedding plans. That gave me time to think."

What Mercy thought was this: She had to put an end to the project. Swiftly, severely, and finally. She did it at a Christmas Eve gathering of the Blaha and Staley families, at the Staleys' mansion in Cedar Rapids. It was dusk, just going dark in the late afternoon, and snow was falling: a winter scene as nearly perfect as Iowa could offer – and Iowa winters are some of the most scenic in the world.

"Michael, this is too beautiful to miss," Mercy said, looking out the window, into the Staleys' vast front yard. "Come for a walk with me before dinner."

How the elder Staleys and Blahas must have beamed, as Michael and Mercy put on their coats and caps and headed out the door. So sweet: the engaged lovebirds enjoying the falling snow with only each other – and their love – for company. Teresa Blaha could hardly wait to utter the "Aww," when they'd closed the front door behind them.

Michael and Mercy had just barely made it down the Staleys' front walk and onto the sidewalk when Mercy let it fall.

"Michael, I'm sorry. I don't love you, at least not enough to marry you, and I will never want to marry you, and I'm not going to. And now that I've told you, I'm giving you back this ring, and we'll walk for a few minutes if you want to, and then we're going back into that house and tell everybody, and call it off."

"Michael seemed really and truly hurt," Mercy told David, next month. "He might have had an idealized concept of who I was – he'd never made any effort to get to know me – but at least he was decent about it and didn't argue."

Mercy and Michael did, in fact, break the news as soon as they were back from their walk. As they had agreed, once the company was assembled in the Staleys' living room, everyone with drink in hand, Michael stood and asked everyone's attention and Mercy made the announcement.

It probably was the best way to do it. Nobody dared to object, let alone make a scene; the announcement had to be accepted. It was. With dead silence for a few seconds, and then Michael's father said, slowly and laboriously, "Marriage isn't something to be entered lightly. If that's the way you guys feel, then you've made absolutely the right decision." And he stood and raised his glass to Michael and Mercy, and said, "I'm proud of both of you." The other adults followed – mechanically, stunned, it seemed to Mercy. Christmas Eve dinner was eaten in near silence; Teresa and Ted Blaha said not a word to their daughter as they drove home – but as they were getting out of the car to go into their house, Ted gave Mercy a tiny smile and a wink.

"That might've been the first time I ever really stood up to my mother," Mercy told David. "Now that I've done it, I'm amazed how easy it was. I mean, I just *did* it. And for the rest of Christmas break she hardly talked to me, just sighed a lot, and finally a few days later she asked me, 'Do you realize you've made complete fools of us? Me, and your father, the Staleys, and poor Michael? I know it wasn't his decision.'

"I asked her, 'Should I have gone through with the marriage just so you wouldn't lose face?'

"And that was when she tried to talk me into changing my mind, telling me how perfect Michael would have been for me. She didn't go crazy; she was calm all the way through it. But I didn't say anything and finally she ran out of gas."

Mercy looked a bit smug, a bit triumphant, as she told David all this. But was she feeling it? Or could she have been, still, afraid of her mother? Afraid of repercussions somewhere down the line? Could she have been feeling guilty because, deep down, she knew that in a way she *had* made a fool of her mother, that she had (at least to some extent) strung Michael along, and turned up her nose at a man who – even despite her mother's approval of him – might indeed have made the ideal husband, the ideal father of her children?

Or might Mercy have told herself that her mother had made a fool of herself, had brought upon herself any embarrassment she might be feeling? And might Mercy have felt guilty for telling herself that?

Anyway, as far as David or anyone else could see, Mercy was in no doubt: She was pleased with what she'd done.

Mercy and David's courtship was slow. Neither of them could have said when or how they made the transition from being friends to being a couple; it happened so gradually over the next year-and-a-half. But by the time they'd graduated and Mercy had gone off to the Peace Corps, in the spring of 1999, it had happened. Mercy would not permit sexual activity, but she had at least gone beyond the affectionate busses of friendship, by that time, and was kissing David as a girl would kiss a boyfriend. David must have been more than a bit frustrated – as any young man would be – by this situation, when he was aware that his peers were having full-on sexual relationships with their girlfriends. But perhaps he contented himself thus:

"She's an exceptional girl," he might have reasoned. "I'm lucky to have her, and I'm lucky to have someone who's got standards and principles. If she's not having sex with me, she's not having it with anyone else, either. Maybe I wish she weren't saving herself for marriage, but if she is, I don't love her any less."

And could it be that Mercy's attitude made her more desirable to David?

Throughout 1998 and into 1999, then, the two of them were in Des Moines together during the school year. Now that they were aware of each other, they spent most of their time together in State City, too, during vacations. But Mercy exposed David to her parents very little. It could be that she still resented her parents enough – or was afraid enough of her mother – that she hesitated to let them see much of a boy she'd chosen without any encouragement from them. Especially a boy who, she could be certain, wouldn't compare favorably in their minds with Michael Staley.

She spent more and more time at the Wainwrights', when she was in State City. She was happier there than at the Blahas' home; she found Jim and Gail more congenial.

"Your home is a lot less high-pressure than mine," she remarked to Gail one day. She had been invited to lunch with the family, and had volunteered to come over earlier to help Gail in the kitchen.

"I feel so comfortable around you and Jim. You're so… *real* and… *unpretentious*. You don't treat your kids like they were something to show off. You don't try to make them perfect. My mother… it's like everything I do is a reflection on her."

Some observers might suggest that at some point, Mercy came to be dating Jim and Gail Wainwright, courting them as potential in-laws, more than she was dating David. That might or might not have been the case. At any rate, it's likely that she felt grateful to David for having brought her into this household, where she felt welcomed and at ease.

Mercy came out of college a Registered Nurse, and went immediately into the Peace Corps. David had majored in Journalism, and he and his college roommate – Glenn Austin, another J-school graduate – took a few months of travel, after their final semester. They were, apparently, pretending to be a couple of young Hemingways, although not working on any specific assignments for any specific publications.

What kind of stories David was working on, if any, has never been established. Maybe he was "finding himself"; maybe he was living his dream of being a citizen of the world; maybe he was just spending his parents' money. He did have a few articles published in the State City *Examiner* – one of those "local boy reporting from faraway places" kind of things – but he almost certainly got no more than a token payment for those.

David's writing wasn't the best, but it was good enough that when he returned to Iowa, the *Examiner* hired him as a full-time reporter. It couldn't have been well-paid, but it was a job, and David was making his living as a journalist, which not many people can do.

Mercy landed back in State City, too, a little more than a year after David did, following her hitch in the Peace Corps. State University Hospitals hired her almost immediately. Possibly she'd laid the groundwork in advance – quite likely her mother pulled a string or two – so that she'd have that job waiting for her.

So, observe this young man and young woman, now back together in the town they'd grown up in, and keeping steady company. It's possible that this – and not two years previous – is when they fell in love. But that's a detail hardly worthy of speculation. It's enough that we know that David and Mercy resumed dating right away, and within a few weeks they considered themselves an engaged couple. In early October of that year, 2001, they disclosed this fact to their families.

20. One Wedding and Another

Once Mercy had made it clear to her mother that this time, the wedding would take place, Mrs. Blaha again threw herself into making plans. This wedding, she resolved, would be even more wonderful than the one she'd been preparing for Mercy and Michael Staley – even if she believed that David Wainwright wasn't worthy of it.

The wedding was set for the end of September of the following year. The fall foliage peaks a little earlier in the Midwest than it does in the Eastern United States, and Mrs. Blaha pointed out that it would be an ideal time for a wedding: even better than June. (June, in Iowa, is either too hot or too rainy, and anyway she wanted a full year in which to make all the arrangements.)

It was shortly after their announcement, though, when David and Mercy began to talk about living together. It made sense, they decided. They would be married soon enough; they were sure of each other; it would save them both money.

Their decision to live together was not driven entirely by economics – and it could have been more Mercy's idea than David's. Mercy clearly resented her mother's domineering nature, and how better to piss her mother off than by going against Teresa's conservative Catholic sensibilities?

There was probably something to Mercy's complaint that her mother considered her a possession, a creation to show off to the rest of the world. The Blaha household had a strong *leitmotif* of perfectionism running through it, and Teresa Blaha was the primary driver of it. We can't deny that. So what better way for Mercy to get back at her mother, now, than by publicly scorning her mother's values, living in sin with a boy she knew her mother didn't approve of?

By all accounts, it did the job. Mercy was living independently, and she could have gradually gotten Ted and Teresa used to the idea of her and David cohabiting, but that wasn't her way. She presented it to her mother as a done deal, about a week before she moved in with David. The reaction was predictable.

"We brought you up better than that!" Teresa told her – more in anger than in sorrow. "Are you doing this just to spite your father and me? I get the feeling you are."

Still the outcry was less bad than Mercy had feared it would be. As she'd done before, she stayed perfectly quiet and let her mother talk till she ran down.

It took Teresa quite some time to get used to the fact that her beautiful, talented, intelligent, gifted daughter was "living in sin." Mercy's father recovered from the initial blow pretty quickly, and accepted the situation. "It's a different world, now," Ted Blaha told his wife, when he'd come home that evening and she'd informed him. "And not so different. It went on all the time, when we were younger than they are."

"It went on, but not with decent people," Teresa retorted. "I shouldn't say 'decent,' but I mean it didn't go on with people who'd been raised right. Besides, do you think they'll ever get married, now? He's getting free butter; why should he buy the cow?"

Ted cocked an eyebrow.

"Okay, that didn't come out right. You know what I mean."

Ted did, he admitted. He, too, feared that David wouldn't ever get around to actually marrying Mercy.

"Not that that would be so bad in the long run," he told Teresa. "He's insubstantial. We both know that. She'll outgrow him."

"And what kind of man would marry her then?"

"Honey, you have to admit there's two things that count for a lot less, these days: virginity and complete games."

"I know, I know. But what if a baby comes out of all this? Is it awful of me to hope she's on the pill at least?"

But consider this: David and Mercy had been boyfriend and girlfriend, on and off, for nearly four years, but they had not yet consummated their relationship.

That's right: Mercy wouldn't give David any. She was saving her virginity for her wedding night: she was resolute. Even after they were engaged, on that point she would not budge. She hadn't even allowed David to get to Second Base. A little feeling under the sweater, okay, but her brassière was the Iron Curtain. His attempts to go further were thwarted, and she never made any gesture in the direction of David's zipper. Kissing, Mercy allowed and participated in with pleasure. Sleeping in the same bed, fully clothed, took place on a couple of occasions. But that was it.

And on their first night together in their apartment... ah, the assumptions people make, the false expectations that can well in the human breast! By common report (David and Mercy both have friends, and they talk), David had the idea that they would live as man and wife from the night they moved in together. He would be disappointed.

Mercy would not allow it. That is, they shared a bed, but Mercy made it clear that no hanky-panky would go on, and no hokey-pokey either, till their wedding night.

Power is a wonderful thing: as intoxicating as any drug ever discovered, and more. Observe: Mercy held utter dominion, now, over both her boyfriend and her mother. This must have been a heady time for her. But the story gets better.

That situation lasted a week, if that. A few days later, Mercy arranged for a woman who called herself a "Roman Catholic Womanpriest" to perform a marriage ceremony in their apartment, with just Jim and Gail Wainwright, Christine and Melissa, and two extra friends each for the bride and groom, as witnesses. It was all legal, and legitimate, so they really were married – but it was done on the sly, because nobody else knew they'd made it official. "Nobody else" included Ted and Teresa Blaha. They weren't told.

It was several months before the elder Blahas were reassured, and not in the way they'd have chosen, ideally. But Mercy did deign, the following September, to submit to a full-on, elaborate Roman Catholic wedding, at Our Lady Queen Of Sorrow, which is State City's biggest Catholic church, as big and impressive as a church can be without being a cathedral. Ted and Teresa laid out something close to $100,000 for the ceremony, the party, the flowers, and all – and Mercy got to act like she was doing them a great big favor by going through the ordeal.

Her parents still hadn't been told she'd already been married. Jim and Gail Wainwright knew, but they kept the secret admirably, and the Blahas never suspected.

Let's not judge the Wainwrights too harshly, though. We might think it pretty horrible, that Jim and Gail would have known about this situation and still allowed the young couple to go on deceiving Mercy's parents. But who knows? Conceivably, Jim and Gail *did* urge David and Mercy, in the strongest possible terms, to spare the Blahas this ridiculous expense. But somehow one has to doubt it. One can't help suspecting that they not only knew, but connived and colluded.

Here's how Mercy might have handled it. If she had wanted to get married, she might have talked it over with her *fiancé* before she moved in with him – if she were so bound and determined to keep her hymen intact till after the ceremony. The two of them might then have figured out how elaborate a wedding they could afford on their own.

Mercy could then have gone to her parents and told them that she and David were getting married, "and here's the ceremony we have planned." If Ted and Teresa had then insisted on paying for something fancier, Mercy and David could have negotiated – being careful not to put themselves in a position where they had to do Teresa's bidding because she was paying for it.

Or, if Mercy and David had wanted to have sex, but had to be married first, then the two of them could have planned a small and quiet wedding beforehand, and told Ted and Teresa that they could take it or leave it.

And the big fancy church wedding that took place after the fact? How, specifically, might Mercy have rationalized it? Perhaps Mercy went through with it, without telling her parents that she was already married, because she wanted to give her mother the satisfaction of the ceremony. She knew that her own big wedding would be a peak event in her mother's life – at least, it would be if Mrs. Blaha got to plan and execute the whole to-do, herself – so why not let her have her fun? It would be a way of making it up to her mother – at least in part – for rejecting Michael Staley, and for marrying someone less to her mother's liking.

But that excuse doesn't hold up. Mercy didn't exactly sabotage her big church wedding, that fall, but for her mother it was like pulling teeth to get Mercy to at least be a good sport. For example, Mercy balked at wearing a traditional wedding dress. She wanted to wear a plain dark dress or suit, and David to wear a suit or a sport jacket. She finally gave in, and consented to the full costume for the entire wedding party – but not before she'd said something mildly sarcastic to her mother, to the effect of, "I'm surprised you'd want me to wear a white dress, considering I've been living in sin."

Mrs. Blaha forced herself to count ten, then sighed a bit, and replied, "The white dress is symbolic of the first marriage – not the condition of the body inside it."

The Wainwrights, relegated to secondary status as mere Parents of the Groom, observed Mrs. Blaha's fussing and spending with amused toleration. Mercy would complain to Gail, now and then, about her mother's general bossiness, her ostentatious plans, her demands on her daughter and future son-in-law. Gail would smile indulgently and advise Mercy to just put up with it.

"It'll be over soon, and then you and David can do whatever you want. Just think of this as your mother's last chance to be in charge."

Maybe Mercy did actually see herself as the poor little rich girl who was attracted to the Wainwrights' more humble, down-to-earth lifestyle. In a lot of ways, the Wainwrights came across as "just folks."

What some people might think funny is that both sets of parents felt Mercy was marrying outside her class. They differed, though, as to the direction she'd taken. The Blahas, for obvious reasons, felt she was marrying beneath her. The Wainwrights, we can be sure, felt she was marrying *up*. They weren't as rich as the Blahas, but they were nicer, in so many ways. The

Wainwrights weren't Catholic; they didn't have that ludicrous foreign-sounding name; they probably watched better TV shows and contributed to higher-toned charities. They belonged to the Friends of the State City Public Library, and they attended Community Theatre productions. The Blahas... well, they went to the football games.

A couple of months before the wedding, Teresa confided to Andy Palinkas how she was handling the whole conflict. This was on a day when she had come downstairs from her office and walked into Rosen's to buy a shirt for David, in honor of his birthday. "It's not what he would have picked out for himself," she said to Andy, "but it's what he would choose if he had taste."

"He's got good taste in women, anyway. I take it the wedding is working itself out, after all?"

"What can I tell you? He's not the person I'd have chosen for my daughter to marry, but she chose him, and she's making the best of it, I hope."

"I guess if you can't talk her out of it, you just have to accept it and look pleasant. I'm glad I've been spared all that."

"I did try, in my way. To talk her out of it. It took me a while to learn it, Lord knows, but I did finally learn that you can sometimes get your child to do something by asking her to, but you can never get her to *not* do something by telling her 'don't.' So I never told her not to marry him. I just tried – as diplomatically as I could, when Mercy and I were in private – to point out things about David that might lead to problems down the road. Which I won't get into now; it's water under the bridge. But that was all I could do, and she's going to do what she's going to do."

"How are you handling the religion thing?"

"Oh, that. If you're going to be married in the church, and one of you isn't Catholic, you have to agree to bring the children up in the church, but it remains to be seen how seriously Mercy and David will take that. I'll do what I can. David has to take instruction in the Catholic faith – which if I know Father Pat will probably consist of the two of them talking about baseball for an hour or so. I love Father Pat, he's a sweet man, but he's Vatican II, if you know what I mean. I'm doing my best not to be overbearing on that subject."

Over the next few weeks, Andy heard from Teresa and from other sources about the wedding preparations. About 10 days before the wedding, at one of their regular lunch dates, Teresa told Andy she'd made a disturbing discovery – or was about to.

"I'm going down to the courthouse after we're done here. That Christine, that sweet little tail-ender of the Wainwrights... I was over at their house yesterday, to discuss the rehearsal dinner with Gail, and while I was talking about the ceremony, little Christine said something like, 'You're gonna do it right this time, huh?' And Gail shushed her and Christine looked embarrassed.

"At the time I didn't think about it; I thought Christine meant maybe my own wedding hadn't been perfect so I was going to do my daughter's just right – which would be something a little girl like her might say. But then I got to thinking. Mercy was always so straight-arrow when it came to premarital sex. We've talked about it, over the years; I'm not as Victorian as I look. And we always saw eye-to-eye on that. She always said she was an old-fashioned girl and she was going to give herself to her husband as a virgin on their wedding night."

Andy knuckled his forehead, not getting it.

"So then I mulled it over, on my way home last night," Teresa continued, "and I said to myself, wait: what if they're already married? What if they got married secretly, so that they could... *do it?* If they did it here in State County, the records will be at the courthouse. And if they did it somewhere else, well, that might take some research, but it can be found out."

"If they did it here in State County," said Andy, "it would've been in the *Examiner*, no?"

"They only report marriage license applications if they

need to fill space. And David works for the *Examiner*; he could keep it out of the paper."

"If they are already married, what will you do?"

"I haven't gotten that far yet."

An hour later, back in the store, Andy took a phone call from Teresa, upstairs. "Can you come up here tonight, after you've closed? I need to unload to somebody."

"It was all there in black and white," she told Andy, that evening in her office. "At the County Recorder's office. All this time. And she never told us. And just to put the cherry on the sundae, they got this Bridget Shanahan, this so-called 'Roman Catholic Womanpriest,' to do the ceremony. Apparently it's legal; apparently whatever they did, they followed the law, right to the letter."

"As I understand it," said Andy, "just so long as they obey the civil regulations, it doesn't matter who officiates."

"That's not the point. This woman is not only *not* a Roman Catholic priest: she's a fraud. Calling herself Roman Catholic. She's outside the Church. She excommunicated herself when she committed that sacrilege. She's persisting in manifest sin. She's putting her immortal soul in terrible danger. She needs prayers. Only I'm so angry at her that I can't pray for her – and I'm ashamed of myself for that. And my daughter is doing the same, by associating with her, by enabling her and being party to that ceremony. *Knowing* that it's illicit."

"You know I don't believe any of that. But yeah, if I accepted your first premises, I'd feel that way too."

"It's not important what I feel; it's what the Church teaches. And I know you don't believe; that's why I'm telling you. I feel dirty just knowing this. How can I face Father Pat?"

Andy inhaled, as though to respond. Teresa stopped him with a gesture.

"I don't want advice. Not yet. Thanks. I just need you to listen while I vent. I don't even know if I can tell Ted. Of course I'll have to, but… That's just the *end*. It might have been

one thing if they'd just done a civil ceremony in secret. But *this*:
I don't know if Mercy did it to show off how liberal she is, or if
this was some way of spiting me and Ted without our knowing
about it..." Teresa stared down at her desk, shaking her head.
"I don't know what to do now."

In the event, Teresa did nothing. She said nothing to Ted,
nothing to Mercy. The wedding went on, a few days later, at
Our Lady. Andy was there: the Blahas had invited him months
before. He tried to estimate the congregation, and guessed at
500 people. It was as perfect a wedding as Teresa Blaha could
have orchestrated.

"May God forgive me," Teresa said to Andy over lunch
a few days later. "And may God forgive my daughter. Only, I
have to take the blame for that. I let her do it."

"Excuse my asking: Why didn't you say anything? Why
did you just let it go ahead?"

"For my own satisfaction. I couldn't call off the wedding; we already had so much invested in it, and I don't mean
the money. I mean emotionally. It was for my vanity. So that I
could see my daughter married in a big church wedding."

"Okay."

"But that wasn't all of it; that wasn't the worst of it. It
was also because I didn't want to be made a laughingstock. I
didn't want to embarrass the family.

"And you know what's the worst reason I had for going
ahead with it? I wanted to see if Mercy really would do it. If
she'd go through with the whole deception. Oh, she did it, and
she'll have to make peace with God for that – if she ever cares
to – but I let her do it. I let her transgress, for my own horrible
reasons."

"It didn't hurt anyone," said Andy. "And it stimulated
the local economy. And it made all kinds of people feel all wet
and sticky – I mean, warm and fuzzy." Andy winked, trying to
coax at least a smile out of Teresa. "And it certainly was impressive."

"I let her stand up there – before me and her father, before the congregation, before God – and lie. And she did it."

"Nothing you can do now. Let it go."

"I did make a good confession, but I had to drive up to Mechanicsville. I couldn't confess to Father Pat; he knows my voice. I put on jeans and an old sweatshirt and went where nobody knows me."

It occurred to Andy that he'd never seen Teresa dressed like that, not even at football games.

"I have no idea which priest I confessed to. He absolved me but I think he was way too lenient. He said the first wedding might have been legal but it wasn't licit in God's eyes, and I was just making sure they were married within the church. He said the only sin I committed was Pride. But I still feel guilty. I knew what I was doing. It wasn't just a momentary weakness. I premeditated it, I deliberated, for days, and I did it. And I deliberately didn't make confession till it was done."

"People premeditate all kinds of sins, extramarital affairs or whatever, and God forgives that, doesn't he?"

"I can only hope. I'll be praying about this for a long time. For God to forgive my daughter. And to forgive me for deceiving Ted. He'll never know. He'd probably tell me it's no big thing."

"And maybe it isn't. Hell of a story, though. Too bad we have to keep it to ourselves."

21. David's Career

"Mercy almost forced her mother to be the star of the wedding," said Bill Longley, in his barbershop, as he shaved the sides of Andy Palinkas' head with a straight razor. (Andy could just as easily have shaven his own head, and he did, six days a week, but We Cut Heads was gossip central, so Andy went there once a week to get the full treatment – a complete head- and face-shave with hot towels and all, and a manicure – and to get updated.) "She made it clear this was her mother's show and she was just going along."

Bill Longley had already explained to Andy that he'd had the honor of being David Wainwright's best man twice – which made Andy wince, because if Longley were telling the story around, Teresa Blaha would inevitably find out that it was no longer her secret.

"This young lady sounds pretty unpleasant," said Andy. "Even if her mother's a good friend of mine."

"Oh, no, she's not, really," said Longley. "She's good to Dave, and gosh, Dave's been my buddy since seventh grade, but I'm pretty sure he's gotta be tough to live with. Self-absorbed, you know. Mercy's not that bad. But she did do one other thing right after that fancy wedding that I didn't think much of.

"They came back from this lavish honeymoon in Europe that her parents paid for, and then a few days ago, Dave came in here for a haircut, except that he was totally white in the face. Petrified. He looked like he'd just been diag-nosed with liver cancer. And he told me Mercy's pregnant."

"I take it he wasn't pleased."

"The way Dave explained it, Mercy told him the birth control just plain failed. Only the pill isn't supposed to fail."

"So she was flushing a pill down the toilet every day?"

"I wasn't going to say that. Especially not to Dave. But it did strike me funny."

"Real funny," Andy agreed. "Real funny that she'd choose to go off birth control on their honeymoon, right when she knew they'd be doing it a lot."

"I guess it saves them a lot of arguing back and forth about when they're going to start a family," Longley observed. "Maybe it was the smart thing to do. He'll love it, once the baby's born. At least that's what they say always happens. He just has to get used to the idea."

That may have been the conventional wisdom, and David did come to love little Juliet, at least in the abstract, although it must be remarked that he paid her less attention than many fathers might think it meet to lavish upon their firstborn. She was an enchantingly pretty baby, and she grew into a beautiful toddler – by which time Mercy was pregnant with another child, this one planned. That is to say, this second pregnancy was planned with the knowledge and consent of *both* parents.

"One of the reasons why my childhood was so messed up," Mercy told David, "and why my mother still tries so hard to control me, was because I was the only child; I'm sure of that. If I'd had a few brothers and sisters, Mom would've had less time to spend breathing down *my* neck. I'd have had to do some big-sister duty, but I'm sure I could have handled it a lot better than what I actually went through."

Which could have been a bit of an overdramatization on Mercy's part, for she certainly had never gone short of anything as a child; she was never unloved, let alone neglected. Undoubtedly, there's hardly a parent in the world who hasn't earned the resentment of his or her children – unless the child chooses to sanctify one parent while demonizing the other.

Anyway, David agreed to have another child. It could have been for any number of reasons. Perhaps he wanted to keep trying till he got a boy; many fathers do. Perhaps he felt that a second child would make his wife happier, so why not? Perhaps he truly wanted another, no matter the gender. At any rate, James Theodore Wainwright, called Theo, came along a little more than two years after Juliet.

Oddly enough – since it was a boy, after all – it was at this point that David seemed to detach himself from his family even more than before. He still had his job on the State City *Examiner* – in fact he had risen to editorial page editor – but now he began to spend more and more of his spare time in the tiny third bedroom of the apartment he and Mercy and the children occupied. It seemed to him that as long as Julie and Theo were so small, it would be no problem for them to share a room, and he needed a space where he could go and be alone with his own thoughts – or so he explained to Mercy. In fact, he told her, he was finally ready to buckle down and get that first novel written.

To Bill Longley, his friend and barber, David explained further: "I feel like I'm helping society, being a journalist – though I admit I would have wanted to end up as a foreign correspondent, or something more exciting than this.

"But I know I have books in me. The one thing about my job that frustrates me is that I spend all my energy writing and editing pretty dry stuff, you know. News. Op-ed pieces. I don't have the time or the energy to devote to *real* writing. I try. I have a room of my own, in our apartment, and I try to work there every day, but it's slow. Sometimes my job wears me out and I don't have the energy for the *quality* writing that I *want* to produce. And sometimes I get writer's block."

But he persevered, did David Wainwright. On and off, he worked on that novel, and came up with ideas for several more – and someday, he told himself, he'd be able to take a year off of his regular job, or even two years, and devote himself to the kind of writing he was meant for.

It was shortly after Theo's birth that Mercy started advising David to do that.

"I could support the family for a couple of years. I could take on more hours – I'm sure the hospital would give me more, or worst-case I could moonlight for a doctor in town – and you could stay home and finish your book. When you have one done, the rest will come easier, and then either you can work for the *Examiner* and write at the same time, or you'll be so successful from your writing that you won't have to have a day job."

"That sounds like a great idea," David replied, "but how do I know I'd have the job waiting for me after a year or two? And how would it look if you were supporting me?"

"It wouldn't be that way. David, you're a brilliant writer. I feel privileged just to be at your side. When we agreed to be married, I agreed to be your... your helpmeet. It's what I want. Just do it; take a year. It would make us both happy. Not just you."

It took a while for David to make up his mind to let this happen. David was sincere in his desire to make it on his own. And he was sincere in his belief that it would be a sign of weakness to accept help from Jim and Gail, and especially from the Blahas. It's pretty certain that he knew how his in-laws – especially Mrs. Blaha – felt about him. There had been times when he'd had to borrow small amounts from his parents, to pay for some necessity – unforeseen expenses do crop up, when you have small children – but he'd always paid it back, always offering a modest interest (which his parents always refused to take), because he was not a leech.

The Blahas often came to their apartment with gifts – nice clothes for the children, and toys that David and Mercy wouldn't have bought them – and do you want to know why David and Mercy and two small children were living in a cramped apartment above a pizza parlor, anyway?

It was because they wouldn't accept the house that the Blahas were trying to let them have for ridiculously little money. The Blahas had picked out a nice little house that would have been just right that family: not fancy, but three bedrooms and a walk-in closet that would have done fine as an office for David, and a small yard besides; it would have been their own house.

"We were going to buy it, and then let Mercy and David buy it from us over 30 years at no interest," Teresa Blaha explained to Andy Palinkas. "You understand what that is? You know, when you have a mortgage on the house, your monthly payment is broken down into principal and interest, and at the start of the mortgage you're paying mostly interest and only a little principal, and then gradually it's less interest and more principal. Ted and I were telling them, 'We'll sell you this house for just the principal.' In other words, added all up over 30 years they'd pay approximately half of what they'd have paid if they'd gotten a regular mortgage through a bank.

"Only they wouldn't take it. Oh, I know what's going on. First there's David the sensitive artist. Too proud to let anybody do him a favor. Especially his wealthy in-laws. And then there's my daughter. Look, I'm no dummy. I know Mercy has issues with me. I know she thinks I controlled her, when she was growing up. So now she gets all bent out of shape whenever I offer to do anything for her.

"That's why they stay in that crummy little apartment. Can you imagine living above a pizza joint in the first place? I mean, I love pizza, but I'd never want to eat it again if I had to smell it 24/7."

"No offense," Teresa added quickly, remembering that Andy had recently bought the building that housed the pizza parlor and that apartment, and was now David and Mercy's landlord. "I know it's a nice apartment. I mean crummy compared to owning a house."

We mustn't be too hard on David and Mercy. An arrangement like that would have put them under an obligation to the Blahas that might have proven intolerable. But it's hard to imagine that they couldn't have worked out some sort of a compromise – accepting a private loan at a favorable rate of interest, for example. It does seem that this refusal to improve their lifestyle, when they had an opportunity to do so, was a way of stroking themselves. It's one thing to resolve to make it on your own, when you truly are on your own. But when you have children, you have given hostages to Fortune.

You may cherish your image of yourself as a rugged individualist, but you now have those tiny people depending on you for whatever they get: food, shelter, clothing, schooling.

They have no choice. And if they have to be uncomfortable because their comfort is less important to their parents than not accepting help from their elders, it's difficult to concede that those parents have done the right thing.

Quite aside from not wanting to be supported by his wife – and not wanting to look like a freeloader in the eyes of his in-laws – it may have occurred to David that if he accepted Mercy's offer to support the family, he'd be home with the children all day, most days, instead of at the offices of the *Examiner*, where he had friends and was generally liked. He didn't hate his job. It was stressful, dealing with daily deadlines and editing the work of writers who were often incapable of writing grammatical sentences – but the job was high-profile, and he got to write for his living. To accept Mercy's offer would be to forsake all that, and almost drop out of society for a year.

On the other hand, he was realistic enough to know that if he didn't devote himself full-time to the novel he wanted to write, it might never be written. Ike Abenafino encouraged him. Ike was a local hanger-on, who called himself a literary agent. David knew him because he drank in the Beer Garden, the same bar that the *Examiner's* reporters frequented, and he usually joined their crowd. He was a little older than David, maybe 35: a short, rat-faced man with tousled black hair, a greying moustache, and a perpetual smart-alecky smile.

David had the impression that Ike didn't make his living entirely as an agent; he remembered hearing Ike mention that he sometimes took temporary jobs at Accutest and at other workplaces around town. But the man did get his clients published, by reputable imprints, according to his website.

"Write it, Dave," Ike urged. "Do it now before you start wishing you had. If it's any good, I'll get it into print."

On the morning of the second Monday in January of 2006, the publisher of the *Examiner*, Bob "Thunder" Karlsson, called David into his office to inform him that the editorial page staff was no longer pulling its weight.

"It's nothing to do with you, Dave. Your work is fine. But the Opinions department can't support you and two assistants. There isn't enough work for three people anymore. We're going to unpaid contributors, more and more. It's the economy, and so many people are willing to write for free; we might as well take advantage. So I'm going to have to ask you to decide which of your assistants you want to keep, and let the other one go."

"It's cold out there, Bob," said David, gesturing toward the window. It was a grey, blustery day, with the temperature below zero.

"I know. There's no good time to lay someone off. I delayed it past Christmas; I didn't want anyone to be unemployed at the holidays. But MRC and Accutest are both going to be looking for temps later this month, so if we have to let anyone go, now is as good a time as any. I want you to think about it, and by noon tomorrow I want you to let me know who stays and who goes."

It didn't take David more than a couple of hours to decide. After lunch he knocked on Karlsson's office door and said, "It'll be me. I'll go."

Maybe he was bluffing. Maybe David believed that if he offered to be the one to leave, Karlsson would find a way to keep them all – and spare David the inconvenience of firing anyone. Or maybe David truly did prefer losing his job if the alternative were to take away someone else's. Or maybe he was thinking that it had been no fun at all, leaving the house in 10 degrees below zero with a wind-chill of about -40, and walking to work, and it wouldn't get any more fun for another couple of months – whereas he could be at home in his bathrobe, drinking hot chocolate while he wrote what he wanted to write.

Karlsson looked astonished, even dismayed. He tried to talk David out of it.

"You've got a family, and you've got a great career ahead of you. This seems crazy to me. That you'd throw it away. And it'd be way easier for Jill or Caleb to find jobs equivalent to what they have now, than for you to do it."

David agreed to sleep on it, and when he left the offices of the *Examiner* that night he had pretty well resolved to stay on, and let one of his underlings go. But when he told Mercy what had happened, his resolve was tested yet again. She gave him the full-on sales pitch, right over the macaroni casserole.

"Don't you see? This is an opportunity! That job is beneath you, David. It's a waste of your life. You'll be growing old at this... this *provincial newspaper*. Is that how you want to spend your life? Writing editorials about zoning regulations? And how long do you think the *Examiner* will stay in business? Everybody gets their news from the Web now. In 10 years they won't even be publishing, and those will be 10 years you lost.

"You're a genius, David. You're a *genius*. And you're meant for something better than that. I say quit and be glad you did. This is your chance for a real *career*. You'll establish yourself, and then... even if you don't write huge sellers, you'll have a reputation, and you'll get a job directing the writing program at some university. Take a year off. It's an investment in our future. Something you're doing for your family, not just for yourself."

The less-pleasant of the two pictures that Mercy painted – of David growing middle-aged in a job that might not see him through to retirement – was probably the more persuasive. So, the next day, David told Thunder Karlsson that he was sticking to his decision, and formally gave notice.

Karlsson didn't feel that Jill or Caleb had the experience to fill David's position, so he hired someone from the Cedar Rapids *Gazette* – who decided that *both* those juniors could be let go without compromising the quality of the editorial pages. And by the time they were informed of this decision, all those temporary jobs at MRC and Accutest had been filled.

David Wainwright shut himself up in his office, in that cramped apartment above Parilli's Pizza Parlor, and wrote. He did write; he did not goof off. He put in, probably, more hours working on his novel in that ensuing year than he would have put in at the *Examiner* if he'd continued there.

His children didn't see much of him. They went to day-care on weekdays, and on weekends they were under strict instructions not to bother Daddy when he was in his room. Julie was barely verbal and didn't understand everything very well, and Theo wasn't even toddling yet, and sometimes David had to holler for Mercy to come and get the kids away from him. He didn't enjoy it, if he happened to be home with just the kids for company; fortunately that didn't happen often.

When David wasn't writing his novel, he was writing in his journal *about* writing his novel, or writing emails to his old college roommate, Glenn Austin (who had stayed abroad, and was living in Thailand), about writing his novel, about the process of writing.

The book will be called *Sarah Strong.* The protagonist is a plain-looking but ambitious society girl, a debutante from one of the "best" families in Boston. She could have married a rich boy and settled into high society, but she feels a higher calling. It's the Great Depression, in 1929, and Sarah Strong has gone to teach Native American children on a reservation in the South Dakota Badlands as part of Franklin D. Roosevelt's Great Society program. Shortly after her arrival, Sarah accepts a proposal of marriage from a man who has represented himself as a wealthy rancher. But when they arrive at his ranch after the wedding, it turns out to be a tar-paper shack on a desolate dirt-farm, which barely produces enough to keep the two of them alive – and no way for her to get away from her husband and his drinking (even though it was Prohibition, he kept a still and sold moonshine to the Native Americans), and his abusive behavior.

I keep writing, and the story emerges as though from an abyss, or as though developing slowly through an ancient glass-plate Daguerreotype. I see this patrician girl from Boston, not beautiful, but beautiful in her firmness and resolve, and I feel the intensity of her decision to leave home to make some sort of difference. I feel her disillusionment and her helpless horror as she realizes her husband has lied to her and enticed her, and now looks at her as property. She will have a hard fight to survive, but the fight will change her life forever.

As I write about Sarah Strong of Boston, Mass., I think of my own dear wife, Mercy of State City, ha-ha. Seriously, how lucky I am to have found a wife who understands that this is work I have got to get done – work that I feel called to do by some higher power that I don't know what it is.

I've discussed the plot with Mercy and nobody else. She brings a woman's eye to things, and allows me a better look into Sarah Strong's soul. At times I feel that I actually become Sarah Strong, a vehicle for a woman who might have actually existed in some time long ago, in some bleak shack on the boundless prairie.

Mercy is eager to know what comes next, and I wish I could tell her but I'm waiting for Sarah to tell me. (I'm afraid Mercy might become jealous if I tell her my creative muse is not herself, but a product of my own imagination, ha-ha!) I hope to have a first draft done before the Iowa snow flies in December – and then we will see what agents and publishers think of it.

Glenn, I'm aware of how badly the world needs me, how my wife and children need me, but I'm so full of emotion now, my mind brimming over with the imagery that develops before me, with the strength of the woman who has burst into my mind with such energy that I am not entirely David Wainwright now, but am actually channeling this new person, Sarah Strong. And in a way I am channeling her abusive husband Richard Jewett: arrogant, barely literate, filled with hatred and prone to violence. Above all, though, I am Sarah, this strong, strong woman – yes, I gave her the name for a reason – who must survive or die.

§

Sarah Strong Jewett has given birth to a son. She had begged Richard to stay with her during labor, but he told her, "It's yours; you take care of it." He took his shotgun and went out hunting. Taking the oilcloth cover from the dining table and squatting on it on the hard dirt floor of their shack, Sarah brings the child forth from her body, feeling unconditional love. She enfolds the tiny baby to her breast which he takes at once, contemplating the miracle of feeding a child from her own body. She sits there in the pooling blood, silently waiting. Too weak to find a knife, when the placenta slides out the umbilical cord is severed by Sarah's own teeth.

To her dismay she realizes that she has made a mistake, bleeding on the oilcloth. If Richard sees it, she might feel the butt of his shotgun. She had felt it before. Yet she sits there, nursing her baby, knowing that now she will be fighting not just for her own survival but for that of this tender new life.

§

Glenn, I've become almost as close to Sarah's baby, Jonathan, now, as I am to Sarah. Jonathan has turned out to be autistic. His father talks openly about drowning him, and for once Sarah stands up to him, informing him he will have to kill her first. Even though there is little that Jonathan can do, he grows up to become his mother's rock – especially as she had to bury three stillborn sons and bring two precious daughters through cases of diphtheria that almost killed them.

If I ever write a sequel, it will be about Jonathan and his struggles with autism. But for the purposes of this book he grows up to be a strapping 15-year-old – but very thin because his father regards him as a "useless eater" and allows him to eat only enough to keep him alive. They are all thin; Jonathan is a living skeleton.

It is now 1945 and the end of the Depression and the War Years. The story is approaching its resolution. It will not be long now before I am done with the first draft. I'm proud of what I have done so far. How I will miss my "family" when this work is done! How I will miss those occasional of moments of bliss, which could come at any instant, even when I'm asleep and I might literally dream the perfect thought, even the perfect word, and I race to the computer to type it in and all of a sudden I'm rolling again, and I can't possibly go back to bed because I've been irresistibly drawn back into this other world of the tarpaper shack and the hard dirt floor in the wilds of South Dakota.

§

They had made ends meet with the liquor that Richard made and sold. But now the war was ending and liquor would be more available on the legitimate market, would the local Native Americans still buy Richard's product?

Sarah had made dear friends with an old Native American woman, Takes-Away-Clouds. From her she has learned how to provide a family with food and other necessities no matter how little there appeared to be to work with. And Takes-Away-Clouds is full of wisdom.

"I have always found whatever I needed right in front of me," she would say.

She tells Sarah, "Peace good. War bad."

"The future, it is coming," she would say.

Prevented by Richard from contacting her own mother for years, Takes-Away-Clouds, full of wisdom, became a mother-figure for Sarah.

Richard resented "that Injun squaw," and claimed that she carried diseases and fleas. But he could not stop the friendship, because Takes-Away-Clouds' tribe were his customers.

§

It's likely you can imagine how the rest of the story went. You've got David's style. Slowly, tentatively, gently, tenderly, *romance* – a fine and noble romance, innocent of lust – grew between Sarah and the stalwart, silent son of Takes-Away-Clouds: a World War II veteran named Declan Two Dogs. Declan was a gifted horse-trainer, and a poet, and an artist. In fact there was almost nothing he could not do. He was kind to Sarah's children, and brought them art supplies and school supplies, and taught them songs in the Lakota language.

Declan begged Sarah to take the children and live on the reservation with him, but she had sworn a sacred oath, to stay with Richard till the author of their story had run out of graphic descriptions of spousal abuse – and so she stayed.

In late November, 2006, David finished the first draft of *Sarah Strong*. The final pages illustrated the consequences of all that had gone before.

The climactic incident was triggered by the most horrific snowstorm that the South Dakota Badlands had seen since the first Lakota tribes took up residence there. Feet of blowing snow, drifting to a depth of several fathoms. Temperatures so low that even Jack London could never have imagined them.

Whatever his faults, Richard Jewett offered a level of customer service that could serve as a benchmark for any business: making deliveries of his homemade hooch in weather like that. The author hadn't set up the character well enough, in some readers' opinions, to make this degree of professional dedication believable, but better authors have made worse slips. And after all, Richard had to be got out of the house, somehow, in order to place him in mortal danger: a drunken fall into a ravine.

Declan Two Dogs – intuitively divining Richard's distress through the sort of sixth sense that's peculiar to noble Indians, and despite the blinding snow and deafening winds – appeared from out of nowhere and somehow managed to pinpoint Richard's exact whereabouts. He dove into the ravine, determined to rescue this undeserving drunkard – but the effort proved too great, and the two men died, the yin-yang of Good and Evil, frozen together in each other's arms.

The following spring, in keeping with the universal idea of life starting anew, Sarah Strong and her three surviving children were adopted by the Indian tribe. She lived on, to be revered forever after as Declan's spiritual widow. Richard Jewett was never again spoken of, but Sarah Strong spent her remaining years as the rock of the tribe, their trusty liaison with the white man's world. "So strong was Sarah Strong," David concluded his first draft, "with a woman's strength."

And so, Glenn old buddy, my book is done. I still have to do a second draft, but in a week, or two at the most, I'll be ready to submit to publishers. I might look for an agent, or I might submit directly myself. I truly believe it is that good and I am humbly proud to have written this work.

Now I have re-crossed the threshold into reality. This writer, for this night, is content.

When David told Mercy the news, over breakfast the next morning, she was appropriately thrilled, but she advised him not to try to sell the book himself.

"Agents are, like, the gatekeepers, from what I understand," she said. "Publishers won't even look at a submission that doesn't come from an agent. If an agent is representing it, it means at least one real professional believes it'll sell."

It irritated David to hear Mercy talk about the literary business as though she knew more about it than he did, but he kept this to himself and admitted that she was probably right.

It took David only a few days to go over the copy and tweak the usage and punctuation here and there: This, he called his second draft, and he decided it was ready to shop. He emailed this draft to Ike Abenafino.

22. David and Mercy Inherit a House

As mentioned, Andy Palinkas owned the building in which David Wainwright lived with his wife and two children. It was a horrible juxtaposition, but David and Mercy's lease on their apartment above Parilli's Pizza Parlor was coming up for renewal shortly after Andy had agreed to buy How Precious from Gail Wainwright.

This was a building that Andy had bought the previous year as part of his ongoing investment strategy, for two reasons. First, Parilli's had been there forever, on a long lease, and wasn't about to leave. Second, the residential units above Parilli's were all renting at well below market. The previous owner had been either too generous or too clueless to get what she could have gotten for them. So, as those leases expired, Andy brought the rents up to market – and anyone who didn't want to pay a market rent could leave. There was plenty of demand for apartments in State City.

"That's outrageous," said Gail Wainwright to David and Mercy, when they came over for Sunday dinner and told Jim and Gail their predicament. "That's not fair at all. He knows none of the people in that building are rich. He's just another greedy landlord. There should be some sort of law that keeps people like him from taking advantage like that."

"Mr. P is an opportunist," said Jim. "He knows he can kick his poor tenants out and still find plenty of people who'll be willing to pay the higher rents. Money isn't everything, but obviously some people don't know that."

"I sometimes think," said Gail, "that it should be illegal to rent houses or apartments for profit, or lend money for interest. They're both such... predatory occupations. It's people looking for ways to take advantage of other people."

"I wouldn't go that far," said Jim, "but there sure are plenty of abuses."

Gail turned to David and Mercy, "I'll bet Mr. P probably jacked your rent up a little extra just because of who you are. Maybe he feels guilty about how he got that great deal from me, or he just decided that all the Wainwrights are pushovers. Either way, he's got it in for us."

"No he doesn't," said Christine. "Mom, he did you a favor, buying that store from you. You didn't even want it."

"Anyway," said Mercy, "my parents have offered to buy a house for us." She recounted to Jim and Gail her parents' proposition. "Which sounds great, but, you know, I hate to be under obligation to my folks. They'd have even more of a claim on us than they do already."

"It's not that great of a house," David added. "It'd be adequate for the four of us, but it's hardly our dream home. I guess we'd be crazy not to take it, though. I mean, it's okay, and it's bigger than what we've got, and cheaper."

Jim and Gail looked at each other.

"Don't say yes right away," Jim advised David and Mercy. "There might be some other possibilities."

A day later, Jim called his son on the phone and told him, "I want you to listen very carefully to what I'm about to suggest.

"Mom and I have been thinking for a long time that once Christine is off to college, we won't need this big of a house anymore. It's a great house, but what we've never liked is that the yard is fairly small. You know how Mom likes to garden. We've had our eye on a couple of houses. There's one over on Mayflower Road and another one further out, on Stuart Drive, that are smaller than this one but with huge yards, back and front, and they'd be the right size for an old couple that might want to spend more and more time gardening.

"And we were thinking that we could move you to a bigger apartment, and help you a little on the rent if we need to, and then when Christine goes to college we could give you kids a real good deal on this house. I haven't seen the house that Ted and Teresa had in mind for you, but I bet you anything you'd find this one more to your liking."

David allowed as how that sounded like a great idea, but the lease on their apartment would be up soon, and the house that the Blahas were offering to buy for them was at least immediately available, ready to be bought and moved into.

"We'll see what we can do about that," said Jim.

So Jim and his son agreed, a few days later, that when David and Mercy's lease ran out, they'd move into the old family home. Meanwhile, Jim and Gail would see if they could find a house that would be right for the two of them, as empty-nesters. If neither of those houses that Jim had mentioned came available, something else was bound to turn up – and Jim, Gail, and Christine would certainly be moved into their new digs in a few months. Till then, Stately Wainwright Manor would be crowded, "But it'll be nice to have the whole family together for the holidays, anyway," Jim observed.

Mercy was thrilled at the news – she had *not* wanted to buy a house from her own parents under such easy conditions, but this was "different" – and their daughter Juliet was intrigued by the idea of living in "Gramma and Grampa Wainwite's house." Conceivably she might have preferred Gramma and Grampa Blaha's, but if she had such a thought, she never revealed it.

Jim had discussed this offer with Gail, of course, before he'd made it, and it served – as he was pretty sure it would – to remove any reservations Gail had had about leaving the house in which she'd spent nearly 30 years.

"All the time you were talking about how we'd get a smaller place after Christine was gone, I couldn't stand the idea of strangers living in this house," Gail told Jim. "But if it's going to stay in the family... and this is probably our one opportunity to keep it in the family. Not to mention it's a way of hocking a goober in Teresa's eye."

Gail seldom made Jim roar with laughter, but that was one of the times.

And so it was that a few days before Christmas, 2006, David and Mercy and their two children moved in with Jim and Gail and Melissa and Christine.

Dear Mr. P,

You prolly noticed that the whole family is moving in here. We're gonna have a full house for Xmas, that is for sure. The story Maman et Papa are telling me is that c'est temporaire. David and Mercy are here till they can find another place because the Greedy Landlord (that would be you) kicked them out of their old place. Just cuz you're so greedy an' selfish an' stuff an' besides you hate hate hate all that is Wainwright. Haha.

Mercy's parents have a house just as big as ours, and only the two of them living in it, PLUS they offered to help Dave and Mercy to buy a house, but Mom insisted that they should stay here and they took her up on it, and guess who had to give up her room? Because mine's the one closest to the second bath, and they couldn't put Melissa out of her old room in the attic, just because. So D&M had to have the room by the bath, and the two kids got the other bedroom, and where did that put me, right?

They get my bigger bed that I paid for, while I hafta sleep in the basement, on my old twin that was in storage, and they get to use my dresser and the desk and chair cuz they need it, right? Besides Maman said "It doesn't make sense to move all that stuff downstairs." So now I don't even have a bathroom on the same floor as where I sleep, and the bottom line is, why? So D&M can tell themselves that they've somehow stuck it to Mercy's parents – and so my parents can tell themselves that they've stuck it to her parents, too.

And it's Bonus that I get moved to the basement cuz it teaches me not to be so spoiled.

That's another thing! Motherdear says to me, "It's the right thing to do!" and I'm like "If it's so important for somebody to give up a bedroom, why don't you and Dad do it?"

And then Dad is like, "You're being over dramatic. I didn't know you were royalty!"

And I'm trying to think of something to say, and he gets this Concerned Parent look, like he's trying to be all Patience and Wisdom and Deeply Hurt and all, and he's like, "I don't know about kids today. I just don't know. I thought I'd seen it all when Dave and Missie were growing up, but you... I don't get it. Just yesterday you were Dad's little angel, and now you're like someone I never met before. When I think of what I went through, at your age, all the advantages I didn't have..."

And I was like, "Dad, I'm sorry, I have to walk away or my head's gonna explode," so I went and sat down cellar which is where they keep me nowadays and that's where I am now.

At least I can sing down here if I'm pianissimo.

I'm still working with Tanya and she has got me so into opera and classical singing. She says I could be a star if I work at it. You know I felt kinda insecure about my talent when I was in that lame band, back in the day, but Tanya is making me feel like maybe I got it after all.

I saw you in Janscombe at the performance of Messiah the other night but you didn't see me. I was at the back and you were at the front. Did you go there to ogle Tanya? Have you asked her for a date yet?

Dear Miss Christine:

I'm sorry to hear you've lost your room. It's not my business but I say it stinks. And you handled your father better than I would have. One thing parents always seem to forget is that their children don't have the same frame of reference. Kids today aren't "spoiled." Just different. But you'll be called spoiled if you're anything other than immediately submissive.

Let's hope David's family doesn't stay too long, and you get your room back. I'm sorry I was the unwitting instrument of your displacement, but I had to get my building operating at market value.

No, I haven't asked Tanya for a date. Jeez! I've not gotten within speaking distance of that lady since her wedding day, years ago, and it would be ridiculous for me to start hitting on her.

Tanya did a terrific job with her solos in *Messiah*. I could tell she had the strongest voice in the ensemble. As I understand it, when you're in a group, your voice isn't supposed to be especially noticeable, but hers was; you could tell that her voice has more power behind it than the other women, and it has this kind of brassy quality to it, like a trumpet, or like a French horn if there were such a thing as a soprano French horn.

And that face, oh, my God, that face, such animation in her face, when she was up there, and that big wide mouth, and the way she held her mouth when she sang was – I don't have the words, again, but in conjunction with her eyes, it made her look like, oh, what? Not a fairy princess, I almost said that but that's not it. She's quite tall, and fairy princesses you don't think of as tall. She looked more like an elf princess, out of Lord of the Rings, because elves were tall. Or like one of those Romanov princesses, but she doesn't look Russian, she doesn't have that Slavic face. She has more of a Baltic face. Which she would be, with a name like Cucoshay. But I've fixated on that huge mouth of hers, and I've started thinking of her as "La Bouche."

Dear Mr. P,

Ooooo, Mr. P, you do have it bad for Tanya. You're crazy. :-D Should I tell her?

Dear Miss Christine:

No way! Please, seriously. I would just embarrass myself.

Besides, she has a boyfriend, so you told me. I'll just admire her from afar, and eat my heart out. Speaking of boyfriends, did you find a nice guy to take you to *Messiah*?

Dear Mr. P,

Sigh… Les Parents don't allow me to "date" yet. Not till I'm 16, which is just a few months away, and in the meantime what they don't know won't hurt them ;-)

No, I went with a group of music nerds from school. But I am kinda interested in a boy. His name is Ralph but he pronounces it Rafe, and he's a year ahead of me and he's one of the preppie student government type. You know, he's on the student council, kinda serious, into politics. We started getting kinda interested in each other this fall. Tall dark and handsome, haha. Curly hair. Real straight-edge type, or he pretends to be. I bet I can make him a little naughty tho. He'll be fun to experiment on anyway. So far we've only kissed but you never know.

Mr. P, listen. Take voice lessons from Tanya! You say you feel bad that you never learned any music. And if you want to get close to her this is your chance. I'm gonna tell her you're gonna call her when spring semester starts. And you better do it! ;-D

§

Dear Miss Cucoshay:

Christine Wainwright suggested that I get in touch with you. You might know me by sight. I'm the guy they call "Sibelius."

[Andy must have apprehended that it might have been painful for Tanya if he'd alluded to having met her at her wedding.]

I'd like to take singing lessons. I do some acting, and my lack of any training as a singer is limiting me, so I would like to learn to sing at least enough so that I could do it on stage without causing embarrassment. Would you be available to teach an older person who is nevertheless a very beginner?

Best regards,

Andrew Gabor Palinkas

DEAR MR. PALINKAS:

OF COURSE I KNOW WHO YOU ARE. THE WHOLE SCHOOL OF MUSIC KNOWS YOU. WE MET AT MY WEDDING, WHERE YOU BOWED AND KISSED MY HAND AND WERE SUCH A GENTLEMAN. UNFORTUNATELY THAT WEDDING DIDN'T "TAKE." I'D LOVE TO GIVE YOU LESSONS AND I'M HONORED THAT YOU ASKED ME. HOWEVER, MY COURSE LOAD IS HEAVY THIS SPRING SEMESTER AND I DON'T HAVE TIME TO TAKE ON ANOTHER STUDENT. IN THE SUMMER, I'LL BE AT A WORKSHOP IN GRAZ, AUSTRIA. IN THE FALL, MY COURSE LOAD WILL BE LIGHTER BECAUSE IT WILL BE MY LAST YEAR, AND I WILL PROBABLY HAVE TIME TO TAKE ON MORE STUDENTS, IF YOU'RE WILLING TO WAIT TILL THEN. IF NOT, I'VE LISTED AT THE BOTTOM OF THIS EMAIL SOME OTHER GOOD TEACHERS YOU MIGHT REACH OUT TO.

I'M GIVING A SOLO RECITAL IN A FEW WEEKS, ON MARCH 4, SO MARK IT ON YOUR CALENDAR. CHRISTINE IS A BIG TALENT AND SHE TOLD ME YOU'RE HER SPECIAL FRIEND. I'VE ADVISED HER PARENTS TO PLEASE ENROLL HER IN THE YOUTH SUMMER MUSIC CAMP AT STATE U. THIS YEAR. IF YOU KNOW THEM PLEASE ENCOURAGE THEM TO DO THAT.

BEST REGARDS,

TITANIA CUCOSHAY

23. David Finds an Agent

David had been warned that it took months for an agent to get back to an author, especially on an unsolicited manuscript. But in this case it was right after the holidays – early January – when Ike Abenafino sent David an email.

Come by my office this afternoon and we'll sign an agreement. I like your book. No, I love it. I can sell it, and I will.

Looking at his computer screen – in his and Mercy's bedroom in his parents' house – David started breathing heavily and swallowing air. He'd always hoped to get a message like this, and he'd always half-expected that it would happen one day, but now it *had* happened, and he could hardly believe it. An agent, a real professional agent, wanted to represent him.

All of a sudden he felt dizzy and started to salivate heavily. He staggered to the bathroom and half-retched a mouthful of spit into the toilet bowl.

For once, his impulse was to run to his children, pick them up, turn about, and whirl them each around in the air – but they wouldn't have understood why their father was so pumped. So David ran downstairs to the kitchen and told Gail. When she'd calmed down, she promised to pass the word along to Jim, Melissa, and Christine. Then David called Mercy at work and left a message on her voice mail. A rather rushed, breathless one, but it got through, because Mercy called him back within five minutes and by then David had gotten so excited he could barely talk at all: it had taken that long for Ike's message to truly sink in.

"I can sell it, and I will."

Hanging up the phone, David began to rehearse in his mind some of the questions he'd ask Ike that afternoon.

Ike's office was in his apartment, a block or so from the *Examiner's* offices, and not much farther than that from the building where David and his family had lived till recently. The apartment was just as one might imagine: in the upstairs of a small up-and-down duplex, full of dirty underwear and empty take-out boxes. It was this clutter that David noticed first. The agent's office was a tiny second bedroom – David wondered how more than one person could fit into it – and Ike indicated that they should sit in the living room. Ike flopped down onto an old Barcalounger, reclined it, and began chuckling.

"Dave, you're a daisy. I'm gonna sell this book for you, and I'm gonna sell it fast, at that. There still might be snow on the ground when we sign a contract."

David sat, trying not to show how overwhelmed he felt. He forced himself not to reply immediately. The three questions he wanted to ask were, "How much will I get? How about movie rights? How about getting it on Oprah's Book Club?"

Ike laughed, as though he sensed that David was trying to maintain a poker face – and as though he was hearing those questions telepathically. David sensed the source of mirth, and began to feel a bit embarrassed. Without further prompting, Ike began explaining the situation to David.

"It looks to me like the most promising way to go, for a book like this, is the trade paperback market," he began. David's heart immediately dropped a notch. His expectations had been for hardback, with a tasteful, dignified dust jacket that denoted "literature." In the "new fiction" section at the front of Barnes & Noble, with a $35 cover price.

"This is definitely a seller," Ike continued. "Lots more women read novels than men, and this is what's selling these days. I'm gonna reach out to some of the bigger trade houses, the ones that publish a lot of books every year. It can't hurt to start with the big names, and if one of them bites, there you'll be, with all their prestige and their marketing support, which is what you want more than anything else. If they market your book for you, it'll do great. If they don't, enh…"

"How much can I expect to make? Just from royalties."

"What should concern us is how big of an advance we can get you. That's always the important thing, because hardly any books will bring royalties over and above the advance. Sure, if a book really takes off, then the royalties matter. But in your case, this is a first novel by an unknown. It's gonna sell. No question in my mind. Will it be a best-seller? Maybe, but best not to count on it. To answer your question, I'd anticipate an advance of between two and ten thousand dollars."

More glow came off of David's heart, which was no longer anywhere near his mouth. His face must have shown it.

"I'd thought it'd be a little more than that. I mean, I know I won't get what Stephen King gets, but, like, I heard that Jonathan Franzen got… okay, not what he gets, either, but I was thinking a hundred thousand anyway. No?"

"No. You got no idea how hard it is to break into the business at all. I'm giving you real good news. This is a salable book and I'm gonna sell it, and you're gonna get paid for it. And it's gonna do well enough that publishers will probably pay more for your next one. Don't worry: We're gonna get you the best deal we can. I'm working on a percentage, here. On 15 percent of nothing, I don't eat. And I gotta eat."

"How about movie rights?"

Ike chuckled.

"Don't get too far ahead of yourself. That might happen, but not till we've sold the book and not till people have read it. And that's another thing. How many people read it might depend on how hard you work to market it. Are you gonna be willing to travel all over the country, one Barnes & Noble after the other, to give readings? If you are, I can promise you, this book could be the worst piece of shit ever to get on paper – and I mean worse than actual shit on toilet paper – but it'll sell if you're out there flogging it."

David walked out of Ike's apartment slightly crestfallen, but still withal pleased. He believed Ike, when the agent said so positively that he would sell the book. And maybe Ike was deliberately setting David's expectations low, so that if there were any surprises, they'd only be pleasant.

There was the issue of traveling. That would be fine with David – he could hardly imagine anything more in keeping with his vision of himself as an important young author – but he wondered how Mercy would take it, and how his in-laws would take it. He could count on Mercy to support his decision, he was pretty sure, but he supposed the Blahas would accuse him of ignoring his familial obligations.

But he would deal with that if it happened, he resolved, and if Ike did, in fact, sell the book to one of the bigger houses, the advance would be a lot bigger too: enough to keep the family in a higher style, while he worked on a second book.

He briefly considered telling Ike to forget about it, and shopping around for another agent who would maybe have a more ambitious vision for how the book would be presented to the public and how much money could be had for it. But David knew just enough to know that he was extremely lucky to have found an agent at all, and doubly lucky to have done it so quickly, on the first try. To find another agent might mean waiting months more, if not years, and with no guarantees. He decided he had to go with Ike.

By the time he'd taken the bus back to Wainwright Manor, he felt only slightly less buoyant than when he'd walked out the door earlier that afternoon. Still, he resolved to tell Mercy that he and the agent hadn't discussed how much he was likely to be paid. And he'd add, "There might be some travel involved, when the book comes out. Lots of mini-vacations for just the two of us."

V. THE PLOTS START MIXING A LITTLE MORE

24. Two Slow Breakups, and a Music Camp

Melissa Wainwright and Leander Washington didn't officially break up; they just stayed apart, and the emotional distance grew greater, the longer the physical distance remained. Melissa, living at home, couldn't quite bring herself to invite Leander down to spend a weekend – especially not after David and Mercy and their family had moved in. There was no guest room to offer him, and what was she going to do: ask him to stay in a hotel, and go there for trysts, but not spend the night? Or spend the night and live with the implications? Many women would have done that, and let people think whatever they would think, but Melissa for some reason wasn't willing to.

It might have been different if Leander had proposed himself for a visit. But he didn't, quite possibly because he had the same reservations. He wouldn't be able to share a bed with Melissa in the Wainwrights' house, and it's not everyone who likes to stay in hotels.

In the fall of 2006, Melissa did travel up to Detroit for a weekend, and she stayed with Leander, but while she enjoyed his company, she told him, "I can't ever see coming back here long-term. Maybe one day we'll find a place where we both want to live." She said this on the Sunday afternoon of her visit, when they were still relaxing in bed following their end-of-visit fuck.

Leander sighed. "You were always a fish out of water here." He was silent for a moment, then he added, "It's something to consider. When you have your Master's, we can start looking for jobs together, someplace. Where would you go?"

They talked desultorily about possible destinations: New England, Hawaii, the Northwest coast. But it was in a joking, idling manner, and they both knew that a lot would have to happen before they could think seriously about it.

They emailed, and talked on the phone, through fall and winter. But less and less. Melissa's week-long spring break wouldn't coincide with Leander's; each resisted asking the other to travel. After several days of silence between them, at the end of February 2007, Melissa sent Leander a blunt message:

Why don't you want to see me at spring break?

I wanted to, but I knew you didn't want to come up here. And your parents wouldn't have appreciated me coming down there for a week. Frankly I assumed you had moved on. If you haven't, okay, I'd love to see you: maybe we could meet someplace neutral. But if we're going to live 500 miles apart for a year-plus, we need to take a break. At any rate we shouldn't feel that we're still in an exclusive partnership. I'm just trying to be realistic and aboveboard. Then we can re-assess, depending on where we both are.

§

Dear Mr. P,

I feel sorry for Missie. She gots nobody to talk to about this cept me, and I admit I don't know enough to do anything but listen, so it's frustrating. She could talk to David I guess but David's a guy and kinda into himself (and kinda clueless if you wanna know the truth), so that wouldn't do her any good. She and Mercy are not that close and anyway Mercy is always working. I dunno how she does it. She looks tired all the time. Mercy I mean. And she won't bring this up with Mom cuz she's afraid Mom will be all "I told you so" and Missie doesn't wanna hear that. And Missie's right. I don't blame her.

Anyway I dunno what to tell her. It seems to me that if Missie really loved Leander she'd find some way to hold onto him but I gotta think that deep down she doesn't wanna hold onto him. And maybe it wouldn't make sense. It's not anything I'm smart enough to figure out. But she's all mopey now. Missie is.

You know what's funny is that she didn't decide to move back here till after she found out Connor was broke up with Tanya. But she's hardly seen him since she got back. I know Mom and Dad would love it if she started seeing him again but they're being cagey.

Meanwhile this guy Rafe is acting more and more like he likes me. Hard to explain but I know he does. I'm gonna try to play it cool if I can. It's almost my 16th birthday (just a month now) so I'll be able to spend time with him after that.

Are you going to Tanya's recital next week? Could you take me? I'll tell Les Parents you're a friend of hers and you're going anyway. That way they won't complain about having to drive me. Of course they'll ask me if you tried to touch me or anything.

Dear Miss Christine:
        Go ahead, ask your folks if I may take you to Tanya's recital. By the way, have they given the okay for that summer music camp that Tanya was telling me about?

Dear Mr. P,
        Re the camp: Mom was all, "Oh, Christine, I don't know," and Dad was like, "Wouldn't you rather be doing

volunteer work or something more constructive?"

Dear Miss Christine:

Oh, crap. I'll figure out some way for you to get them to let you apply. We might have to be tactful, but I'll think of something.

Christine went to Tanya Cucoshay's recital – but not with Andy, because Jim and Gail, when Christine proposed letting Andy drive her there, decided that they might like to hear their daughter's teacher perform too. "Even if she did double-cross poor Connor," Jim added. "That was such a shame. But maybe it was for the best – for Connor, I mean. You never know."

So, on a Sunday afternoon, Christine sat with her parents in the Chamber Auditorium of the Janscombe Center – the smaller recital hall where soloists and small groups performed – and saw Andy sitting by himself in the front row as Tanya sang Purcell, Mozart, and Schubert in the first half; Smetana, Tchaikovsky, and Canteloube in the second. (Also, in the first half, Tanya sang a song written by Gareth: one of his ghastly poems, set to a tango by Astor Piazzola.)

When the performance ended, Tanya took her bows and went backstage – then in a minute or so she emerged from the side door that connected the backstage to the auditorium. Dr. and Mrs. Cucoshay were there to embrace her first; others gathered near, waiting their turns to congratulate her. The Wainwrights were among these; Andy Palinkas hung behind them, also waiting.

"That was great," Andy exclaimed to Jim and Gail. "She's going places, you can tell. You know, Tanya's a good friend of mine, and she was telling me the other day that she was hoping that Christine gets into that summer youth camp at the School of Music. I think it's wonderful that you've decided to send Christine there. I've heard so many good things about that camp, and you're to be commended, both of you, for giving Christine all this encouragement."

Jim and Gail just looked back at Andy.

"I understand those camps are pretty intensive," Andy continued. "They keep the kids incredibly busy. It'll be a great way to keep Christine out of trouble during the summer." He winked at Christine. "We mustn't let you run around loose, after all, Christine. You'll break too many hearts."

"So you're a friend of Tanya's?" Jim asked, and Andy must have noticed a tinge of suspicion in Jim's expression.

"Oh, all the music students know me," said Andy. "I'm the ubiquitous presence."

Tanya and Christine hugged each other hard, and Tanya grabbed Christine by both arms and gave her a little shake of affection as they both laughed.

"Thank you for coming, Christine," Tanya said. "Hello," she said to Jim and Gail, smiling less effusively but offering each of them her hand. "So nice of you to come."

The Wainwrights congratulated Tanya and headed for the exit, and Andy stepped forward.

"Mr. Sibelius!" Tanya exclaimed.

Andy didn't kiss Tanya's hand this time, but shook it, with both of his, and said, "I enjoyed it like I can't tell you. The Canteloube especially. You put so much energy into it. You totally rip."

Tanya thanked him, and added, "Yes, I love Canteloube. So fun to sing." and that was their conversation.

Dear Mr. P,

THANK YOU THANK YOU AND MERCI BEAUCOUP for saying what you said to Les Parents yesterday. They said I could apply to the camp, and I did this morning, just barely in time to make the deadline, and I am pretty sure I'll get in. You know what? I think Mom and Dad are afraid of you. I don't mean afraid of you for my sake. I mean THEY are afraid of you. I dunno why but they are.

Did you get a chance to talk to Tanya? I saw you were still waiting to shmooz with her after we left. Did you ask her out? ;-)

Dear Miss Christine:

No, of course not. There's that boyfriend, you know. I saw him, too. He was standing near, kind of hovering, so I assume that's her BF. It was the guy who played Escamillo last spring. Only he's way way way the hell younger than she is, isn't he? And he's prettier than most girls. Is an old bald man gonna compete with that? Yeah, pull the other one. Besides, you could kind of see from his body language, the way he was standing there looking at her, that he's more or less her slave. (As I might be if I were his age and had a girl like that. Good God.)

I did talk to her, long enough that she'll remember I was there. But a handshake is all I'll ever get from her.

So glad I was able to help with your parents. I sure hope that camp turns out to be worth our little conspiracy.

Dear Mr. P,

Yeah, that's her BF. I call him "(sigh) Gareth." The sigh before you say his name is very important cuz he's soooooo dreamy. Yeah you're right, he's pretty like a girl. Like he's too pretty almost. He's a real good singer. Can I tell you a secret? You're not the only person crushing on Tanya. I hafta admit I've been kinda in love with Tanya ever since I started working with her. I'm not a lez and obviously she isn't either but I want to kiss her. Just once. I mean in a romantic way. I'm gonna make that my project for the fall. (sigh) Gareth will be out of the way.

Dear Miss Christine:

My goodness! That's an ambitious project. But didn't you tell me you have a BF too? And how did you know (sigh) Gareth will be gone? Did they break up this morning or something?

Dear Mr. P,

No but (sigh) Gareth is gonna graduate then he's gonna go to Boston to get his masters at the New England

Conservatory. And Tanya's going to Graz and then coming back here. Yeah, I'm pretty sure Rafe is kinda interested in me, and me in him, but we'll see. Anyway I just wanna kiss Tanya once.

Realistically, Tanya and (sigh) Gareth must both have known that their romance wouldn't last. As it was, they were coupled for a year and more. It must have been a rewarding relationship. We can't escape the notion that Gareth was probably unable to believe his luck, for that year-plus.

There he was, constantly in the company of the most beautiful woman on the campus. In his own mind he had, in effect, rescued her from the sack of shit she'd married, without having to resort to violence. And for that year-plus, he got spend as much time as he wanted with this amazing, enchanting woman. He got to look at her naked almost every day. He got to be seen with her. He got to take her home to show her off to his family, and be taken home to be shown off to hers. He got to drive into the country with her, and take her for walks on old dirt roads, and sit on a hillside with her and just touch her, kiss her, look into those perfect, amazing eyes. He got to kiss the little crease at the corner of her mouth. And – one would presume – Tanya gave his little Cub Scout a workout whenever he wanted her to.

Tanya would have gotten the same out of it – or rather, the female analogue. This was the boy she'd maybe hoped Connor would have been: this pretty, barely-grown boy who worshipped her, wrote her bad poetry that she didn't care was bad, made love to her as often as she wanted him to – in a way she'd never experienced with anyone else. Gareth brought such emotion, such ardency to the game.

Still, Tanya must have been more realistic about the situation than Gareth. Gareth, from the way he talked about the relationship to Tanya and to others, may have seriously thought that they'd be together forever. It's not likely that this is what Tanya had in mind. Or maybe she did have fantasies;

maybe she thought it could happen; maybe she'd have liked it to happen.

But more likely, she knew that her future and Gareth's could not be tied to each other. For one thing there was the age difference. She had 11 years on him, nearly 12. She must have enjoyed the energy and the passion with which he courted her. But she must have realized that he was still a boy – more of a boy than Connor, even – and must have known that it couldn't work, if she and Gareth tried to stay together despite the various forces that would try to pull them apart. Sometimes his immaturity may have annoyed her, although it must have charmed her and amused her more often. Sometimes his passion may have cloyed.

They got on each other's nerves surprisingly seldom – possibly because, although they were together as much as possible, they maintained separate living quarters. They bickered hardly at all. But it must have been self-evident that the natural course of events would separate them.

That's the way of music students. A bachelor's degree doesn't suffice, if you want to make music your career. You have to get the post-graduate degrees, and usually that means seeking the best program that will admit you – wherever that is in the world. Tanya knew all along that Gareth was looking at programs outside of State University. Sometimes she would look hurt when the subject came up; sometimes she would have no reaction, as though she were accepting the inevitable. She never urged Gareth in one direction or another.

It was right around the time of her recital, when Gareth arrived at Tanya's apartment late one afternoon and announced – with considerable excitement and glee – that he'd been accepted by the New England Conservatory for the following year. Tanya smiled, and bestowed a congratulatory kiss.

But then she looked away from Gareth, and shrugged, and said no more.

Tanya must have fallen hard for Gareth. He was so pretty and romantic. And such a boy. One might also suspect that she tried to hide, from herself, the degree to which she'd fallen for him. Or maybe, after all, she'd merely been amusing herself with him for a year. Maybe he'd been what she needed at the time: an excuse to get away from Connor; someone who showed her the kind of appreciation that Connor never did; someone who adored *her*; someone who wasn't seeing her as something he'd settled for and now was saddled with.

Maybe she never did see a long-term future for herself and Gareth. She was experienced, and realistic. She knew that musicians move around; they have to. It couldn't have come as any shock to her when Gareth did the same.

But she had an ego. Singers do, especially sopranos. It must have rankled, that Gareth was choosing the New England Conservatory over her. That she was running second to something or someone – as she always had, it seemed to her.

Gareth must have sensed this, because he put his arms round Tanya and said, "Two years is nothing. I love you."

Tanya embraced him back, but didn't speak.

And she never, for the last few months that she and Gareth were together, said anything to suggest that she wished he wouldn't go. Nor did he say a word to suggest that she might join him there, as soon as she'd completed her degree at State University. And possibly each was disappointed in the other, that neither had fought harder to keep them coupled.

Whatever was going on, it remained undiscussed – and remained at least a partial mystery to both of them.

25. David Sells a Novel

"Dave, we got it," announced Ike Abenafino over the phone. "It took a while, but we got a firm offer. I even got them to go a little higher than their standard rate for a first novel. And if you sign now, and we get the ball rolling, it'll be out in a year."

David Wainwright, sitting at his desk in the bedroom he and Mercy were sharing in his parents' home, felt almost the same rush of excitement he'd felt a few months before, when Ike had agreed to take him on as a client. It was late May, now, and David had been starting to think he'd never have this conversation – even though Ike had warned him that while he *thought* a publisher would bite quickly, it *could* take a while. A year, even two. But it would sell eventually, Ike kept insisting.

"You sold the book."

"You're fuckin' A right I did. Congratulations, Mr. Professional Novelist."

"Who to? How much?"

"The imprint is American Romance. And the advance is $4,000, which is right in the ballpark I told you, and like I said it's more than they usually pay. They're real enthusiastic, Dave. They raved. And they can't wait to see your next one."

David felt himself deflating.

"So you come out of that with $3,400, clear, plus any royalties over and above that," said Ike. "Realistically, that's as good as we're gonna do. You like?"

David didn't like. A little over $3,000 for a year's work. And a year, at least, before his book would be on the shelves. And at least another year to write another book, which would probably not net him a whole lot more – while he waited a year

or more for *Sarah Strong* to come out and then spent the following year marketing it, traveling from bookstore to bookstore,
full-time.

Also, the name of the imprint – American Romance –
filled him with suspicion.

"What kind of marketing support will they give me?"

"Probably what they usually give to a first novel by an
unknown. They'll send out press releases, a few review copies,
and see what happens. For a book like this, it's in-store display
that matters. And it'll get shelf space, don't worry about that."

As he listened, David googled "American Romance."

"Are you talking about the American Romance that's a
division of Harlequin?"

"That's the one."

"Harlequin?"

"Something wrong?"

David did his best to stay calm. "I'm just surprised. I
just… I'm surprised that that was where it ended up. I would
have thought it would have been picked up by… I don't know,
a university press or something…"

"You're trying to say, a more literary-type publisher?"

"Yeah. Frankly."

"Frankly, I tried the big houses. Random House,
Crown, Doubleday, Bantam, Knopf. Those were long shots
right from the get-go because you haven't got a name. You
never published any fiction before. It was real unlikely that any
of them would have been interested. And as far as any of the
university presses…"

Ike paused, and considered.

"It's not the kind of book for that market," he said at
last. "We could have gone there, but it would have been a
complete waste of time."

"But that's the kind of book this is. This is literary fiction. It's not pop fiction. And it's not a Harlequin romance!"

There was another long silence at the other end of the
line. David had to ask Ike if he were still there.

"Yeah, I'm here. Gimme a second to think."

David gave Ike a very long second.

"Dave, I might've misunderstood your own concept of what this book is. You say this is literary fiction, you know, a novel that you write mainly to impress other writers."

"I want it to be a big seller, of course."

"Yeah, but you don't see this book as popular fiction like, I dunno, Stephen King. You see it more like, oh, John Irving? Or Hemingway? Or, like, Dickens and Tolstoy and those guys?"

"That's how I hoped it would be received. That's what I meant it as."

"Okay." Ike sighed, and paused again. "Dave, this is a good book of its kind, but I'd call it genre fiction. Nothing wrong with that. Lots of genre fiction does real well and becomes classic. Novels are like whores and politicians: if they survive long enough, eventually they become respectable. Hell, Dickens' stuff was considered pop junk, when he was writing it.

"So, it's not to say that this book of yours might not become a classic, years from now. But any book has got to stand the test of time. I don't care if it's Barbara Cartland, or the Bible. If this book is as good as you can make it, then put it out there. Give it a chance to become a classic. Let people read it and make their minds up. This is your opportunity. You knew you weren't gonna make big bucks on your first book..."

Actually, David had still been hanging onto the dream that he might.

"... so be glad that it's going out, getting read. Dave, believe me, for what this book is, this is as good a deal as you're gonna get."

"But what do you mean, 'genre fiction'? It's not a romance novel. Not like we use that term."

"No. This is abuse porn."

"What?"

"Evidently you wrote genre fiction without being aware you were doing it. It's abuse porn. It's a book that'll appeal to the kind of woman who loves to read about other women be-ing abused. And believe me, there's a lot of 'em out there. Be-cause a lot of women are abused, and a whole lot more women aren't abused but they like to think they are. So they'll identify with this Sarah chick. They might also secretly get a kick out of seeing her abused because deep down, women really fucking hate other women. And they'll all jump up and cheer when her husband dies like a fucking animal, and they'll cry when he takes that Indian guy with him. It's like, this book's got every-thing. You got a winner here. It won't sell in bookstores, but it'll do great in supermarkets and drugstores."

David had to accept the deal, he decided, and he did accept it. He could say he'd sold his novel. He'd never again have to be an "aspiring novelist." Now, he *was* a novelist.

But he was still worried about how he would tell Mercy, and he had to think about it all the way home. The speech he prepared, for when Mercy asked him about the money, was, "The advance does sound kind of small, but Ike says it'll sell, so the royalties should be pretty high. I guess with a book like this one, per-copy sales are what you make money on, so we can hope it'll come to a lot more money in the long run. Especially when it's got a major publisher backing it up."

But David wished he hadn't agreed to let Mercy handle the finances in their marriage, or maybe he could have found a way to pretend that the advance was bigger. When he gave Mercy the news, when she got home that evening, she didn't immediately ask about the money, but naturally she wanted to know who was publishing the book.

"You're going to have to laugh. Harlequin! But it won't be one of those cheap Harlequin romances that you see at the Hy-Vee. It's one of their more serious imprints. It's called American Romance, and they publish the type of book that ap-peals to a different reader, a more literary reader, you know?"

And then Mercy asked about the money, and David gave her the prepared explanation. And if Mercy were skeptical of David's description of the publisher, or disappointed at the size of the advance, she didn't show it. She threw her arms around David and whispered, "My hero."

§

"I almost had to go get stitches in my tongue," Teresa Blaha reported to Andy Palinkas. "It's funny: Mercy was able to lie to us about her wedding, no problem, but she couldn't bring herself to lie about the advance her husband got. And then she rationalized. It's just a first novel; he's bound to make more off the royalties; it'll open doors for him. I didn't say a word. But I'm pretty sure she *heard* criticism and condemnation, because I wasn't all whoopy-hollery.

"Then I went on the Internet and did some research, and I discovered that that advance really is right in the ballpark, for a book like that. If you want to make any kind of an income, writing romance novels or whatever you call what he does, you have to crank one out every month or so. That one took him a year at least. Mind you, I haven't read any of the drafts. It could be good literature for all I know."

"But it does look like Mercy's going to be the breadwinner in that family," Andy remarked, "if he's going to keep on writing full-time. Unless, like you say, he can produce, what, a dozen books a year? But, if Mercy's okay with it..."

"But how long will she be okay with it?"

26. A Reunion

Dear Mr. P,

We're having a Memorial Day cookout here next Monday. The family plus Mercy's family, and the Lowes.

Connor and his baby and his parents. Can I invite you? I
want there to be one person I can hang with.

Dear Miss Christine:

Have you cleared it with your parents? If you haven't, ask
them first, and for Heaven's sake *don't* tell them that you've already
asked me, or they'll feel that they have no choice.

But Christine did tell Jim and Gail that she'd already invited Mr.
P – for that very reason. Certainly, she invited him partly so
she'd have some congenial company. But perhaps also she felt
that this would be a small way of discharging an obligation that
she felt to Andy since he'd used his diplomatic powers to get
her into the summer camp.

"Oh, Christine, you *didn't*," Gail moaned. "Someone
who knifes us in the back every chance he gets? What on Earth
possessed you to do that?"

"He got you out of that store, didn't he?" Christine replied. "And he only saved my life once, but maybe that's another time when he stabbed you in the back."

Christine was immediately ordered to her "room" – i.e.
the basement – for that remark.

Nevertheless, a week later, Andy Palinkas was there, in
the Wainwrights' front yard, on that Memorial Day evening –
since otherwise Jim and Gail would have had to order Christine
to uninvite him. He'd brought a salad of macaroni, tuna, and
white beans, and Jim Wainwright had set up a couple of folding
tables and was grilling burgers.

Ted and Teresa Blaha were there, and three generations
of Lowes: Mr. and Mrs. Lowe, who were about the Wainwrights' age; Connor; Livy. All three of the Wainwright children were there, plus David and Mercy's two little ones. The
Blahas, Andy, and Christine sat at one table, along with David
and Mercy; Jim and Gail sat with the elder Lowes, Connor, and
Melissa. The children mainly just ran around. Mercy tried to get

Juliet and Theo to play with Livy, but neither of them found her very interesting.

"Mercy gets frustrated when kids act like kids," Teresa Blaha muttered to Andy. "Mercy, let me take care of her for a bit," Teresa called to her daughter. She got up from the table and walked over to where Mercy was hovering over the children, and scooped Livy up in her arms.

"What a pretty little thing you are," said Teresa, and she carried Livy back to her seat and held her in her lap.

"Isn't she pretty?" Teresa asked Andy and her husband.

"It remains to be seen," said Andy.

"Oh, Andy. Don't you ever get tired of being such a Grinch?"

"Never."

"It figures that they'd be friends of Andy's," Gail said to Jim, with a baleful look at the other table. "The Greed Brigade. I hope Christine isn't giving them more to gossip about."

"I was two years behind Andy in high school," Teresa said to Christine. "I went to Visitation, but I knew Andy a little because we were both in speech and drama. He was a wonderful actor. We're all so glad he's gotten back into it."

"I never saw you act back then," Ted Blaha remarked. "But Teresa has told me. And we sure do enjoy seeing you perform now."

"Are you still gonna take voice lessons this fall, Mr. P?" Christine asked.

"I guess so. If Tanya can take me." Andy turned to Teresa. "I'm sure you remember that I couldn't sing a damn note, back in high school."

"I only heard you sing once – in *Oklahoma!*, remember?"

"I was hoping you'd forgotten."

"How could I forget that? You were so scary as Jud!" Teresa turned to Christine. "Andy was a better actor than a singer. But he sure could act."

"And on your lap," Andy said to Teresa, "is the daughter of Christine's teacher – and my future teacher, I'm hoping."

"Oh, that cr... that girl Connor married? That's your teacher? Is she all right, now?"

"I guess so," said Christine. "She doesn't talk about it."

Teresa looked around to make sure no other Wainwright was in earshot. Her own daughter was occupied with her children, and David had excused himself from the table a few minutes ago.

"I never heard the whole story," Teresa said, softly enough that only Andy, Christine, and Ted could hear. "It does sound awful. A mother abandoning her child like that. But all I know is what your parents have told me," she added, looking at Christine. "I guess we can't judge unless we know her side."

Christine looked uncomfortable, and squirmed in her seat. Teresa glanced around the yard.

"Speaking of abandoning children," Teresa said, turning back to Andy, "Our son-in-law the budding author. Gone up to his garret to work on his next masterpiece. Or to contemplate his navel. I wish he'd spend more time with his family. Oh, I'm sorry, Christine, I'm not the most diplomatic person, am I?"

"It's okay," said Christine. "It's not like I don't notice."

"And he especially can't stand to be with Ted and I for long," Teresa told Andy. "Ted and me, I mean. His children are so burdensome, and we... well, Ted and I are so *uncultured*."

Andy shrugged.

"It looks like Connor's situation is working itself out," Teresa remarked, nodding over at the other table. "I didn't know Jim and Gail were that well acquainted with the Lowes."

"Missie, show Connor our flowers out back," Gail said, at the next table. To Connor, she added, "We have our rose garden out front here, but out back is where the real variety is. And you haven't been over here in the spring since you and Missie were in high school, have you? It looks like Livy's being taken care of."

"And you two," Gail added to Connor's parents, "You've never been over here at all, have you? Can I offer you a tour of the house?"

It was a lovely back garden. Both Jim and Gail had put a lot of their time into it, over all the years they'd lived in that house.

"It's gotten even more... I don't know, fancier, than the last time I saw it," Connor remarked to Melissa.

"My folks are talking about moving out of here before too long. They're looking for a smaller house with a bigger yard where they can go crazy. And then the plan is to sell this place to David and Mercy. Which, okay, I'm kind of jealous about, but they're the ones with the family."

"Want to go for a walk along the creek?" Connor asked. "Like we used to?"

Dear Mr. P,

Oh Joy! (sarcasm, kinda) I might be getting a real bedroom before too long. Ever since that Memorial Day cookout, Missie and Connor have been hanging out, some. It's been more than a month now and Missie is starting to talk about how she ought to get her own place. She doesn't say it, but she wants her own place so she can have S-E-X. That's what I assume. Les Parents are over the moon about her hanging out with Connor and they're all, "Yes, get your own place, we can help you with the rent." But the joke will be on them if she invites Leander to come down here and visit in her very own apartment.

Either way, if she does move, maybe I'll be invited back into the family space. Maybe, if I behave. Not my old room, but upstairs. Prolly cuz Les Parents think it'll be harder to sneak Rafe upstairs than into the basement. I haven't done that yet but you never know. And then there's that. Rafe and I have been doing stuff. Not all the way yet, but any day now.

Dear Miss Christine:

Do what you will, but be sure to use birth control. How are
you liking the music camp?

If Melissa wants a job, to help her pay her rent, I could
probably find something for her part-time at Rosen's Silhouettes.
The pay won't be great, since it's retail, but it'll at least be some
money coming in, just as a stop-gap, and she'll meet people, and your
folks won't have to help her. Have her contact me. I'll give her an
interview. She's poised, she's nice-looking and well-groomed: exactly
the kind of person we could use at a bridal shop.

Dear Mr. P,

No worries. I know what to do. And I am lovin the
camp. It's not a real camp since I still live at home and
just go to classes every day but it's great. I'm getting
private and group lessons. And guess what? My teacher
for the summer is Tanya's Professor Jespersson. She is da
bomb. And Professor Riding is our choir director and he's
teaching us about oratorio voice which I gather is a lot
different from chamber voice and opera voice. Tanya is
gonna be shocked when she comes back and hears me sing.
I am really making progress.

But the courtship of Connor Lowe and Melissa Wainwright,
much hoped-for in some circles, progressed only very slowly
that summer – if it progressed at all. "Courtship" is not what
Connor and Melissa thought of it as, at first, or so they pretended. They told people, "It's just friendship." Melissa visited
Connor's house now and then, maybe once or twice a week, to
help with Livy. Connor and Livy became regulars for Sunday
supper at the Wainwrights'.

Most student apartment leases start on August 1, in
State City, and that was when Melissa moved into a one-
bedroom on the southwest side of town – geographically a bit
farther from Connor's house than where she had been living,
but she had privacy there. And in any case, she said, she was

going to have to buckle down to her studies this coming year if she were to complete her degree, so it couldn't hurt to live nearer to the campus and the library.

It didn't please Jim and Gail when Melissa informed them that she was thinking of financing her move with a job at Rosen's Silhouettes.

"I don't see why Mr. P thinks that's going to make us feel beholden to him," Gail remarked, when Melissa informed the family of this possibility one evening at the dinner table. "But I can't think of any other reason why he'd just hire you out of the blue like that."

"He said he needed somebody who's good with people. And probably he thinks because I've been a teacher I could do it. And Connor says he's fine to work with."

"Maybe," said Gail. "But Mr. P has this idea that he should control us. He's always doing something or other to try to put us under his thumb. Why encourage him?"

Thus advised, Melissa turned down the job offer.

27. Rearrangements

Dear Mr. P,

Looks like the upstairs bedroom thing is not gonna happen after all. And pretty soon you and I are gonna see less of each other. Les Parents went and bought a house. Yeah, all that talk about one day when they were empty nesters they'd get a smaller place with a bigger yard? I guess I don't count as one of their kids because they did it now. And they didn't even tell me about it till it was a done deal. They just did it. Now they tell me. They went and closed on this place that's way over on Rockefeller

Avenue that has a huge huge yard where they can garden – but guess what, it only has two finished bedrooms and Ma Chère Maman says she needs the second one for a sewing room.

So we're moving there in September and guess where that puts me again? Right. Dad says he's gonna fix up the basement for me with a full bath and carpeting and finished walls so it'll be like my own apartment. But that's gonna take time and cost money so I'll believe that when I see it.

I feel like a piece of furniture that they can't throw out or give away. I hate my life. Not to mention that I hafta do a lot of babysitting for La Nièce and Le Neveu. Melissa did some of that while she was here but now it's all on me. It's not like it's Mercy's fault cuz I know she works hard and Dave is no help but still I shouldn't have to do all this kid-watching. At least Mercy pays me. Mom said she shouldn't feel like she had to but Mercy insisted so I can't be too mad at her.

Only good thing is that Rafe and I are Doing It. Sometimes he has his house all to himself for a while, not that he needs real long :-P. And we find other places to be together.

Les Parents don't know this, but they sometimes make remarks about "maybe you're spending too much time with Rafe."

Only, Les Parents can't complain about me seeing Rafe cuz he's exactly the kind of boy they would think is a catch. He's a year ahead of me and he's prolly gonna be president of the senior class when the school year starts. Plus he's in band and he plays basketball and he's such a straight arrow (everybody thinks). And the couple of times I've had him over here he acts all somber and grown up and Mr. Most Likely To Succeed. You prolly know the type. Les Parents are Very Impressed with him. (gag)

Wonder how they'd like it if I told Rafe I live in the basement.

Dear Miss Christine:

I went to high school with a Rafe. I envied him. You'll find a Rafe in every high school in the world. Seriously, it does sound like even if he's not "Mr. Right," he's "Mr. Right Now." A good catch for this time of your life. Not necessarily for permanent. I know it sounds shallow of me to say this, but it does you good in the long run if you hang out with the "élite" kids in high school.

I know I'm going against conventional wisdom here, but I believe it's probably healthy enough for kids your age to experiment sexually. Just be sensible, don't be too promiscuous, and don't get preggers. I have to admit, though: I'm envious and bitter because I never got to do any of that sort of thing in high school.

Now, with regard to your housing situation:

It's hard to trust parents. Usually they don't plan to double-cross a kid, or behave with deliberate malice (although sometimes they do). Usually, when they fail to do right by one or another of their children, it's through sheer thoughtlessness – but I will allow that sometimes parents can be so egregiously thoughtless that it almost looks like malice.

This is a big reason why I've never regretted missing out on parenthood. I know it sounds like sour grapes when I say it, because the truth is, I never met a woman I liked to that degree, who also thought that I was good enough for her. But even if I had gotten lucky and found a girl to marry who also wanted to marry me, I would not have wanted children. Because I know I would not have treated my children right. I might have wanted to, but I know that I'm selfish, self-absorbed, and inconsiderate.

Here's something you might try, if you want to stay in your current house and get your own room back. I warn you, I'm pretty sure the chances of this working are slim – I have to assume that your parents' minds are made up, and you say they've closed on the house, so it's theirs – but it's worth a try.

Suggest this to them: "Mom and Dad, it'll be two more years before I go away to college. I've tried to be a good sport about living downstairs. But now you're going to take me out of the only home I've ever known, and put me in the basement of this other house that I don't know anything about, in a new neighborhood where I don't know anybody.

"I know you want Dave and Mercy to have this house, and I know you want to be sure they've got someplace nice to live, and since I'll only be here for another two years, do you think you could let Dave and Mercy and the kids move into that other house, and pay rent on it, and just trade houses when I go off to college? That way you could still finish that basement, but since it'll be a rental you can deduct that expense from whatever you make on the rent, and that way you'd pay less tax."

I don't know if what I've given you here is not diplomatic enough – or not rough enough. But it's an idea. You should tinker with that message if you're going to use it at all. And like I said, it's not likely to work. But if you state your case politely and reasonably they'll at least hear you out, I hope.

§

Dear Mr. P,

I memorized what you told me to say and I tried it last night after dinner word for word before they could go settle down in front of the TV. As calm as I could. And Mom's official diagnosis is that I'm bewildered. You believe that? I'm bewildered about whether or not I should kill her. I said what you said I should say, and they both kinda look at me for a few seconds and then Mom was like, "Oh, honey, you're upset. We understand. We know this move must be bewildering, but we're going to try to make it easy for you."

She pretends to be all kind and understanding while she's doing nothing but dismissing me, and meanwhile

Dad is there with that goofola smirk on his face, and he's like, "It's demand, demand, demand, isn't it?"

Demand, demand, demand because I object to sleeping in the basement, and getting up every morning and putting my feet on the concrete floor. Oh, they did back down on that, at least. They said I can have the second bedroom till the basement is fixed up for me. Mom says, "I guess I can wait to have my sewing room." Like she's some big marter (sp?) making the big sacrifice for her ungrateful daughter.

And you know, why should they have asked me how I felt about this BEFORE they closed on the fucking house? No reason why I should have expected that.

Oh, but it gets better.

Mom said, "Actually Dad and I had talked about how maybe you could stay here, if you wanted to. We had a feeling that you might not be happy about moving, and we talked it over with Dave and Mercy, and they agreed that if you'd like, you can stay here with them, for your last two years of high school. Would you like that?"

Again, can you believe that? I'm saying to myself, Yeah, sure, if that was all there was to it. Except I'll be taking up their space and eating their food, and in return I get to be maid and nanny and general house-slave for three meals and a room. FOR MY KEEP.

That would be a BIG WIN for everyone but Li'l Chrissy. Full-time live-in help for Dave and Mercy, and meanwhile Mom and Dad will be FINALLY FREE of this parasite (me), two years before they thought they would be. Dandy, right?

Meanwhile I won't have any social life or anything at all for my last two years of high school. No thanks.

God, I can't wait to get out of this town, and never see any of them again. OK, Melissa I feel sorry for. Her life is gonna suck if she ends up with Connor. And it's gonna suck double-awful worse if she DOESN'T end up with Connor, cuz she's prolly bright enough to know that Mom and Dad expect her to marry him, and it'll be The Big Letdown for them if she doesn't, and they'll be all disappointed and stuff. If there's one thing that Missie doesn't wanna do it's disappoint Mom and Dad. Because they think David's poop doesn't stink, and all Missie wants is for them to feel that way about her poop too.

Anyway I bet she's gonna marry Connor, and she has no idea how bad it'll suck, but, God, it's her own fault. Whatever she does, she does because she thinks she owes it to Mom and Dad. I can just be glad I won't have to live my life that way.

Oh, and that wonderful basement apartment that Dad's gonna build me in that little house? I can tell you right now what's gonna happen. You think it's ever gonna get built? Not hardly. First it'll be at least a month after we move in before I'll feel right about asking him when we're going to get going on the project, and then he'll say we're not quite moved in yet, or some shit like that. Then it'll be too close to Thanksgiving. And then too close to Christmas. And when Christmas is over, Mom will say, "Gosh, Christine, does it really make sense to go to all that trouble and expense when you're gonna be off to college in barely more than a year, and who knows how often you'll be here after that?"

So they're prolly gonna make a few improvements down there like maybe a toilet and a shower stall, then I'm gonna be spending the next couple years living down there in an unfinished basement so Mom can have her sewing room, and I don't even know if I'm gonna get my own furniture back or if they're gonna make me give it to Dave and Mercy.

Yeah. "You're bewildered." Tolly. Sorry to go off like this but who else am I gonna tell? Please don't tell me I'm spoiled, I get enough of that here at home, only I don't feel like I can call it home. Not this house and not the other one.

Dear Miss Christine:

You're absolutely correct about what would happen if you lived with David and Mercy. You'd end up having to do quite a lot of the housework and child-wrangling, and I'm sure David and Mercy would keep a closer eye on you than your parents would, because they'd consider themselves responsible for your behavior – and they'd want to make sure you didn't get away with anything that they didn't get away with when they were kids. Believe you me, your parents might be a burden to you, but they'll give you a lot more leeway than D&M would.

So all I can advise you to do is bear it. I'll miss having you around the neighborhood.

Oh, by the way, Tanya will be back from Graz in a few days, right? So, I'll see if I can nail down some lessons with her.

Also by the way: it's "martyr." But I give you full credit for knowing the word and using it correctly.

28. Melissa and Connor's Romance

Christine had been mistaken, or at any rate not entirely right, about Melissa's motive for wanting to move to a place of her own. It's more likely that it was a matter of Melissa's self-esteem being on the line. The idea of being her age and "living at home" must have galled her, especially in view of the way her teaching career had at least temporarily failed. Melissa probably wanted to establish to her satisfaction that she was a person in her own right. To Connor she said, "I feel like I haven't been a success, so far. Like I've let myself down."

This was when she and Connor were strolling around Connor's neighborhood one evening, with Livy. Melissa had taken a shine to Livy, who was pretty in a more exotic way than a two-year-old ordinarily is, and had more of a personality than most two-year-olds. Livy was bright, and stubborn, and perhaps Melissa saw in Livy the girl she wished she'd been.

"Don't say that, Melissa," said Connor. "You're a success. You're a great person. You're great with Livy. And you're working on a post-grad degree, and that's more than I ever did. Don't ever think you're any less than what I think of you." And Connor smiled, bashful, as though he wasn't sure whether he'd said something clever or something dorky.

It wasn't a romance: not for quite a while after they'd walked alongside the creek on Memorial Day. Neither of them had tried to take it further, then, or for a long time afterward. But through that summer and into the fall, Melissa and Connor started seeing more and more of each other.

Much of their activity was centered around Livy. When she could spare the time – which was pretty often, till classes resumed in the fall – Melissa would come to Connor's house and prepare lunch for him and Livy, or they'd all go out, usually to the Welcome Inn.

Connor told Melissa a lot, at first, about his divorce.

"I haven't been dating anyone," he told her, on another of their evening walks. "I don't want to leave myself open to another disaster like that, because I couldn't take it. I might have to get used to being a bachelor – at least for a while." He looked rueful. "And if I wait a couple years, by then all the good women my age will have married someone else."

Melissa felt uncomfortable at this, but she gave Connor a little touch on the arm.

"It'll work out. You're too good a man to be alone for long."

"It hurt so… so *much*." Connor had groped for a stronger word than "much" but hadn't been able to find one.

"Her loss," said Melissa. "This beautiful little girl, and this wonderful husband – and it wasn't worth anything to her."

Connor nodded. "I'll never understand it. I know I must have done something wrong; nobody's perfect. But I tried to love her, I did. I'm sure she'd tell you if you asked her. But you have to understand, she's paranoid. I think she's delusional. She made up an awful lot of stuff that just wasn't happening. As though she was looking for a reason to break up the marriage. She told me later she'd been having an affair since before Livy was born, so it all made sense. When she told me that."

"So maybe she wasn't crazy at all," Melissa suggested. Just... calculating."

Connor, it's almost certain, sincerely believed that he'd done his best in that marriage, that he'd done nothing seriously wrong, nor given Tanya any real reason to be discontented. And could he simply have forgotten the conversation he'd had with Melissa at the old abandoned church, when Livy had been a tiny newborn?

And could Melissa have forgotten that conversation? Or did she somehow truly buy Connor's story about how he'd done everything he could to hold that marriage together?

"Tanya almost never sees Livy," Connor complained to Melissa once. "She came over for Livy's second birthday, in May. And she hasn't seen her since then. I had to twist her arm to even get her to do that. Or, no, she couldn't even make it on Livy's actual birthday; she came by the next day. She stayed about half an hour and she asked Livy if she knew her. Livy said she did, but I'm not sure she even has the concept of "mother." She just knows she's seen Tanya here and there.

"Oh, she tried to be nice. Tanya did. She talked to Livy like she'd talk to a grownup: She doesn't have any idea how you interact with someone that age. She tried to get Livy to sing with her. You know, she sang some children's songs and Livy seemed to enjoy that, but it seemed so artificial. Like something Tanya was doing because it was what she thought she was supposed to be doing. And she kissed Livy hello and goodbye, but not like a mother would kiss her child. And she brought Livy presents that are too old for her. Like a toy piano and a picture book that's supposed to teach her about music."

"She'll have them when she's old enough to appreciate them," said Melissa. "And Tanya must have meant well. She just doesn't understand where Livy is in her development. How could she know when she never sees her?"

"Good point."

"Anyway, don't be too hard on Tanya. She has herself to live with, after all."

Melissa didn't hear much about Connor's breakup, after that conversation. It seemed not to interest Connor to talk about it anymore. Melissa supposed he was over it, now. Part of her wanted to tell Connor about Leander, but part of her suspected that he would rather not know. It was early in the fall, when romance starts brewing in many hearts, and when Connor and Melissa still hadn't done anything more physical than a few friendly embraces, when Connor asked her to dinner. He took her to one of State City's fancier restaurants – Vautrin's – rather than the "family" places they usually patronized. Livy would be spending the night at his parents' house.

When they were seated, looking at the menu, Connor said, "Funny, isn't it? A fancy date like this after all this time."

"Is that what this is?"

"What else would it be?"

Connor must have immediately thought, "Oh, my God, what if I've made a mistake here and she starts giving me the 'friends' speech?" It must have been a huge relief when Melissa said, "Yeah, it's just been a while."

"I should have tried harder to be a better boyfriend back in high school," said Connor. "We could have kept seeing each other through college, and maybe... maybe we'd have saved ourselves a lot of heartache.

"Neither of us was ready, back then. We had to experience life first."

"But you never came close to getting married, did you?"

"Not really." Again, Melissa thought for an instant about telling Connor about Leander, and immediately decided it wasn't worth mentioning.

"Do you think you might want to be married, someday?" Connor asked.

"I guess I never thought I wouldn't be. Someday."

It's hard to say whether Melissa was thinking of Connor as husband material, at that point. Connor was probing, trying to get an idea of whether she was at all into him in that way, and Melissa could not have been so clueless as to not figure that out. Or could she have been? At any rate, after they'd ordered and the waiter had brought them each a glass of wine, Connor asked, "What kind of a guy do you think you might like to marry?"

"Someone just like my dad, of course." Melissa laughed to show that she meant it. "How about you? Not somebody just like Tanya, right?"

"She'd have to be good with children, obviously. And I would hope that she'd want children of her own. I certainly hope Livy will have brothers and sisters someday."

"I want... the best way to put it is I want someone who likes the simple things," Connor continued. "I married somebody who wasn't satisfied with that, and look where it got me. Although I got a wonderful little girl out of it. And I'd want someone who likes the outdoors. Camping, hiking. Someone who likes having a nice comfortable home. Someone who likes to dance. That was one thing I did like about Tanya... at first."

"Aww."

"And I want someone who'd commit for life. Someone who's faithful forever, and means it when she says it."

"That's so important," Melissa agreed.

Who can know? Maybe Connor told himself he'd always been true in his heart to Melissa, and that that was what mattered.

Or, just as likely, Connor convinced himself that he had truly made a lifetime commitment to Tanya: a commitment that he would never have broken – but then Tanya had shown herself faithless by walking away. Maybe Connor told himself that he'd only had that conversation with Melissa at the church, a couple of years before, because he knew that Tanya had already damaged their marriage beyond repair. By then, Connor may have reasoned, it was inevitable that Tanya would leave him – one day. (Even if it did take almost another year for Connor to make it happen, some observers might have added.)

It's possible that Melissa had some similar rationalization process going on in her own head – but it's more likely that she didn't think about it at all, except to hear Connor's statement and agree with him.

"I've been cheated on too," Melissa said at last. "It's an awful feeling… when you find out that you can't trust a person you trusted with everything."

After that they spoke very little, during the meal. When they'd ordered dessert, Connor dared to say it:

"It's something to consider. You and me. One day. If we're ever ready."

"Maybe it is," said Melissa. "But we'll have to let life take its course. And if it's meant to be, it'll happen."

Connor took Melissa's hand on the way back to his car, and she didn't resist.

29. Christine Looks for Love

Maybe because it's a college town, and the new crop of students comes sweeping in at the end of the summer: Andy Palinkas invariably reacted to fall in State City the way most people in most places react to spring. Andy hated hot weather, and didn't mind the violent Iowa winters – and besides, all the students and faculty were out of town in the summer and nobody bought clothes, so June and July were his slowest months, and he tended to get depressed about that, too. Thus he looked forward, each year, to the death of summer. The beginning of each school year, for him, was a season of renewal – and a season when even an old bald man's fancy lightly turned to thoughts of love.

Andy Palinkas remarked on it to Teresa Blaha, over lunch one day in late August, during the first week of classes.

"This is the time of year when I'm more aware than ever of my lack of any romantic prospects. Every year. It never changes. Every year, for some reason, I'm fleetingly hopeful in the fall – and by December I know it'll never happen for me."

"Because you don't want it to happen," Teresa retorted. "I won't say you're selfish, because you're not, but you don't have any room in your life for anybody but you."

"Maybe not now. I'm set in my ways, now. Probably there's no way I could get married. I'd like a nice girlfriend, though. I'd like to be coupled."

"In theory, you'd like it. You could find someone if you wanted to badly enough."

"If I were willing to settle for someone I don't love."

"Love comes," said Teresa. "You come to love the person you're with. You don't fall in love with them first, and then become coupled with them."

"It's true that that has never happened to me. I mean, I've never become coupled with someone I was crazy about. I can't help suspecting that it happens to other guys. Guys who have more to offer a girl than I have."

"Like you have nothing to offer a girl? You're rich enough. You've got taste, you're cultured, you're a gentleman – mostly – and you're tall, and you're not that bad to look at. And you're extremely nice, whether or not you like to admit it."

"On paper, I'm great," Andy agreed. "I have someone in mind. I just might make her my quarry for this fall."

"Anyone I know?"

"You know her by reputation, anyway. Christine Wainwright's vocal coach. Used to be married to Connor Lowe."

"Oh, Andy, why do you do things like that to yourself?"

"Because women are going to reject me anyway, so I might as well be rejected by one I'm attracted to, rather than one I know I'm just settling for."

Teresa sighed. "Okay. Knock yourself out."

"On another front, I guess the senior Wainwrights are out of that house, now. How's Mercy liking it?"

"It's a nice house," Teresa conceded. "I'm sure they'll love it there now that it's less crowded. And it's certainly more house than they could have afforded on their own. It does hurt my feelings that they'd take a special deal from Jim and Gail but not from Ted and I. Ted and me. But the Wainwrights can do no wrong. Ted and I are just an annoyance to her, by comparison. And I'm sure David knows we weren't happy she chose him. Although we do our best to be nice to him."

Teresa thought for a moment.

"But at least they're not all together in the same house, now," she said, "so maybe Mercy won't be influenced by her... *adopted parents*, so much. Not that I accuse Jim or Gail of doing anything terrible, but they must have had something to do with how their son turned out to be such a good-for-nothing."

§

Andy did indeed engage Tanya Cucoshay for voice lessons. Obviously, he did this on the remote chance that he could use these lessons to court a woman nearly 30 years younger than he, but he didn't have a lot of luck with that. Not at first. Because she was so occupied with her doctoral studies and her regular teaching duties, Tanya gave private lessons mainly in the evenings and on weekends, and Andy was slotted at 6:00 on Saturdays: just in time for him to close Rosen's and drive to the Janscombe Center, where Tanya held court in one of the practice rooms. (She was now a graduate assistant, so she had the privilege of giving private lessons there.) Then at 6:30 her next student would show up, and Andy would be on his own.

Tanya, as we've seen, was inclined to tend to business at these lessons, and Andy rarely had an opportunity to chat her up. He had to content himself with making eye contact, smiling when he remembered to, and making a courtly bow as he left the practice room.

It was early in their acquaintance, around mid-September, when Tanya mentioned to Andy that the School of Music would be holding auditions for the Christmas opera, which would be *Amahl and the Night Visitors.* "They need people all ages, for the chorus," she said. "You ought to get into it."

"I would," Andy replied, "but that's the busiest time of the year for me. I can't commit to a show then. You should mention it to Christine, though."

"Oh, I did," said Tanya. "They'll probably want a boy soprano to play Amahl if they can find one, but they don't grow on trees around here. Christine's going to be really, really big one day. I'm so envious of her voice."

At the next Rotary Club luncheon, Andy told Jim Wainwright that his daughter's talent was coming in for praise, from an authoritative source.

"That's good to know," said Jim. "I never could understand that kind of high-brow music. That's more your bag."

"Anyway, Tanya says Christine's going places," said Andy. "It's great that you keep encouraging her. You're doing just right."

Jim shook his head.

"We try. She's at that age, you know, when it's hard to talk to her. We do the best we can with her."

"I miss seeing her around, now that you've moved," Andy said. "I understand she had mixed emotions about that. Has she adjusted to the new place?"

"Hard to say," said Jim. "It can't have been that big of a thing for her, but girls that age, I guess they always have to have something to complain about. You've never had kids, so you never experienced it, but it's kinda sad, when they hit that age when they don't want to be your little girl anymore. All of a sudden, you just don't know them."

§

Dear Mr. P,

So I've at least got a toilet, sink, and shower stall down here now, so I'm in the basement and Mom has her sewing room, and when I'm down here it's easy enough to sneak out at night. Mostly to see Rafe but sometimes to do other shit too. Now that I'm working with Tanya at Janscombe I'm meeting a lot of people and there's this grad student who taught at the music camp last summer who seems to kinda like me. He might wanna see me in THAT way, nahmean? For now I'm staying faithful to Rafe but you never know.

You know I'm not too sure if I even like Rafe. For one thing he kinda smells like a wet dog, and he's not that good in bed, not that I'm all that experienced (not at all actually) but I guess I was hoping it would be more, I dunno, more spectacular than it is. He doesn't eat my pussy the way I was hoping he would. He says it's "not

manly" and he won't try it. I don't have an orgazam with
him fucking me and that's another thing, I'm too shy to do
it for myself where he can see, so if I wanna take care of
business I hafta do it later.

Plus he makes funny faces all during the ballgame
and it's not that nice to look at. And once he was doing it
to me and for some reason it just didn't feel right at the
time, like not painful but like I wasn't in the mood and I
wasn't liking it at all, so I asked him to stop but he kept
on going, and I asked him again but he was about to finish
so he kept going till he finished, and I guess it wasn't
rape cuz he was already in when I decided I didn't want
him in me, but still I felt kinda used and taken advantage
of and like he didn't respect me.

Plus he's so arrogant. He truly thinks he's the
most intelligent person in the world. He even says so. He's
not but he says so. He also says he's "a radical" only he's
not a radical either. He's for Barack Obama for President
so that makes him a Democrat like the rest of us. I'm for
Hillary and he says the Democrats will never be dumb
enough to nominate her. He says women don't have the
"emotional makeup" that you need to be President. Which
kinda makes me feel insulted.

I think I stay with Rafe outa habit and maybe the
social prestige (am I using that word right?) and maybe he
feels that way about me too, but being w/o a BF would
suck, so he'll hafta do till I meet somebody more my
speed. I feel like I'm getting too grown up to deal with
boys my age. I should hook up with a college guy. And
that's a good reason to take Tanya's advice and get more
serious about singing, right?

Dear Miss Christine:

It sounds like you're experiencing a normal part of growing
up. Rafe is your first boyfriend and it's becoming obvious that he's
not your one-and-only forever. So, be with him if you want to be, but

don't expect it to last – especially since it sounds like you have no reason to want it to last. I know nobody likes to be reminded that they're young – unless they're old – but face it: you're 16 and you have a lot of adventures ahead. No reason to take life too fast. Andante, okay? And be careful about getting involved with older guys. I'm not saying don't, but I'm saying be careful. There are lots of creeps out there, and even more young men who are not creeps but will not take a 16-year-old seriously. (And yes: you used "prestige" correctly.)

Dear Mr. P,

I feel like the cat that swallowed the canary. I swallowed something anyway. That grad student? We hooked up last night. I told Les Parents that I had choir practice tonight when I tolly didn't. I borrowed Mom's car and drove to Janscombe where Greg was. I took him for a walk by the river and we sat by the boathouse and talked for a while then we made out and it was way late so there was nobody around, so I started playing with his wiener and sucking on it but it wouldn't get hard, prolly he was nervous or something so I told him don't worry and we went back to kissing and I was playing with him for a long time, felt like 20-30 minutes or something and finally he started getting hard so I sucked on him again and this time he busted in my mouth. I was afraid somebody was gonna hear but if anybody did they kept quiet. Anyway that was my first time I blew a guy all the way and it was kinda neat. I dunno if I wanna see him again cuz he's not all that interesting except that he's kinda into me. Even Rafe has a bigger one. But he got a nice blowjob out of it so he can't complain about the transaction even if we never do anything else.

Dear Miss Christine:

OK, but be careful. It sounds like this guy's harmless but you don't want to arouse expectations. Also, this is going to sound stuffy and old-fashioned, but let's face it: I am stuffy and old-fashioned. It's just not a good idea to be sexually promiscuous. It might be fun in the short run, but it can have consequences you don't want. Maybe I'm just saying that because when I was your age no girl would even look at me. I'm ashamed to tell you this, but I never kissed a girl till I was 19. So I feel bitter and resentful when I hear about teenagers having sex. But enough of my whinging.

    I know nothing at all about this "Greg" guy. But if you're 16 and he's what, 23 or 24 or even older? He might be fascinated with you temporarily but this might not be the time to get involved with him. But you say you don't want to, so, no worries. But I'd advise against leading him on, if you're not into him.

Dear Mr. P,

    Yeah, you're right, he's fascinated. Now he's like making puppy eyes whenever I see him in Janscombe and texting me a lot but I don't wanna get involved with him. That was just for fun. I told him I'd be his friend but now he's acting like he's all in love with me or something. We only had that one little encounter, I dunno that you could even call it a date, we just kissed a while and I blew him and I guess that made him think we were a couple. I hate to disappoint him but that's all I want to do with him.

    And guess who else is taking lessons here at State U? My old frenemy Léa. She still sings but she's focusing more on violin now and she's getting private lessons in that, like me. I don't tolly dislike her now that we're not in the same band, and it doesn't hurt that I'm starting to think my voice is better than hers. And I don't have any interest in violin so that's fine with me.

    Big news is, I'm auditioning tomorrow for "Amahl." Tanya said I should, so here goes nothing. Wish me luck.

Dear Miss Christine:

    Yes, Tanya told me you'd be a natural. Good luck to both of you! As for this Greg, you've just learned something, which is that

boys are just as romantic as girls, at least some of them are. Some
guys, even if you pay them only a little attention, will think that
you're into them – and they'll fall in love with you, or think they're in
love. I know it's fun to have sex (or it can be, at any rate) and fun to
be naughty, but be careful of people's feelings.

      You're smart enough to know how to run your own life, so
I'll shut up now and wish you luck again. I'd pay to see you as Amahl
even if I don't like that opera.

Dear Mr. P,

      OMG OMG I've been cast as Amahl. I'm bad! I'm a
bitch! I'm the star of A Bitch And The Bitch Followers.
And she might have told you already but Tanya will be my
mother. I gotta love it, an opera with two big parts for
sopranos and I get to work with my teacher. It's gonna
be a lot of rehearsal, though! Eight weeks starting mid
October. I'm sure Les Parents will be tickled, only not so
much. They'll prolly be like, "Can't you do high school
stuff like a normal teenager?" And they'll be all about
how it means driving to and from Janscombe every night.
But I've already told Tanya to call them and tell them
how glad she is that she'll be working with me. That
should keep them pacified.

      I hope I'm not being too nosy and if I am you can
tolly tell me but I have to ask you about this cuz we've
been talking about sex and you sound like you know about
it but I can't imagine you ever having sex. With anybody.
Mom and Dad say you're "that way," and that's kinda
funny since they think you're a perv who's trying to have
sex with me, right? If you are "that way" I'm tolly cool
with it, but I'm curious. Do you have sex at all?

Dear Miss Christine:

      First, congratulations on Amahl. I'm sure you and Tanya
will challenge each other and turn in incredible performances. I
can't wait to hear you.

Now, re your question. I like women. Unfortunately, most of them, like you, can't imagine me having sex! (Or if they can, they have to go wash their brains out with Clorox.) I know lots of people think I'm "that way," and I know your parents think I like sex with children, but it's just my bad luck that I give off those vibes – and that most women catch them. I don't know what it is, exactly, that I do to set their creep-alarms all a-jingle-jangle – but I do it.

That's why you never see me with a GF. I do have sex, but less and less as I get older, and it was never frequent. I haven't had anything like a GF since before you were born.

I've always known a few women in the State City area who will pretend to be my GF for a couple of hours, in return for a small financial consideration, if you know what I mean. If I want to have sex, that's what I do. If a nice girl were to come along and want to be my GF for free, that would be great. But as the Irish playwright Brendan Behan observed, "The difference between paying for sex, and getting it for free, is that getting it for free costs more."

30. Andy Looks for Love

Andy Palinkas never could explain it to himself. His fascinations with various women had always gone according to a pattern, all his life long. He would conceive an attraction for a woman, an attraction that would quickly become obsessive, without that woman having done anything at all to encourage it – and he'd be able to think of almost nothing else. The woman would not only fill his fantasies, but would create – or rather, Andy would allow his mind to create – an almost unbearable anxiety, longing, and despair. Because, always coupled with the attraction, were two ideas: first, that he could win that lady for his very own if only he played his cards right – and second, simultaneously, that she was utterly unattainable, that nothing, *nothing* that Andy Palinkas could do would suffice to win her. This is the concept that George Orwell referred to, in *Nineteen Eighty-Four*: the ability to hold, simultaneously, two contradictory ideas in one's head.

Andy had been like this, ever since he first started taking an interest in girls. He'd fixate on someone, and it would always be someone he couldn't have – someone way out of his league – or else he'd surprise himself by making himself interesting to a woman, but then he'd commit some *faux pas*, early in the courtship process, that would put him squarely and permanently in the "friend zone."

So there he was, in transition from middle-aged to old; never married or even close to it; never having had any but fleeting, ephemeral relationships that either he walked away from because the lady wasn't challenging enough, or the lady *ran* away from because Andy put her off or scared her.

Some of these infatuations were stronger than others. His obsession with Tanya Cucoshay became one of the worst he'd ever experienced.

So far as Andy could tell, Tanya was not an exceptional talent. He knew he'd heard stronger soprano voices, just in State City. Andy pretended to himself that he was attracted to Tanya partly because she was such a wonderful singer, but in truth, that had almost nothing to do with it. She had a big voice, a powerful voice, a professional voice – but not an exceptional voice. Her technique was excellent – not outstanding. She did have wonderful energy. Andy enjoyed hearing her sing, but that wasn't what his attraction was about.

The brutal truth is that Andy's attraction to Tanya was all about her personal desirability. Her looks, partly, but even more her *presence*, which he'd noticed years before, the first time he'd seen her in a chorus. Plus, he told himself he was catching a vibe, for want of a better word. Not a vibe directed at him, but one that told Andy something about her personality.

Different vibes from different women attracted Andy. In Tanya's case, it was her awareness of her own pulchritude. Just from the way she put herself together, the way she carried herself, it was clear to Andy that she knew how she looked, knew that she was compelling. And yet, Andy sensed that coupled with that self-confidence was a painful, constant insecurity about her looks. A wee bit too much makeup; too much rouge on the cheeks in particular: that tipped Andy off. He'd never seen eyebrows more painstakingly tweezed and penciled. She tried too hard with her clothes. Perhaps Tanya, too, held two contradictory thoughts in her mind. And Andy wanted to give her a good talking-to about wearing the wrong colors.

Andy liked to pretend that he never allowed himself to form a close relationship with a woman because deep down he was a solitary man – maybe slightly schizoid – who preferred to avoid that type of commitment. But also festering in Andy's mind was the belief that his solitary personality was itself, to some extent, a pretense: a rationalization, a lame excuse to evade the horrid truth of the matter. That truth, Andy told himself in his most self-hating moments, was that he was simply not a good enough man to attract the kind of woman who'd be acceptable to him. It wasn't about his worth as a *person*; it was about his worth as a *man*.

During his first few weeks working with Tanya, Andy told her only a little about himself, his business, his interests in music and theatre, his friendship with Christine Wainwright – but he managed to hint that he didn't like Christine's parents.

"Tell me about it," Tanya said, with an eye-roll, making it clear that she, too, had a story waiting to be told. (And Andy did get to hear that story, eventually.) It was that eye-roll, that brief revelation that she had feelings on the subject, that instant in which she shared a confidence, that made Andy hope that he was establishing more than a business relationship with Tanya.

This was at the end of a lesson, and Andy was leaving –
but when he saw that eye-roll, he felt he had to find an excuse
to linger, if only for a few seconds. Tanya still sat at the piano.

"So you'll be working with Christine for real, in December," he said.

"I'm kind of intimidated by that. She's a huge talent. She
could go way farther than I'll ever go – if her parents let her."

"It's not so much that they don't want her to succeed,"
Andy told Tanya. "They just don't like the inconvenience. And
the possible expense later. But if we can keep pointing out to
them that her musical career will keep her busy and out of their
sight, they won't interfere."

"It's good that she's got you. I've got nobody. My
mother, but she doesn't understand where I'm coming from."

"No boyfriend to lean on?" Andy figured that if he
wanted Tanya to at least start thinking of him as a confidant, he
might as well ask the kind of question a confidant would ask.

"I was with someone till this summer. Then he went off
to do his post-grad. Oh, I knew it couldn't last; he was more
than 10 years younger than me. But it's so hard to meet anyone.
And when you meet them they're not worth knowing."

And so it was that Andy went home and checked the
School of Music's calendar of events, looking for something
that might interest Tanya. Next day, he got up the nerve to
email her with the suggestion that they ought to attend a solo
recital by the oboe professor (the one Andy knew from Rotary)
on Thursday evening, and get a bite to eat afterwards.

"Here it is just a few hours away from our date, and La Bouche
hasn't called or emailed to cancel yet," Andy remarked to
Teresa Blaha at Rotary, a few days later.

"She probably won't," said Teresa. "It sounds like she's
eager, from what you say."

"What the fuck would she want with an old bald guy?"
Andy demanded, in an undertone so that their tablemates
wouldn't hear. "But, damn, I feel like I've got a championship

fight coming up tonight, or some such. It's as though I've never been on a date before. And I almost haven't. Not in years. I'll just have to figure out how to show complete absence of desire, without coming off like a eunuch."

"Just act like a friend. You can show appreciation for form, features, and function without being a letch. You also have age working for you. Older men who've never been married always hold a certain attraction for younger women."

"Really? This one could do way, way better than me."

"Some women hope they'll be the one who finally breaks down the barriers. Think of Annette Bening and what's-his-face."

"La Bouche is hotter than Annette Bening," said Andy, "and I'm no Warren Beatty. I know she probably just accepted my invitation because she thinks I'm interesting. But you never know. Anyway, you miss 100% of the shots you don't take."

Teresa looked at Andy sidelong.

"Ooh, quoting an inspirational poster. You've sunk to a new low."

"At least it was Gretzky, not the Dalai Fucking Lama."

Teresa tsk'd.

"Email me when it's over," she said.

§

OK, so I'd rate it as Not Disastrous. I picked her up at her apartment building, and drove her over to Janscombe, and of course I felt like a hell of a fellow, arriving with this incredibly hot young lady as my escort. Lots of the music faculty saw us there. Call me shallow, but that COUNTED. Being seen with her like that. Fuck, yeah, it counted.

And she definitely seemed to understand that it was a "date." Was impressed that I opened the car door for her, set her chair in the restaurant, helped her with her coat, etc., all of which I do as a matter of course, but she says nobody does that anymore. (I took her to Vautrin's, BTW.) The conversation went fine as far as I could tell; she seems bright enough. And when it was over I took her home, walked her to the main door of her building, and saw her safely inside. I dared not try to kiss her goodnight or anything; hope my no-touch policy didn't send her the wrong signal.

Also, it's clear that she doesn't regard that other boyfriend – the one who just recently left town – as anything serious. I'm sure there's a story about that, and maybe I'll hear it later if there's ever a second date, which is doubtful.

I explained, early in the date, that I'm pathologically shy like Laura Wingfield, so she'd be warned if I made some awful *faux pas*, but I don't think I did. She was complaining about the size and quality of the dating pool in State City. She's ravishing; I'd think she'd have no trouble at all. Mind you, in a college town, 30something is old, but still...

I don't have a handle on her personality, but haven't found anything objectionable yet. She seems easy-going. Told me about other guys she's dated lately, and yeah, I'm not bad by comparison. But, f'Chrissake, the age difference. And she could easily be dating doctors, full professors, and them kind of trashy people.

Andy:

It sounds like your date went very, very well. A little old-fashioned, but you're an old-fashioned kind of guy. When you're with me you're usually so relaxed and fun to be with. If you behaved that way with your new crush, you're on quite solid ground.

Sounds like you may have a winner here. Just don't ruin it by getting too obsessive. Continue casual and relaxed, let it take its own course, and don't push. Maybe you're in for a nice, long courtship. Right up your street! Slowly, slowly catchee monkey.

Stay cool and keep breathing.

Teresa

§

Shit. I went to our lesson Saturday and acted cool. Didn't ask her out again. Waited till Tuesday to email her, as follows:

> Re next weekend: Home game on Saturday. The Cats play U. Des Moines. Any desire to re-schedule your Saturday afternoon lessons and come with me? (Then we could head back to your studio for MY lesson.) Failing that, maybe on Sunday there'd be a movie you're dying to see? I'm easy. Let me know what works for you.
> Best,
> Andy

She took two days to get back to me, and just now I got this from her:

SORRY, I'M COMPLETELY SNOWED UNDER WITH COURSE WORK THIS WEEKEND. BUT SEE YOU FOR OUR LESSON AS USUAL. THANKS FOR ASKING!

I'm dead, ain't I?

Ohhhh, Andy.

Yeeeeeaaahhhh, you're doing it already.

You bombarded her with a bunch of choices of things to do this weekend, basically saying you'll jump off a cliff if that's what she wants to do. Little creepy, that, at this point. That's a conversation you have with someone you've been seeing for a while, not someone you've only had one date with.

I know you're now chewing your lip trying to think how to fix all this. Don't. Nothing you can do that won't make it worse. You've dug yourself into a bit of a hole here. Not a horribly deep one, but a hole nonetheless. Now you have to just wait and see whether she decides to help you out or leave you there.

I do not think you're dead already but BACK OFF.

Do NOT contact her again -- except for your lessons. Let
her make the next move. You've already made enough
of them. If she doesn't, yeah, then you're pretty much
done for. But if you let some time pass, then find some
reasonable pretext for contacting her very innocently,
you stand a good chance of picking back up with
her. Time will tell ... which I know is the worst possible
thing to say to you. Now you're going to spend every
second obsessing about this ... sigh.

   I fucking hate myself.

   See? I knew that's what would happen. I should
have kept my mouth shut. It's just that I've watched this
happen to you so many times ... and I know you're a
good guy, not a stalker or rapist or any of those other
things, and that these women are missing out on some
fun if they only knew. You just have to stop shooting
yourself in the foot before you even get a chance with
them.
   All is not yet lost with this lady and I sincerely
hope I'm being the Voice of Gloom and Doom. Either
way, though, my very dear friend -- you have something
going for you in that you have reached the age where
you can play the distinguished older gentleman who is
allowed more quirks and eccentricities than younger
men are, and you're single. Buck up, kiddo. Another one
will come along any minute.
   Assume that this one is done. Now let's just all
sit back and see what happens next. She might surprise
you! And ask some of your other female friends what
they think. My view is distorted by too much cynicism
and not enough warm fuzzies (not that I was ever all
that warm and fuzzy, but whatever warm-and-fuzzy I had
when I was younger, it is rapidly disappearing in my old
age).

As hard as it is, your only choice now is to wait it out. Go to your lessons, and don't ask for another date till I tell you it's OK to do it.

§

So, for more than a month, Andy did just that. Then, in late November, he emailed Teresa for permission:

> The State City High School choir is giving a recital on the afternoon of December 2. Christine Wainwright is a member of that ensemble – and a student of La Bouche, just as I am. So, I'm thinking that right after Thanksgiving vacation I can send La Bouche a chatty but not-very-long email and end it with, "I know how busy you are, but I just bring this up because it probably isn't on your radar... if you decide to go, I'd be delighted to take you for tea afterwards."

I see nothing wrong with contacting her about it. You know Christine, and La Bouche knows Christine. A common interest. A thing you'd be attending even if you'd never met La Bouche. Nothing contrived about it.

However, I would handle it differently. I'd just write about a week before and ask if she's planning to attend (make the assumption that she already knows about it). If she asks what you're talking about, you can explain; if she doesn't ask and just answers yea or nay, it doesn't look like you're stalking her.

Don't invite her out afterward ahead of time. Wait till you're there. Yes, you run the risk that she has made other plans, but if you invite her out ahead of time, you run the risk of her choosing not to attend, so as not to have to explain why she can't go out with you afterwards (if that's what she chooses). At least this way, you can have the chance to be at the same function at the same time and have the opportunity to show her that you're not some creepy stalker.

§

Holy shit. Guess who showed up at Christine's concert. Guess who sat right next to me all through it, walked around with me at intermission, and went backstage with me to congratulate Christine. Guess who let herself be seen as my escort as we greeted Jim and Gail Wainwright. Guess who went for afternoon tea with me afterwards and spent more than two hours telling me a lot of her personal shit. I mean it was a LONG talk, and she told me a LOT.

Especially about her marriage, and she told me some stuff about some mutual acquaintances of yours and mine that would cause your eyeballs to rotate counterclockwise.

And then... and THEN...

She told me how she's definitely single now because that boy-toy of hers came back here to visit her a few weeks ago and "We had a big fight because he wants me to stay pure and chaste for two years while he does whatever he's doing, and I'm not going to do that when I know there's no future in our relationship. So he said I wasn't the girl he thought I was. I guess I won't be seeing him again."

Oh, my. Oh, my goodness me.

And after tea, when I drove her back to the school parking lot and dropped her back at her car, guess who initiated a hug and gave me a little kiss on the cheek?

I'm sitting here kind of stunned. I am not believing this shit. I am not believing it. I'm about to burst.

Wow! I'm going to keep that message because I love the joy that's coming through the computer as you relate what happened today. You sound so amazed and stunned and happy and incredulous all at the same time. It's delightful!

Again, I TOLD you this could happen if you played your cards right. And you have done. You have moved very firmly into the "nice guy I am comfortable spending time with and enjoy running into" segment of

her acquaintances. You gave her room to make up her own mind about you and she made it up favorably. This is very cool. As you say, you now have to move from the "friend" designation to "possible boyfriend" category, but that's easier than the first hurdle. Now keep doing what you've been doing -- give her lots of room to continue to get comfortable -- and at some point, SHE is going to invite YOU to join her at a concert or something. And that's when you're allowed to begin to let her know that you're very, very interested in something more than just friendship.

What she was doing, when she was telling you her personal history, was testing the waters. She wanted to make sure you weren't going to judge her or react poorly to something. She was confessing to you. Making sure you still approved of her. She was saying, "Hey, if you want to be a bigger part of my life, this is what I'm about. This is the kind of baggage you'll have to deal with. Are you up for it?"

Unless you're Tom Cruise or Russell Crowe, a woman wants to be friends first. She has to know that she doesn't have to worry about her physical and/or emotional safety. That takes time. But you've got a lot more leeway now. You can contact her more regularly. You're allowed to outright invite her for coffee or other low-key activity without worrying that you're smothering. The hug showed that she now feels closer to you. Why? Because she revealed lots of her personal stuff and you didn't run away screaming.

You really do have her right where you want her. Just keep being as patient and careful as you have been. She'll come to you if you give her enough room. You have the advantage. Just don't press it too hard.

31. Melissa and Tanya – and Olivia

It was late on a Saturday afternoon, at the end of the semester, and Tanya Cucoshay was at the Westdale Mall, on the edge of town, doing as much Christmas shopping as she could get done before she had to meet Andy Palinkas at the Janscombe Center for his lesson. Then she'd had to reschedule her usual 6.30 lesson, because when she was done with Andy she'd need to walk over to the other end of the complex, to Yolande P. Janscombe Auditorium, to get into costume and makeup and get warmed up for the next-to-last performance of *Amahl*.

Tanya's Christmas list wasn't long: her parents; Danuta's family; Livy; and she'd get something token for Connor, as she'd done the previous Christmas. This was her last opportunity to complete her shopping. She had one last performance of *Amahl* on Sunday afternoon, and after that she'd be driving back to Indianola to spend nearly a month with her parents between semesters, traveling with them to visit Danuta.

Connor was a tea-drinker, so Tanya stopped into Teavana and picked out a boxed assortment of loose teas, and a mug with a stylized "C." She was coming out of the store with this, about to head out to the parking lot, when she heard – a few yards off to her right – a child cry, "Mommy!"

Tanya was horrified: not at sight of Livy, but at the sight of Melissa, pushing Livy in a stroller. It was like being hit. In that instant, her suspicions were confirmed: all of them.

Unsteady, not looking at Melissa, Tanya walked over to Livy, crouched down to Livy's height, and embraced her lightly. "I'm glad to see you, honey."

"I see Santa Claus!" Livy exclaimed.

"You mean you just saw him? Or you will see him?"

"We just saw him," said Melissa. "Didn't we, Livy?" Tanya still didn't look at Melissa.

"Well, I'm going to go see Santa Claus right now and tell him to get you something extra," said Tanya to Livy. She straightened up and acknowledged Melissa for the first time.

"Just so you know, I got this for Connor." Tanya showed Melissa the contents of her bag. "So we don't duplicate." She made as if to move off.

"Mommy, Mommy!" Livy cried again, waving her arms at Tanya, evidently wanting her to stay.

"I guess she wants to see me," Tanya said to Melissa, in a slightly apologetic tone. She crouched down again and put a hand on Livy's arm.

"We're supposed to meet Connor at the food court in a few minutes," said Melissa. "You could join us."

"No, thank you. I have to be someplace." Tanya turned back to Livy. "Do you enjoy being with Melissa?"

Livy looked puzzled.

"You like Melissa?" Tanya quickly shifted her glance up to Melissa, then back to Livy. "Is Melissa nice to you?"

"Yeh! Daddy like Melissa."

"I'm sure he does." Tanya patted Livy again.

"I help Connor look after Livy sometimes," Melissa explained. "I moved back here a little over a year ago. Connor and I are such old friends."

"Yes, I know. You were at our wedding. He told me a lot about you, over the years. I know he thinks highly of you."

"Well, we hadn't seen each other in a long time. Before I moved back here. We're just getting re-acquainted, now."

"I'm sure," said Tanya again, still crouching at Livy's level. She turned back to Livy.

"Honey, I have to get going now, but I'll get you something nice for Christmas, okay? And I'll see you soon." Tanya again embraced Livy lightly, and brushed her daughter's cheek with her lips. She straightened up.

"Good seeing you again, take care," she said to Melissa, and walked off.

"Bye, Mommy," Livy called after her.

Tanya barely held herself together as she drove to Janscombe. She walked into her practice room a few seconds late. Andy was there, sitting in a chair beside the piano. He rose, smiling, and bowed from the waist as Tanya entered.

"I never thought this would happen," he said. "That I'd beat you here." Ordinarily Tanya would have smiled and said something jocular, but this time she looked grim, and Andy noticed that while he'd have expected her face to be a bit flushed from the cold, this was different: her face was blotchy-red, so that the streaks of rouge on her cheeks looked paler. She appeared to be having trouble shucking off her coat, and Andy stepped over to her and helped her with it.

"God, my hands aren't working." Andy looked: Tanya's hands appeared rigid. Andy took her coat from her and placed it on the chair he'd been sitting in. He put his left hand on Tanya's right and flexed her fingers for her; her hand was freezing cold. Andy rubbed each of her hands, turn-about, with both of his, and in a few seconds Tanya was able to work them.

"It's not that cold out," said Andy. "What have you been doing?" He noticed that Tanya was breathing irregularly.

"Just give me a minute." Tanya sat down on top of her coat, and put her fingertips to her forehead.

"I'm sorry," she said to Andy, looking at the floor.

"Tanya, what's the trouble?" Andy crouched down, as Tanya had done for her daughter a few minutes before, and put his hands on her arms.

"It was true. The whole fucking thing was true," Tanya whispered. Andy looked mystified. He assumed at first that it must have been something to do with Tanya's career: that she'd suffered some sort of professional or academic disappointment.

"My precious ex-husband, and Christine's sister," Tanya explained. "Melissa."

Andy sat down on the edge of the piano bench. His and Tanya's knees were almost touching. "What happened?"

Tanya had told Andy, weeks ago, the story of her marriage and her suspicions about Connor's feelings for Melissa. Now she told him about the meeting at the mall, in detail, remembering as much dialogue as she could.

"I mean, I don't hate my daughter. I knelt down, I petted her, I talked to her – not that she can talk a lot.

"And there was that fucking bitch, being the good stepmommy-in-training, standing there *judging* me. And asking me if I wanted to join her and Connor at the food court. I had to leave in case I did see Connor. I didn't want to rip him a new one in front of Livy and point out that I'd been right all along about how he'd lied to me about Melissa."

Tanya's face, which had almost returned to its normal sallow color, flushed again.

"Oh, I'm not really mad at *her*. But my ex-husband. All that time he kept telling me I had nothing to be jealous of, and I tried and tried to believe him – tried to believe that I was just being paranoid – but even paranoid people are right sometimes."

"I hope Melissa turns out to be everything he wants," Tanya concluded, with her voice starting to catch. "Because if she isn't, it won't end well for her."

Tanya's face squinched up and tears started rolling.

Andy whipped out his for-blow handkerchief and handed it to Tanya. Then he had to embrace her; he couldn't not. He leaned forward in his seat and guided Tanya's head onto his chest. She hugged back and sobbed, heaving. Andy held her, stroked her hair. He wanted to kiss her, certainly, but knew it would be indecent to try to. So he sat quietly, holding Tanya, not being able to help wondering whether anything might come of this.

It took about two minutes, no more, for Tanya to get her tears under control. She placed her hands on Andy's chest and applied just the least pressure, and Andy knew enough to release her, although he kept his hands lightly on her elbows for a few seconds. Tanya used his handkerchief on her eyes, and blew her nose.

"I'm sorry," she said. "Thank you." And she leaned forward again, looking right at Andy, and put her arms round his neck and squeezed hard, and kissed him on the cheek. Andy kissed her back, and was still debating with himself whether to move to her lips when Tanya started to slowly pull back. Andy relaxed his embrace, too, and looked into Tanya's speckled eyes and smiled – clearly inviting Tanya to do whatever she felt like doing – and Tanya smiled back, simpering. And that seemed to break the moment – at least *for* the moment, or at least Andy was hoping that it was only for the moment.

"I'm sorry," Tanya said again. "Laying all this on you. And now we've used up almost all the lesson and then I've got the show to do. I won't charge you for this one."

Andy touched her hair, lightly. "Don't be silly. I can afford it; you can't."

"He always said I was no mother, and he's right. She's better off without me. All I'm good for is singing, so I'll just do that. Though I wonder if I'm kidding myself about that too."

Tanya blew her nose again.

"Now I've got to go perform. And everybody's going to see I've been crying."

"Go wash your face. Cold water, if you're worried about that. I'll wait here."

Tanya left the room, shutting the door behind her, and was gone for about five minutes. As soon as she'd left, Andy started analyzing and assessing the situation. First of all he could hardly believe it had just happened. Second, he didn't know how to proceed. He was afraid of following up too strongly, being too eager; on the other hand he didn't want to feign less interest than he felt. He knew he was supposed to be assertive, be the man, be forceful without being forcible, so to speak. But above all he didn't want Tanya to say to herself, "What in God's name was I doing, making myself so exposed, to that old man?"

Andy didn't know how he would prevent Tanya from thinking that, if she *would* think it. He also didn't know of a way to find out, if she were *not* thinking that.

Tanya opened the door and let herself back in, and began gathering her coat, hat, gloves, and bag.

"Thanks for letting me vent," she told Andy. "And I'm sorry about the lesson. Guess I'll see you next week. Or no, I won't, because I'll be going home for Christmas right after tomorrow's *matinée*." She tried to smile. "No final exams for me this year. So I'll see you in January. We can probably start up again on… the 11th?"

"Break a leg," said Andy, as he put on his overcoat. "I'll be there tomorrow, so I'll see you once more before you blow town, even if you don't see me."

Andy wanted to say, "I could take you somewhere to celebrate, after that show," but he stopped himself since, he told himself, Tanya was almost sure to be occupied. He didn't want to give her the opportunity to turn him down.

And then Andy put his hand on Tanya's cheek, lightly, and moved his face a little closer to hers – and Tanya put her face against his chest, and put her arms round him, under his coat, and squeezed hard. Andy reciprocated, applying (he hoped) exactly the same amount of pressure.

"Hugs are nice," Tanya murmured into Andy's shoulder. Then she relaxed her grip; Andy relaxed his – but she maintained eye contact as she went to open the door, and briefly held Andy's left hand in her right as she opened it.

"I can't walk with you. I really better dash." Tanya locked the practice room door and hurried down the hall at a near-run, in the direction of the auditorium.

Andy was not dancing on air, as he left Janscombe. You'd think he might have been, and he was indeed elated, but he was barely bright enough to understand that he'd caught Tanya in a weak moment. For him to assume that he still held any advantage would be absolutely fatal to any hopes he might have had.

He would have to wait four weeks to see her again, and during that time he couldn't imagine anything he could do to make himself more sexually or romantically appealing to Tanya – if she were thinking of him in that way at all.

Still, Tanya Cucoshay had put her arms round him, and kissed him. She'd squeezed him, hard. She had to be into him at least to some degree, Andy reasoned, but he could conceive of no way to capitalize on it.

Andy celebrated, that night, by stopping by the Hy-Vee on his way home and buying a 16-ounce New York strip, taking it home, and consuming it along with a Caesar salad and a massive baked potato, loaded. He drank Johnnie Walker Black on both sides of that meal, slept ecstatically, and woke up the next morning only a trifle hung-over.

§

"David and Mercy were afraid Juliet would be too young to appreciate it, can you imagine?" Teresa whispered to Andy, as the three of them walked from the auditorium to the parking lot that Sunday afternoon, after the final performance of *Amahl*. Juliet was glowing. She'd been enchanted by her Aunt Christine's singing and acting. "They went without her on Friday night. She might not have seen it if I hadn't offered to take her today. And your girlfriend is certainly a beauty. Even all dowdied up for that part."

"My girlfriend, I wish. But you never know. I've got an update for you on that, by the way, when the little pitcher can't hear us. Including some Wainsnark."

"Has it ever occurred to you," said Teresa, "that you and I are involved in a feud? We're allies in a power struggle, aren't we? Jim and Gail and their evil spawn have got their claws into my daughter, but I'm trying to protect my grandlings from their clutches – and you keep on trying to rescue their little accident."

32. Christmas, and After

It was unfortunate for Andy Palinkas that this incident happened right in the midst of his busiest time of year, and that Tanya was out of town for a month thereafter. Otherwise it might have been resolved in just a few days, and Andy would have been saved a lot of anxiety and agonizing. As it was, he had to run a multi-store operation during Christmas rush while replaying that encounter over and over in his mind and wondering how he could follow up on it once Tanya was back in State City.

As long as his parents had lived, they'd flown out to California to celebrate Christmas with Andy's younger brother and his family. Andy had never accompanied them: He had too much work at that time of year, he'd explained. If the Blahas were hosting on Christmas Day they'd invite Andy. If they were otherwise occupied, Andy would cook Christmas dinner for one of his paid escorts, or spend the day alone. This Christmas, David and Mercy Wainwright were hosting both sets of in-laws, and they didn't invite their next-door neighbor.

"I should have asked them to invite you," Teresa told Andy, a few days before the event. "But they're always accusing me of meddling, and I'm sure that's what it would have been, to them, if I'd brought it up. But do come and have Christmas Eve at our house."

"Thanks," said Andy. "I expect I will. And don't worry about Christmas Day. I'll get a ham from Swiss Colony and have it all to myself for a week or two. And it's one day for me to be alone and decompress between two crazy shopping days."

Dear Mr. P,
    So this was our first Christmas dinner at the house

that doesn't belong to us anymore. I mean the house that
Mom and Dad pulled me out of so they could have their
precious garden. Mercy is now the *châtelaine* (and thanks
for teaching me that word), and we're just guests there.

I don't wanna be a drama queen because it wasn't
all that weird, but one thing really did piss me off.

You know, being Amahl earlier this month was
HUGE for me. A major opera role at the State University
School of Music. That is HUGE. That's like I'm feeling all
grown up and adult now. And then at the dinner yesterday
I got put at the kids' table. This is the reality.

Mercy said she meant it as a compliment cuz she
knows I'm reliable and good with kids.

I wanted to say, "What if I said I minded?" But
you know, it's HER house now, and I'm such a fucking
pleaser.

What made it just a little bit less bad is that
Mercy's mom actually apologized to me after dinner. She
was like, "I'm so sorry, I was inconsiderate. I saw how
uncomfortable you looked at the kid's table and I should
have offered to trade places with you. If I'd been here
earlier I'd have told Mercy to let me sit there. That's a
grandmother's job."

So I gotta admit I kinda like Mercy's mom after
all. No one else in our family does, so I might as well.

Dear Miss Christine:

I bet a lot of people would tell you you're spoiled if the kids'
table is the worst thing that happens to you – and they'll probably
tell you you're ungrateful and unreasonable if you resent it. But I'm
not going to tell you that. It does matter. You and I understand that
childhood is not for everyone. I find the whole concept of the "kids'
table" objectionable. Kids are part of the family and they should be
included. The kids' table was a gross indignity, when I was a kid –
even when I was very small. I couldn't stand children, even then. I
couldn't stand being a child, and I stopped as soon as I could! I hope

the food was good at least. And yes, Mercy's mother is very nice. She's your friend, more than she lets on.

Dear Mr. P,

Meh. The food was fine. Mercy's mom brought a lot of it and she's a pretty good cook. And I guess she taught Mercy. One thing I forgot to tell you. I am 99.99 percent sure my sister and Connor finally DID THE DEED on Xmas night. She came over here this morning by herself to help Mom with some stuff, and guess what? I know how a girl acts the morning after she's Made It Official with some guy. I've seen enough of my friends.

§

Dear Tanya:

Hope you had a wonderful Christmas and New Year's, and I hope you enjoyed your travels. I look forward to a full report. As you might imagine, I didn't have time to do a lot of celebrating, since Christmas is my busiest season.

I should tell you: Christine thinks the world of you. You give her encouragement and support such as she doesn't get at home. So you can be proud of the impact you've had on her life. Other than that, I don't have much to tell you except the holiday season was insane and I can now look forward to a slight lull for a couple of months. So I've been working on my singing. Scales and intervals, over and over again, more than repertoire, like you advised. And working on "Zueignung." But if you're not there to criticize me I have no way to tell: Am I singing decently, or am I just grooving my bad habits? What's up with you, anything?

Andy

DEAR ANDY:

THANK YOU FOR YOUR NOTE. I GUESS I HAD A GOOD TIME OVER THE HOLIDAYS. I SAY "I GUESS," BECAUSE FOR A LOT OF IT THERE WAS THIS FEELING OF GUILT HANGING OVER

EVERYTHING. IT'S NOT LIKE MY PARENTS MADE A HUGE THING
OF IT BUT EACH OF THEM MENTIONED AT LEAST ONCE THAT
IT WAS TOO BAD THEY COULDN'T HAVE THEIR MISSING
GRANDCHILD WITH THEM AT CHRISTMAS. THAT'S WHAT THEY
CALL MY DAUGHTER: THEIR MISSING GRANDCHILD. LIKE THEY
WANT ME TO FEEL GUILTY BECAUSE I DEPRIVED THEM. I'VE
NEVER WANTED CHILDREN. MY PARENTS KNEW THAT ABOUT
ME. I TOLD THEM THAT, WHEN CONNOR WAS TWISTING MY
ARM, AND I WISH THEY HAD BACKED ME UP BETTER. OR
RATHER, I WISH I HAD HAD ENOUGH SENSE TO LEAVE CONNOR
THEN. I SHOULDN'T BLAME MY PARENTS FOR THAT.

    IT MAKES ME FEEL GOOD TO HEAR YOU SAY THAT,
ABOUT MY INFLUENCE ON CHRISTINE. I DON'T KNOW IF IT'S
TRUE BUT IT'S NICE TO BELIEVE IT. THAT'S THE KIND OF
RELATIONSHIP I LIKE. NOT ONE THAT'S FORCED ON ME.

    ANOTHER THING: MY PARENTS HAVE THE WRONG IDEA
ABOUT MY MARRIAGE. THEY HAVE THIS IDEA THAT I THOUGHT
I COULD MAKE A MAN OUT OF CONNOR BY MARRYING HIM.
WHAT THEY DON'T GET IS THAT I NEVER WAS INTERESTED IN
MAKING A MAN OF CONNOR. I THOUGHT HE WAS A MAN. IN MY
WAY, I IDOLIZED HIM. I ADMIRED HIS MATH SKILLS, BECAUSE
PART OF ME WISHES I HAD PURSUED A CAREER IN MATH. I'M
NOT AN ARTY PERSON. I CAME TO MUSIC THROUGH MATH, IN A
WAY. SO I COULD TALK WITH CONNOR ABOUT THAT AND I
THOUGHT HE WAS BRILLIANT. I TRY TO EXPLAIN THAT TO MY
PARENTS AND THEY LAUGH. THAT'S PROBABLY MORE THAN
YOU WANT TO HEAR. BOTTOM LINE, I SHOULD HAVE MARRIED
SOMEONE WHO WAS SURE ABOUT THE CHILDREN THING. AND I
WAS WRONG: HE WASN'T A MAN. DOUBT HE EVER WILL BE.

    WATER UNDER THE BRIDGE.
TAKE CARE,
TANYA

Dear Tanya:

    You're right: water under the bridge. Don't beat yourself up
about having done anything wrong. You didn't. That's all I'll say. See

you in a little more than a week now.

Andy

So Tanya still was confiding in him somewhat, Andy reflected, and he could not get that enormous hug out of his mind. A woman does not, he reasoned, make that kind of gesture to someone with whom she has a purely avuncular relationship.

And so it was that for his next lesson, in mid-January, Andy arrived armed with a bouquet of Pat Austin roses, which are orange-colored, and brown and green tea roses, in an olive-green glass vase. Tanya was already in the room, seated at the piano, so Andy bowed and presented them to her.

"These are to welcome you back. I thought roses would be nice, but I wanted to get you some that were appropriate to your coloring, so I had to work with the florist to get exactly the right combination of exotics."

Tanya made the appropriate noises of appreciation.

"You know, red and pink and white and yellow aren't right for you," Andy continued. "You're a total autumn. You're copper, right? All earth-tones in your hair and eyes, and..."

"... and my awful washed-out complexion."

"Not a bit. Subtly colored. Anyway," (Andy began to trip over his own tongue) "it's... it's because of my profession. That I notice that kind of thing, I mean. So I hoped you might enjoy this little arrangement."

"That's so sweet of you to think of me." Tanya touched Andy's arm in what appeared to be real affection.

"You deserve it." Andy put an arm round Tanya's shoulders and embraced her briefly. Since she was sitting, her face only came to Andy's chest, but she put her face there and hugged back. Then Andy released her, with a kind of goofy grin on his face as though he were abashed.

"So," he said, "I've been working on *Zuuuuuu-eignung*."

And they proceeded with the lesson as though nothing had happened.

"By the way," said Andy, half an hour later, as he put

his overcoat back on and prepared to leave, "I see where one of your fellow sopranos is giving a recital on Wednesday night. Miss Greenhow. I'm going to be there. Want to come along and support her? Take you to dinner afterwards if you'd like."

"I think I'll skip it. I used to go to other people's performances, but I got sick of them never coming to mine. So I don't go anymore. But thanks for asking."

Andy shrugged, and wondered for a moment whether he ought to kiss Tanya goodbye. He knew he shouldn't, but he did: He bent down and gave Tanya a smooch on the forehead. Tanya giggled and gave Andy's arm a little squeeze. "See you next Saturday, then," Andy said, and left the room without looking back.

Andy may have been naïf and immature for his age, but he wasn't stupid. He was reasonably sure, as he left the Janscombe Center, that he'd failed – and that moreover he should not have tried in the first place. Maybe, he told himself, if he'd made not the slightest gesture of interest or affection toward her, Tanya might have made a move in his direction – but that would have been a pretty outlandish "maybe." Andy got into the new ice-blue Grand Marquis he'd bought himself for Christmas, and drove home to catch the Rivercats' basketball game on TV.

That night, after the game, after a late meal, Andy went into his back-room office as usual, and found this on his server:

DEAR ANDY:

    I NEED TO CLEAR THE AIR ABOUT OUR FRIENDSHIP. I AM GETTING THE IMPRESSION THAT YOU'RE ATTRACTED TO ME, WHICH IS FINE, BUT I CAN'T OFFER YOU ANY MORE THAN FRIENDSHIP.

TANYA

Dear Tanya:

    Gee whiz, it's taken you this long to get that impression? I'm disappointed, it goes without saying, but I realize there's not a damn

thing I can do about it. So, I'm glad to be friends. See you in a week.
Andy

There was more torment going through Andy's mind than he revealed in that email – but as it was, he just took two glasses of whiskey that night, instead of his customary one, before going upstairs to bed. He felt pretty calm, then, but he woke up the next morning from a dream he couldn't remember, saying out loud, "I fucking hate you." He sat up in bed, dazed, and repeated:

"I fucking hate you."

Andy stared at the bedroom wall.

"My God, you suck." Andy continued to speak aloud. "You've never been anything but repulsive. You ought to fucking shoot yourself." And Andy might have done just that, if he hadn't feared that when Tanya heard about it, she'd have thought it was about her, and would have rolled her eyes, or something.

Andy shuffled into the bathroom, muttering, "Fuck you. Fuck you. Fuck you. Fuck you." He repeated this phrase as he pissed. "You son of a bitch," he said to himself as he stepped into the shower. "Who the fuck did you think you were? You make me fucking sick."

And thus, Andy continued to unimaginatively and repetitively berate himself as he shaved, dressed, took breakfast, took a shit, and took himself to work. This improvised cantata went on, under his breath, as he got out of his Grand Marquis and walked from the downtown parking ramp to the front door of his store; it didn't let up even as he nodded hello to one or two acquaintances he passed on the sidewalk.

"You should fucking croak," Andy concluded, as he unlocked the front door of his store and stepped inside. "Worthless motherfucker."

And there was nobody he could talk to about it.

"Who the fuck were you kidding?" Andy demanded, as he turned on the lights and began setting up the store for the day's business. "Piece of shit. Just stop. Stop fucking embarrassing yourself."

And it was only then that Andy realized that it was Sunday, and that he shouldn't be opening his store at all. He stood there, alone in the middle of his sales floor, slack-jawed.

He closed his eyes and sighed, a long sigh.

"Stupid fucking bald-headed cunt," he muttered, and commenced shutting down the store again.

One can only judge by Andy's correspondence or conversations on this subject. He had made himself temporarily insane in his obsession. Insane, that is, if you assess with an impartial eye the intensity of this obsession, and his delusion that he could ever have had any chance of success.

And what's also psychologically interesting is that the drama of this obsession with Tanya Cucoshay had gone on *entirely* inside Andy Palinkas' shiny bald head. As an event – as anything more than a concept, a dream – it had never been. The drama had never happened. Andy had got himself into a lather over nothing at all.

33. Winter into Spring

Dear Mr. P,

I'm hanging out more with Evil Léa lately. She's a real good musician, and she's so cool and so pretty and I look up the her even tho I'm still jealous of her like a couple years ago but I don't resent her like I used to. It's tolly, what's the word? I know my crush on Tanya was always just a silly fantasy. Léa is like a substitute crush if I can't have Tanya.

I'm spending less time with Wet Dog. He didn't get me anything for Valentine's Day, didn't say anything sweet to me, so fuck him. Or not. Fucking him was never any treat.

C'est si bon que vous et moi parlons en français. Il faut que je pratique. Evil Léa and I have been working on singing songs with guitar and violin — it must be way hard for her to sing and play the violin at the same time but she does it — and we're going to form a duo called Les Sœurs Papin. If you don't get the reference, google it; il vaut la peine. It's so chouette it would take the hair off your head if you had any.

I hafta admit, sometimes I'd like to go all Papin on my family, but that alas is a dream that is destined to go unfulfilled since I'm not crazy enough to want to end up in prison. I'm not ready to go lez full time, specially not with a big fat dyke who might kill me!

Tho I gotta admit, I still think sometimes about experimenting that way. It might be kind of chouette to kiss another girl just once and have her actually kiss me back. Maybe one day I'll work up the noive.

But yeah. Killing my parents. I spend time planning it. I'm not going to, cuz even if I hate them sometimes they're more valuable alive than dead. Maybe when Dad's retired, when he isn't bringing home the bacon anymore, I could do it, before they spend all their bucks on their non-productive years. That would be a smarter business decision.

I'd disappear for a few days first, if I were to do it now. Run away or fake my own death. Then I'd double back and do the deed. But I'd be sure to get caught somehow. They always get you. No, this is just a dream. A beautiful, delicious dream.

Mon Dieu, Mlle. Christine:
I think the word you're looking for might be "sublimation."

That's taking an ideal or impulse that you can't act on (whether because it's impossible, or socially unacceptable), and substituting something else that's more realistic or inoffensive.

I did google les sœurs Papin, and yikes, it is a great name for a musical duo, bien sûr, but I'd advise you not to tell your folks who the original gals were, or it'd freak them out. You're not the only teenager to think those thoughts about murdering your family. I thunk them too. You bet I did. I never acted on them, obviously, but I had some dandy fantasies. Don't worry: you're way more normal than I ever was.

Dear Mr. P,

It's too bad we're not next door nabes anymore, or Evil Léa and I could come over and let you hear what we're doing. We worked out a cover of "Carolyn's Fingers" where I do the high parts and Léa sings the low parts and it's just smokin'. You know the song? Here's a link to the original video. It's gonna be the Papin Sisters' signature piece. Maybe we'll come play it for you anyway.

One reason I call her Evil Léa is that Les Parents don't approve of her cuz first of all she was in that band with me playing "headache music," and then cuz I used to be mad at her for trying to be the leader so Mom and Dad kinda blew that out of proportion and decided she was Teh EEEvil, or at any rate they decided she wasn't nice, and then they know that her parents are divorced like that counts against her.

Honest, Les Parents really do think that way. If a kid acts up, it's because they're from a broken home, or "not from a good family," and if a kid acts up who is from a "good" family, it's "Oh he would never do that" or "He musta gotten involved with some bad kids." Never possible that the kid was just a shit. Not if his family was OK.

So they don't like Evil Léa for MY sake which is kinda ironic, right? Since they don't like ME for THEIR sake! But she's talented and we have fun working on music

and besides she's beeyoodeeful and I like looking at her. I
am gonna kiss her one of these days.

U know, Léa's mom is kinda trashy. And her dad is
married to somebody else now and Léa doesn't see him.
Her mom isn't bad, she's nice to me but she's trashy. She
has the grossest BFs, guys with scary teeth and that
weird way of talking that they get from being in prison or
whatever. She is gonna end up beaten to death in a motel
room if she isn't careful. But she wants Léa to get on all
these shows like Americas Got Talent, cuz maybe she
thinks Léa's gonna support her if she does this stuff, and
she's pushin pushin pushin Léa into all this shit and Léa is
embarrassed.

But how can I criticize her? Léa's mom I mean. I
wish Les Parents were pushin pushin pushin me too! But if
they were, maybe I woodent push myself so much and I
woodent work as hard as I do. Confusing, huh?

On another topic. It looks like my big sis is getting
pretty serious with Connor. Like marriage-serious. It's
funny, when I see them together they don't act anything
like they're in luuuuuhv. Believe me I've seen it when a
couple is really into each other and they're just not doing
that. Missie and Connor are like old people. Or not even
old people, cuz old people sometimes act like they love
each other. Missie and Connor act middle-aged. BO-RING.
But maybe they enjoy being bored together. I sometimes
think Les Parents are like that.

§

What struck some observers about the courtship of Connor
and Melissa was the inevitability of it: how Melissa was not
sparked, but simply convinced that all she had ever wanted had
been right in front of her, in plain sight, and now, miraculously,
she was being handed this second chance that she could not
even think of letting go. Or perhaps she was convinced that it

was the will of God, or of the Fates – or of whatever she called Destiny – that she marry Connor after all, and that she would defy Destiny at her own peril. Rather low on the list of possibilities is that she might have truly loved Connor – loved him to the point where she truly desired to marry him and spend a life with him.

It's interesting to consider how Melissa and Connor rubbed along, for the couple of months after Christmas. Suffice it to say that while Melissa didn't move in with Connor, the relationship was indeed conjugal from Christmas on, and Melissa spent more than the occasional night at Connor's house.

Melissa and Connor had agreed not to get each other anything extravagant for Valentine's Day. Connor had asked Melissa, a couple of weeks in advance, if she would like anything in particular, and she'd said, "We're not at a place where we should be spending a lot. You know what I need? Take me to the Mall and I'll pick out a couple pairs of stockings, and that'll be my present. Seriously. And I'll get you something about as fancy as that. And I'd be okay if we just stay home and hang out, that night."

And that's what they did. After they'd put Livy to bed, they microwaved some popcorn and settled down to a movie: *Love Actually*. They sat snuggled on the couch, and when the movie ended, Connor sighed with contentment.

"It's taken me forever to get to where I can trust again," he remarked, "after last time. But, you know, I've always trusted you."

Melissa snuggled closer and put a hand on Connor's arm, as though to encourage him.

"It might be time to start talking about marriage," Connor said. "Someday."

"It does make sense. We're comfortable together. And my family certainly likes you, and I like your folks."

"You get along great with Livy. I'm amazed how you do it. She's… I'm sure she'd hate to lose you. I don't know what she'd do without you."

"Aww."

"And you'll have your Master's this spring, so you won't be busy with classes anymore..."

"I was actually thinking about going on. Getting into the Ph.D. program, if I can find the money for it."

"If you lived here with me and Livy, your other expenses would be pretty low," Connor said. "That might be a consideration. So, Melissa, do you think you'd be... could we... be a family?"

Melissa thought for just a few seconds, and took a deep breath and let it out again.

"Yes, we could."

"Wow," said Connor, to the room in general. He appeared genuinely flabbergasted – and very pleased. Then he gave Melissa the biggest, happiest smile she'd ever seen from him – and she'd known him a while. "I'm glad."

Melissa put her head on Connor's shoulder.

§

Dear Mr. P,

Léa and I are working on a repertoire that we can play at school and around town, and maybe one day if we get good we can get professional gigs. Course we won't be old enough to play in bars for a while.

And guess what? We kissed last night. Like I mean seriously kissed like I'd kiss a guy only it was nicer kind of. Mr. Wet Dog is not a good kisser even tho I've tried to teach him. Anyway Léa and I are working on the Flower Duet from Lakmé. Do you know it? I can pick out the tune on the acoustic guitar and she can add to it with the violin. She sings the mezzo part. She's good but I'm better. ;-)

But she's better with her instrument than I am with mine so we're even. Also we're getting better at "Carolyn's Fingers." And we're doing an instrumental piece

called "Ashokan Farewell" for violin and guitar. Here's a
link to a recording of it.

I dunno if I'm feeling romantic toward Léa or
what. I kinda do have a crush on her cuz she's just as
talented as I am in her way and she's sooooo pretty and
maybe it's cuz Les Parents don't like her. They don't say
that exactly, but they're all, "Are you sure it's a good
idea to spend so much time with Léa?" Because she's from
a "broken home" I guess. Gimme a break.

So it's like I admire her and at the same time I
want to take care of her. I dunno.

Dear Miss Christine:

It's good that you're working with Léa. It sounds like you're
both talented enough that you'll push each other, and each of you
has your own area of superiority – and that's good because you won't
make each other insecure. It's too bad that your parents have that
attitude. My advice is to let them see that you have other friends,
and downplay the fact that you're with Léa a lot. What they don't
know won't hurt them.

§

Dear Mr. P,

OMGOMG, I ate her out. She is a squirmy girl.
Then she ate me out and I had the hugest orgazam! And
then she kept going and I had ANOTHER orgazzy! I didn't
know that could happen but it's nice to find out, right? I
think I'm in luhv. So different from Mr. Wet Dog. Dunno if
I'll ever go back. (At her place and her mom was out so
we had plenty of time to fool around.) Is this crazy?

Dear Miss Christine:

I wouldn't call it crazy at all. You're hurting nobody and
you're evidently enjoying it. Besides, you never were enthusiastic
about Mr. Wet Dog, were you? Now you have an excuse to drop him

entirely. If you tell him you've left him for a girl, that will inflict a lot of pain, so you'd better not let him know that part.

I'm not surprised to hear this. Nothing's quite as sexy as musical talent, am I right? It sounds like you and Evil Léa are just experimenting, but if a real romance blossoms, will you go public with it?

Dear Mr. P,

I hadn't thought about that but there's no reason to, is there? It would just buy us a lot of trouble from a lot of different people. I dunno am I being a coward to think that way?

Dear Miss Christine:

No, you're being realistic. As you suggest, you haven't any reason to advertise what you do in private, and close friendships between teenage girls are pretty common. So, just be cool.

§

"Guess who was in the store this noon, looking at engagement rings?" Ted Blaha was relaxing in the Blahas' living room, in his vast overstuffed armchair with its upholstery of climbing roses. Teresa Blaha handed him a scotch on the rocks, and sat down with her own glass in the adjoining chair. She thought for only a few seconds.

"Melissa Wainwright and... whatsisname?"

"Who else?" asked Ted. "It looks like fate will be fate."

"Did you wait on them?"

"Are you kidding? I wouldn't have missed it. The young man actually gave me a heads-up the other day. He brought in the ring that his first wife gave back to him, when they broke up. So that he could trade it in, without Melissa finding out. Makes sense, of course; it just made me laugh."

"At least he didn't offer Melissa that same ring."

"Oh, he would never have done that," said Ted. "That rock would be kryptonite to him. Not to mention it's awfully small. No, he wanted me to put a price on it, and then he'd bring Melissa in to look at rings, and she'd never know that he'd be doing a swap.

"But you know what else struck me, when the two of them came in today? They were in and out in maybe an hour. You know the process. It doesn't go that fast. It can take days, or weeks. But they looked at three designs, maybe four. I told them, 'Take your time, take all the time you want; it's a big decision.' Melissa came in evidently knowing she wanted white gold. Other than that, she just approved of the design that the young man picked out. And the stone."

"So what did they decide on?" Teresa asked.

"It'll be a nice set. Plain, but nice. One-point-five total carat weight. Center stone's a princess, just over a carat, with a 20-pointer on either side. SI1 or 2, depending on how hard of a grader you are. I to J color. Just white enough to go with white gold. And the rings are substantial. You notice them. Matching wedding band for the groom."

Teresa sighed again. "I guess it's their business."

"Oh, but listen, it gets better. That young fellow gave Melissa this ultra-earnest look – like this – and he said to her, 'They look like they're built for a lifetime.' Not like the adjustable gumball-machine rings he bought for his starter marriage, you know."

"And this event that God won't recognize" (Teresa produced just the barest hint of a sardonic smile) "is when? Did they say?"

"End of July, beginning of August, they said. Oh, wish them well."

"I hope they'll be happy," said Teresa. "And I hope God can forgive them. Not just for this, but for what they did to that poor other girl."

"Oh, you can't believe everything Andy Palinkas tells you," said Ted. "Take it with a grain of salt, anyway. He's sure to put the worst possible spin on it."

"Yes, I know how Andy feels about her. That first wife. He still brings her up, every now and then. Apparently he's still taking lessons from her. Just to torture himself, I suppose."

VI. A ROMANCE, A MARRIAGE, AN ELOPEMENT, A WEDDING

34. Tanya Finds Love

Through the rest of the winter and spring of 2008, Andy Palinkas continued to take voice lessons from Tanya Cucoshay. The State City Community Theatre was supposed to perform *Oklahoma!* in July. Andy had been in that show once before, long ago – in high school, when he'd played Jud Fry, which actually calls for an unpleasant singing voice – but he thought this time he could play old Andrew Carnes, which is a minor singing role. So, he and Tanya started working on various Rodgers & Hammerstein tunes to prepare him for the audition.

For a while, Andy still clung to the notion that he and Tanya could somehow, would somehow be together – but he clung to it the way a tiny child might ruefully play with the scraps of a burst balloon, knowing the futility of it. Andy felt his infatuation dissipating, and he hated to see it go, because he had so enjoyed worshiping Tanya – perhaps he'd even perversely enjoyed the pain of worshipping her – and he realized it was most likely that this diminution of his feelings for her was purely his way of defending himself psychologically.

Tanya no longer had a 6:30 student, so Andy would usually stay and chat for a few minutes after their lesson. Sometimes they'd have a snack together in Janscombe's little café. Aside from his usual clumsy gallantries, Andy avoided any expressions of affection – save that he and Tanya now would always embrace lightly when they parted. It wasn't something Andy forced. Tanya would open her arms to Andy as they said goodbye. Andy never presumed to do more. What had happened months before, might not have happened. It was never hinted at.

Tanya didn't talk about her love-life, if indeed she had one, and Andy never asked, nor suggested that he wanted to hear anything about it. Tanya's personal demons didn't surface much – till after Jim and Gail Wainwright announced the engagement of their daughter Melissa to Connor Lowe, early in the spring.

"I suppose you've heard the big news by now, about my ex and Christine's sister," Tanya remarked to Andy at the end of their next lesson.

"Yeah, I may have heard something. Are you better with that, now?"

"I'm over it. I have nothing to complain about. Except for a few wasted years. That's what I have to get over now. I have to jump-start my career and I'm afraid it's too late. I've lost too much time. I finish my coursework this summer, and I'm just praying that by that time I'll have a job lined up. Teaching or joining a company or both. I'll still have to write my dissertation, but I can do that anywhere. I've had a lot of personal shit bubble up from worrying about that, about what I'll do next, where I'll find work. I've been trying to work through my self-esteem stuff."

"*You* have self-esteem stuff? Whatever problems you've got, I can't imagine they'd be due to any defect in yourself."

"Just holding on to old shit that doesn't really matter, but it's still keeping me from being me. Like that review. I told you about that old review, right? Being told that I have no business singing opera. And just these overall feelings of being a failure. This is a hard field. Lots of rejection. By stupid people, usually. I can't let other people's opinions be the truth."

"My opinion is, you're terrific. But what do I know?"

"Thanks. And it doesn't help that the guy I was dating just stopped contacting me altogether. So I've been feeling rejected in that way, too."

Andy hoped he wasn't showing any reaction. He'd known it was going to happen eventually – that Tanya would reveal to him that she'd found someone else – but that didn't make it any easier when she did let it fall.

"If he's not contacting you, he's probably not worth it."

"I already told myself that. Doesn't do any good. I didn't do anything, so I don't know what's up with that. I can't make him call me."

"Too goddam true."

"The last time I had any contact with this guy I took a big risk emotionally. I... revealed myself, I guess. And now I feel pretty stupid."

"Oh. You gave him the old 'I want to be with you forever and bear your child'? Or some such?"

"Nothing like that! I just told him he meant a lot to me. But apparently I don't mean that much to him. Bastard."

"Jesus. I know one guy who'd be glad to hear that from you. If he isn't, fuck him. Or rather, disdain to fuck him."

Tanya shrugged, and this time she seemed to initiate her farewell embrace with less enthusiasm than usual.

It was a couple weeks later, after another lesson, when Andy got up the nerve to remark that if Tanya were feeling down about herself, well, Prokofiev's birthday was coming up, on the following Wednesday, and Andy could think of no nicer way to celebrate it than by going out to a fancy dinner with a brilliant and erudite singer, so would she be free on that evening, or on an evening proximate? Tanya laughed.

"I'm not sure I'm allowed to," she said. "I'm seeing someone. And he's asked me not to date anyone else."

"What, you replaced that guy already? The one who was giving you the brush-off?"

"No, it's the same guy. He got over it, I guess. Or changed his mind. Anyway we're officially a couple. People can't believe it when they see us together, because, you know, he's so much older than I am. But, there it is."

"Oh," said Andy. "Someone in the School of Music?"

"A violin professor," said Tanya. "Aubrey Cavendish. He's actually almost retired. I hadn't known him except by reputation. But he gives private master classes, in what he calls musical energy, or the spirituality of music, and Miss Jespersson suggested that I should sign up for one this semester, just to, I don't know, just to put a little more *something* into my singing – and Aubrey and I... it's amazing how we hit it off. He's the most spiritual man I've ever met. He's become my life-teacher."

"He's a violinist, not a singer?"

"Yes, but these aren't classes in any one instrument. He criticizes your energy. Your spiritual presence. He's an incredibly deep person."

§

Andy knew who Aubrey Cavendish was. He'd attended many of Cavendish's recitals, over the years, and those of his students. Cavendish had obviously once been an extraordinarily handsome man, in a Christopher Plummer sort of way, but these days he looked more than slightly disheveled and dissolute on the rare occasions when he was seen in public.

Cavendish was older than Andy: mid-60s. He wore his dyed-black hair rather long, dramatically backswept. He had the bright smooth skin that comes from daily use of cold cream, and the preternaturally deep lines in his face that suggest similarly frequent use of opiates.

Andy asked his table-mate, the oboe professor, about Cavendish at the next Rotary Club luncheon. The professor said Cavendish was "a giant" – figuratively, since he was of ordinary size. A giant as a teacher, maybe, Andy supposed, but if he were a giant as a performer, why wasn't he widely known outside of academia?

It was news to Andy that Cavendish had retired, but not surprising. Cavendish's recitals had become erratic, and much inferior to those of the other violin faculty, over the years. Even Andy – who for all his concert attendance didn't know much about music – had noticed. The man sometimes seemed drunk.

"That guy," said Teresa Blaha, a few minutes later, as she and Andy walked from the Marriott back to their building. "Cavendish. He had to retire, from what I heard. If Tanya's with him, she's not the kind of girl you'd want to be with."

"That's cold comfort," said Andy.

"He was more or less forced out. Mostly because of the sexual part. He's been married five or six times, you know. Not to mention all kinds of affairs. And the rumors, about what he did with these women. Too disgusting to talk about. Who knows? Maybe one of them didn't get the grade she was hoping for, so she turned him in. Anyway, he lives way out past the landfill, in this old house he won't take care of. It was a wonderful old house once. I feel sick when I drive past it, now."

Oh, the stories about Professor Cavendish. Andy hadn't known most of them, till he heard of Tanya's involvement with the gentleman, but then he did some research, and discovered that Cavendish was far more of a local legend than Andy had imagined – and Andy had always thought he knew most of what there was to know around State City.

Aubrey Cavendish had apparently won high – but never highest – honors in the most prestigious competitions, early in his career. A third at the Menuhin; a third at the Tchaikovsky; a second at the Prague Spring International. He'd toured full-time, for a few years, but the rap against him had been that his playing showed more flash than substance. He'd been a flamboyant-looking young man then, with long wavy hair that he'd toss dramatically as he played, and he favored touches of bright color – an orchid *boutonnière*, a pocket square – to accent the white tie and tails that were a soloist's customary concert attire.

He was from Wyoming, had grown up on a ranch there. As a young sensation, he was often photographed playing his violin on horseback, wearing a cowboy hat and a bandana – and sometimes no shirt. "The Jim Morrison of classical violin," one critic dubbed him, and it stuck. Cavendish would later claim he'd longed to shed that image, but one wonders how hard he tried to do that.

Cavendish then joined the State University School of Music in the early 1980s, and was its best-known violin professor. He was already on wife number two, then, and he eventually married wives three and four – both of them graduate students of his – and, finally, wife five, a young flute professor from whom he was currently separated.

Erich Korngold's Violin Concerto was his particular showpiece: "The piece he bags all his wives with," one colleague called it. His interpretations of Mozart were also highly regarded. And for many years he was, indeed, a performer worthy of the State University School of Music. But as mentioned, his career fell short of the Olympian heights he'd probably foreseen for himself. He continued to perform worldwide, mainly in academic settings, but rarely with the finer orchestras or in the more prestigious venues. Critics continued to insist that his talent and artistry didn't match his showmanship.

Cavendish had published several books in which he explained his ideas of musicianship. These included *The Presence of the Musician*, *The Spirit That Moves Music*, and *The Tao of Music*. Andy Palinkas spent an afternoon at the State City Public Library, scanning them, and came away feeling that the author hadn't said anything – although he conceded that he might just not have been knowledgeable enough to understand the author's profound ideas. The opening paragraphs of *The Presence of the Musician* will do:

> The fight to find truth in our music is unquestionably one of the most daunting personal obstacles any musician will face in life. Even when we believe that we are being true to the music we're playing, there often seems to be an underlying motive in our playing or singing that is kept secret even from ourselves. Secrets get in the way of truth. Yet, is it a secret when we are blind to what we do? If you clearly see the effect the secret has on you, and the effect it has on the people hearing your music, how blind are you?
>
> To be self-knowing, self-aware, to understand why we do what we do and how we get in the way of realizing our full musical abilities, is what this book will teach you. Is it possible that if you carry, within the depths of your inner life, the secrets that keep you from producing the music you're capable of producing – since music is an expression of the self – aren't you, then, estranged from revealing the real you? When you don't show you, then how can you ever be in a satisfying relationship with your music? How can you show truth and integrity in your music?
>
> And what is musical truth? What is musical integrity? How do we hold ourselves to standards we set for ourselves?

Cavendish's old house got more ramshackle, and received fewer visitors, as he got older. His alcohol use, always heavy, became intense, and his performances in concerts and recitals deteriorated. Several of his students complained that he wasn't always fit to teach. Some of them switched to another studio – which would have been unheard-of, some years before, when it was a signal honor to be admitted to Prof. Cavendish's studio.

By the 2006-7 academic year, his shortcomings had become too evident to ignore. He'd been unable to fulfill his performance obligations – not only did he give up performing; he gave up practicing – and only two new students had applied to his studio for the following year. The Director of the School of Music persuaded Cavendish to accept Emeritus status, as an alternative to facing disciplinary action in response to the many complaints regarding his personal conduct.

He still taught those invitation-only master classes – the Director had insisted that they be off-limits to undergraduates – in which he discussed the "spiritual processes" of musician-ship. His few remaining students evidently found him brilliant on that topic. But by the time he and Tanya Cucoshay became acquainted, in January 2008, Cavendish hadn't played a note in a year. "My instrument mocks me," he explained to Tanya.

But somehow, he bagged her. He didn't even need Korngold to help him.

"And that's the guy who's better than I am," Andy told Teresa. "That's the guy who's, I dunno, more of a man than I am, more desirable than I am."

Andy had great fun tormenting himself, imagining what sex between Tanya and Prof. Cavendish would look like. Tanya straddling that flabby, alcohol-reeking geriatric. Trying to stuff his arguably hard-ish old peewee into herself whilst twiddling her own nipples and heughing in feignèd ecstasy. Tanya kissing the old man afterwards, running her fingers through the luxuri-ant dyed hair, with his expended slime drooling down her leg. And this – *this* – was more desirable to Tanya than anything Andy could offer.

§

"So you're getting started on your dissertation now?" Andy asked Tanya, after a lesson early in May, as the spring semester was winding down. They were sitting in the Janscombe café.

"Almost. I'm supposed to defend my proposal to the committee at the end of the summer session. So I've got two more months to worry. I've done a lot of the research, and I can write it wherever I end up going. Not that I'm getting any help from anybody. Miss Jespersson, you know, she's a singer, she's not a scholar. Aubrey was giving me some advice, when he was sober. But now he's not speaking to me again."

"Count your blessings, and add one. How did you offend this time?"

"I did nothing. He claims he heard from someone that I kissed a boy at the tango club last weekend. Never mind that I didn't. And who would have told him anyway? Now I'm getting the silent treatment. And of course I can't call him."

"Why the fuck would you want to?"

"Oh, you know, I worry. The last time I was at his house he was throwing-up drunk. I mean leaning over the railing of his front porch and heaving into the rosebushes. Plus, he's using again. I'm not totally stupid; I know the signs when I see them. You know, that was part of why he never had the concert career he'd hoped for. But he'd promised me he was only into alcohol, now. He told me he hadn't used in years.

"I confronted him about it, the next morning when he was in condition to talk. And he just said, 'My life circumstances are such that it's what the doctor ordered.'"

Tanya paused and thought.

"I always run second. I wasn't Melissa. I wasn't as important as Gareth's goddam Master's degree; I'm not even as important as Aubrey's… heroin. And Sally Greenhow's going to go farther than I will. Christine will go *way* farther.

"Come to think of it, that's probably why Aubrey made up that story. About me kissing some guy. Of course it was. Of course it was. Because he could use that against me, to shift the focus away from what he was doing."

"What in God's name do you see in him?"

"I told you. I'm one with him spiritually. He's my guide. My life teacher."

Andy shrugged, and tried to smile.

"And here I've been comforting myself with the idea that you just weren't interested in me because I was too old."

Tanya shrugged back, with a little head-toss.

"Sorry."

"If it's any comfort to you," said Andy, "I'm sure he'll get back in touch with you before too long, and the two of you will be blissfully coupled once again. He's just manipulating you. But you know that without my telling you."

"He's in a bad place right now." Tanya looked sorrowful. "And I have to be realistic about our relationship. It can't last. He puts down my singing. He tells me my energy is 'insincere'; he tells me my voice isn't coming from integrity. He says he feels jagged vibes when I sing or even when I'm silent. And maybe that's his truth. I have to try not to let it be my truth."

"He's fucking with your head."

"I wonder if it's because he's so sad about not being able to play the violin. So he's another one who's telling me I don't have the talent. As long as we're talking about the mystical stuff we're fine, but when we get onto music he can be so negative. He's hurting my self-confidence pretty badly."

And thus Andy understood what it was that Tanya saw in Aubrey Cavendish. Andy knew that if he said anything more that was critical of Cavendish, Tanya would be likely to defend him, to rationalize. So he forced himself to say nothing.

"Anyway," Tanya continued, "after this summer I'm out of here. I've got to be in a big city. Seriously, whenever I go to a performance at Janscombe, I think of how I'm missing really good performances, professional performances. I've got feelers out all over the country. There's a conservatory in New York that might give me my own studio. If that doesn't work out, I'll try Boston or San Francisco. But I'm not staying here."

Andy rolled his eyes. "Even if this fellow were to propose to you? It'd be a lifetime opportunity for spiritual growth, wouldn't it? Not to mention I'm sure he'd provide great nurturance of your career. In the long run."

Tanya continued to look serious. She gave no indication that she'd caught Andy's sarcasm.

"I told Aubrey I'd stay if he wanted to marry me. But I

don't know for sure if I would have. He's such a sad person now. I wish things could have worked out with him, but they just can't. Not realistically. My soul will always be close to his, but he has too much sadness to work through."

"His position isn't all that bad. He's a drunk, and a junkie, he's an old man falling apart – and he treats you worse than he treats his dog's shit – and you're sitting there waiting for him to call you. I'd trade places with him in a heartbeat."

Tanya looked away from Andy, then looked back.

"You'll find someone," she said.

"Actually, no. I won't. I'm 60 fucking years old, and all I'll ever be to any woman is a friend. I've spent all my life hoping and hoping and hoping. I don't hope any more. Congratulate yourself. You were the last woman I'll ever hope for."

"So why do you suppose that is? That you've never had any luck attracting anyone?"

Andy sighed, and thought about this for a few seconds.

"I'm not sure I know exactly. I've always had my suspicions of why, but I've never actually *known*. If I did know, and if it were something I could change, I'd change it. The truth is, you probably know what the problem is, way better than I know it. You were the one who had to make the assessment, when you knew I was attracted to you – and you weren't attracted to me. Whatever it was that I did, or whatever it was about me, to make you decide you weren't into me, you can bet that I've turned off an awful lot of other women in approximately the same way."

Tanya looked away from Andy, and shifted in her seat.

"Don't waste your time thinking about it," Andy advised. "Whatever is… is wrong with me, it's my fault. Nobody else is to blame for failing to see what a great guy I am. They can't see what's not there. And my defects are too deep to operate.

"But anyway, I'll miss our lessons. I'll miss having you around. And just so you know: I envy you that dissertation. You're luckier than you might think you are."

35. David's Career Evolves Further

"I could shoot myself," Andy told Teresa Blaha, over lunch at the Mainliner a few days later. "Sincerely, I could. I'd like to. Rather than deal with this constant, unchanging humiliation.

"I mean, what did I expect? Did I think she would settle down here in State City, and live with *me*? Or did I expect to sell my business and travel all over the world with her – as her manager or some such shit? But what I can't get over is that she'd have stayed in State City for *that* broken-down old fuck, but not for this slightly younger old fuck who's still in pretty good shape all around."

"She's a silly woman," said Teresa. "And that's all there is to that. I don't find her interesting. Our little Christine is a much bigger talent. Let Tanya go as far as she likes, and quit being so stupid about her. And for heaven's sake stop talking about killing yourself.

"Seriously, if you're having those kind of thoughts, get some help. Listen, Andy, maybe you don't care about your immortal soul, but I do. If you chose suicide, you'd be placing your soul beyond redemption, because you'd be turning away from God's mercy. Giving yourself no chance to repent and reconcile with God. And besides, you'd be missed. I'd miss you. And Christine would miss you. Would you do that to Christine?"

"You'd look after her. Although maybe I'll wait till she's off to college. Anyway it's just not worth it. I've made myself a laughingstock to myself. I can't bear it. This shame: that's what it is. I'm so ashamed of myself, of what I am."

"You've never had a serious girlfriend, ever, have you?"

"I have hookers."

"Oh, please!" Teresa straightened up in her seat and drew her head back as though from revulsion, but she also looked slightly amused. "You do *not.*"

"It's true. It's what I do. I can't attract women without paying them, so I pay. And that's an improvement. There was a time when I literally couldn't pay to get laid. I used to scare hookers. I lost my virginity when I was 23, to a *very* brave one, and you know what she told me afterwards?"

"Do I want to hear? Where did you find someone to…"

"This was 1971, thereabouts, when things were more free and easy. Well, *free*, for anyone but me. You know, everyone was having sex with everyone, back then…"

"I certainly wasn't."

"Yeah, but you're the misfit, Miss Perfect. C'mon, you know what it was like. Everybody was fooling around, whereas all I could get was the occasional date with a girl who thought I was *nice*, and who had other guys to take care of her sexually. Anyway, what that first one told me, it's embarrassing, actually, and I'm kind of horrified to tell it, but it's interesting, and maybe relevant to my plight, whatever that is. She told me she was terrified the whole time we were doing it. She was afraid I might hurt her, maybe kill her – and you know why? She said it was because I was so *gentle.* Not because I was hurting her, but because I *wasn't!* So, you see, I can't win."

Teresa shuddered.

"Yeah, it is kind of horrifying, isn't it? So, she and I would get together every few weeks, as I could afford it, and eventually she came to trust me, and when she left town – after her husband got out of prison – she referred me to colleagues of hers. By then I'd become kind of attached to her, so it was a wrench, but you get to a point where it's like hiring cleaning ladies. If you like one, you stick with her till she gets arrested or blows town or gets married and leaves the business. If you don't hit it off with her, there are others."

"You talk like women are a commodity."

"Not a bit. No more than operatic sopranos are a commodity; no more than professional athletes are a commodity. You do the best you can. If you meet a nice girl who wants to get emotionally involved with you, maybe marry you one day, great. If you can't, you look for alternatives. It's not using hookers that I'm ashamed of. It's *having* to use hookers."

"I'm sure you've never considered abstinence. Don't you have any idea of what a difference there is between just sex, and Holy Matrimony? Having a family?"

"No more than you do. And it's not just sex. There's companionship involved, too, sometimes. I mean, we might do normal things like just talking, or going to movies, or I cook them dinner. They tend not to be terribly intellectually stimulating, these ladies, but now and then they surprise you."

"Andy, you're crazy. But it's not so bad for you, never being married. Marriage isn't easy. Oh, Ted and I have worked things out. Ted and I are great, always have been. But it did take some effort, and it always will, as long as we're both alive. And look at all the others. Your friend, there. Tanya. And how it worked out with the man she married. And I'm afraid Mercy's not having an easy time with David right now."

Andy raised an eyebrow.

"I wish Mercy would tell me what's going on." Teresa leaned closer to Andy and spoke more confidentially. "I don't know. And my intuition tells me it's because she doesn't want me to know. Maybe it's all okay, but it doesn't look like it to me. Maybe she can't stand to admit to me that they have problems. Maybe she's afraid I'll say I told her so. Or maybe she's staying with him to spite me. I wouldn't put it past her."

"You never know. She might be content. Much as that might disappoint you."

"She doesn't look it. She looks tired. All the time. And she's always talking about how poor they are, and refusing any help from us. David is just not a provider. I wish I could tell Mercy to come down from her cross long enough to give him a good kick in the pants."

§

David had been working on the first draft of his second novel since early 2007, the day after his first meeting with Ike Abenafino, and in a burst of energy he wrote about half of a first draft in the next month. It was to be titled *Four-And-Twenty Blackbirds*. It was set in England, and on the high seas, and on the coasts of Africa and the Americas, in the 17th century. The protagonist was a young man who'd signed onto what he supposed was a merchant vessel, but turned out to be a pirate ship that also carried slaves from Africa to the New World.

During the spring and summer of 2007, after his agent had made it clear to him that getting his first novel into print and onto the shelves might be a long, slow process, David had hit a phase of depression during which he got practically nothing done on *Four-And-Twenty Blackbirds*. He tried to write it – but he didn't see the point of it, if his first novel were still a solid year away from being exposed to the populace and the literary community. During this time, he did write: mostly vignettes and sketches that might or might not find their way into that new novel, or some future work. But he could not focus on a particular goal.

In the late summer of that year, though, something seemed to light a fire under David. It may have been buying his parents' home, plus the realization that he was still a long way from being able to support his family as a writer, that impelled him to at least try harder to produce a second book. Slowly, over the next few months, he went back to his new work-in-progress, and by fall David felt he was back on track.

He also resolved that his second book would be the kind of literary novel that Ike – or, more likely, some more prestigious agent with more pull, and more talent – would be proud to show to the major literary imprints and to university presses. *Four-And-Twenty Blackbirds* would be a story of the sea in the tradition of Melville and Conrad, he told his friends and family. But his first draft, which he completed in December, was far from Conradian or Melvillian in length: approximately 60,000 words.

He raced through a second draft over the Christmas holidays, then sent the manuscript to Ike with strict instructions that he wanted it pitched to major literary houses. He sent it to several New York-based agents, too.

§

David never heard a word from any of those other agents. Nor, for several months, did he hear back from Ike. But in early May of 2008, when American Romance at last emailed him an edited proof of *Sarah Strong*, David had a good reason to phone his agent. This happened, as a matter of fact, the very day after Teresa had had that lunchtime conversation with Andy.

"Ike, what can I do about this?" David demanded. "I'm looking at this file they sent me – and I just forwarded it to you – and this is not my book. It's not the book I wrote. They ripped the guts out of it. I mean, I don't want to have my name on something I didn't write! What am I gonna do about this?"

"I'll take a look at it," Ike replied, "but, you know, there's always gonna be some edits. No writer gets to see his book published just like he wrote it."

"This isn't just 'some edits.'" David's voice started to rise. "They took all the poetry out of it. They changed the time-line. They even took out that last line I wrote, that summed up the whole story: 'so strong was Sarah Strong, with a woman's strength.' That's not in there! What can we... ?"

"Not much you can do, Dave. They bought it; they're probably not doing anything that's not allowed in the contract. I can look at it, but I'd bet that whatever changes they made, they knew what they were doing. These guys are pros; they know what works and what doesn't. Sure, if you want, you can call them and try to negotiate, you know, try to get them to leave in some of the stuff you feel strongest about – but, you know, 'kill your darlings' is what editing is all about."

"What if they refuse? Can I make them? Can I sue?"

Ike laughed. "Sue Harlequin? You could try; you'd get nowhere. You think they don't do the same to all their authors? Especially the first time, I'd bet. You'll get more experienced, you'll get a better feel for just what they want, and you'll need less editing. Seriously, Dave, let it go. Publish and be-damned, right? Look over the changes they've made, and let it be a lesson for your next book. And speaking of your next one, I might have some good news. I've gotten a nibble from Phoenixfire Press; they're a division of Phoenix House."

"Phoenix House?" David tried not to let himself feel elated. "Really? Phoenix House?"

"Thought you'd like to hear that," said Abenafino.

But then, as he'd done when his first novel was sold, David googled while he had the agent on the phone.

"Ike, I'm looking at my computer here… That's the Young Adult division of Phoenix House."

"That's your niche, in the long run," Ike said. "They'll want you to re-work this manuscript here and there, take out the sex parts and punch up the fight scenes. I mean, you have to consider your audience. They're 11, 12 years old. And put in a 'magical Negro' character to teach racial tolerance – I'm kinda surprised you forgot to do that – but they say they'll run with it if you're willing to do those rewrites. They're willing to hold off for a few months while you work on it.

"Oh, and that's another thing. They want you to find a way to change the main character into a girl. You know, she disguises herself as a boy and runs off to sea, and they want her to end up like a sort of 17th-century Uberwoman. Because as the book stands now, it's for boys, and boys don't read. Not anymore they don't. They want this to be about a tough teenage girl, 'cause girls are your readers. You gotta make 'em feel 'empowered.'" (Ike made air-quotes, which David couldn't see.)

"You think this is a *children's* book?"

"Dave, don't take that attitude. Lots and lots of writers got seriously rich and famous writing for kids. Madeleine L'Engle, Robert Louis Stevenson, Robert Cormier, Judy Blume. Hell, Harper Lee wrote one children's book and she never had to do another thing as long as she lived!"

David considered for a few seconds, and felt a little better.

"What kind of money would we be talking about?"

"Well, they won't make us a firm offer till they see your rewrites. But I'm guessing it'd be in the same ballpark as last time, maybe $4,000; *maybe* I can work it up to five or six but don't get your hopes up. Count on four."

"Seriously, that's all? I mean, this isn't a first novel. And they want me to rewrite it on spec?"

"Publishers just aren't paying the big advances nowadays, except to the really big names," said Ike. "But maybe I can talk them into paying for a tour, once it's published – a few cities if you're up for it – and that should sell you a few more books, and you'll find it's easier to write to the Y.A. genre when you've done it once. And when you learn how to crank 'em out fast, and you get a reputation as a reliable producer, you'll get the higher advances."

"Ike, that's not what I want to do with the rest of my life. Cranking out crappy little Y.A. novels or Harlequin romances. I'm a writer; I write novels. Not crap."

"Look, Dave, this is what you write, now. And that's fine, but if you want to write something else, you'll need to learn how to do it. U. Des Moines has a great M.F.A. fiction program; I don't need to tell you that. Apply there. Or apply here; the program here is almost as good. You'll have a published novel you can show them."

David didn't reply. He was afraid to tell Ike what was on his mind: that *Sarah Strong* might not be powerful enough writing to get him accepted into either of those programs.

"You know what might be better for you? If you want to be more of a literary writer? Fuck the M.F.A. Go for a Ph.D. in English Literature. Spend a few years learning from the masters. When you've done that, you might have a better idea of what goes into serious literary fiction."

David said nothing.

"You could still write. "You're getting there. Maybe while you're studying you could experiment, you know, write some short stories, get them published in reputable literary magazines, build yourself a reputation."

"They don't pay."

"Just a suggestion. But seriously, think about going back to school. You'll have a marketable skill, you'll probably catch on at some college, and even if you don't, you'll be qualified to teach somewhere. Meanwhile, kiss *Sarah Strong* goodbye and be glad you're a published novelist. And get to work on that next draft of the new one. You're almost there."

David dreaded having to talk the whole matter over with Mercy – the situation with his new book, the size of the advance (if the book were even accepted after a rewrite), his future prospects, and Ike's career advice – but there was no way to avoid it. The more he thought, the more a few years in graduate school made sense to him – and appealed to him.

To his surprise, when he did bring it up, over dinner that evening, Mercy didn't appear angry or disappointed. Just doubtful as to whether they could afford it.

"I believe in you," she told David. "But maybe you do have to learn more. It's a process. It might be worth it, if you got a degree. And I'm sure my parents would help, if I put it to them the right way. Though I hate to ask them for anything."

David's lips tightened.

"Yeah. What'll they think of me?"

"Honey, don't worry about that. We could ask Jim and Gail first. My folks might never have to know."

"We'd have to involve both sets of parents, one way or the other. Maybe it's not a good idea after all."

They agreed to sleep on it.

§

Undoubtedly, Teresa Blaha could be assertive. She spoke with a loud voice; she wore bright colors; she had decided opinions about this and that – and she wanted the best for her daughter and grandchildren. What she thought was best, anyway.

The tension between Teresa and her daughter had been in play since Mercy was barely toddling. Mercy's refusal to marry the boy her mother had picked out for her certainly didn't help. Then, Mercy started dating David, and who knows? Maybe Teresa dropped a remark to the effect that David didn't seem like such a great catch, to her. Or maybe she phrased it more strongly. Maybe she flat-out suggested that David was a lightweight, an overgrown child who wanted to play the sensitive artist instead of going out there and making a living. And you know how that goes: If your daughter brings a young man home, clearly infatuated with him, you mustn't dream of criticizing him. If you do, you'll have a son-in-law, sure as can be.

That's probably what happened here. Even if Teresa Blaha would insist that she'd been the model of tact and circumspection all along.

And let's not forget Ted Blaha's complicity, or guilt if you prefer, in this matter. Ted Blaha is a nice fellow, a fine fellow. Nobody has ever had an unkind word to say about him. He's a low-key guy who tends to his business, and if there was ever a man in State City who had less artifice about him than Ted, bring him out and show him to us. If you're just-plain-folks, though, you tend to be uninteresting.

If you're bright and curious, like Mercy, and if you have ambitions that rise above being like your parents, then you'll resent having a father like that – at least till you get old enough to appreciate him. He'll be an object of scorn to you; you'll feel that you have to live down your background. You'll be ashamed to let your friends know that you came from such a dull household, that your old man is such a clod, and nothing but a jeweler.

Now, along comes David, who probably struck Mercy as a romantic, an intellectual: everything Ted and Teresa were not. Idealistic. David was a journalism major, and if you don't know it, journalism majors tend to be very earnest. Annoyingly so. They often see themselves as budding crusaders for social justice, exposers of wrongdoing, champions of the downtrodden: deeply committed to whatever they're deeply committed to. Not much humor to them. Some of them are clever, or witty, but they're not good for many laughs.

They can impress you, though. David impressed Mercy, and she must have been flattered by the fact that David obviously liked her. Oh, it's easy to see how they got together.

Under other circumstances it might have just been a college romance, and they'd have drifted apart, gone in directions that would have led to different outcomes for both of them. But when Mercy considered her parents, and how her greatest fear was to end up like them (and when she considered their attitude toward David), could that have confirmed her belief that she'd be taking the right course by hewing to David's?

Perhaps, at first, Mercy had had visions of the two of them going out and fighting the good fight all over the world. Mercy would cure yaws or beriberi, in some godforsaken jungle in Bumbolumboland, while David wrote exposés of how America's Big Bad Corporations had made common cause with the corrupt King Bumbolumbo to strip the land of its resources and leave the inhabitants to starve.

What might strike some readers as more astonishing, though, is how Mercy developed such a crush on Jim and Gail Wainwright. It seemed to wash away any ambitions that she might have had to realize those high-minded ideals.

At some point in the process, it appears, Mercy decided that she wanted to grow up to be Gail Wainwright. Why else would she have got pregnant so quickly? It's just not plausible that that was an accident.

Maybe Mercy feared, somehow, that David regarded their marriage as ephemeral. Maybe she feared that once the romance of the thing was over, that once he had had her, sexually, he would lose interest in her and abandon her – if not physically, then at least emotionally. Maybe she wanted to avoid the unpleasantness of having to discuss when and how they would start a family. Maybe she dreaded the excuses that David might bring up for not starting one. Maybe she wanted to get the suspense over with, present David with a *fait accompli*, and proceed from there.

Didn't it occur to her that starting a family immediately would preclude that romantic crusading life she had once envisioned? Or could she, by then, have abandoned that ambition as a childish fancy? Maybe two years in the Peace Corps had gotten it out of her system. Might she, by the time she took her marriage vows (the second set of them, anyway), have adopted a whole new ambition: to be just like her in-laws?

Perhaps, also, she'd realized at last that David had a somewhat underdeveloped sense of responsibility. Perhaps she got into a family way in hopes of immediately, abruptly, reforming him. Albert Einstein once remarked that a woman marries a man thinking she can change him. A man marries a woman thinking she'll never change. Both will be disappointed.

§

Mercy, that night, felt she had nobody to whom she could confess her situation. If it had been about anything else, her first move would have been to call on Gail. To her, Gail was almost as much a mother as her own real mother was – and certainly wiser than her own mother, in Mercy's opinion. More down-to-earth. But to go to Gail, to admit that she was becoming disillusioned with Gail's son?

And to go to her own mother, and admit that she needed help supporting a man who should be supporting his own family? And to hear what her mother might have to say about the Wainwrights in general?

She thought of Nina Cermak, the older woman who ran the little in-home daycare center where Juliet and Theo sometimes spent their days. (And that was another thing: Mercy couldn't dismiss from her mind the idea that David was being self-indulgent, insisting on daycare for the children so that he could write.) Nina wasn't the brightest woman Mercy had ever met, but she was calm, and kind, and she'd listen.

Mercy had never – despite years of temptation – gone into David's computer and snooped his writing. But at four o'clock on the morning following that conversation about David's future – unable to sleep with all that was on her mind – she'd wanted to see what else David was working on. He'd said Ike Abenafino had advised him to try short fiction; maybe Mercy could look at whatever David had going on, and advise him without disclosing that she knew more about his writings than he thought she did.

Mercy held herself together surprisingly well through most of that day, after having discovered what she'd discovered – possibly because she was too stunned to react otherwise, at first. She'd gotten the children up and dressed without waking David; she'd driven them to Nina Cermak's house; she'd put in her shift at the hospital. But by the time she arrived back at Nina's to pick up the children, late that afternoon, she was unable to hold it in any longer.

Nina Cermak was a plain-dressed, plump, grandmotherly type, somewhere in her late 60s. She lived in an old house full of antique dolls, cuckoo clocks, and other "eccentric but charming old lady" stuff. She was known around town as a wonderful kid-sitter, but she could never take more than a few children at a time, so Mercy and David had been lucky to place their two with her. Teresa Blaha had slipped Nina something extra for the privilege, although Mercy never knew that.

Mercy was still trying to decide, when she walked into Nina's house that day, whether or not to confide in her, but all it took to set her off was Nina asking, "Mercy, are you okay?

You're *white*. Jesus Christ, you're shaking." And Mercy was. The children were in Nina's back yard, with a few other children and Nina's assistant, and the two of them, for the moment, were alone.

Mercy began shaking harder.

"God, *sit*," said Nina. "Tell me what the fuck it is."

"I was always so in control." Mercy's voice was barely above a whisper. She stayed on her feet. "I always was so sure that everything would work out so well; I thought I knew how to react to anything, and now something has happened that I don't know if it can ever be fixed and all of a sudden I need to talk to somebody – honest, I can't remember a time in my life when I felt I *needed* to go to someone else about a problem I was having…"

With that, Mercy just plain sagged down onto Nina Cermak's davenport, as though she'd been knocked off her feet. She bent over nearly double, her face near her knees, her shoulders rising and falling as she sobbed. It may have been the first time she'd cried with such helplessness and abandonment since very early in her childhood.

Even Nina, who had seen a lot in her life, was alarmed. She sat down next to Mercy, and embraced her, something she'd never have thought of doing before. She held Mercy in her arms, rocking her, for about a minute, and it was another couple of minutes after that before Mercy looked like she might be able to speak coherently.

"Is it David?"

Mercy nodded, averting her face.

"The kids are fine, outside. I'm listening."

Mercy composed herself, and told Nina – haltingly at first, then more fluently – about the paltry advance David got for his upcoming book and *might* get for his second, and his desire to redirect himself toward a post-graduate degree.

"And I didn't say anything, last night, but my reaction was, 'How are we going to afford that?' And considering how he's done so far, what's the guarantee that he'll make it in academia? How can I believe he's ever going to be a success now? I had faith in him, oh, God, I still have faith in him, I have to – but then this morning something else happened."

Mercy went into her shoulder bag and brought out a few sheets of paper.

"I printed it out. I had to take it to work with me and read it again, and see if it was really as… I don't know, I don't want to say '*bad*,' but to see if it really meant what I thought it meant."

"I found three stories." Mercy handed the papers to Nina with her face averted. "There might be more."

Nina read.

My Asian Girlfriend

She removed her t-shirt, and there she stood before me: naked to the waist; incredibly feminine despite or even because of her flat chest. She had long, flowing, straight black hair, flawless golden skin, black almond-shaped eyes, and a sweet, pouty mouth.

Slowly she removed her jeans, and was about to take off her panties, too, but I told her, "Stop. Those are mine." And she giggled. I gently pushed her back onto the bed, on her back, and I kissed her lips, her neck, then slowly drew off her panties.

She had only a little pubic hair, like you'd see on a very young girl, black and silky. And a nice big dick. Not abnormal, just big, uncircumcised. A beautiful, beautiful cock. And no other body hair aside from just that little bit of hair above her cock and balls, because she was a beautiful Thai girl. I'd never seen anything I'd ever desired as much; I wanted her; I wanted to suck her big cock and make it hard. I wanted the two of us to be naked together with no inhibitions, not hold anything back. It was a longing.

I wanted to taste her semen, I wanted to feel her burst and shoot her hot juice into my mouth, but at the same time I wanted to see my beautiful Thai girl have her orgasm; I wanted to see her body tense and her big red cock start to twitch, so I kept stroking it, up and down, slower, and she started breathing harder and I knew she was getting ready so I kept playing with her, gently, and watching closely, and all of a sudden she moaned, so softly, and her cock surged in my hand and this little puddle overflowed her belly button and I watched her spurt again all over her hairless belly while I caressed her balls and milked her cock to get every sweet drop, then bent down to drink it off of her. It tasted floral, of roses, violets.

"I wasn't sure what I would do," Mercy explained as Nina read. "I just knew I had to print it out."

"If you have to go to somebody with this, you might start with your husband," said Nina. "But really, is it that big of a deal?"

"Nina, he's *gay*. You can't tell me this is just fiction. And there are others. Including one about his college roommate. That's a guy I knew; I recognized the description. And even if he never did it with him, he obviously *thought* about it a hell of a lot. And here's one about some other guy – about David imagining being... *taken from behind*... by some biker type. Just look at that writing. It's his best work. Way better than anything he's ever had published. For the first time, I can really feel his... his passion. I can see his soul in this. How will I talk to him about it? How? Or maybe I should just leave."

"It might be fiction," said Nina. "Is there a reason you wouldn't talk it over with David – before you jump to conclusions? Maybe he was just being a writer. That's what writers do: they imagine stuff."

"I'm sure that's what he'd tell me, if I confronted him."

"So, give him a chance to."

Mercy thought, gazing out the window.

"Maybe I should just leave," Mercy repeated, the way people do when they want to make it clear that it's a question they want the other person to answer. "Just take the kids right here and now, and never go back."

"There's a reason you'd have to do that? Like, you'd be in some kind of danger, or the kids would be? I'm asking."

"No."

"Then is there a reason why you wouldn't talk this over with David first?"

"You mean aside from it being really, really unpleasant and embarrassing?"

"Well, yeah, aside from that." Nina laughed, and Mercy conceded the least ghost of a smile.

"Where would you take the kids?" Nina asked. "Or would you just walk out, and leave them with David?"

Mercy looked shocked that Nina would even mention such a thing.

"So you'd take them to your folks' house?"

"Oh, God."

"Would that be so bad?"

Mercy sighed. "I don't especially want to walk into my parents' house with my two children trailing behind me, asking for charity because they were right all along about the guy I married. And have them tell me they told me so."

"Would they do that? Take them one by one. Would your father say 'I told you so'? Or anything like it?"

Mercy considered. "No, he wouldn't. He wouldn't say it. He'd think it."

"But he wouldn't say it, right? Wouldn't give you any shit? Wouldn't blame you?"

"Probably not. He doesn't talk much."

"And how about your mother? She doesn't seem like the type to do that. Or I don't know, maybe she does seem like that type. Would she?"

"Depends on what mood I'd catch her in. But she sure wouldn't be happy about it."

"Can't expect her to be, can you? So, don't just up and leave. Take your mom to lunch, tell her you need her advice. She'll know what it's about, without you telling her. At least, she'll know it's about your marriage, so she'll be prepared."

Mercy walked out of Nina's house a few minutes later, with the children, feeling slightly less desperate. By the time she'd driven halfway home, though, her imagination had gotten the better of her again, and she was in a state of horror. Her mind's eye actually brought up the image of a stone building crumbling in mid-air and slowly falling to the ground, as though her marriage were being professionally demolished. She could see the disgrace of it – she would be just one more divorced woman who couldn't hold her family together – and she couldn't bear to imagine what it would be like, bringing up two children with no husband to help. It didn't cross Mercy's mind, then, that that was not too far removed from where she was already.

Another point: how would she look to Jim and Gail? How could she explain the reason why the marriage had failed, if indeed it were to fail? And what would be Jim and Gail's reaction? It would be *she* who had let *them* down, she supposed, and not David who had let *her* down, or deceived *her.* Mercy would be the faithless one, the abandoner of her family.

The children were being quiet in the back of the car – tired out, probably, since they usually found a lot to do at Nina's house – and it was too quiet for Mercy. She wished they would start acting up, would start doing something, anything, so that she wouldn't have to be sitting there in the front of the car with nothing but her personal demons to keep her company. She almost turned around and snapped at them to be quiet before she remembered that they were being quiet.

Once they were all in their house – *their* house, now, not Jim and Gail's – it was close to dinnertime, and for once Mercy was just as happy that David hadn't done anything in the way of getting the meal started. She was glad of the distraction of preparing food, and glad that David was barricaded upstairs as usual and had to be called down to eat.

It wasn't hard for Mercy to ignore David during dinner – he didn't notice – and then he went back upstairs and it was time to get the kids ready for bed, but when that was done, Mercy could not stop thinking her thoughts. The TV gave her no distraction, not this night.

She went up to bed, waiting for David to join her, which she knew could be soon or late. On this occasion it was near midnight when he entered the bedroom. Mercy had been trying to read (probably a self-help book titled something like *The Semi-Absent Husband And How To Love Him*), but hadn't been able to focus. She sat propped up in the bed, staring at the book rather than reading it, turning ideas over and over in her mind.

She waited till David had undressed, brushed his teeth, and gotten into bed before she spoke.

"I found out something terrible today, David."

"Hm." David apparently supposed she'd heard something unpleasant or saddening.

"Something about us."

"Hm." David still apparently wasn't getting it, and looked like he was about to fall asleep.

"It's something so terrible that I'm not sure our relationship can survive it."

This got David's attention. He didn't sit all the way up in bed, but he scooched himself into a half-sitting position against the pillows, and looked over at Mercy.

"What?"

"It's too awful. I can't tell you."

"*What?*"

Mercy gazed sorrowfully up at the ceiling.

"What do you mean? It's so awful you can't tell me? How am I supposed to do anything about it if you won't tell me what's wrong?"

"I can't. I can't talk about it now. Maybe tomorrow."

"Wow." David chuckled, bitterly. "I've seen you fight dirty before, but this is a new one. But just in degree. I know what you're capable of, and I'm not playing your shit. If you want to tell me what the problem is, you can; and if you don't want to, I'll assume it can't be anything bad, and I won't worry about it."

David slid under the covers and curled up, his back to Mercy. In truth he was upset, and wondered what the issue could be – but he decided he would do as he said he would do, and although it took him a few minutes longer than usual, he did fall asleep, and didn't dream.

Five o'clock in the morning, more or less, was the hour at which Mercy decided to discuss the matter. She shook David awake and announced, "Okay, we've got to talk about this now." David made the protests one might expect from anyone awakened for interrogation in that manner, but Mercy insisted, "I can't wait any longer. It has to be now." She had already gone to her purse and extracted the incriminating documents, and now she commenced a dramatic reading of "My Asian Girlfriend."

"And there's more, as you know. I've printed them all out, and they're in a safe place."

David, still bleary-eyed and thick-tongued, demanded to know what Mercy had been doing, snooping his computer.

"That's no longer an issue. The issue is that I found these. And I don't think we can be married anymore, in fact I know we can't be. You're gay, David, and that's your business, but you married me under false pretenses."

David protested with some vehemence that he was not gay, and that the documents Mercy was wielding were fiction.

"That's what writers do," David said. "We imagine things and write them down. That's what I do for a career, re-member?"

"Bullshit!" Mercy repeated to David the same argu-ments she'd given Nina the day before: in effect, that this writing was too well conceived, too lovingly crafted, to be anything but wish-fulfillment at least, and actual memoir at worst.

"It was going into a novel. I was imagining a character."

"You were having those thoughts. You obviously wanted to have sex with Glenn, whether you actually did or not. You paid too much attention to the writing; it's too believable. And it's pretty good writing for once in your life. If it had been made up it would have been written worse."

"Oh, fuck you," David cried, and at that point he forgot that the children were asleep, and gave an impromptu speech that lasted for a couple of minutes about how he was pretty sure that Mercy had never had any confidence in his work, that she'd never shown his work the respect that she'd pretended to have for it.

"You've always resented my being a writer, haven't you?" he demanded. "You're embarrassed that I don't get bigger advances; you're embarrassed that you have to work; you're embarrassed by the fact that I'm a writer. And now that I'm on the edge of producing something really strong, really artistic, you have to sabotage it by sabotaging our marriage."

"That is *so* not true," Mercy protested, and went into the bathroom for her shower, saying before she shut the door, "I think we're done."

David sat on the edge of the bed, too flummoxed to move, and when Mercy came out of the bathroom she said to him, in a somewhat kinder tone, "I've been told that we're all bisexual to some extent. But honestly, I always did think there was something between you and Glenn – not necessarily that you were having sex, but that you wanted to at least."

"No! No!" cried David. He threw his underwear across the room and stormed into the bathroom to take his turn in the shower. His denial was too vehement and inarticulate to be believable, Mercy told herself.

When David emerged from the bathroom, Mercy had dressed and left the house. She'd taken the manuscripts with her. She hadn't prepared breakfast, or awakened the children.

She'd got in her car and driven to the hospital, leaving David to deal with the rest of it.

As Mercy drove, she again considered the questions Nina had asked her, about her parents, and decided that in the final analysis, her mother would have to know – and probably could advise, if only she, Mercy, could tell the story calmly.

Mercy only had a four-hour shift that day, so she called her mother as soon as she arrived at the hospital, and Teresa, although only half-awake, immediately guessed why Mercy wanted to meet her for lunch.

"Come over here," she told her daughter. "I'll be home. Then we don't have to worry about anybody hearing us."

§

"Who knows?" asked Teresa, as she took the chicken tetrazzini out of the oven. "He might be telling the truth. That might be all there was to it, just his imagination."

"But it's all making sense now," said Mercy. "Those travel pieces he wrote, about sitting up in the night in their hotel room and hearing Glenn breathing in the bed next to him… those were love-letters."

"I have to admit I never told you this, but I always did wonder if David was a little bit… funny." Teresa got a salad out of the refrigerator and carried it into the dining room, where the table was set for the two of them. "That doesn't have to be a deal-breaker, though. Plenty of people have those… inclinations… and still marry someone and have children and they just, I guess you'd say they sublimate that part of themselves. This is probably his way of letting out some of what he's been bottling up. He might not even publish it. I'm thinking it's probably harmless – or at any rate nothing to worry about."

"But that story was so *graphic!*"

Teresa gave a long, helpless shrug. "You know that sort of thing goes on. And I'm sure people think about it, a lot more than actually do it. Look at it this way: If he'd been writing a murder mystery, and he described killing someone in some horrible awful way, would it upset you? Would it make you think he'd literally been killing people?"

"No, but this is... different."

"I can see we'd better have a glass of something with this." Teresa took two wineglasses out of the china cupboard.

"Maybe this is only because you'd been suspecting something like that, and this confirmed it," said Teresa after a couple of minutes, once she'd dished everything up and she and Mercy had said Grace. "You always thought so, just a tiny bit, didn't you?"

"No! Honest, I swear I never did. And I've got pretty good gaydar." Mercy reconstructed the conversation she'd had with David earlier. "Well, actually, I did tell David, this morning, that I'd suspected it. But that was after the fact, you know, I was telling myself – and telling him – that I'd suspected it at the time, but to be honest I never did."

"But, honey, if he were a more successful novelist, and he used something like that in his book, would you think anything other than that he was just being creative?"

"Well, no, maybe not. But he's not. Successful."

Teresa nodded.

"Maybe these stories aren't the only thing that's bothering you. Do you think you might be more upset with him for not being as good a writer as you hoped he'd be? Not as successful?"

"Mom, I was pretty sure going in that I'd out-earn him for a few years."

The two women ate in silence for a while, and it's likely that both were thinking, "Yes, but not by this much. And not with so little hope of that situation ever changing."

"Are you having other problems?" Teresa asked.

"Just the usual."

"Honey, you look exhausted. Your Dad and I worry."

Mercy sat silent for a moment, hanging her head.

"I didn't get any sleep, the last couple nights."

"I don't just mean now. You look worn out whenever we see you."

Another pause, and Mercy sipped the Gewürztraminer while she considered.

"I have to be the mother and the father. David is no help. I know approximately how much paying work he has, and it's hardly any. He could manage his time better, but I don't believe he needs to. He has his column in the *Examiner*, and then he's got his novel that netted him... You know how much he got, and I was ashamed to tell you. And he'll get the same for the next one, if they even decide to buy it; that's not a sure thing yet. He avoids Julie and Theo. If he plays with them for 10 minutes on a Saturday, that's being a great Dad. I make the money, I do whatever needs to be done for the kids; it's like he only had kids in the first place to show that he had them..."

"Now, wait a minute. Who decided on her own to have the first one?"

A pause.

"Okay. That was an accident. Truly."

"If you say so. He doesn't believe it was."

"But he was so happy when Juliet was born..."

"Don't ask me to explain men to you. I could try, but it would take a while."

"... and now he'd rather not have them around, except as decorations, and sometimes I feel exactly the same way. Because I have to do all the parenting. Almost all. I have to do the disciplining when they need it. I have to do the picking-up-after, the baths, the laundry, and sometimes I wish I could hold David's head in the toilet for a long time. Only it's getting so I don't even want to touch him, I'm so angry at him. He's a free-loader – an entitled freeloader."

Teresa seldom denigrated David to her daughter in an obvious manner, but she usually couldn't avoid at least insinuating her disapproval, when the opportunity to do so presented itself. This time, though, she held back. She just kept eating, and gave Mercy the least bit of a prompting glance.

"Maybe I didn't know what love was when we got married," Mercy said. "Maybe David didn't either. This is all making me wonder about what it's going to be like when – I don't know, when I'm your age and feel like I've wasted my life by doing what I thought I was supposed to do."

Teresa must have had a jumble of reactions, in her mind, when her daughter said that. She was tempted to ask, "Do you know what love is now?" More than once, in conversation with her husband and with one or two close friends, Teresa had confided that she believed Mercy was less in love with David than she was in love with the idea of marrying a man her parents didn't like, and then *showing* them. And later on (Teresa would add), even if Mercy had to admit to herself that she'd made a mistake – that her parents had been right in not approving of David – she would never be able to admit it to anybody else.

"It seems to me that if I ever do end this marriage, this is my chance," said Mercy, "and if I don't take it now, it'll be too late to ever change my mind again."

"Do you want me to tell you it's okay to leave him? Or do you want me to talk you out of it? Do you *want* to leave him?"

"Sometimes I do think I'd be a lot better on my own. I feel like a doormat, and I feel like it's less David's fault than it is mine. I let myself in for all this. First by marrying him, and telling myself what a privilege it was to just tag along by his side because he was so wonderful."

"What was it that made him so wonderful? You never did explain that to me."

"He was so enthusiastic about everything. Especially me. Yeah, sometimes he acted more like a 10-year-old but that was part of it. And I loved the way he'd talk about what a great writer he was going to be, how he was going to study the masters, and turn out stories that would be better than Dickens, better than Joyce or Hemingway. And I believed him."

"And now you can't, anymore?"

"You know, I closed my eyes to it. To the fact that he really *was* still 10 years old and wasn't going to grow up. And that he... I won't say he can't write, but he's not *good*. He's good enough to write columns for the *Examiner*. But no better than that. I kept telling myself, if he were to make a success, it wouldn't matter what I did. I could have... a career that wasn't just doing what I'm supposed to do. I could do something fun with my life.

"And that's another thing. I hate being a nurse. It's what I got into because I was supposed to. Supposed to help people. That's what life was for, that's what everybody told me – not just you and Dad, but the way they taught us in school, too. I hate nursing. I can't tell you how I hate it. I'd rather eat glass than ever work another shift. But what else can I do, now?"

This was more of a surprise to Teresa than anything Mercy had told her about her family situation. She almost asked Mercy, "What else would you want to do?" but she stopped herself, forced herself to stay focused on the issue of the marriage.

Teresa considered telling her daughter, "Give him time," but she had to admit that Mercy was right: a lot of time had been spent already. Besides, Teresa wondered whether that would be useful advice.

David was past 30, now, and not every successful writer has "made it" by age 30 – far from it – but they usually have shown promise by that age. Mercy was right, Teresa told herself. David's columns in the *Examiner* were utterly ordinary: like those that can be found in any small-town newspaper. There was no possibility in Teresa's mind that David was anything but an amateur, who might continue to get piddling advances on his books now and then but would never be able to crank them out in volume, nor invest the time and effort it would take to market them.

"Another thing," said Mercy. "If he goes on a tour, to promote his book, he'll be even less help than usual – not to mention I'll be wondering who he might be *with*, in his hotel, and what sex that person might be. And now that I know he's probably gay... What if he brings home AIDS or something?

"And I'm afraid that if I ask him to contribute more to the household – at least helping more around the house, if he can't bring himself to get a job or go back to school – then he'll say I'm trying to hold him back, that I'm taking him away from his work and keeping him from doing what might support us later on. But if he would do that, if he would only be a full-time house-husband. That would be a start. I could live with that."

"Then tell him that," said Teresa.

"I'm afraid either he'll agree to it, and then not hold up his end – or worse yet that he'll agree to it and *do* it. Then I'd have no reason to complain. And I'd be stuck in a marriage with someone I'm not sure I love anymore."

Teresa removed their plates, went into the kitchen, and began making coffee. Mercy followed, went to the sink, and washed the plates.

"Thank you, dear," said Teresa. "Listen, do you maybe feel that you don't love him, because you're so busy resenting him right now? Maybe you'd love him the way you used to, if you could get him to... I don't know, meet his responsibilities. Or make him see that he does *have* some responsibilities."

"I feel like what we have now isn't even a friendship," Mercy replied. "It's two people stuck together because we have these children to bring up – only that's all *my* job, and if it's all my job, what do I need him for? Why can't I cut him loose and let him do whatever he wants to do with his life? One less mouth for me to feed."

"You could. Honey, whatever you decide to do, Daddy and I will support your decision. You know that, right?"

Mercy hadn't known that. She'd doubted it, till just that moment. Maybe because she hadn't expected to hear what Teresa had just said, she couldn't bring herself to voice a "yes."

"You married David till death do you part," said Teresa. "Not 'as long as love shall last.' Honey, marriage is a life-long project. It has to be worked on, always. It's going to

need work as long as the two of you are together, and there'll
be bad times when it needs a *lot* of work.

"You could walk away; a lot of people do. I wonder if
that's good for them, though, in the long run. Oh, I'm not telling you that society will break down if you and David split. But
it will have an effect on Julie and Theo, you can count on that."

§

Mercy came home that afternoon still undecided about whether
to continue in her marriage. She found that David had taken
the children to Nina Cermak's place, and he was at home – in
his attic, at his computer.

"I don't know for sure what I want or what would be
best for all of us," Mercy told David. "But one thing to consider is maybe we should separate while you think things over,
or get counseling, or experiment, or whatever else you feel you
need to do, to help you decide whether you're gay or not."

"I am *not*..." David started to shout, then lowered his
voice. "I am *not* gay. This is my house and I'm not leaving...
And I don't want to be separated. God... Mercy, we're *married*.
We made a commitment and I've never had any second
thoughts, never."

Mercy looked skeptical.

"If you want to stay married," she said, "we at least
have to get couples therapy – and still I don't know if we
should live together right now." (Mercy was about to say that it
might be best if they saw a lawyer as well; then she decided she
might see one on her own, and what David didn't know
wouldn't hurt him.)

"What'll it do to the kids, if we separate?" David demanded. "It's not me who's asking for a separation."

"And it's bad enough that you told your mother about
all this," he added. "How am I ever going to face her again?
What'll *my* parents say, if we split up because you think I'm gay?
What'll they think of me? And what'll they think of you?"

Those questions left them both in silence for several minutes. Conceivably David feared, on reflection, that if Mercy insisted on a separation, and told Jim and Gail the reason why, his parents' sympathies might lie more with Mercy and the grandchildren. They might even encourage Mercy to stay in that house – while David moved out and took some time to "find out who he was." And by this time Mercy, too, may have been thinking that she might come out of this looking like the innocent party even in Jim and Gail's eyes. Might David and Mercy have simultaneously envisioned that same scenario?

"Another thing," Mercy said. "If you and I are going to continue living together, you have to start pulling your weight. We're just barely keeping up our house payments, on just my salary, and I don't know if you know it or not, but real estate prices are way down now. Our mortgage might be underwater. If it gets called in, and we default… Your parents co-signed the loan. Do you want to make them pay it off? Or would you rather go to my parents for help?

"So you need to get a job. It doesn't have to be a big job, but it has to be something. I need you to contribute at the *very* least $20,000 a year to our family, for now, and probably more later as our expenses get higher. If you want to keep writing, that's great, but you're not making any money from it and we have to face that you're never going to."

This seemed to hit David harder than the accusation that he was gay. The blood drained from his face; he opened his mouth; his stomach heaved; he began to retch. Mercy absolutely gasped aloud as she saw this.

"Put your head between your knees, David." Mercy stepped over to David and pushed between his shoulder blades to get him to bend. It took a minute, but David recovered without fainting or vomiting. He straightened up only somewhat, so that he was still bent almost double, and rocked rhythmically back and forth in his chair, head hung, eyes closed.

"It's not the end of the world, honey," said Mercy, almost gently. "It just means getting a job. And while you're looking, I'll need you to be in charge of the house. I can't come home at night and feel like I'm starting a second shift. I can make you a list of things that need to get done every day, every week – I can give you a to-do list every day, the night before – but you'll have to commit to doing it while you're at home."

"You think I'm a failure."

"Honey, no. You've sold a novel and you're about to sell another, and how many writers can say that? And you'll sell more. You're just not at a point where you can make a living on your books. We have to face it. A lot of famous writers have to take other jobs. They have to be professors or whatever."

David wanted to rail at Mercy that she just didn't want him to succeed, that she just wanted him to submit, that now that she'd gotten the two kids she wanted, she was looking to cut his balls off and turn him into a drone. It was in his mind to say that, but he was too spent. He sat there, shaking his head.

"I know I've overloaded you with things to think about," said Mercy. "I'm going to help. I'll work out a to-do list, like I said, and I'll make a list of where you could apply for a job."

§

For the next several days, while they didn't separate, they found it convenient for Mercy to sleep on the living room couch. David offered to sleep on a pallet in the attic, but Mercy said that since she was the one who wanted a separate room, she would allow him to stay in their bed. They also agreed to go separately to counseling: not couples therapy.

(This was for the same reason that Connor had given Tanya, a couple of years before: "I don't want the two of you ganging up on me," David explained. Mercy, who knew at second hand about the husband/wife team that Connor and Tanya had employed, suggested using them, but David said he wouldn't want to discuss these matters in front of another married couple.)

David also surrendered to the idea that he was going to have to bring in some money – even if he wanted to go for a post-graduate degree that might pay off in the future.

He applied for his old job at the *Examiner*, but was told that the newspaper was barely keeping afloat as it was. Thunder Karlsson, the publisher, was being let go; the *Examiner* wasn't hiring any editorial personnel.

Mercy suggested that if David wanted to consider going back to school, he might apply for a clerical or research job at State University, so it would be easy for him to work (maybe part-time) and go to classes.

What galled David in particular was that he had to be *seen* looking for employment – as though proclaiming to the world that his writing career had failed. Following one job interview, he stopped into the Gilded Lily because it was the nearest bar, and he wanted a glass of beer, and he just wanted to look around, see what the place was like: maybe work it into a scene in his next novel. And he figured that since it was three in the afternoon, it would be safe enough. The place would probably be deserted.

Not quite, as it turned out. There were about 10 customers in there, and two of them were old high school acquaintances of David's – not friends, just acquaintances. David drank his beer quickly, hoping not to have to interact with anyone but the bartender – but his former schoolmates saw him, and greeted him, and he had to acknowledge them.

"Dave Wainwright!" cried Jim Pew, walking up to the bar. "I hear you're a novelist now! Congratulations!" He put out his hand, and David shook it.

"In here doing research for your next one?" Pew asked, laughing.

"No: Dave's walking on the wild side," cried the other former classmate, Marty Richards, half-singing, in a loud nasal whine. "I'm gonna te-ell."

"No… no, just in for a beer." David tried to keep his voice quiet and pleasant although he feared that he was sounding vehement. He wanted to smash Marty Richards to the floor and kick and stomp him to within an inch of his life. "Just thirsty, is all."

And he walked out the door, but not before he heard Marty whine, "I'll bet."

It was a week later when David walked into We Cut Heads for a haircut, and saw that Bill Longley was finishing his work on that same Marty Richards.

"Hiiiii, David," Marty crooned, with a laugh in his voice, drowning out Longley's quieter greeting. David barely nodded, and seated himself in the corner of the shop to wait.

Marty said something to Bill in an undertone, and giggled. David could feel his ears getting hot.

"Buh-byyyyyyy-ee!" Marty sang to the room in general, as he did a pirouette and sashayed out of the shop. Longley swept off the vacant chair, and motioned for David to take his place.

"Boy, that guy," David sighed, before the barber could ask him what he wanted done. "I saw him in a bar the other day, I'd just gone in there for a quick beer, and he sees me and starts making all these insinuations about how I was in a gay bar and was in there cruising, and…"

"What, the place on Cypress Street? The Gilded Lily?"

"I don't know the name of the place but it was on Cypress Street I think. A little shorter than usual, okay? Weather's been hot lately. Yeah, I'd never been in there before, I don't know if it was a gay bar or what, maybe it was, but that guy… Jeez, he was giving me grief. I mean, I just was in there having a beer, and he starts pretending to make inferences. As though I didn't have a wife and two kids. I don't understand why people like that have to mess with other people."

"I guess they don't like it if you want to keep your private life private," said the customer in the next chair.

"That's it," said the barber who was working on him.

For the next week, it seemed to David that Jim Pew, or Marty Richards, were in several places at once. Everywhere he went in State City, it seemed to him, he'd run into one or the other, although perhaps his imagination exaggerated the reality.

Marty he certainly did see again, a couple of days later when he walked into Rosen's to get some socks just as Marty was on his way out with a box under his arm, and Richards wailed, "Hiiii-yeeee!" and winked at David as he passed.

"Yeesh, that guy," David muttered to Andy Palinkas, who'd come up to assist him. "He gives me the creeps, that guy. You know, the other day…"

A few days after that, on the street, David happened to run into Thunder Karlsson, the erstwhile publisher of the *Examiner*, now living on his severance package. Karlsson told David he was working on getting his real estate license.

"That's something you might want to try," Karlsson suggested. "You know what'll drive the housing market here in State City over the next few years? Gay marriage. The state Supreme Court is probably going to rule next spring, on whether it should be legal in Iowa, and they're almost sure to uphold it. You'll see tons of gay and lesbian couples moving into Iowa to establish residency and get married, and it'll be a gold mine for the real estate business because those people will mostly be pretty well off, you know, professionals, a lot of them, and if a broker can get a reputation in that community as someone they can work with…"

"What, you think I'd be especially good with gays and lesbians? Somebody told you the rumor too?"

"What rumor?"

"Oh, what that guy, that Marty Richards, has been saying about me…"

"Only it's not true at all," David concluded his story. "I didn't even know it was a gay bar, and I certainly wasn't cruising. Apparently Marty is one of those gay guys who likes to pretend that any guy who's straight is secretly gay, and maybe he gets some sort of kick out of making stuff up about people…"

It was a few days more, after that, before Mercy mentioned the matter. David had come home late that afternoon feeling up-beat, since he'd had what he felt was a pretty successful inter-view for a 30-hour-a-week clerical job at the State University admissions office – right near the buildings where most of the English classes were held, so he might be able to work and go to school with no strain – and Mercy was already home, but the children weren't.

"I took the kids over to Mom and Dad's so we could talk," Mercy told him. "They're spending the night there. I need to know. Are you officially 'out,' now? Because if you are, okay, fine. You are what you are, and I don't judge you for it. But if you're... you know... *looking*... If you're cruising the gay bars trying to meet people, I need to know that. And if you're look-ing for another relationship, same thing. We're going to have to re-think our arrangement, then."

David was almost shrill in his demand to know what Mercy was talking about, and who'd been talking to her.

"I can't even remember exactly where I heard it." (Whether Mercy was telling the truth, about that, is anyone's guess.) "But what I heard was that you'd told several people that you had been... looking for action... and the assumption was that you and I were getting divorced because you'd decided you were gay. And like I said, if you are, you are, but..."

It was the nth time David had told the story in a couple of weeks, but it was the first time he'd told it to Mercy. He had told it with slight variation each time, to Bill Longley, to Andy Palinkas, to Thunder Karlsson, and to others, but this time, talking to Mercy, he described his brief visit to the Gilded Lily as accurately, and in as much detail, as he could remember it. He added that Marty Richards was spreading the story mali-ciously because that is what that kind of gay guy likes to do, for some reason: pretend that every other guy is secretly gay, and try to "out" other people whether the information is accurate or not. David summed up his case with great feeling.

Mercy was silent for a few seconds when he'd finished. Then she said, "Okay, I believe you."

David stepped close to Mercy and made to embrace her, and she allowed it, and in a second or so she was hugging back, and they were kissing, and then...

Let's draw a discreet curtain over what happened next, but it happened quickly and with great energy, right there on the living room carpet. David partly wanted to do it, but partly also he was sure that he had better do it. Anyway, it got done.

And Mercy missed her next period.

36. Christine's Vacation

A loud squabble about her future – following a years-long accumulation of grievances large, petty, and in some cases imaginary – triggered Christine's disappearance. The last email Andy Palinkas received from her, prior to that event, ran thus:

Dear Mr. P,

Les Parents just went over the line. Both of them but Daddydear especially. I was kinda thinking out loud at dinner tonight about where I might wanna go to study music after highskool, and Dad was on his usual shit about "are you sure you wanna focus on music?" You know, the standard speech about how music is great for fun but it's no way to make a living, right? And then I was talking about how I might wanna apply to Eastman, Juilliard, Curtis, the New England Conservatory, and places like that, and Mom was, "I dunno, honey, those places cost an awful lot. If you have your heart set on studying music, why not here? State University is every bit as good as any of those other places."

And yeah, Mom might be almost right about that but the point is I WANT TO GET AWAY from this place. But I couldn't say that of course. But it made me mad because Melissa went to a pretty expensive college in Minnesota and they didn't mind, and Dave just took a whole year off after college, so what's the prob with me going to Juilliard or Eastman, right? Or at least applying there? I'm gonna apply to all those places anyway but it pissed me off that they're dismissing my ambitions and not wanting me to be as good as I can be.

So I'm like, "I'm good enough to sleep down in the basement, or address Missie's invitations, or sit at the kids' table at Christmas. Don't you give any kind of a shit about my future? Or are you still pissed off because Mr. P didn't let me drown?"

And that seriously made them mad cuz they don't like you at all and they're always putting you down and THAT'S WHY. And it really pissed them off cuz I called them on it.

So that's when Mom yelled, "That's it. I'm done. I'm sick and tired of you holding that over our heads when you know it was an accident. I'm done with you, young lady. I don't even want you in this house!" And then Dad got up out of his chair and kinda stood over me and says, "Apologize to your mother. Now!" I dunno if he would have hit me but that was the closest he ever came to it and it scared the shit out of me. So I said sorry real fast and ran outa there and now here I am at my computer trying to figure out what to do.

Who knows whether matters would have fallen out differently if Andy had been near his computer that evening? But he was at a recital, then to dinner with several of the music faculty, and didn't get home till nearly midnight, when he went to bed without checking emails. By the time he read that message, the next morning, Andy supposed the situation had become less volatile, so he typed a few words of commiseration and added:

I'll have to ponder this. I'll do my best to advise you, as always, if you want me to - but for now I hope it's blown over. Keep a low profile and stay out of your parents' way for now - and go ahead and apply wherever you like if you can do it without their signature. I don't know how that stuff works. But keep me in the loop.

By then, Christine was no longer in her parents' house. And, as we've seen, it was several days before Andy was informed – by the police – of her disappearance. Andy had thought it strange that he didn't hear from Christine that Monday – they exchanged emails more days than not – and stranger still that Tuesday and Wednesday went by with no word. On the Thursday, Detective Sgt. Brown visited his store.

It was later that same day – in the afternoon, after his lunch with Teresa Blaha – that Andy remembered the email exchange he'd had with Christine a few months ago: the one in which she'd discussed the possibility of disappearing for a few days, then doubling back and murdering Jim and Gail.

That email, Andy told himself, was several months old: the police might not have looked that far back when they were searching Christine's computer. Andy had assumed, when he'd received that message, that Christine had just been blowing off steam – which is why he hadn't remembered it for several hours after hearing that she'd gone missing.

But now she had indeed disappeared, following another family unpleasantness, and it occurred to Andy to *not* tell the police, to let the scene play itself out and let Christine do her worst. The fantasy of Christine hacking Jim and Gail to pieces – or gouging their eyes out and beating them to death with a hammer, which is what the Papin sisters did to their victims in real life – might have briefly amused him. But Andy told his assistant manager to take over, and walked the two blocks to the police station to talk with Sgt. Brown.

"I don't know exactly when she sent it," Andy told the detective, when he was seated in Brown's office. "February, March. This may be way off base; I'm sure she was just talking. But you never know."

"Thank you. I don't know what we can do with this information, but it does change things up quite a bit. You didn't think about warning her parents when you got this email?"

"Of course not. People say crazy shit like that all the time and they don't mean it. I didn't believe for a second that she was serious. Not to mention that she was saying that kind of stuff to me specifically because she knew she could trust me. And that's another thing. When you find her, *please* don't let her know that I told you anything. That I pointed you to that email. Tell her you found it on her computer yourself."

State City police were now operating on the possibility that Christine Wainwright – possibly with her friend – had not gone far. They might, Sgt. Brown warned his subordinates, be in the State City area still, possibly within easy reach of Jim and Gail Wainwright's home. They might be armed; they might be dangerous. Brown didn't contact Jim and Gail, that evening, to warn them to be on their guard. He didn't have enough information to assume that Christine was contemplating violence against them. But he had to consider the possibility. That night, and all through the next two days and nights, there was increased police presence around Jim and Gail's little house. It wasn't obtrusive – no cops on foot patrolling the neighborhood – but police prowlers drove by the Wainwrights' house every few hours, and more frequently after dark.

This was a neighborhood into which the police almost never had to venture, so it was noticed – and when Jim noticed it, on Saturday morning, he said to Gail, "What are they doing around *here*? *Here* is not where she is. What a bunch of boneheads!" He must have considered phoning the police and telling them to get on the ball and stop patrolling *his* neighbor-

AMBITIONS

hood, but if that idea did occur to him, he thought better of it.

And then it was over. Sgt. Brown, on Sunday at around noon, called Jim and Gail to tell them that Christine and her friend had been found.

The two girls had taken their musical instruments with them, which reinforced the detectives' idea that they'd run off together, and were planning use their musical skills to fund the adventure. Even after Andy Palinkas had come to him with his news, Brown suspected that that was still the more likely scenario, rather than any attempts at violence.

The word had gone out, to police stations nationwide, about two missing teenaged girls. Christine and Léa stayed under the radar for a few days, but inevitably some policeman, somewhere, was going to question two girls who had no identification, who were busking on the street and evidently sleeping rough.

The pinch took place in Austin, Texas, where the two were spotted at an outdoor festival – where they'd gone hoping to be "discovered." They were, too, but not in the way they'd hoped. The police didn't get any information out of Christine or Léa, but a quick check indicated that they matched the descriptions of the two missing Iowa girls, and they were taken into custody.

Dear Mr. P,

So here I am back in State Fucking City. Sorry I couldn't be in touch for a few days. I suppose you know by now that I skipped town for a while. Would have stayed away forever but we got caught. I'm staying with Melissa at her apartment tonight till they all decide what to do with me. Execution is the most likely. Anyhoodles, I got back this afternoon and I def did NOT want to spend tonite at home and I don't guess Mom and Dad woulda wanted me to. Prolly they need a day or two to get used to the idea that I'm still alive after all. I'm sure it was a blow to them. I keep turning up like a bad penny, don't I?

But at least Léa and I had a little vaycay, and I learned a lot about police procedures when they're dealing with runaways.

Léa and I had been talking about this for a long time. Taking a little road trip I mean. After that last conversation with Les Parents that I told you about, I decided it was time, so Léa and I took off that next morning. Took Léa's car to Cedar Rapids, left it in a lot and took a bus down to Austin. The Austin Folkfest was coming up that weekend so that's how we chose it. Won't bore you with the deets but when the cops picked us up and found out who we were they said we could choose to go back home or be kept in juvie hall there till they found us a foster home and even then we'd prolly hafta go home eventually. So we decided one was as bad as the other so why not go home. The devil you know, right?

I asked the cops how they gonna get us home, who pays for it, and they were like, "We see if your family can pay for it, and if they can't we put you on a bus. With an escort if we think you need it."

So here's what surprised me. Les Parents said they'd buy me a plane ticket and they also said they'd pay for Léa's because her mom can't exactly afford it. Which I had to admit was nice of them but I would never have guessed they'd do that.

From what I gather there's been a lot of back and forth about where I'm gonna stay now. I'm not crazy about going back to that house and God knows whats gonna happen if I do. The cops asked me if my parents had abused me and I told them they hadn't, because to be honest what they do to me isn't abuse. Being an asshole isn't abuse. I could stay with David and Mercy like they offered before but it would be the same problem. I'd be a servant. I could stay here at Missie's apartment because she's almost always at Connor's now, but Les Parents would never agree to that and prolly Missie would be thrilled about it only not.

Here's what's super crazy, tho. The Blahas called Les Parents and offered to let me stay with them for at least a few days till everything calms down. That's what Missie told me but she made me swear not to tell Les Parents that she told me.

You know Mom and Dad don't like the Blahas at all. Almost as much as they don't like you. And wouldn't it be too cool if I did stay with them, and people found out I was staying with them cuz I couldn't stand living with my own family? I'm peeing my pants thinking about that. Anyway gotta jet. Missie ordered a pizza and it's here. Tomorrow I'm spozed to meet Les Parents to negotiate.

§

"Christine, Mom and Dad don't hate you," said Melissa as she opened the pizza box and she and Christine sat down at the kitchen table in her apartment. "If it's any help, I used to think they hated me, too, sometimes. Everybody feels that way about their parents when they're growing up, at least once or twice."

"They never wanted me," said Christine. "But I didn't do it on purpose. I didn't decide to get born so I could mess their lives up. Or yours."

"It'll get better," said Melissa. "I know Mom's all caught up in the wedding right now and she's acting like she's got a new granddaughter now that Livy's part of the family…"

"No, no! That's not the problem. I don't want anything from Mom, except maybe respect. I want to get *away* from all this. You know what was the best part of Austin? The attention. We were playing on the UT campus, and in parks, and people were really listening, like they were into it, and clapping and cheering like I've never heard for street musicians. There's just nothing like it. Singing and getting recognized for it. It's what I want to do, and they're not going to stop me. I don't want to be pushed to be someone I don't want to be, just because Mom and Dad would approve. And because it'd be more convenient for them."

At this point, Christine had to pluck up her courage to go on – she was a guest in her sister's apartment and her all-around situation was pretty dicey considering what had just happened – but she felt she had to proceed.

"I don't want to end up like you or Dave. I'll get through high school. Somehow. And after that I am *so* far away from here. State University would be perfect for me if it wasn't in the same town as Mom and Dad. But I've got to get *way* away, for a *long* time."

"Dave and I both went away for a while. And we both came back. We wanted to. What's so bad about that?"

"Did you want to? You don't act like you want to be here. It's like you're doing all this because you know Mom and Dad want you to. Marrying Connor, too. Like they haven't been scheming to get you two back together – ever since they found out he was engaged to Tanya."

"Christine, that's not true at all!"

"I was here when you weren't; I saw it. But maybe I saw it wrong. Anyway, tomorrow I'll tell them what's on my mind."

Now, that is really interesting. Granted: Jim and Gail had hoped at various times that Melissa would end up marrying Connor, or a boy much like Connor. They never made a secret of that. However, we must be fair. No evidence exists – none – that Jim and Gail Wainwright wanted to prevent, sabotage, or undermine Connor's marriage to Tanya, let alone that they ever actively tried to do any such thing. It must be admitted: Jim and Gail were almost certainly innocent of such a charge. And yet this was Christine's narrative. She was insistent on the point. It's what she believed – or at least it's what she wanted Melissa to believe.

§

Indeed, as Christine had told Andy, the Blahas had offered to let Christine stay with them – "Just if you need some time apart for a few days," as Teresa had said to Gail Wainwright over the phone. "I hope you don't think I'm interfering, and if you want me to mind my own business just say so."

Gail had thanked Teresa for the offer, graciously enough, and might well have considered taking her up on it. Christine, though, after that meeting with her parents the following day, decided to stay with the people who (in her perception) wanted her least. She made this choice, we have to suspect, for a complex of reasons – the main one being that at least she could, now, intimidate Jim and Gail into giving her all the freedom she wanted and not discouraging her future musical career. In effect, she was perpetrating a sort of blackmail – not that it was entirely unjustified.

The showdown took place in the Wainwrights' little house, on the following afternoon. Christine had insisted that Melissa be present for the conversation – mostly because she feared she'd just be railed at, and probably punished in any number of ways, if she were left alone with her parents for this first meeting since her disappearance. And the fear of physical harm hadn't entirely gone away either.

As Christine recalled it – and not to anyone's surprise – the meeting was pretty awkward. The four of them sat upright, Jim and Gail together on the living room sofa, Melissa and Christine in chairs, as though they were strangers to each other, and adversarial strangers at that.

Jim opened the business session by clearing his throat. Gail said, "Well."

"Well, I'm back."

"Christine, we want to be fair," said Gail. "If you feel we're not treating you right, we're willing to hear what you have to say."

Christine tried hard to keep her voice low and calm, and for the most part she succeeded.

"First of all, Mom and Dad, both of you, I need you to

start treating me like I'm worth something to you, instead of a problem you're trying to deal with. Second, I'm going to be a star and you're going to support me just as much as you supported Dave and Missie in whatever they decided to do. And that means I'm going to apply to all the conservatories I want to apply to, and I'll look for scholarships and make it as little of a hassle for you as I can, but I need you to get behind what I want to do with my life.

"Third, Léa and I are a couple, at least for now, and you're going to have to get used to that. The bottom line is, I won't be the mistake in this family. If that's what I am to you, then you should be glad I was trying to arrange for you not to be inconvenienced."

Jim and Gail sat silent for some seconds – like they'd been turned to stone, Christine reported later.

"Honey, we never meant to give you the impression that you were a mistake," said Jim at last, and no doubt he meant it. "Please don't think that."

"It's true you weren't planned," Gail conceded with just a bit of a smile. "But we were very happy to have you and we love you just as much as we love Dave and Missie. Truly."

"Then I need you to show it. I need you to be glad that I'm doing what I'm doing, and not complain about what it'll cost you or how it's a pain in the ass. Or how I'm a pain in the ass. Okay, maybe I am sometimes, and I'll try to… I don't know, not be such a diva if that's what I'm being. Only I don't think I am most of the time."

"We saw a lot of your emails," said Gail. "The police showed them to us. It's like you're living a whole other life. You're like a person we don't know."

"We didn't know what to make of it," Jim added. "We just don't understand it. We were pretty shaken up. To find out all this about you."

Christine shrugged. "It's who I am."

"And everything you told Mr. P," said Gail. "About us. How *could* you?"

"I wish there were some way he could be put in jail," said Jim. "This is as much his fault as anybody's."

"How? Because he listened to me when you wouldn't?"

"He knew what he was doing was inappropriate," said Gail. "He can't have *not* known that. Encouraging you to... have sex. Taking advantage of you to... to find out everything he could about us, so he could do whatever he wants to do to us..."

"What's he ever done to you?"

"Plenty," Gail snapped.

"The point is, he was using you to get information on us," said Jim. "It's not about what he might have done with it, but he was using you. Don't you see that?"

"I don't think he was," said Christine. "And he's not the only person I've ever told stuff to. Léa knows almost everything Mr. P knows, and so do some of my other friends. But, yeah, Mr. P does know a *lot* about us."

Again, Jim and Gail both did a little take.

"I've been talking with him forever." Christine looked stern. "Mr. P knows all the shit on this family, and I mean *all* the shit. And he's seriously pissed at you."

Another idea popped into Christine's mind.

"I want to be able to tell him things are better and that he shouldn't be mad at you, or at any of us."

It's likely at this point that either Jim or Gail, or both of them, were about to forbid their daughter any further contact with Andy: restricting her email and Internet use, taking her cell phone, and so on. But it probably occurred to them just as quickly that it would be impossible for them to prevent her communicating with anyone she wanted to be in touch with – and counterproductive to their goal of reconciling with Christine, if they tried it.

"I don't want us to fight," said Christine. "I want us to get along. And I want you to be proud of me. One day."

"I feel like some of this is my fault," Melissa put in – probably trying to take the heat off of Jim and Gail. "I didn't pay enough attention to you when you were growing up. And maybe I acted like I resented you sometimes. I wasn't always very mature, I guess. But I think it's great that you want to sing. Mom and Dad do too."

And as Christine recollected the conversation, it sort of wound down from there, with no real resolution but no more recriminations either – and by the time the afternoon was well along it was decided that Christine would collect her stuff from Melissa's apartment and move back in, and they'd all try to get along better.

37. Melissa's Decision

"It's true. Christine gets treated like she doesn't matter," Melissa conceded. She was at Brett and Beverly Norton's house. It was a Sunday afternoon; Brett and Connor were off playing golf and Melissa and Bev were sipping mojitos in the back yard, and watching Bev's two children and Livy.

"Mom talks way more about raising her grandkids than she talks about Christine. Including mine that haven't been born yet. And that's another thing. My kids that I'm inevitably going to have. I feel like I'm following a script. Like everything seems to be *happening* to me, rather than me making things happen. Like, I don't know, like fate is just sweeping me along.

"I like to think of myself as someone who goes out there and makes things happen, but maybe I've been kidding myself all my life. If I were making this happen, I'd think I'd feel excited about it. Marrying Connor, I mean."

"You're not? Feeling excited?"

"Sometimes I remind myself that I should be excited. And then I am, but only a little, and only for a little while. Like I'm *willing* myself to be excited because I'm really not. Mostly

I'm just… like, numb, like I'm passing through life on one of those moving sidewalk things in an airport. Like when Connor and I were picking out the engagement ring. He showed me a couple of designs and I couldn't even give him my opinion. Didn't know what I wanted; just couldn't get into it. Wasn't feeling it."

"That should raise a flag, don't you think? If you're not feeling it."

"I love Connor, but I never think about it. That's something you shouldn't have to think about. I do love him. In my way. I love the way he loves me."

Bev shrugged. "Then the other kind of love might come. You just have to let it."

"I hate that, though. I hate that I don't feel what I want to be feeling. The way I've felt about other guys."

Bev considered for a moment, got up, and walked across the yard to where her children were playing – to give herself a few seconds to think, most likely. The children glanced up, wondering why she was suddenly standing next to them. "Doing okay?" she asked, and walked back to Melissa.

"The thing is," said Bev, sitting back down, "is that the two of you seem so unemotional when we see you together. Like you're actors playing an engaged couple the way you think maybe an engaged couple would act."

Melissa gave a barely noticeable start, and looked hurt.

"Do you really know Connor that well?" Bev asked.

"What? You know I do." Melissa laughed her you-can't-be-serious laugh.

"I mean, yeah, you knew him in high school, but people change. Do you know what he's going to want from you when you're his wife? Or what he'd want from anyone he marries? What do you do together, besides take care of Livy? Do you and he have any other stuff you like to do together? Well, aside from *that*. Do you even know what his interests are? Or does it matter to him what yours are?"

Melissa was finally starting to get irritated. "Are you trying to talk me out of getting married?"

"No, just telling you maybe you ought to think it over a little more. And take some time."

"Connor and I know where we stand with each other," said Melissa. "At least Connor loves me. That's more than I could say about some of the others I've been involved with. We've talked over all the important stuff, and we agree on it."

"When the two of you were dating in high school, I thought you were great together," said Bev. "And I thought you'd probably end up together. Even when he was married to Tanya, I had a feeling it wasn't going to last. But frankly? That marriage made me see things about Connor. I don't mean he's a bad guy; I don't mean he's wrong for you. But I saw how he was with Tanya, when Tanya needed him."

"What? What are you talking about? He's always been so solid, and dependable, and look how good he is with Livy!"

"Yeah, with Livy. But he wasn't so good with his wife. I'm not saying there wasn't blame on both sides. But that was kind of an eye-opener for me: how he treated Tanya. He wasn't supportive – and it was because he was still obsessed with you. That's something else you'll have to deal with. Tanya used to say Connor was in love with a fantasy Melissa. Tanya and I were never super-friendly – I don't think she trusted me all the way, because I was Connor's friend – but we did talk, here and there. And she opened up to me a little more, toward the end. And that's what she told me. And maybe she was right. Maybe you and Connor don't really know each other."

"It's been almost 15 years we've known each other! Anyway, it's kind of late to put off the wedding now." Melissa forced a small laugh. "July 27. Gosh, just five weeks now."

§

A wedding can take place on any day of the week. People used to avoid scheduling a wedding on a Sunday because the hairdressers and florists and other concerned parties were closed, but with more businesses open on Sunday now, and with various mobile services available – hairdressers willing to make house calls at a moment's notice, and so on – Sunday's as good a day as any.

Better, in some ways. For one thing, there's usually less competition, on that day, for reception venues and for the various artisans, such as caterers, photographers, and the aforementioned hairdressers. For another, you can often get a price break on that day, if you're hiring a hotel ballroom or a limo.

A little-known savings usually comes on the liquor. Since people have to get up and go to work on Monday morning, they won't punish the alcohol quite as severely as they might have done on a Friday or Saturday.

Finally, if a lot of the guests are coming in from out of town, you can hold the ceremony on a Sunday afternoon, letting them travel home that night or on the next day, Monday, when many airlines offer cheaper fares. So, Sunday, July 27 it would be.

Melissa did not get her wedding dress from Rosen's Silhouettes – even though her friend Bev managed the store – nor did she steer her bridesmaids thither. Andy Palinkas had told Bev not to expect that commission. But as mentioned at the beginning of this story, the Wainwrights were still looking for bargains on the male costumes less than two months before the event. When Jim Wainwright had hinted that he was looking for a favor from Andy – if not free rental of the tuxedos, then a deep discount at least – Andy had disappointed him.

"We can give you a package deal on the tuxes," Andy had told him, "Although if it's a daytime wedding, tuxes aren't appropriate. You'll want full morning dress, or sack coats – or just plain dark business suits would be acceptable unless it's a very formal wedding. If you wanted to go that way, I could sell a suit to whichever of the groomsmen don't have something appropriate, and then they'd have something they could keep a long time. Or we could rent you the morning dress, which would be slightly more expensive than tuxes. But, it's all whatever the bride wants. Have her come see me."

It was generally felt, among the Wainwright family, that Andy had just been feeding them a line about morning dress being more appropriate so that he could upsell them. Melissa did come to see Andy, a few days after Christine had returned to them, to look at his offerings, and she had decided on tuxes after all – grey ones, with ruffled blue shirts.

"That's a 1970s look, what you're asking for." Andy tried his best not to let his disapproval come through in the tone of his voice. "The ruffles and all. We used to rent an awful lot of outfits like that, back around 30 or 35 years ago, for high school proms. I never quite understood them. Besides, it's best if the men are as plain and conservative as possible. I would recommend white shirts for the gentlemen, and certainly no ruffles; the ladies can be as colorful as you want them to be. But that's just my opinion. It's your day."

"I want the colors for the whole wedding to be mostly blue," Melissa explained, "except for my dress. Black tuxes would be all wrong."

"If it's grey you like, I'd still recommend morning dress. Tell you what: I'll give you a deal. I'll rent the gentlemen morning dress for the same price I'd charge for the tuxes. Just so I can sleep at night, knowing that everyone is *comme il faut*."

"Maybe we'll be back; we'll ask around a few other places," Melissa replied.

"Glad to serve you anytime. And in any case, every best wish."

§

Dear Mr. P,

The wedding seems to be going along according to schedule, and I dunno whether I should be happy for Melissa or not. There's a crapload of stuff that doesn't get mentioned. Stuff like how I'm just barely smart enough to realize that Missie doesn't seem nearly as happy as when she was with Leander, who I liked a lot the one chance I got to meet him.

You know what's another thing I'm figuring out? All of Missie's efforts to finally get the praise she wants from Mom and Dad aren't gonna change a thing. That praise ain't never gonna come. She thinks Connor loves her and maybe he does for now but he showed Tanya what kind of a husband he can be. He's not gonna be that bad to Missie cuz Missie is so passive and so eager to please and she'll do whatever it takes to keep Connor with her and make Mom and Dad feel halfway okay with what she's done with her life. But she's gonna end up with a husband who's not gonna be as crazy about her as he is now, and a step-daughter who I'm pretty sure is gonna start talking about how Missie's not her real mommy, and then Missie will start having kids of her own who are gonna wear her out and make her feel like a prisoner – just like it was with Mom – and Les Parents are still gonna blow her off so they can fawn over Dave and Mercy. Connor's gonna get more respect from Mom and Dad than Missie will.

And I'm not kidding, what I said about Mom. It took me a while to get it. She likes to make people think she's such a Mom with a capital M, you know, so into it, but yeah, she really does feel like a prisoner. Like she did what was expected of her and now she hasta act like it's all she ever wanted.

I gotta admit, Li'l Chrissy is glad she's the bad seed in this family. It'll be a lot easier for her to grow in some other garden. Way the fuck away from here.

§

It happens more often than a lot of people would think: a young lady, a few weeks away from her wedding, calling a former boyfriend out of the clear blue. And it could happen for any number of reasons, and with any number of motives. When Melissa called Leander, about a month prior to her scheduled ceremony, he sounded distinctly cool. When Melissa began the conversation with, "Hi," Leander just replied, "Oh. Hi," thus forcing Melissa to state her business.

"Just thought I'd call and, like, tell you how things are going," she said. "I'm getting married."

Silence for a few seconds, then Leander sighed.

"I assumed you'd met someone, a year ago, when the emails stopped coming. I wish you well."

"Don't you want to know the story?"

"I'll listen, if you're dying to tell it."

That took the wind out of Melissa's sails a bit, so she gave Leander a considerably shorter version of her news than she'd probably planned to give him.

"You don't sound excited," Leander commented.

Again, Melissa couldn't think of anything to say for a few seconds, and Leander asked, "Are you?"

"Yes, yes, of course I am."

"Are you getting the jitters? Cold feet?"

"Not really. No. No. I just wanted to... you know, I wanted..."

"Closure?"

"No, I don't know that I mean that. I mean we just stopped communicating. We never talked about it."

It wouldn't be useful to reproduce the entire conversation here. More revealing would be a list of what Melissa and Leander didn't discuss. They didn't talk about their respective careers. Nor about how Leander's parents had felt about Melissa, nor about how Jim and Gail had felt about Leander. They didn't talk about whether Leander had any marital prospects. They didn't recriminate. The dialogue, for the next few minutes, consisted of a sort of pushing and pulling in which they both acknowledged that they could have tried harder to keep their relationship going, but conceded that it would have been problematic, and probably not productive, if they had.

Melissa finally said, "It's too bad. It was nice while it lasted. You know, I'm sorry."

"If you're sorry," said Leander, "are you sure you're okay with doing what you're doing? Or did you call me to give me a chance to talk you out of it? It's just now starting to dawn on me. You ran back to State City to chase this guy. Didn't you? Not that I hold that against you if that was what you wanted to do. But I don't understand what you want from me, now. If you want anything from me."

Melissa hesitated, then blurted it out before she could think better of it. "You could come down here to see me."

"No, sorry. Not while you're engaged. Not when you're getting married in a month. If you were single and unattached, maybe we could talk about it."

"So I've got to break off the engagement before you'll see me again? You could just come for a *visit*, you know?"

"Melissa, that's crazy. I've moved on. I can't just jump when you call. I can't go down to see you just to *see* you, and I'm not going to put my life on hold for you. That's not a reasonable expectation. I'll always listen if you want to talk – but my life will go where it goes, and you'll have to make your decisions without putting me into the equation."

Silence for a few more seconds – then Leander spoke again.

"If you want me to come down there for a visit at this point, then you need to think good and hard about what you're planning to do next month. You need to determine who you are, first. Then find someone who *fits* who you are. Not marry someone because he wants to and because your parents approve of him. It's almost like you're doing this to please other people. Like you don't want to disappoint this man – Connor – and maybe you want to show your parents that you're worthy of them. I wish you would do whatever you do, to please *yourself* – whether that's marrying this guy or someone else."

"It wouldn't have worked between you and me," said Melissa at last. "I'm doing the right thing. Thanks for letting me sort it out. Let's do keep in touch though, from now on, okay?"

"My email and phone are still the same," said Leander. "Whatever you decide, I hope it's the best for you."

It wouldn't have been hard for Melissa to find a rationalization following a conversation like that. One line of reasoning might have been to say to herself, "Connor is there for you. Is Leander? Is he fighting for you? Did he ever fight for you? Connor has always been there for you."

Yes, Connor had, indeed, always been there for her – an imaginary and cynical interlocutor might have said to Melissa – except during his marriage, but perhaps it could be argued that even while he'd been married to Tanya, Connor's heart had remained constant.

"This was meant to be," might have been another of Melissa's arguments to herself. "Every event, all of it, it just fell into place as though Connor and I *had* to be together, as though the world wouldn't be right unless we *were* together."

And yet the doubts must have persisted in Melissa's mind; they must have almost deafened her. Did she love Connor? Or did she feel an obligation to him because of how he felt about her? Or an obligation to her parents because of what they obviously wanted her to do? Or an obligation to motherless Livy?

That remark of Bev's must have stuck in Melissa's mind: "Tanya used to say that Connor was in love with a fantasy Melissa. And maybe she was right."

Here is what Melissa might have asked herself, but probably never did: "Does Connor think, has he ever thought, about what *I* want? About what *I* need? Has he ever asked me about *my* goals, *my* ambitions?"

And then she might have asked herself, "Do I know what I want or need? Do I have any goals, any ambitions?"

But maybe those questions aren't important to everyone, and maybe they don't need to be.

Some observers of this situation might wish that Melissa would not marry Connor, that she would spread her wings and fly away, instead. And another writer – someone presenting a fictionalized account of this story – might give in to the temptation to write it so, for the sake of a happier ending. It would have made the book more politically palatable, and more salable as a movie. And it would have made most readers feel better.

But an honest storyteller must tell the story as it happened – and would Melissa have done that, really?

When she'd added everything up and looked at all her options, the possibility of flying, so to speak, might not have been compelling to Melissa. She might have wanted it, but not badly enough to do it. She may not have wanted anything badly enough, all her life long. It could be that the thing she wanted most was a negative: to *not* displease her parents. So that's what she did. She avoided displeasing her parents. She probably knows she'll never be their star. But she won their approval by capturing the prize they'd set their sights on.

Also, what about Connor and Livy? If Melissa had backed out of the marriage, would she not have been letting them both down? Connor, who'd come to rely on her to be a mother to his little girl, and Livy, who probably depended on her more than anyone else might have guessed? What would they think of her, and would they ever forgive her, if she left them in the lurch after raising their expectations so high? That must have been what Melissa was thinking.

And by marrying Connor, Melissa would have spared herself the never-ending hints that it was so unfortunate that she wasn't married yet, and, gosh, we wonder if she ever will get married. What a nice family she might have had with Connor and that poor little girl of his, but it's her life…

38. The Wedding That Might Have Been

"So, the wedding will be starting just as I'm pulling out of town forever, tomorrow," Tanya told Andy as she locked the door to the practice room and the two of them headed down the corridor, to the exit and the Janscombe parking lot. They might have been the only people in the building. Technically, Tanya should already have handed her keys over to the proper authorities. The café was closed, since the summer term was now over.

Tanya's course work was done. She'd defended her dissertation proposal the previous week, and now only had to write it – which, she told Andy, couldn't possibly take more than a year or so. Most of her stuff was packed and ready for her parents to haul back to Indianola. Tanya herself would be off to New York City the next day – permanently, she hoped.

"Be glad you're making your escape," said Andy. "Now you can get your career on track."

"Maybe," said Tanya, as they left the building. "This conservatory position is kind of a gamble. It's not what I'd have chosen, ideally. But it's a start and I can look around. Meanwhile I'm finally done with the most horrible years of my life. At least I hope that's what they were."

"Oh, come on. You met me. That'd make up for all the rest of it, I should hope."

"It was fun getting to know you. I hope we can stay in touch."

Andy at this point felt the impulse to tell Tanya, "It's not too late. You could stay here – stay here as Mrs. Palinkas, I mean. You'd only have to put up with me for 15, 20 years, and

I'd subsidize your career. And there'd be enough for you to live on after I kick off."

But he didn't say it. For one thing it would have struck Tanya as an absurd proposal, probably a repugnant proposal. And she certainly would have taken it as an offer to do business.

Andy's nearly-new Grand Marquis and Tanya's much older, dilapidated Hyundai Elantra were parked side-by-side. Andy and Tanya both stood there, next to their cars, and they both apparently had the same thought: to take a long look back at the Janscombe Center, and the State River beyond it, and the otherwise empty lot.

"The headquarters of my personal Hell," Tanya remarked.

"You were Carmen there. Nobody who heard you will ever forget that."

"Yeah. I was Carmen in State City. Oh, well."

Andy had another impulse – to put his arms around Tanya and hold her to him – and this time he indulged it. And somewhat to his surprise Tanya hugged him back, as though she welcomed his embrace, and just for a few seconds Andy got to hold Tanya as he might have held a wife, pressing her face to his chest and stroking her hair.

Then he gave Tanya a little kiss on the cheek and she gave him one back, and they locked eyes for just an instant, and Andy said, "All the luck in the world."

"You too." Tanya got into her car, and she and Andy drove off in opposite directions.

§

Dear Mr. P,

OMG, Mr. P, you won't believe what happened.

That was the craziest buttstabbinest wedding evah. If you can call it a wedding since it didn't quite go off as planned.

Hey, it's Missie's Big Event, so I wasn't gonna say anything about the groom's party wearing tuxes at a day wedding. You warned her about that and she didn't listen. If that had been the only thing that was wrong it wouldn't have been so much fun.

OMG, Mr. P. Everything was going pretty OK at first. There was the groom's side of the church and the bride's side (this was at First Presbyterian. That's where Connor's parents' go. It's bigger than the Methodist church we go to twice a year, so it won the big contest to host State City's most coolest social event evah), and there was Connor up at the front of the church waiting for the bride, with his friend Brett Norton standing with him, and the groomsmen and bridesmaids all up there waiting, and Mom up at the front looking all glowy and like she was gonna cry, the way Mother of Bridezilla is spozed to look, and the Lowes were there too but I thought they looked kinda glum and resigned. That was just me thinking it; I can't know what they were feeling.

Livy was sitting with Juliet and Theo and Dave and Mercy, and the Blahas were there too, up near the front. Evil Léa and I were toward the back. I told Mom I wanted to sit at the back cuz I'd be able to hear better that way and maybe she was OK with it cuz I had Evil Léa with me and that might have been more than Mom could handle if we were right up front with the fam.

Anyway if Mom was looking glowy, you shoulda seen Connor waiting up there by the altar. It was almost embarrassing, he was all red in the face and he had this kinda moony look, like he was looking to the back of the church like maybe he was almost a teeny bit worried that Missie might not show. Then the organist starts playing "Here comes the bride, all fat and wide," ya know, and Daddydear is leading Missie up the aisle and yeah, she was smiling all right but she wasn't glowing, ya know? Like, I can kinda read Missie's emotions cuz I've known her a long time and yeah, she's glad the wedding is turning out nice, but if she's really truly happy about marrying Connor I'll swallow my own head.

And then just as Dad and Missie get to the altar and the music stopped, Livy yells out, real loud, "MY DADDY IS MARRYING A HO! I WANT MY REAL MOMMY!"

Gosh, Mr. P, Livy is only three and I didn't think she could talk so well yet and I am amazed she knew what "ho" means. (Maybe she doesn't, but I don't know who taught her the word.) But anyway that's what she said and everybody in the church heard it.

You ever hear complete silence? I swear it got so quiet in there that I could hear my blood flowing.

And then Livy yells, "Daddy, she forgot to tell you about her black boyfriend!"

(How did Livy know about the black boyfriend? I sure didn't tell her, tho it mighta been fun if I had, and it wasn't anything Mom and Dad would have shared! Could she have second sight or something?)

And then Evil Léa, right next to me, yells, "Missie, don't do it! You really want to sleep with that guy for the rest of your life? Don't you miss big black dick? Connor, how are you gonna compete with that?"

And I yelled, "I'm sorry, Missie, I didn't mean to let it slip about the black guy. But, yeah, Connor, that guy was so hot."

You shoulda seen the look on Mom's face. Missie had her back to me so I couldn't see but Connor looked like he just got hit with a baseball bat.

I know Mom and Dad have been keeping it real quiet about Leander, and for all I know maybe Connor thought Missie never had any other boyfriend besides that guy she was with in college, right? I woulda hoped Missie woulda told Connor about Leander but you know what I bet?

I BET SHE NEVER DID.

Anyhoodles, the next thing we hear is this great big loud Tarzan yell from up in the balcony, and I look up there and it's Leander! Only he's wearing nothing but a leopard skin. And he leaps down from the balcony to the floor of the church. Perfect aim, he got the floor and didn't hit a pew. And he landed on his feet, you know what they say about "those people" and how they're more like monkeys.

And Missie yells out "Leander!" and runs back down the aisle to him and jumps into his arms, and the organist starts playing "Jungle Boogie" while the two of them run out of the church hand in hand and everybody just stands there looking gobsmacked except for me and Evil Léa. We were jumping up and down and laughing and yelling after her "You go, Missie!" And I could see that Mrs. Blaha was laughing and yelling with us.

And Livy was still yelling "I want my real mommy! Daddy is a poop!"

Only, not. None of that shit happened.

What actually happened was, Livy tolly behaved and didn't make a sound. Maybe she didn't understand what was going on. Everybody else tolly behaved too.

You know, Dave and Mercy got married Catholic (I mean the second time they got married when they had a church wedding with a real Catholic priest in public) and I kinda like that ceremony better cuz it's like set in stone and the priest didn't say any extra stuff besides just the ceremony, nahmean? But for this one they had Pastor Merlyn from the Presbyterian church. Dunno if you know her. Big woman, looks like a man. And she was going on with this big long speech about how marriage is a lifetime commitment and not something to enter lightly.

And I wanted to yell out, "Yeah, Connor, not like the first time when you were only kidding!"

Only I didn't. And Mom was wiping her eyes all
thru it and I was facepalming in my mind only of course I
didn't do it for real and nobody saw that I was cringing
and yecching inside except that just before the vows
started I took ahold of Evil Léa's hand and prolly nobody
else in the church noticed it and maybe Evil Léa thought I
was trying to be romantic only I wasn't! I had to hold
Léa's hand so that I didn't start screaming, was all.

OOOOO I was frustrated that I couldn't stop this
thing from happening.

Then the minister said she now pronounced them
man and wife and they kissed. And then Connor did a fist
pump right there in front of everybody and then he took
Missie's hand and I swear he was about to RUN down the
aisle only Missie held him back and they ended up walking
down the aisle after all. I know they didn't rehearse to
do the run thing, but it must have been an impulse of
Connor's but thank God Missie stopped him. It might be
the one and only time she ever puts her foot down with
him but maybe not, you never know.

And then we get outside in front of the church and
everybody is milling around and Mom comes up to Connor
and gives him a great big hug and says, "It's about time,
you two!" and then she hugs Missie, and I'm saying to
myself, "Yeah, Mom, you've been working up to this for 10
years or so and I still can't figure out why you wanted it
so bad but you got your wish anyway."

I wish I could stop being so mean about this but I
can't. Because you know why?

Cuz what Connor said back to Mom was more than
a million times worse. He said to Mom, "Finally it's come
true. After 10 years of dreaming of it."

Yeah, he said that.

So he was dreaming it was actually Missie, when
he proposed to Tanya. He – I gotta guess – dreamed it
was Missie standing next to him when he and Tanya made,

y'know, that VOW thing. And then when Tanya had her baby, maybe Connor was dreaming that one day Missie could be the baby's mommy for real.

AND NOW SHE IS!

Isn't that wonderful?

But maybe it's OK. At least Tanya escaped. I guess the marriage fucked her up a little, but she escaped. Mom and Dad got their big wish, the most wonderfullest son in law evah, and Missie got her big wish, making Mom and Dad sorta-kinda proud of her at last. Dave and Mercy got that great big house to be happy ever after in.

And now you're prolly thinking, Li'l Chrissy is gonna complain that she's the only one who didn't get anything out of this and she's been shat on once again. And I kinda wish I could tell you that, cuz like a lot of sopranos I like to make it all about how tough it is for MEEEEE. But you know what? Honestly I can't complain. Not now, anyway.

I think it's gonna be OK for me. I've only got one more year of high school and I can get thru that easy enough. For one thing I'm gonna start this fall as one of the coolest girls in the school, cuz of the runaway and partly cuz I've got the hottest girl in the school for a girlfriend. That's funny, right? I'm the coolest and she's the hottest.

It would be different if I was a guy. Being lesbian has a coolness factor but for some reason that doesn't apply to gay guys. Boys have to keep it to themselves unless they want to buy themselves a lot of shit. And if I was a boy I would never have gotten such a hot girl!

On the other hand Léa and I might keep it quiet at school this fall, and act like we're just besties, and just let people speculate on whether we're doing the nasty or not. Might be more fun to keep it a mystery. Haven't decided.

Anyway it's not forever. I really like dick. It's not like I'm a lesbian per say. I'm trysexual. You know. "Try" anything. And like I say, having Léa for a GF is partly a business decision. It's a way to be one of the cool kids for my last year of high school. I deserve it, finally.

And I think I put the fear of God into Les Parents. They are gonna pretty much let me do whatever the fuck I want for as long as they have to have me living w/them. And then next year I'm GONE and we can all be HAPPY.

Believe it or not, Mr. P, I'm almost happy now. As close to happy as I've ever been. And I know it's gonna get better as I get older. The most important thing is, I'm optimistic for once in my life!

39. Il Faut Imaginer

Christine's ambition, and her enthusiasm for her vocation, were stronger than David's, and certainly stronger than Melissa's. Her industry was greater. Yet on some level Jim and Gail resented her ambition: considered it an annoyance, almost a personal affront. Possibly this was part of the general resentment that Gail, in particular, felt toward Christine for having had to bear her, and bring her up. For having been deprived, by Christine, of years in which she could have been doing something more fulfilling. Or maybe Jim and Gail were more tolerant of ambition in a boy, while deeming it unseemly for a girl to have aspirations outside of certain careers.

It could even be that in their perverse way, Jim and Gail thought they were protecting Christine by steering her away from her ambitions, on the principle that tall poppies get cut; nails that stick up get hammered down.

Or might Jim and Gail have been merely *normal*, all through the years of child-rearing: not much better or worse than other normal parents? Could it, indeed, have been Christine who demanded too much, had unrealistic expectations? And might Andy Palinkas, in observing and relating this story, have been too eager to think the worst of Jim and Gail, whatever they did? The reader must be the judge. And the reader, we must admit, is getting an incomplete narrative: not an entirely disinterested narrative.

It was a source of great satisfaction to Andy that Christine had finally gotten the better of her parents. It also has tickled him half to death that he has managed to write this highly biased, jaundiced, and tendentious account of how she did it. "*Il faut imaginer Sisyphe heureux*," Andy likes to say, but what if Sisyphus had caused the story to conclude by letting that one big stone roll down the hill – and instead of pursuing it, pushed a few more down the hill *after* it, starting an avalanche?

"Rocks fall, everyone dies." It's a shame more stories can't end that way.

This is the summer of 2015, seven years after the fact, when Andy relates this story, so he knows; he has seen.

Less than a month after Connor and Melissa got married, David had to call his parents and his parents-in-law with the news that Mercy was in the hospital – as a patient.

"We were going to tell you guys in a few days, after all the excitement from the wedding had died down," David told both families. "But now she's miscarried, and it's pretty bad."

Mercy had started hæmorrhaging severely, and all of a sudden, David explained. Thank goodness she'd been on duty, at the hospital, when it happened. It looked like she was going to pull through, David reported, but she'd lost a lot of blood.

Teresa Blaha immediately called the attending physician and asked to know the whole story, but was told that laws regarding doctor-patient confidentiality had to be observed.

"But I'm her *mother*!" Teresa had protested – to no avail: Mercy was an adult.

"I've had miscarriages," Teresa told Andy Palinkas, some days later. "She was far enough along for there to have been such severe complications – which means that she would have known she was pregnant – known it for long enough that she'd have told me she was. *If* she'd wanted me to know. And somehow it sets something off in my mind, that she was so conveniently *right there* in the hospital when it happened. Oh, I don't doubt that something went terribly wrong. I believe that part. But…" Teresa looked down, and shook her head.

"I can't bear to think it. I won't think it. I'll pray for her. And for the little child."

"You're assuming facts not in evidence," Andy said.

"Maybe if I'd done things differently. It's ironic, isn't it? If I hadn't been so… over-involved, I guess, so control-freaky… Mercy might have turned out more the way I'd hoped. At any rate, maybe she wouldn't have ended up in the situation she's in. I feel so guilty."

David and Mercy still live next door to Andy Palinkas. They haven't had any more children, but they've reconciled. Mercy has come to accept the fact that David has these various parts of him. David does love Mercy, in his way, and sporadically he tries to demonstrate it. Another part of him wishes that he had, at some point in his life, had the courage to act upon his fantasies – and often, when he's making love to Mercy, she wonders what David might be fantasizing about. A third part of David wishes simply to be left alone. That's the part of him that withdraws to his garret – and when he does that, sometimes Mercy misses him and sometimes she doesn't.

Oddly enough, David occasionally consoles himself in the arms of other women. Mercy daydreams about finding a man who might appreciate her more than David does, but she never tries to do it – because of the persistent belief that it would be wrong. If she suspects that David is unfaithful to her, she never mentions it to him or tries to find out for sure, because she would rather not know. In recent years their marriage has become even more distant, although never hostile.

A cynic might suspect that Mercy secretly has yearned,

for years, to cut herself loose from her husband. But she'll consider it her duty to stick with him for the sake of the children; for the sake of her own sense of martyrdom; so as to simultaneously spite, and not disappoint, her mother; so as not to feel that she has failed; and, perhaps most important of all, so as not to alienate Jim and Gail.

The rumors about why David and Mercy's marriage went upon the rocks in the first place haven't gone away. To this day, people smile behind their backs, and remark, "Apparently they decided to stay together once he'd decided he wasn't gay after all – or at any rate not *that* gay."

Jim and Gail never knew about that issue. They never heard a word about the rumors, or about Mercy confronting David. Neither did Christine or Melissa, for that matter.

David got that clerical job at State University, and started taking graduate courses in English. Ted and Teresa Blaha insisted on helping with tuition, and David and Mercy agreed, with little discussion, that it didn't make sense to refuse.

David has not gotten a degree yet. His nearly-full-time job, plus a wife and family, have prevented him from taking more than one or two classes per semester. He's a perpetual student – but he tells Andy Palinkas he enjoys being one.

David has published no more fiction. He never got around to revising that second novel, and he's reticent about revealing that he's had one published. Class-related materials take up most of his writing energy. He does sometimes note down interesting or funny anecdotes about his job, or the people around him, hoping that someday he might use them for a novel, or perhaps a memoir. He's also talked about writing a non-fiction book about marriage and child-rearing.

Slowly, though, David has begun organizing his thoughts and notes, and doing some more serious writing again. He continues to occasionally publish an op-ed piece in the *Examiner*, but in general, David tells his friends, that kind of writing is "crap." David is older now, and he's not stupid.

"I've learned a lot in grad school about how to be not just a writer, but an artistic writer," he told Andy recently. "An æsthetic writer. I feel like I'm ready, now, to make a name for myself as a writer of *literary* fiction – *timeless* fiction. I've been feeling inspired by writers like Nicholas Sparks and Joyce Maynard, lately – almost like I'm their literary soul-mate. So I have to say I'm feeling positive. I'll have a career as a novelist after all – and it won't be about the money. It'll be about the legacy I leave. You know, my literary reputation 100 years, 200 years after I'm gone. It's just a matter of finding the time."

Mercy has realized her ambition to get out of nursing. Although she never would have imagined that it would happen, she asked her father if she might join the family business – starting small; she didn't want any special favors – and work toward an executive position. Ted Blaha was delighted. He let Mercy do exactly that, and gave her time to take business courses at State University. Mercy never developed much liking for retail, but she has discovered a natural talent for selling. She has good management skills, and she finds the jewelry business far less stressful than nursing.

Ted and Teresa Blaha are still both in good health, and not likely to go to Glory for a few years yet, but they'll have to leave their fortune to someone. Mercy and David are likely to end up very well off. One wonders how they'll handle the loss of the poverty to which they've clung for so many years.

Mercy, although she continues to love and admire Jim and Gail Wainwright, has come to appreciate her own parents. In her private thoughts she has had to admit that this new-found respect had its beginnings in the talk she'd had with her mother when she'd feared that she and David would have to split.

Indeed, there came a time when she realized – with some reluctance – that at last she felt more comfortable with her own parents than she did with Jim and Gail. Partly, it's because her mother has softened her attitude toward Mercy. And it's partly because Mercy has come to enjoy the order, the slight formality, the touches of grace that she finds in her parents' home, and which she tries to introduce in her own.

The Wainwrights, Mercy has to admit, can sometimes be smug about their lack of affectation. "It might look like it's easier to live the way they do," Teresa said to Mercy one day, "and I'm sure it suits them – but think of all the effort they put into being just plain folks." And Mercy had to laugh.

"We'll never be perfect," Teresa added, "but it's fun trying to get it close."

Perfection, or close to it, might have been what Connor Lowe thought he had achieved at last, on the day he was wed to Melissa. His master plan to marry the girl of his dreams had been realized. And now the reality has been with him for seven years. Jim and Gail still think he's the perfect son-in-law, because that's what both Connor and Melissa want them to believe. To admit of any problems in that marriage would only serve to reduce Jim and Gail's high opinion of both of them.

Also, Connor doesn't want to admit that his master plan contained one huge flaw: He made Melissa up.

Melissa didn't pursue her doctorate. She still hadn't found a teaching job in the State City area, when she got married, and wasn't sure she could justify the cost of several more years of school, when college professorships in English were getting harder and harder to come by. So Connor suggested that they might as well start a family right away – and there'd be time for Melissa to pick up her career again one day.

Melissa and Connor have two children – a boy, then a girl, aged six and four, now – to go with the daughter Connor had with Tanya. Melissa soon saw herself falling into the same pattern as her mother, especially when Connor announced that since he was making plenty of money, there was no need for her to look for a full-time teaching job. She had enough to do, with two small children, Connor told her. "And I like taking care of you, so you can take care of me," he added.

Connor is awfully old-fashioned, as Melissa has discovered. He may also have been mindful of what happened when Tanya desired a career. Perhaps he said to Melissa, "I want our house to be a home."

It's unlikely that Melissa needed to be persuaded, the way Tanya had had to be persuaded. More probably, she was willing enough to forgo the drudgery of teaching, which was a career she'd never liked even though she knew she was supposed to like it. She probably figured she could manage the life of a stay-at-home mom better than her own mother had done.

She didn't. Gail, at least, had kept herself busy, day in and day out – with housework, if she had nothing else going on, and with her gardening, political work, book clubs, and handicrafts projects. Melissa had none of these to fall back on – and once she was into the groove of motherhood, she had no great desire to acquire any hobbies or develop any passions.

Plus, Connor was gone most of the day, after the first two years of marriage. Connor's father was looking ahead to retirement. Connor would take over the family business in due course – and for now, Connor told Melissa, his day trading practice was growing to the point where he needed an office away from home, and an associate or two. Teresa Blaha gave Connor a good deal on a small space down the hall from her own suite, above Rosen's.

Melissa still daydreamed, now and then, about the novels she thought she had in her. She'd read her brother's book, of course, when it came out. She'd hated it.

In fact, Melissa told Bev Norton, once she'd read *Sarah Strong* – knowing that Connor would never give it a look – she'd waited till the next time she'd had to move her bowels, then taken the book into the bathroom, ripped out a few pages, and used them for a certain purpose.

She knew she could write something better. But it's hard, with a houseful of small children. David, at least, had been a self-starter. Melissa didn't quite know what she would write about. And she enjoyed flaking out in front of the TV whenever she had a few minutes to herself.

She gained some weight, particularly after her second child, and while she wasn't exactly fat, she thought she was sloppy-looking. Her clothes got too tight and it was easier to get new stuff than to slim down.

Melissa took to relaxing, in the afternoons, by putting a little white rum in her 7-Up. It was no big thing, except that she would sometimes fall asleep in her armchair and the laundry would be only half-done that day, and Connor would notice it. And it wasn't long before he noticed that rather a lot of white rum was being consumed. And that things got broken, and that the housework wasn't always getting done, nor meals cooked, and sometimes he'd have to whip up pancakes or scrambled eggs for the kids, and finally he got into the habit of bringing half-prepared foods home from the Hy-Vee.

Melissa never heard from Leander again. She did scout him on Facebook, a few years after their final conversation, and saw that he'd remarried and had a baby son. For the next week or so, Connor wondered why his wife was so sad and weepy, even though she told him it was "nothing." Connor suspected that whatever hormonal problems might have brought this mood on, were only made worse by Melissa's drinking.

Connor did eventually force himself to have a talk with Melissa about that issue. He would have liked to mention that she ought to pay a little more attention to her figure, too – but, one thing at a time, he told himself.

In the midst of that conversation, which was not going in a direction he was liking, it occurred to Connor to ask Melissa, "Would you be happier if you went back to work?"

Melissa didn't have to think for even a moment. It wasn't easy to find a teaching job, but looking for one kept Melissa busy for a few months. Then she got one – teaching at a small rural high school a few miles outside of State City – and she's evidently happier. She's cut her alcohol consumption way down, generally sticking to one drink a day, and she seems to have lost weight, probably just by keeping busy. She isn't rated highly as a teacher, but she gets by.

Connor never found Melissa as attractive, after their second child, as he once had. Melissa tolerates his occasional sexual advances but she's never able, herself, to rouse much enthusiasm. Mainly, Connor and Melissa get along by staying out of each other's way and focusing on their children.

Little Livy, by the way, has never been a problem for Melissa. Melissa doesn't exactly love her – for one thing the girl is growing up to look too much like Tanya – but she goes out of her way to treat Livy kindly, always asking herself, "What would I do if she were my own child?"

Livy's a serious girl for her age – although capable of humor – and she's always respectful to her stepmother, who reciprocates. Livy and Melissa's relationship is reserved, but never less than cordial and affectionate. It could be that Melissa feels grateful to Livy, for having picked up some of the slack with regard to housework and child-minding during the phase when Melissa was drinking a little too much. And for never having complained to Connor. And maybe Melissa's a little afraid that Livy might still say something, someday, to someone.

Livy slowly grew distant from her father, as he and Melissa started having other children. She came to believe, rightly or wrongly, that Connor considered them his "real" children, while she, Livy, was a child he was taking care of because it was his duty. But in fairness to Connor, we have to say that he never overtly favors his children with Melissa.

Jim and Gail Wainwright have never quite been able to get used to Livy. Out of her hearing, in conversation with other people, they sometimes refer to "that strange child of Connor's." When she's around, they all but ignore her. Livy notices this, but being a small child she can't think of a tactful or useful way to mention the circumstance to Connor or Melissa, so she says not a word about it – to them.

Livy enjoys seeing her mother every year or so. Tanya always invites Livy to come and stay when Tanya visits her own parents in Indianola. Since Dr. and Mrs. Cucoshay will have no contact with Connor aside from what's absolutely necessary ("I might not control myself if we were face-to-face," Dr. Cucoshay says), Livy has never gotten to know that set of grandparents very well. She barely thinks about the fact that they're her grandparents, but she likes them fine.

"Maybe when you're a little older, you can come see me in New York," Tanya tells Livy.

Tanya also reminded Connor and Melissa, when Livy was about five, that it was time to get Livy started on music and dancing. They took Tanya's advice – Tanya was pretty insistent about it – but they don't pay a lot of attention to Livy's efforts in those areas, or care much whether she practices.

Livy is 10 now. Tanya texts or phones her every week or so, to ask about her music and dancing, and to remind her to practice hard. (Tanya is tactful: She knows that all of Livy's emails automatically go to her parents, as well. Melissa and Connor took a lesson from Jim and Gail's experience with Christine). Livy has started getting more interested in dance, and she can play the piano a little, but now that she's old enough to carry a tune, she gets the most enjoyment from singing.

Tanya returned to State City a little more than two years after leaving it, to defend her dissertation. She is now Dr. Cucoshay. But so far, the degree has not brought her a job that justified the time and expense she put into earning it. She has had rough going, financially. That conservatory position in New York turned out to not be a remunerative or secure job. It was like being a real estate or insurance agent: The office is a place to hang your hat; after that, you're mainly responsible for finding your own clients. Or students, in this case. Tanya wasn't much more than a glorified private instructor. It took a while for her to start making enough money to pay her bills. She tried to supplement her income by giving tango lessons, and she started organizing tango parties at various bars and clubs in the city. It's been hand-to-mouth, for her.

Just lately, though, Tanya has been building a reputation as an especially good teacher for girls who might be a little more talented than most – or whose parents think they are, at any rate. By marketing herself as someone who only has time for "serious students with ambition," Tanya has upped her prestige, and created a bit more demand. She's starting to make an okay living at last, and she seems, after all, to have established a career in music – even if it doesn't look like the career she'd envisioned.

In a recent email to Andy Palinkas, Tanya reported that she keeps applying for jobs at colleges and universities all over the country, and taking any opportunity to sing professionally.

I STILL DON'T LIKE CHILDREN. I WILL NEVER LIKE CHILDREN. BUT EVIDENTLY THEY LIKE ME, OR RATHER THEIR PARENTS DO. AND I SEEM TO HAVE A TALENT FOR TEACHING THEM. BUT I WISH I WERE NOT TEACHING TO PAY MY RENT. YOU KNOW WHAT THEY SAY. THOSE WHO CAN, DO...

I'M GETTING TO THE POINT WHERE I CAN'T BE TOO PARTICULAR WHERE I LIVE, SO LONG AS THE JOB IS RIGHT. AM I BETRAYING MY STANDARDS? I'M AFRAID I AM. I GUESS I COULD GO BACK TO INVESTMENT MANAGEMENT. I'D HAVE TO START MY CAREER ALL OVER AGAIN, AND I'M GETTING KIND OF OLD FOR THAT, BUT I'M SICK OF NOT HAVING ANY MONEY, AND THAT'S ONE FIELD WHERE I KNOW I COULD EVENTUALLY MAKE SOME. BUT I HAVE THIS TEACHING CAREER NOW, SO I KEEP HOPING AND HOPING. POOP.

Andy never did offer Tanya the solution he'd wanted to suggest years before: come back to State City as Mrs. Palinkas, endure it for a few years, and end up a financially secure widow, still relatively young. He knew Tanya wouldn't give it even an instant's consideration – and he told himself that in any case he was too bitter, now, to really want it to happen. But maybe he was just saying that.

Tanya almost always has a man in her life, but she's mistrustful. When she meets a man she likes, she avoids getting too close to him, because she can always tell if there's something that would prevent him from being her lifetime partner – or, just as frequently, she'll go to the other extreme. She'll meet a man who looks like he might be The One, and she'll build all her hopes on him. Then either he'll tire of her, or decide she's not worth the effort, or she'll finally hold up a hoop that he can't or won't jump through – or Tanya will discover that she's running second, once again, to someone or something else.

She almost never discloses to anyone that she has a child.

Christine's last year of high school was (Christine told Andy) "the happiest year of my life so far." Christine and Léa were inseparable. They were in Drama Club together, and in choir, and they tried to form a jazz combo with a couple of other girls but it never got off the ground. When they went to the prom, just before graduation, they each went in the company of a nice boy, and privately referred to their dates as "Beard One and Beard Two."

Christine didn't get into any of the truly élite conservatories to which she applied, but she was accepted at Arizona State University, which she decided was good enough – and certainly far enough from State City. Jim and Gail had assumed she'd be going to college, and they'd set aside some money for her, but they made it clear that there wasn't much left, now that they'd already helped two children through college and were getting near to retirement, so their contribution would have to be supplemented by scholarships and loans. Andy discreetly helps Christine with her expenses, now and then.

Christine sometimes has a boyfriend and sometimes a girlfriend, or sometimes both, or several of both. Sometimes she has a part-time job and sometimes not; sometimes she makes extra money by giving lessons – almost always to children – and singing at weddings. During her time at Arizona State she had to admit to Andy and to Tanya that she sometimes got sidetracked by the party scene – it took her an extra semester to graduate – but she told them not to worry: she was putting in the practice.

Christine went back to State City at Christmas and for summer break, after her first undergraduate year. Her sophomore year, it was just for Christmas – and after that, she decided she needed some time away from the family. Like, a long time. She almost never contacts Jim and Gail, now, although she always gets an e-mail or text message on her birthday, and a reminder near Christmastime that "you're always welcome."

Christine has just completed her first year in the Master's program at the University of Hawaii at Manoa – "almost as far away from Les Parents as it's possible to get," as she remarked to Andy. She's trying to decide what to do after next year: focus on performance, or work toward a doctorate and an academic career.

I'm thinking I could move to the east coast or go to Asia. There are all kinds of singing opportunities for white girls in Tokyo or Hong Kong. I hope I don't end up like Tanya. But that's how it's starting to look. I have so many doubts about my abilities and how far I can get with them. Sometimes when I'm in a recital or opera I blow myself away with how good I am – then other times I remind myself that I'm only in Hawaii, not out East. And I feel like if I went for a career in Asia it would be like how so many American athletes end up in Japan or Canada or Australia – because they can't cut it in the States, and the whole world knows that's why they're there. Maybe that's the wrong attitude; I don't know. I don't have any idea how good I am at this point, and who knows whether I'll ever get any better than I am now? But I won't find out unless I keep trying, I guess.

Jim and Gail Wainwright are moving toward retirement, living happily in their little house across town in which nothing much ever happens. They travel, now and then, and they'll probably live long enough to see their grandchildren having children of their own. It's clear that they love each other. Neither of them, probably, could imagine a life without the other. In general, they're able to look back with satisfaction.

"I'm so glad everything worked out for that family," Bill Longley once remarked to Andy Palinkas while shaving Andy's head. "If anybody deserves a happy ending, they do. Jim and Gail can be proud of themselves. Dave and Mercy had their little misunderstanding, but I'm sure that that's all it was. Dave was my best friend in high school, and if there'd been any of that sort of thing go on, I'd have known.

"I'm glad it worked out for Connor and Melissa, too. We all are. They were meant to be. They've got a marriage every bit as strong as Jim and Gail's. And it's nice to see it happen, when you think about that crazy woman Connor married the first time. I never was able to figure that out – except she was really good-looking. I'm sure that had a lot to do with it. Anyway, good riddance; she's probably working a strip club someplace.

"The only one I can't figure out is Christine. You know, she was such a sweet little kid. But she was the baby, so I'm sure they indulged her. She probably came to expect all kinds of special treatment, and when she didn't get it, well, you know the rest. I guess we can just hope she'll shape up one day.

"She and that first wife of Connor's might have had the same problem, you know? Spoiled. Entitled. It's funny how one Wainwright would turn out so different from the others, huh?"

"It's funny how people are perceived," Andy replied. "You never can tell how the perception lines up with reality."

Teresa Blaha echoed Longley's final remark in a conversation with Andy, just recently, when she was in Rosen's to buy a present for her husband.

"I can't understand it, how Christine turned out so different from the others," she said. "I liked her; I always wanted to get to know her better. I would try to reach out to her at family gatherings and so on, but she was never very comfortable around me. Almost as though she were afraid of how her parents would react if she got too friendly with me."

"Send her an email," Andy suggested. "Cultivate her. I bet she'd reciprocate. Believe it or not, Christine's a pretty lonely person. Maybe she wishes she'd gotten to know you, too."

"She's the only one of that bunch I ever gave a sh... the only one I had any use for," Teresa said. "And I actually miss her. The rest of them... I force myself to get along with them. I don't approve of divorce, but I can't help having my fantasies."

And Andy Palinkas? He has his fantasies, too. He plugs along, doing his best to keep Rosen's in the black – and scaring the ladies, presumably. He remains a fixture at the Janscombe Center, and backs the State University Rivercats all the way when football season comes along.

He has never been able to hope for it again – as he told Tanya he never would or could, again – but he can still dream that one day, old as he is, another Tanya might come along to break his heart. *Il faut imaginer...*

Il faut imaginer Sisyphe heureux.